I0543845

IMAGE OF DECEIT

This book is a work of fiction. Names, characters, places and incidents are products of the author's imagination. Any resemblance with real persons, living or dead, is entirely coincidental. Business establishments, events or locale used in this novel are either products of the authors imagination, or used fictitiously.

Copyright © 2013 by Jill Shannon.

Cover art by Dave Iversen
Cover Design by Sheenah Freitas

All rights reserved. No part of this book may be reproduced or transmitted in any form or by any means, electronic or mechanical, including photocopying, recording, or by any information storage and retrieval system, without permission in writing from the Author.

Printing History

Paper Mill Publishing

Paperback edition / July 2013

E-Book / July 2013

ISBN-13: 978-0615827117

ISBN-10: 061582711X

IMAGE OF DECEIT

A MYSTERY

JILL SHANNON

To Dave.

Because of you, I have the freedom to chase dreams. This one belongs to you.

To my parents, for teaching me to love books.

"You just can't explain crazy." Detective Hall speaking to the press.

1

She'd fallen asleep on the old couch and woke in a crunched fetal position with her hands tucked between her knees. She sat up and rubbed at the imprint of nubby fabric on her cheek. Her body protested fast movement as she stumbled toward the counter and fumbled a ringing phone to her ear.

"Hello?" She blinked hard and reached to rub a hipbone bruised by the old couch springs.

"Is this Mrs. Hudson?"

"Who's calling?" She cradled the phone against her shoulder and filled a glass with tepid water from her workroom sink. It didn't sound like the voice of the persistent reporter from the newspaper, but she wasn't awake enough to be sure. Probably a telemarketer.

"This is Detective Hall, with the San Diego Police Department. I need to speak to Big . . . Ahhh, Mrs. Lars Hudson."

Bygie caught the stumble. "It's Bye-Gee. What's this about?"

"Is anyone home with you, Mrs. Hudson?"

She set the glass down without taking a drink. Must be the reporter on a fishing expedition. "I'm not sure how it concerns you, but, yes. I'm entertaining the local high-school marching band. They stopped by for snacks."

"I'd appreciate cooperation, Mrs. Hudson. We have a serious problem."

"Let's start with a badge ID and phone number where I can call you back, Mr. Detective." The bloodhound reporter would have to find another trail, she'd had enough of his hunt and gather phone calls. Hubby Lars needed to make the harassment stop.

"Please stay at your residence, I'll meet you there. In the meantime, call to confirm my credentials." He recited a bunch of numbers. "Tell them you need to verify, Detective Tom Hall."

He disconnected without giving her a chance to respond.

She snorted. "What a fake." She tossed the phone onto the countertop, knocking over the untouched glass of water.

"Shit!" She mopped the spill and tossed soggy paper towels in the trash.

Her life was pathetic. She should have called quits on her marriage years ago, but instead, she stayed married to a liar to avoid the embarrassment of telling her family she'd failed. "Damn it." Leaning against the counter, she squeezed her eyes shut, rubbing her forehead. She felt a year's worth of tired. So much for taking little steps like the damn self-help book suggested. It said to start small, so she did. Her first baby step toward self improvement was to quit swearing. She'd been doing damn well, until last night when Lars told her why the reporter was calling their house. Why the same guy parked at the end of their driveway and stood by his car, staring at their house.

Yesterday, when the reporter showed up again, she called Lars at work. In an unusual burst of agreement he rushed home, pulled in behind the car and jumped out to confront the guy. She observed their heated conversation of exaggerated arm movements through her studio window, waiting for Lars to come and explain what the reporter wanted. Instead, both cars backed away. A big fat nothing returned to give her an explanation.

Her husband waited until evening to come home and purge a sordid story. He was afraid of an investigation and begged forgiveness.

Not this time.

Heading out the door of her second floor art studio, she ran down the outside steps through a drizzle of rain. At least that's what they called this annoying mist in Southern California — rain.

Having spent most of her life in North Carolina, Bygie expected rain to pour in hard, abrupt bursts, falling so thick it formed a continuous, cleansing sheet. The spring rain in Southern California adhered to travel brochures touting the dry climate and the output was minimal spits. Water spots of shine that made everything around it look dirtier.

Her studio sat above the unattached garage and was intended to be a granny-flat. The exterior staircase, on the opposite side of her home's front door, gave the illusion of privacy to anyone coming and going. Parents forced to spend their golden years, living in a box above their loving children's parked cars, could sneak in and out after dark in an ironic game of pay-back.

God, how depressing. If I had children, that's probably where I'd end up. Sleeping away my retirement with help from exhaust fumes.

Walking around the front of the garage, she made a bet Lars wouldn't be home. The bastard would stay gone as long as he dared. She had plenty of questions for him. When Lars told her why a reporter was showing interest, Bygie listened to her husband with tears streaming. When he reached to touch her, she twisted her back to him and left without a glance. She walked to her studio in over-controlled, herky-jerky steps, and spent the night on a throw away couch. Lars drove away after she left and as far as she knew, he'd never returned. It's not likely she would have missed his car pulling in beneath her studio to baste her with sleeping fumes.

Groggy, with a lack of sleep hangover, she stepped through the front door. She stopped in the large entry and listened to silence. Flinging her over-shirt onto the staircase post, she walked up four steps to the kitchen. Without stopping to make coffee, she continued down a hall towards the master bedroom. Stripping for a shower, she kicked her dirty clothes into a pile. Lars could deal with it when he got tired of tripping over them. He could pick up after her for a change.

In the master bathroom, she turned on the shower and reached in to feel the temperature, waiting for warmth. She felt guilty for wasting water, but hated stepping into a cold shower. With grim determination, she watched the source of an oft repeated argument flow down the drain.

"Why are you outside the shower? Letting the water run? Don't you realize how much you're wasting? It's ridiculous." Staccato bursts of wisdom.

The last time he'd shared his view, she'd snapped back, mimicking his cadence, "Its cold. I'm not getting in. Until the water's hot. I'll conserve by flushing the toilet. Every third time I use it."

"Always a smart-ass answer, isn't it?"

He was right. What drew them together in the beginning was now a wedge. In the early years, Lars was attracted to her smart wit and sense of humor — until he felt it directed towards him. Now, her conversations with him consisted of small, stinging barbs.

Stepping into the shower, she let the pressure beat against her neck, loosening taut muscles. Turning to face the spray, tears mingled with water. She braced her hands against the tile wall, pushing hard, refusing to cry. She rotated her shoulders, using the warm pressure to ward off the pending migraine. Her head throbbed in perfect rhythm with her heartbeat and the morning's interrupted dream flashed.

A wavy image of bodies entwined, contoured into a sculpture of limbs and baby skin butts. The male shape recedes into a murky form, but focus on the female remains razor sharp. She glows with a uniform finish of perspiration. Her skin is consistently tan from head to toe, absent of annoying bikini lines. Her breasts are obvious imitation, filled with baseball mounds of silicone, fashioned into the ideal, man-made, shape. Lengthy, toned legs, wrap below the man's waist, a post coital jailer's embrace. One possessive hand lays claim, covering the man's flaccidity. Thick blonde hair hides the face tucked under the man's chin.

A recognizable chin.

Grabbing a bar of soap, Bygie scrubbed hard to rid herself of the dream. Extra time in the shower left her feeling human, but she pictured Lars tapping his watch to indicate how long she'd taken. He could skip a shower of his own to make up for her wasteful insensitivity.

Using a lightweight towel to dry off, she grunted. Another example of a routine gripe. Lars preferred his towels to be thick and luxurious. She was supposed to take cold, abbreviated showers, while he wrapped himself in an acre of energy-consuming dryer time.

The ringing doorbell made her jump. She clutched the thin towel to her chest.

Crap. Who the hell was at the door? Damn it, I was going to quit cussing.

Hurrying to the bedroom, she pulled on ragged jeans and a comfortable old sweatshirt, one Lars wanted her to throw away. He didn't want her wearing anything that looked shabby; he thought it beneath their burgeoning status in the community.

"Right," she stabbed back, "who cares what I wear around my own house? If I want to walk around naked, I can." At one time, the word naked would have been said as an invitation to a truce. Now the thrown gauntlet shouted 'don't you dare touch me'.

Hurrying to the door as it rang again, she ran fingers through her wet mass of tangled hair. She could see the outline of someone through the frosted glass. The pain over her left eye intensified, she was in no mood to be friendly. She fell back to her Southern heritage and a favorite redneck expression. *I'm gonna open a can of whoop-ass on the reporter.*

Bygie jerked the door open.

2

Dwarfed by the large frame filling the doorway, Bygie stepped back and narrowed the door opening. The man standing on her porch stood over six feet tall, a solid hunk of intimidation. If this was a reporter, it meant they'd been up-graded to first class news. It wasn't the same skinny creep she'd seen at the end of her driveway.

"Mrs. Hudson? I'm Detective Tom Hall, from San Diego PD. I spoke to you on the phone." A demanding voice, but sunglasses hid his intent.

Bygie stood and stared. She'd forgotten the call. When it ended with an abrupt hang-up, she assumed it was the re-porter. *Ass-u-me, emphasis on me.*

"Mrs. Hudson?"

She tucked a glob of wet hair behind her ear. Embar-rassed, and feeling defensive, she came across cool. "Yes, I'm Bygie Hudson. Could I see your badge, please?" She repeated the line from a television show, and it worked.

When he reached to his back pocket, his windbreaker opened enough to reveal a holster at his waist. She tightened her hold on the door handle, ready to slam it. He pulled out a black leather holder, too thin to be a man's wallet and flipped it open to show her his flat badge and police identification.

She squinted at the contents, pretending she'd know real from fake. Not knowing what else to do, she swung the door wide, allowing the scary giant with a gun to step in.

Bygie led him through the entry and down two steps into a formal living room. Pitch perfect in presentation, the room looked stiff and unwelcoming. She spent little time in there, it didn't reflect her taste.

High-backed, thin legged wing chairs flanked a cold and uninviting marble fireplace. Instead of burning logs, it held an impressive array of candles arranged on copper stands. Facing the fireplace stood a hump-back sofa that looked as uncomfortable as the chairs. Uninspiring art hung in dark wood frames. The drapery choice for the floor to ceiling windows imitated an English castle drawing room.

"Have a seat, Detective. What can I do for you?" She watched him scrutinize each available place to sit until he settled on one of the chairs. It offered no comfort but had a clear view of the room and the front door. He took off his windbreaker and draped it across his knees.

His polo shirt was her favorite shade of blue, a word she liked to feel roll off her tongue. Nervous energy had her repeating the word. *Periwinkle. Periwinkle. Periwinkle.* Catching herself, she blushed. She headed towards a chair, but took a seat on the matching ottoman, regretting the decision as she landed. She felt small and childlike. She straightened her spine to compensate.

"My partner will be joining us," Hall stated. "I apologize for the delay."

His manner had the warmth of a dead fish. He still had sunglasses parked in place and what she could see of his face was an empty canvas. She couldn't warm to anyone who didn't smile.

"I don't have much time." She picked at a hole in the knee of her jeans. "I'm pretty busy. Could you tell me why you're here?"

"When did you last speak with your husband?"

"Uhhh, early last evening? I worked late in my studio and fell asleep there. He wasn't here when I came back to the house. He'd left for work. Why?"

"Back to the house? Where is your studio located?"

"It's here, above the garage. I work a lot of late nights. What's this about?"

"So your husband was home most of the night?"

The direct question caught her, "Uhhh, I don't know for sure. I was focused on a project."

"If he left, what would he have been driving?"

"His Mercedes, a big SUV thing. Why do you want to know? Has he let speeding tickets go unpaid? I'll make sure he calls you."

The sound of the doorbell made her jump.

Hall removed his sunglasses and revealed dark, flat eyes. "That should be my partner. Would you like me to answer the door?"

Bygie believed the detective was here due to the mess Lars was in.

Hell, he probably knew more than she did.

She rose, heading to the door on shaky legs, feeling so ashamed of her husband she could kill him.

***

The woman didn't look like a detective. Her friendly manner and young age were the opposite of heading-towards-full-gray, Hall. In judgmental fairness to stern non-smilers, Bygie also judged people who smiled too much. They used the happy face to put you at ease . . . right before they moved in for the kill.

Detective Ruby Wilson was an impressive five-foot-eight and had enough weight behind the height to be curvy, in a good way. Pink-glossed lips, bright blue eyes and light blonde hair added to the attractive package. Bygie dropped her eyes. Wearing ripped jeans and her old sweatshirt, she screamed civil servant more than the chemically-addicted blonde ever would. She hunched in defeat.

Lifting her gaze, she met Wilson's eyes and corrected her posture. Her sweatshirt, wet from her hair, was making her neck itch. Reaching to run hands through the tangles, she dropped them to her lap in resignation. Too late to worry. She glanced between the detectives. Hall's steely eyes felt invasive, so, like a big girl, she avoided them.

She spoke to Wilson. "You should know up front, I stay out of my husband's business. He's the one you should be talking to." Her fingers picked at lint on her sleeve and harvested little balls of fluff.

"Mrs. Hudson," Wilson glanced at Hall, then continued. "We're sorry to be delivering bad news. Your husband's vehicle was found last night, overturned off Highway 67." The young detective swallowed hard. "It appears he lost control due to the wet road and rolled down an embankment. I'm so sorry."

Bygie looked back and forth between them. Ruby Wilson looked as if she felt bad, but Hall's face remained stony. The only sound in the room was a distant hum of air conditioning.

The information sank in.

Her headache throbbed.

She lifted hands to massage her temples, asking the question with eyes closed.

"Is he dead?"

She opened her eyes and locked on Hall.

With his affirmative nod, Bygie troubled the detectives.

She started laughing.

3

Tom Hall left his office and trudged to his old minivan; he stooped to unlock the door, the auto unlock gizmo was on the fritz. A fan belt whined as he backed out of the space.

Tom fought hard for other people's rights, but he sucked at dealing with personal turmoil. When his ex-wife wanted a new catering vehicle during their divorce, he gave in and considered it alimony. He traded in his late model sedan for a box truck and in consequence, inherited her old mini-shitty-van that smelled like food.

His cell phone rang as he reached the gate exiting the parking lot. Caller ID shouted work. It was his partner, Ruby.

"What's up? No matter what it is, I'm heading home." He sounded angry all the time, but didn't give a shit. She'd learn to deal with it.

"Ahhh, sorry to bother you. This is Ruby. They called to let us know Hudson's autopsy is finished. The toxicology report will be a couple more days. Should I stop by in the morning to pick it up? It's no trouble."

When Tom found out he'd been assigned as an FTO, field training officer for a green recruit, the blame rested on his shoulders. Climbing the occupational ladder backwards, he'd walked away from ten years in homicide and requested a move back to vice. The pinch in the pay difference meant he wouldn't be getting a new car anytime soon. Being teamed with a rookie partner was an additional slap for making a stupid move.

Ruby had graduated top of her class, and before the ink was dry on her certificate, she was snatched out of the academy and straight into vice. Her physical attributes were an asset, but her history was far from perfect. The public had no idea a rough background didn't disqualify a person from becoming a police officer. If the applicant is truthful, and past mistakes weren't felonies, it could be a damn fine reason to hire them. It's harder for a suspect to bullshit a person who's been in their shoes.

Tom had taken to operating under the principle a person was guilty until proven innocent. His twenty-year career in law enforcement had skewed his view. His new partner would need to prove herself long before Tom trusted her.

He also didn't expect her to last long. The reality of the day-to-day grind was far different than television, but the Hudson case brought excitement. Vice cops don't handle car accidents and death cases, and Ruby was thrilled to be involved in something different.

Tom forced himself to sound less angry.

"That'd be great, grab the autopsy report on your way in. I'm going to stop and see our laughing widow, Mrs. Hudson, in the morning. We've given her time to deal with her husband's death; it's time to start getting answers. She lied when we talked to her, she knew damn well her husband had gone out and stayed out."

"I could meet you there," Ruby offered. "I mean, if I could help or anything. I'm sorry, that's dumb. You don't need me."

Ruby had an annoying way of apologizing for everything.

"We've got too much on our plate to double up. I'll be the bad guy and push for answers. If that doesn't work, you can do a follow-up call, try a softer approach. Grab the autopsy report and I'll meet you at the station when I'm finished at Hudson's." He added, "Tell the M.E. thanks for rushing it."

"Sir?"

"Skip it. Do me a favor, quit calling me sir. It pisses me off and makes me feel old." Tom thought he'd get by with only one apology, but she came through as expected.

"Ahhh, okay. Sorry to bother you, sir . . . ahhh, Hall, I'll see you in the morning."

Ruby tried hard, but Tom hated babysitting and assigning tasks. He was not a role model for a good F.T.O. He left her instructions, but otherwise spent as little time with her as he could. He worked with her, end of story. He didn't have to bond with her. He didn't want to hear tales of her childhood. If she had a boyfriend, he didn't want to meet him. He wasn't interested in getting a drink after work to discuss cases. Not with her, not with anyone.

Maneuvering through heavy downtown traffic, the laughing widow occupied his thoughts. Ruby and Tom had done preliminary background checks on the Hudsons. Everything on the couple came back clean, but it didn't mean much at this point. They'd only scratched the surface.

Calling the mortuary, at Tom's bidding, Ruby learned there would not be a big, country-club funeral. She was struck by the cheapness and thought it reeked of money-grubbing. A solid theory when you added the widow's strange reaction to his death. Maybe she couldn't stop laughing long enough to sit through the service.

Tom had taken part in his share of notifying families of unexpected deaths, but Bygie Hudson's response was one for the record book. Her abrupt burst of laughter was not a prelude to hysteria. Dry eyed, she asked if her husband was alone in the car.

Who did she think was with him?

He looked forward to finding out more in the morning. The lady was an enigma. Wearing work jeans and a stained sweatshirt, she didn't fit his image of a rich, stay-at-home wife. He'd expected California plastic, not someone sans makeup and dripping wet hair.

Putting widow Hudson on hold, Tom turned into a busy supermarket. Other drivers drove like maniacs to find front row parking. They cut in front of him to horn in on a perfect spot, anything that required as little walking as possible. He hated coming here. The ease of a drive thru was his usual choice.

When his divorce was fresh, he'd spent more time at his desk than he did in his empty house. Not anymore. Now that he was training Goldilocks, he left work early to get away from her irritating cheerful presence. He could get more done at home without answering questions, each one frickin' apologized for.

Parking at the unused back half of the lot, Tom headed inside to buy what amounted to a home-cooked meal. Something in a box. This was a time he missed his wife; the woman sure knew how to cook. She'd kept the fridge stocked with tasty leftovers.

Towards the end of their marriage they rarely saw one another, both worked long hours. Most nights, Gloria was catering an event by the time he straggled in the door. One time he came home, walked straight to the stove and served himself a plate of food. He'd just forked in a bite full when Gloria walked around the corner, scaring him enough to spit out his mouthful.

He hadn't noticed her vehicle when he pulled in and parked behind it.

Tom didn't fault Gloria for having drive and ambition; it's what attracted him to her in the first place. He watched as her business thrived, smug that her independence allowed him more time for what was important. His job.

Inside the store, Tom headed straight to the middle aisles, he knew exactly where the boxed meals were. He didn't waste time going after fresh fruit or vegetables; they spoiled before he ate them. Compared to the junk he ate from grab-n-go's, a gourmet dinner meant hamburger with a boxed pasta and pre-packaged seasoning. Grabbing the first one he came to, he headed to the meat counter.

"Hi there, handsome. What can I get ya? We have fresh shrimp on sale, or maybe you'd prefer mahi-mahi?" The female voice parroted a seductive tone. The nametag on the woman behind the counter said 'Becky', his girlfriend from junior high.

Girlfriend was not an apt description. Tom had been strong-armed by Becky's older brother into taking her to their eighth grade Valentines dance.

They both smiled.

"Hi yourself. I didn't know you were back to work. Isn't it too soon?" Tom asked.

Becky had given birth to her third daughter two weeks ago. "I'm back part-time. Between breast-feeding and changing diapers, this is a break." She watched Tom's face turn red at the mention of breast-feeding. "Oh geez, you can be such a dork. You're a tough guy when it comes to work, but mention feeding a baby the natural way and you go all school-boy."

"Come on Bec, lower your voice." He glanced around. "You know I'm happy for you, but I don't need to hear the details." He leaned in close, "I don't ever want to watch the birth video, got it?" He couldn't imagine a husband wanting to share film shot during the birth of his child, but Becky's husband offered the play-by-play every chance he got. It gave credence to Tom's theory that having babies burned brain cells. Willing to show a birth video proved it.

"Geez, for such a big guy, you're a real wimp." She winked at him. "You're never going to have babies for yourself, if you don't get out. I wish you'd let me fix you up, I mean with a date, someone you could take to dinner and a movie."

She'd tried to arrange a blind date with one of her friends, but he was adamant in his refusal. Tom had crawled into a protective shell when Gloria left him and the shell turned to concrete by the resignation bomb of his old partner. It dealt a blow bigger than the end of his marriage, which spoke volumes he didn't care to examine.

"Maybe later. For now, all I want is hamburger so I can go home and feed myself. If I feel the need for therapy, I'll stop by and have a beer with you and Joe this weekend." He'd meant to get by and see the new family member. He offered a lopsided smile. "If all the women were as good as you, Bec, there'd be a whole bunch of happy men in this world."

Becky accepted the compliment from one good friend to another. He waved goodbye and promised to visit over the weekend. He grabbed milk on his way to check-out.

Standing in line to pay, Tom studied the people around him. During their marriage, Gloria accused him of looking for bad guys on his time off. The argument festered and hung between them. Being off duty didn't mean he turned off a switch. Of all people, it shouldn't have been hard for her to understand. She never quit looking for new recipes.

He scanned the row of checkers and shoppers. Not seeing anything out of the ordinary, he shrugged away a niggle at the base of his skull and chalked it up to lingering thoughts of a birth video.

4

Bygie sat at her kitchen table, chin in hand, staring at her laptop. She'd been reading an article entitled *Highway 67 — Is it Our County's Most Dangerous?* It listed the high number of deadly accidents on the heavily traveled road, citing the recent fatality of Lars Hudson as an example.

The detectives were careful to use the word 'assumed' in discussing the accident. "Assumed" he'd been going too fast for the rain-slicked road. "Assumed" he'd lost control. "Assumed" he hadn't stood a chance when the vehicle plowed down the steep embankment.

The accident was discovered when infrared on a night-patrol helicopter detected something burning. The vehicle had caught fire during the roll-over, but was slow to burn in the damp, misty weather. While Lars had suffered burns, most of the trauma occurred before the fire started. They believed severe head injuries had meant instant death, but the autopsy was needed to verify all of the "assumptions.

On file, his California Notary fingerprints saved her from an awful identification process. She had yet to cry, she was too damned angry. Unshed tears pooled inside, forming deep caverns of sorrow, leaving her a soggy mess on the inside with a brittle exterior.

A man from the yellow-page selected mortuary, had made an information seeking visit to her home, offering sympathy and hand pats that she wanted to swat back. When the funeral planner found out she wasn't agreeable to a send-off of the century and that she wasn't purchasing a coffin costing as much as a house, he left. Papers were faxed to her; she signed and faxed them back. The age of technology. No need to go out, simply sit behind a keyboard and order a cremation. The hand-patting-sympathy-charged man changed to brisk-business-type-man, when he emailed to let her know the autopsy report was needed before a death certificate was issued.

The obituary announced there would be a private, family only, ceremony. She decided to take his remains to North Carolina for final burial, back to the place they both called home, or at least she did.

She pleaded with her only remaining relative, her sister, to stay put in North Carolina. It took lengthy, persuasive phone conversations before Jane relented. Bygie told her Lars was killed in a car accident, but didn't mention an investigation into his over-time activities. The open wound would have to scab before she discussed it.

"Jane, I'm fine. Well, not fine, not at all, but I'm hanging in there. Once everything is organized, I'll come home. We'll hold a private ceremony." With a sigh, she added, "It's been way too long. I need to come home."

"Will you be coming back to see me, or is it an excuse to hunt for sea shells?" Jane said, trying to lighten the mood. "If you keep taking our shells, there won't be any left for us regular folk. You better lower your standards and use west coast clam shells instead."

Losing herself in the moment of routine conversation, Bygie pictured the seashells she used in her artwork. "Don't worry, I'll only take the best, leave my cast-offs for the uneducated tourists to find. Have you been saving any sea-glass for me?"

"Got a big ol' jar full. I told the kids you'd pay them ten cents for every piece they found, they covered the beach like a swarm of bees."

Picturing her niece Holly and nephews Ian and Robert, she smiled, but it felt foreign. "Tell the kids hi and give them a hug, I'll see ya'll as soon as I can." Her southern accent was markedly evident when talking with family.

"Love ya, sis. I know it's too soon but please, please, consider moving home. I miss having you close."

"Love you, too."

Her sister had always been her champion, the one to encourage her first clumsy attempts and call it art. Still, Bygie kept Jane at arm's length, the pattern she began after marriage. The physical miles between them made it easier to put a happy spin on her life.

Lars didn't have any relatives to call, but maybe that'd been another one of his lies. She didn't know what to believe.

Lars and Bygie shared ownership with two other men in Oceanview Mercedes, a successful dealership located on prime real estate along the San Diego coast. The partners didn't question her decision to keep the burial private and she sensed their relief. For all she knew, they were involved in the same after hour activities as Lars.

One thing was certain; they hadn't wasted time in offering to buy out the Hudson's share in the dealership. The partners had placed a condolence call worth seven figures. She'd already made a decision, but wanted them to sweat. In the past, when she complained to Lars that the men were condescending towards her, he blamed it on her over-active imagination.

His comment was condescending as well.

Bygie's life had dramatically changed as the car business soared. The first time Lars appeared on television in a dealership commercial, they'd watched it at home, together. They tossed light hearted jokes that he was famous.

Gradually, her world eroded with his consuming need to be recognized. His list of appropriate things grew larger. Join the right clubs, shop at the correct stores. Use a decorator. The harder Lars pushed, the more Bygie withdrew. She rarely asked how sales were and took to wearing old, comfortable work clothes most of the time. A big stand for normalcy.

The wife of each partner dutifully called to voice sympathy. Each sent massive bouquets of identical flowers, the appropriate thing to do. It'd be hard to catch either of them doing anything inappropriate. Bygie hadn't bonded with the women, and it pissed off Lars when she referred to them as Mitzi and Bitsy.

"Mitzi and Bitsy spend their days getting massages or manicures. They have so much Botox I can't tell if they're happy or sad or pissed off. They carpool their children to private schools and get facials. What do I have in common with them? I'd rather spend time in my studio."

In the beginning, she'd tried to fit in with their lifestyle but quickly tired of speaking in a voice an octave higher than normal, as if it made her nicer than she really was.

"Oh my gosh, red polish?" She couldn't care less.

"For God's sake, Bygie. I'm only asking you to try harder. Most women would be thrilled to spend money with 'the girls'. Lord knows, your hands do need pampering." He motioned to her dry, chapped skin, and torn cuticles, effects of her art. "Quit your little hobby."

The words cut the ever present wedge between them into a chasm.

When her little hobby helped pay bills, he called her an artist.

The couples were forced to attend social functions together, but with nothing in common, Bygie felt excluded, an outsider. After each event, she obsessed over why it bothered her to feel left out.

Snapping down the lid on her laptop, she pushed away from the kitchen table. She'd spent the day procrastinating a dreaded task. She was forcing herself to leave the house, make a necessary trip out for groceries and refill a prescription. Fear of running into unexpected questions had kept her secluded.

"How are you coping with your husband's untimely passing?"

A truthful answer was the saddest epitaph of all.

I was planning my divorce when it happened.

She backed out of the driveway, heading to a grocery store located a distance from her own neighborhood. She wasn't worried about running into friends; she had few personal acquaintances. Her days were spent in her studio, and no one knocked on the door asking her to come out and play.

She strayed from her normal grocer because clerks at that store recognized her as that car-commercial-guy's-wife and would have heard of his death.

She parked and walked into a busy supermarket, her hunched shoulders forming an artificial protective shield. She pushed her cart to the produce aisle, keeping her eyes downcast, avoiding contact. Her outfit for the day was comfortable, but not clothing that car-commercial-guy would have appreciated.

Her long hair was pulled into a high pony-tail and shoved through the hole of a drab blue ball-cap. Boot cut jeans were tucked into a comfortable pair of old, flat-soled boots. She wore a man's faded, button-up shirt over a plain white tee. The shirt had belonged to her father and was one of her favorites, one she remembered him wearing. It offered a small source of comfort.

Her small frame looked gaunt under the baggy shirt; jeans that were tight days ago, hung loose. Stress took a toll, and rather than snack her way through it, she forced herself to eat. Food was simply a necessity. When she was working, eating was a bothersome task that interrupted her flow. Lars enjoyed dinners in fancy, expensive restaurants, but they were agonizingly slow for her. While she enjoyed a break from cooking, posh wasn't what she craved.

"It all has the same result, Lars, a full stomach. Instead of sitting through a two-hour dinner, let's grab fish tacos and go to a movie."

"You really don't get it, do you? I work hard to take my wife out to a restaurant where we can sit down without wiping lettuce off the chairs and getting salsa stains on our elbows. All you do is complain. I don't know why I bother."

"I appreciate how hard you work, I do. I thought it would be a nice change, more relaxing." She smiled. "We used to go to movies all the time, remember when we snuck food in and someone complained because of the smell?"

"It's not a fond memory, Bygie. All it reminds me of is how hard we struggled. Not much fun then and it sure as hell wouldn't be fun now." He reached into a pocket for his money clip, tossing a ten dollar bill on the counter. "Here you go, have a taco on me. I'm going out."

If going out for dinner with Lars was a battle, in the end, staying home became one too.

"God, Bygie," he'd mutter. "Can't you make something more creative than eggs? I would have eaten before I came home if I'd known that's all you were making."

Her answers were snarls. "If I knew when you planned on arriving, I would have stopped to make a meal more fitting to your refined taste."

She never knew when he'd get home, had quit caring enough to ask. When she did cook a decent meal, optimistic that a marinated chicken could fix what was wrong, it'd be dry as jerky by the time he came home.

Shaking off the memory, she picked out fresh fruit and vegetables, along with cheese and eggs. Nothing sounded good. She tossed in a box of crackers and quit.

Pushing her cart to the check-out, she joined the throng of shoppers in line to pay. As she stood waiting, a tingle of dread ran across her neck. Lifting her eyes long enough to scan the people around her, she didn't see anyone looking her way.

Deciding she was acting paranoid, she pushed her cart forward to pay.

***

When detective Ruby Wilson first noticed Tom in the grocery store, her instinct was to say hello, but she held back. Keeping her distance, she watched him buy meat and flirt with the girl behind the counter. She eyed him as he moved through the store, trying to get a handle on the man she spent most of her time with.

She was good at giving men what they expected. A childhood filled with more fake-dads than hugs had taught her well, men were darn easy to manipulate. Her partner was proving hard to figure out; she irritated him no matter what she did.

He was in for a big surprise if he thought he could run Ruby off. She'd made an immense change in her life, she had big dreams and important plans and was not going to let one grouchy S.O.B. get her down.

At the check-out line, Tom's demeanor changed. He was scrutinizing the shoppers. It didn't take long for Ruby to see what had his detective antennae quivering. Bygie stood two aisles down, in over-sized clothes that looked like cast-offs. She was small enough to be hidden from Tom's view by the high display of gum and candy. Why would Mrs. Hudson be shopping so far from her own neighborhood. Slumming?

***

Bygie clenched her teeth while waiting for her prescription to be filled. The one-stop convenience of a pharmacy in the grocery store was a great idea, but she wanted to shout at the pharmacist. Tell him to grab the damn bottle and count out the migraine pills.

Returning to her car, she took a deep breath then dry swallowed a headache tablet. All she wanted to do was go home and hide. She knew she'd have to face the mess Lars left behind, but the longer she ignored it, the stronger she'd be. Maybe.

Multi-tasking as she pulled into her driveway, she hit the garage remote while fishing around in her purse for house keys. Knee driving, she grabbed her purse in frustration and put it on her lap. Looking up, she slammed on brakes. What on earth was that? She stabbed at the garage door remote, trying to get it to reverse. As it lowered, Bygie clutched her stomach. Painted across the outside of the door, in big red letters, was a message.

Whore. Keep your mouth shut.

5

Eyes glued to the ugly words, she dug through her purse, groping for her cell phone. Her quick intake of breath was audible. *What if someone was watching her?*

The last of the evening light was fading. She turned her headlights on, then snapped them off. They felt like a beacon. Finding the familiar shape, she clutched the phone to her chest. Scrambling through the mess again, she found Hall's card. Using the weak light from her cell phone, she studied the numbers.

She double checked that her car doors were locked, useless really when the top was made of canvas. *A knife could cut right through . . .* she phoned Detective Hall, the big guy who never smiled.

"Whatever you're selling better be good, my supper's getting cold."

Bygie wanted to hang up, but was more terrified of who'd been at her house than she was of the detective.

"Officer, I mean Detective? This is, Bygie Hudson, we met a couple days ago?" Her words exited without a breath. "I need you to come to my house, I mean if you can. I'm scared to get out of my car."

"Slow down. You're in your car?"

She felt dumb for calling.

"While I was out, a nasty message was painted on my garage door." She blurted over his next question, "it says 'Whore, keep your mouth shut.'"

A moment of silence on Hall's end was too long for By-gie.

"It shook me some, but I'm okay. Sorry to bother you, it's a stupid prank." She cut the call before he could say another word. And wondered what to do.

Her hand jerked when the phone in her hand rang. "Hel-lo?"

"This is Hall. Lock your car doors and sit tight until I ar-rive. I'm on my way."

***

As a precaution, Tom called for backup, wishing he could call in a fifty-one-fifty for a mental welfare check. What game was she playing? Maybe a visit to the mental ward would get her talking. Not knowing if her husband was home or not on the night of the accident, was full of shit, she was covering for him. Now this. He'd already formed an opinion on the garage door message.

It didn't ring true. It's not the way a person would be warned to keep their mouth shut, that type of threat was done privately. It would not be a public display painted on the outside of a garage door.

All the same, as he pulled into the exclusive area known as Stony Point, his eyes swept the area for anything unusual, not that he could see much past his headlights.

The Hudson home sat off a steep, single lane road that twisted and turned, snaking its way up the granite hillside.

Running past a cluster of homes on the lower end, the of-fering dwindled to an occasional driveway the higher it climbed.

The long strip of asphalt driveway he turned onto was marked with dim solar lights. Belted on the right by a col-umn of towering Cypress trees, the left of the driveway was guarded by a vertical wall of granite, topped with massive boulders. This wasn't an area of San Diego where homes played slip-n-slide during the rainy season, but a big earth-quake would cause some damage.

One boulder shaking loose would flatten anything in its path.

The large multi-level house sat to the right of the garage, hanging out over the edge of a precipice. The soaring view of distant mountaintops, heading towards the Mexican border, was blanketed with heavy fog, giving off an eerie reflection of remote city lights. The daylight view was one of distant homes surrounded by synthetic islands of green. California moats of artificial turf.

The drastic change in heights gave Tom the sensation of being too small to be of any consequence. Ocean temper-tantrums he could deal with, not large, bull-dozing rocks and sharp drop-offs.

Parking beside the black and white patrol, he nodded a greeting to the two officers standing alongside. He was surprised to see Bygie's car. He'd expected her to drive a flashy, expensive Mercedes from their dealership, but she sprung out of an older Mazda Miata.

Bypassing his mini-shitty-van, Tom elbow-guided Bygie to the backseat of the patrol car.

Hall leaned in, "Stay put until we know it's clear. Do you have your keys to the house?"

She held a mess of keys hooked to a seashell. "It's this one." She pulled the correct key to the top of the ring before handing it over.

"Do you have an alarm system?"

Her face turned red, "Yes, but it's not on."

"Is there a reason someone would be in your home, or on your property?

"No. I'm here alone."

"Does anyone else have a key, a housekeeper maybe?"

"No, I'm the housekeeper. Lars had house keys on his key ring too."

Hall, nodding before shutting the door, reminded her to sit tight.

Staying away from a direct approach to the garage door, he came at it from the side, squatting down to level a flash-light onto the asphalt. He moved the beam around, looking for footprints that may have been left in dust. No luck. Inspecting the painted words, he slipped on a vinyl glove, reaching out to touch the still tacky paint. Pretty fresh. He sniffed the end of his paint coated finger to determine what type of paint was used. Water based paint, oil based, lacquer, they all had a different smell.

He motioned for the patrolmen to cover him as he climbed the outdoor staircase towards Bygie's studio. The combined flashlight beams looked carefully for any sign of foul play and found nothing. Tom tried the key Bygie had indicated, wondering if it worked the studio lock as well. No luck. He made a note to have one of the officer's check inside before they left. They trailed back around the front of the garage and climbed steps leading to the front of the house.

He motioned for the officers to cover opposite, outside corners of the home. It allowed each patrolman to cover two sides of the house and keep an eye on Tom's back. Working his way towards the rear of the house, there wasn't much to see. The back of the house was a fenced swath of ground that dropped away into a deep canyon. It'd be hard to scale without leaving marks and impossible to do a thorough search by the beam of a flashlight. He'd send someone from Forensics out in the morning.

Tom walked as much of the perimeter of the property as he could, looking for footprints, or signs of a broken window. Nothing. They regrouped at the large front door. The keyhole didn't exhibit signs of having been tampered with, no unusual scratching. Hall inserted the key, and clicked the tumblers loose. With guns drawn, held two-handed below the sight line, they entered the house, guns, heads and bodies of all three men sweeping all directions as they entered.

One of the officers headed down a short flight of steps that led to a lower level of the house. The second officer walked straight ahead through the entry, stepping down into the formal living room. From there, he could keep the front door secure as well. Tom headed up steps that led to a kitchen and dining area. He checked the surroundings, then continued down a hall, finding the master bath and bedroom. Other than clothes on the floor and the unmade bed, nothing looked disturbed, but they'd need Bygie to confirm it.

Once the property was deemed clear, Tom returned to the patrol car and had Bygie point out the key to her studio. The uniforms carefully checked the space, while Tom stayed with Bygie to collect pertinent information. It didn't take long to clear the one-room studio and once the officers received information for their reports, they left.

Tom escorted Bygie from the car and accompanied her inside to look around.

6

Bygie wondered if she'd read Hall wrong. He'd given the impression of a stern kindness when he arrived at her home, not at all what she expected. Watching him and the other officers check her property gave her a feeling of security.

When all was clear, he led her to the front door and asked her to look around, see if anything appeared out of place. She was embarrassed by the mess her house was in. She hadn't summoned enough energy to clean. Other than her own scattered mess, everything looked fine, untouched.

She made a good-mannered offer of coffee, but was caught off guard when Hall agreed. She busied herself making a fresh pot, ill at ease with the detective watching every move. They took a seat at her kitchen table, Bygie cradled her cup, soaking the warmth into her cold hands. The message on the garage door shook her. What did it mean? She hoped the detective sitting across from her would find the answer.

Starting to believe she'd judged Hall too hastily when they met, he flipped the switch and turned back into bad-ass detective.

"If I checked, is it possible I'd find you use the same color of paint in your artwork? A possible match to the red tone used to paint a message on your garage door?"

He asked the question in a conversational tone, as if he were asking for cream and sugar in his coffee.

Her mouth fell open. "What? Are you kidding me? Of course not." She didn't even use paint in her work but was too surprised by the question to correct him.

The friendly tone disappeared. "There's something not right here, Mrs. Hudson. If someone wanted to scare you, they would have violated your space. They would have entered the garage, or broken into your home." He waited for her to make eye contact. "What they wouldn't have done, is write what amounts to a childish message on your garage door."

She snapped back. "Childish? It may seem childish to you, but it isn't to me."

"Maybe you felt a need to muddy the investigation? You know, your husband was involved in a pretty dirty business."

Bygie flinched. "I didn't know a thing about his dirty business, as you call it. I mean, I only knew what he wanted me to know."

"So you had knowledge of his activities?"

"No! That's not what I'm saying." She fiddled with the napkin under her cup, tearing off small pieces and rolling them into balls.

"You expect me to believe you had no idea what your husband was doing? He glanced away, shaking his head. "Any one of the characters he associated with could be responsible for the little message on your door. Unless you have pissed off teenagers for neighbors?"

"No, we don't. Maybe. I don't really know the neighbors." The privacy of her home now felt like isolation. "I don't know why this was done. I hardly had a chance to talk to Lars, I mean, we hadn't been . . ." her voice trailed off, finding it hard to admit how strained it'd been between them. "Well, we weren't close."

"Weren't close?" Tom echoed, his eyebrows raised. "Last week, the paper ran a picture of the two of you at the dealership." His eyes gave away nothing.

She stood from her chair, circling to stand behind it, using it to put a barrier between them. Hyper-aware of Hall's eyes tracking every move. "Pictures don't tell the whole story."

She wanted to shout, but took a deep breath instead. "Lars put on a front. He'd pretend we were the perfect couple. I, well, I . . . followed along. I found it easier than fighting. It's like I . . ." she fumbled for the right words, her palms up as if the answer would drop in from above.

Tom raised his brows, "You expect me to believe you followed the party line?" He lowered his gaze, then brought it back with such force, she took a step back. "Don't take me for a fool. My experience tells me you wouldn't be an easy pushover."

Silence filled the room.

"If you expect me to believe you knew nothing of your husband's extracurricular activities, you'll have to do better."

Her taut energy drained, she groped for the chair, sitting back down.

"Tell me the truth." Hall stated. "Maybe I can help you out of this mess."

She slouched, laughing softly, disbelieving.

"Look," Tom paused, demanding her attention. "I need you to be honest. If there is any way I can help you get out of this situation, I will. Don't try to cover for your husband; you'll only make it worse." He impatiently leaned forward, "I'm sure these aren't people you want to be involved with."

Bygie studied him while he made this plea for honesty. Taking a deep breath, she put her arms on the table and leaned forward.

"Listen, Detective. I'll tell you exactly what I know. When a reporter started calling our house, or when I'd see him parked out in front, of course I asked Lars. At first, he brushed it off as interest in him running for city council."

She sagged back, humiliated. "I'd stayed out of his life for so long, I didn't question it." She pushed hair back from her face, irritated she wasn't able to get across how little she had to do with her husband. Embarrassed to be explaining her marriage to a complete stranger.

A cop no less.

"The night of the accident, he told me a portion of the truth." Bygie's anger at her husband came back with a rush, adding color to her cheeks. "I'm sure there's more to the story, Lars put a spin on everything." She hugged her arms to her chest. "One thing is certain. I don't know anything beyond what he told me on the night he died. That's it."

"It doesn't make sense that he'd leave. If he explained his money-making venture the night of the accident, as you claim, I'd assume you'd have plenty of questions for him."

"Money making? I thought what he was doing cost money." She snorted in repulsion. "You're mistaken. How could he turn something that disgusting, profitable?"

"So you knew your husband spent time with other women?"

Her body jerked. "Plural? You're telling me more than one?" She felt sick to her stomach. "He admitted to a one-time slip-up with a . . . he said 'professional girl.' He told me a reporter found out and was trying to ruin his reputation by making it public."

"The news didn't surprise you?"

"Of course it did."

"It's hard to imagine any woman hearing such sordid news would return to work like nothing happened."

"I didn't return to work, I couldn't stand the sight of him." Her voice rose. "I couldn't stand arguing anymore." She clasped her hands on the table, her knuckles white. "I walked to my studio, mad and disappointed and confused and . . ." her voice trailed off as she worked to reign in her temper. Lars was dead.

"You never questioned why he was gone so much? I imagine he was out most nights of the week."

"Lars treated customers to late dinners or had some function to attend." She shrugged, "I didn't question when he came home. He didn't need an explanation, it's the way our marriage had been for a long time." Bygie wrapped her arms around her middle again, feeling stupid. She'd accused him of cheating, but never believed he'd stoop low enough to engage a hooker.

What a fool she'd been.

This time, Hall was the one to bark out a laugh. He slapped a hand on the table. "You're trying to tell me you led separate lives? I find that hard to believe. Your husband was a visible man, with his TV commercials and awards and all. His partners said he had a good marriage. It can't be painted both ways. Good or bad, you get to choose only one."

Her cheeks flamed at mention of the partners. She'd bet they were amused at trying to describe her marriage. She wasn't the Stepford wife they each had at home.

"Our marriage wasn't textbook." Hearing the words out loud, she couldn't believe how dumb they sounded. "I attended social functions with him, but they were few and far between in the last year."

"How about the fundraising dinner last month?" He noted her look of surprise. "I've spoken to people who were there. They believed you made a nice couple. If you cared so little for your marriage, why would you agree to go at all?"

Bygie didn't answer. There wasn't a plausible reason. Why indeed? Why had she stuck around?

"Come on, that's a load of crap," snapped Tom. "Maybe I could see the marriage you're painting if you weren't a strong, independent woman. I hear you're pretty successful with your art."

Bygie stared back, mute.

Not getting anywhere, Tom switched tactics, leaning forward, his forearms crossed on the table in front of him. Lowering his voice, he asked, "Maybe this started small, an experiment that got out of hand? You wouldn't be the first couple to try and add spice to their private life."

She was slow to recognize the meaning behind his words. She startled to her feet. "What?" This time she did yell. "You've got to be kidding me. I wouldn't be involved in that. We did not try to add spice to anything. That's sick." She was shaking with anger, heavily fueled by embarrassment. "I didn't know what Lars was doing, aren't you listening? What kind of woman do you think I . . ."

Tom interrupted, "That's what I'm trying to find out."

"You believe I'd sit at home while my husband was out running around with another woman? Women?" Her gut churned. "Prostitutes? Hanging out with whores?" The dream of her husband, wrapped in arms that weren't hers, was a harsh reality to face. She cried with her hands pressed hard against her mouth and the ache in her chest painful.

She listened to Detective Hall say words she didn't want to hear.

Her husband had been running an escort service through the dealership.

"Is there anything you can add to help clear this up?"

Bygie looked at the detective, ashen faced, tears streaming. "I can add that Lars enjoyed first class, and I didn't fit his high standard. Prostitutes were better than me."

7

"Oh baby, yeah do that. Do it harder." Greasy was reclined in the front seat of his car with his favorite girl, Sugarlips. She sure did live up to her name.

"Do ya like it honey? I got more moves than you've ever seen. Hang on baby."

Greasy groaned his response as her mouth headed back to work.

He'd been picking her up twice a week for months, finding her on a stretch of El Cajon Boulevard, looking forward to a quick release in her warm, inviting mouth. Being caught with a hooker didn't worry Greasy. He'd spent eight long years covering crime and knew when, and where, prostitution stings were going down. A perk in having a reporter's desk smack dab in the middle of the police department.

Robert 'Greasy' Tucker thought he'd made it big when he was assigned a desk in the press room of the San Diego PD. He figured it'd be a matter of months before he broke a big story. Once that happened, there'd be no looking back.

He'd be sought after for TV interviews and write a bestseller covering his life as a true crime reporter.

The stupid dicks that called him Greasy wouldn't be laughing then. He'd be sitting in a chair next to Nancy Grace, her right hand man for sniffing out crime. The lady was so damn hot.

But it hadn't happened. He hadn't factored in the expertise of the P.D. in covering up juicy news. They fed bullshit to the press, even when you had a desk in the center of it all.

Take the sting operation on the boardwalk area of Pacific Beach. Pansy-ass families had complained girls were selling their wares and wanted them out of the neighborhood. No one would find that story in the press. Hookers trolling for tourists wouldn't be good PR.

What Greasy really wanted to know was how the girls were spotted. He'd made many a mistake of hitting on the wrong college girl.

Greasy renamed Pacific Beach to Bikini Fantasy Land. Co-ed's lying around in miniscule strips of fabric, and when they dressed to go out for the night, they wore short skirts and bared mid-riffs. Nothing much to cover the days hard work of tanning. They dressed the part of girls looking for a roll, but acted offended when he approached them. How the hell was he supposed to know the sleazy bitches weren't begging for a good time?

No wonder he needed the ministrations of Sugarlips, Greasy was a man who needed relief. He was frustrated.

Sugarlips and Greasy developed a relationship, of sorts. Each time they met, she lingered awhile longer in the front seat of his car, simply talking. She'd slump down below dash level, needing to stay out of sight, keep her head down where the money was — in the lap of her johns. If her pimp found out she sat and talked for awhile, she'd be in for a hell of a beating.

Greasy rarely paid attention to what she said. He'd sit back and relax after his sweet release and let her natter about stupid shit, tuning most of it out. She'd spell out her dream of moving up in the world of hookers, entering the glamorous world of well paid call-girls. Her ambitions didn't run any deeper than turning tricks for bigger money. Greasy tuned out her dreams and replaced them with visions of his success.

His impatience with her word vomit changed after spending an entire night with her.

A damp fog had moved in, blanketing the streets with chilly air and the cold night cut into Sugar's business. Her pimp was out of town, clearing the way for a night of partying between the pair. They'd spent the night putting away a bottle of sour mash whiskey in a cheap motel room that rented by the hour. Greasy, grudgingly, had kicked in more than his usual twenty-five bucks to cover her time off the street.

Not too much though. The night was cold and he'd figured Sugar wouldn't make shit on such a miserable night. She was damn lucky to have him.

The skinny reporter had dozed while Sugar spilled a continual flow of chatter. He'd wanted her to be quiet, keep her mouth shut. She could open it when he wanted her to, and it wouldn't be for talking.

***

"Listen, this could be big for me. Isn't it great? I'd get off the street." She giggled a laugh with elements of a smoke alarm. "Rich men would be set up through a big time car salesman guy. No more walkin' up and down the El. I'd be makin' real good money."

"Sounds like changing pimps to me." Greasy rolled over to face the wall. "Don't ya need sleep?" She was dreaming if she believed anyone would pay more than a few bucks for her services. Sugar was good, but Greasy kept his eyes shut tight while she worked her magic. Nothing worse than looking in the face of a used up whore.

"I mean, listen, it's high-class stuff." Sugar continued, ignoring his pleas for silence. "These people all have big bucks. I can feel the dough rollin' in." She elbowed Greasy's back. "The girl hookin' me up? She got in on it and promised to hook me up too. We're friends from way back."

Greasy snickered, picturing the two girls together. "I gotcha.'"

"Aww, you naughty boy. I can tell what yur thinking." Sugar reached over and tweaked his nipple. "Naw . . . not like that. We got busted one time, musta been ten years ago. I hadn't seen her for a long time when I heard she was lookin' for me. I figured she'd want me to join her holy-roller church, I had no idea she stayed in the business at all."

"Promising you the golden nest, I mean golden egg?" Greasy gave a sarcastic laugh. "She gonna hook ya up with the big bucks, huh? Guess she's still walking the streets."

"She ain't on the streets, that's what I'm tryin' to tell ya. She's lookin' real good and gettin' paid high dollars to shack up with fancy guys."

Greasy played a good angle, "Maybe you oughta hook me up with her, huh? Maybe get a discount?"

"You're so bad, why you gonna need anything else when you got me? Sugar will take care of ya jus' fine." She pulled him around, slid down under the covers in one fluid move, and put her mouth to work. Greasy swore she kept talking while she did her magic.

The girl was a real pro.

The next morning, Greasy had sat slumped at his desk, looking through police reports. Over-indulgence with Sugar had taken a toll. He was only thirty-seven but looked fifty. The hard life he tacked on to the end of every work day, along with the bad luck to have inherited his mother's side of close-bred DNA, left little doubt his looks would continue to erode. His appearance looked disheveled and he reeked of alcohol.

The snotty bitch at the desk next to his had turned her back on him when he walked in. Greasy peered at her. One day, she'd regret acting so high and mighty. When he made it big, he'd make damn sure she'd never get time in front of a camera, the little prima-donna fuck.

He pushed back from his desk to put his feet up, and daydream about good treatment from Sugar. In place of the whore's face, he pictured the face of the blonde working next him. Bits of conversation with Sugar drifted in. Something to do with high class johns? He sat up so fast he had to lean forward and hold his head between his hands to stop the pounding.

What exactly had Sugarlips said? Did she mention a car salesman at a Mercedes dealership? Sounded like bullshit, but now that he'd leached some of the whiskey, the story could be worth checking out.

If there was any truth to his personal hooker's ramblings, he needed names. Sugar didn't have the goods to earn one cent more than what she got on the street. But, that didn't mean there wasn't truth behind the story. Maybe she did have a friend who was a high falutin' looker-hooker.

It'd be one hell of a story, one he'd been waiting on forever. High-class hookers meant johns with money and guys with money made great news when they tumbled.

No one wanted to see rich bastards fall more than Greasy.

He left his desk, in a hurry to find Sugar.

Winking at the female reporter on his way out, he didn't notice her shudder.

He drove down El Cajon Boulevard, spotting Sugar on her usual corner. He cut off another car in his haste to get to the curb. In his mind, the story had grown to award winning proportions. He leaned towards the passenger seat as the window lowered.

"Hey, Sugar," he yelled out, getting her attention.

She sidled over to the window and took a good look in the backseat. "Not working for the cops now, are ya, honey?"

"Geez, Sugar, cops don't have to answer truthfully, why bother asking?" He gave her his most charming smile, one he'd practiced for years in front of a mirror. "Get in, babe. I need to talk to you."

"That all you got in mind? Talk?" She gave a high giggle. It sounded worse undiluted by whiskey. "Miss me already?"

"Let me buy ya a coffee."

Sugar had a heart of gold, twined with a whore's heart. "I need 'ta earn more than coffee."

"Come on. I'll give you the going rate. Get in," Greasy pushed opened the door for her, from the inside.

Climbing into the front seat, Sugar made sure her skirt rode up thigh-high. She reached over, putting a hand on his lap. Greasy let it linger then brushed it away as he pulled away from the curb. He needed to keep his mind on business.

"What's up with you honey? Got a girlfriend all the sudden? I won't tell." She reached over again, stroking his thigh.

"Don't do that Sugar. I said coffee. In this traffic, you'll get us killed."

"Aren't we grouchy today. I know what would cheer ya up." She made a smacking sound with her lips.

No one could tell Greasy that hookers didn't love their job. He was being a decent guy, trying to buy the girl a cup of coffee, offering to pay her wage without earning it and she was still begging for it.

"I need to talk to you. I have questions about last night." He pulled into the lot of a run down diner that sat between a ninety-nine cent mart and a liquor store. "Come on, I'll even spring for food if you're hungry."

A smile lit up her face. "You takin' me to lunch? Have you gone sweet on me, honey? This like a regular date, huh?"

The run-down looking restaurant had seen better days. If the entry was any indication of cleanliness, eating a meal could present a health risk. Fingerprints covering the glass door were a solid smear of build-up.

They sat down in a sticky, red vinyl booth that had been repaired with matching duct tape. The tape had rolled in on itself and now held a collection of body hair and crumbs. A waitress came over with a limp rag and made a lazy swipe around the salt and pepper shakers, leaving a bunker of crumbs banked against them. The table-top was left with a lingering scent of disinfectant. Taking plastic menus from under her armpit, she slapped them on the table without a word, then snatched them back as if they'd steal them when they only ordered coffee.

"I can't stay long. My guy will be back looking for me, but this is soooo sweet! We had ourselves a good time last night." She fluttered her eyes. Under the table, she slid off her shoe and put her foot up between his legs. "We could have us some fun right here."

"Stop it. I told you, I want to talk." Greasy was having a hard time turning down the action but he was sore from last night's partying.

Sugar sat back, stared out the grimy window with her arms crossed.

"Come on Sugar. You wore me out last night." Greasy tried out his earnest look. "I've been thinking and I came up with an idea that could benefit both of us." He had her attention now. "I really need your help to make it work."

Sugar flashed a sprig of hope, "You been thinking 'bout us?"

"Of course, what kinda man do you think I am? I want you to have a better life." He stretched his arms across the table, palms face up. Sugar uncrossed her arms, placing her hands on top of his.

"You need to get off the streets, Sugar. You're too good for that. I worry when you're out there." He gave her hands a squeeze. "You wouldn't mind being famous, would you?"

"What is it? Tell me. Don't leave me sittin' here and wonderin'. Ya know I can clean up real good. I'd make you proud." Sugar beamed.

"I need to meet your friend, the one you mentioned last night. Is she still willing to set you up with high-class johns?"

Confusion clouded her eyes. "Why you wantin' to know about Lizzie? What's she got to do with you an' me?"

"It could be one hell of a story, Sugar. One we write together. A real book."

"I don't know how to write. Who's gonna write it? What story ya talkin' 'bout anyway?"

He answered through clenched teeth, "I'm a writer, Sugar. You know I write for the paper."

"I didn't know that meant you could write a book. Don't you just copy down what they tell ya at the police station?"

Greasy bit back a retort. He let go of her hands. "No. I don't copy anything down, I write the stories myself." *Stupid whore.* "I want to write your story, you and your friend's. What's her name, Lizzie? If she's doing the tango with rich bastards, we'd have a story to sell. This could be real big." He slumped back. "That is, if any of its true. For all you know, Lizzie made it up to impress you."

"No, it's true, Lizzie wouldn't lie to me. She's workin' out of some fancy house and has a lady that sets her up with guys loaded with dough. They got so much business they're needin' a couple more girls. That's why Lizzie was lookin' for me."

"What lady does she work for, Sugar? You didn't mention a lady or anything about a house. You said a car dealer guy was behind it."

"Well, yeah. I don't know all the details yet. The guy, Hudson someone, books the rich dudes after they buy an expensive car. Lizzie was driving a real nice car herself. Honest-to-god, you won't believe it. A Mercedes. Can you imagine? " Her head shook back and forth. "When she met me, drivin' that car? I didn't even recognize her."

"The car dealer? Hudson? Are you sure that's his name?"

"Yeah. Hudson. I think. He sells Mercedes, or maybe Cadillacs?" Her eyes widened. "Wow. If I work it right, maybe I can get me one of those fancy cars. I could drive you around. I always wanted a blue car with a top that . . . ."

"Sugar, stay focused," Greasy snapped.

She sat back. "I was only trying to tell you my dreams. I thought I was important to ya."

"You are, that's why I'm here. Come on, tell me about the house."

She pouted.

"This is for us, Sugar."

She crossed her arms and stared out through dirty glass. *Damn party whore, she better open up.* "I want this for us, Sugar. Come on, trust me, tell me what you know. Let's make this happen."

She lifted her chin and answered without looking at him. "I would get to dress up, show up at a fancy house, and treat men with my God given skills. There," she turned to glare at Greasy, "now ya know."

"We need to know the location of the house, Sugarbear."

"Aww, there you go callin' me Sugarbear. I swear. I dunno why I put up with you. You get me all mad and then go callin' me somethin' sweet as that."

"Of course you're my Sugarbear. Find out where the house is and I'll check it out, make sure it's safe for you to be there."

"I dunno. Lizzie never said. It's a real sweet deal tho."

"Did you make a plan to see her again?"

"She said she'd check back with me in a coupla' days, see if she could get me hired on. I told ya, we go way back."

Greasy smiled. *Friend Lizzie probably saw how bad you looked and didn't know what else to say.* "Do you have a way to get in touch with her? It's important to talk to her."

"What ya need her for? She's not gonna be telling you anything 'bout the men she's seeing. That'd be like cuttin' her throat."

"I know, Sugar. There's no way she'd squeal names. She'd end up in trouble herself." Greasy slouched back against the sticky vinyl, shaking his head. He snapped a finger and shot forward. "I got it. She wouldn't want to give up names, unless . . ."

"What? Tell me."

"Unless she could afford to quit the business for good." He smiled, leaning in across the table. "I'm looking out for your best interests, baby. You know how much I care. I'm sure your friend is as nice as you."

"I don't know. I'm not thinkin' Lizzie would tell ya anything. She's got herself a sweet deal, no need to go and ruin it. If her johns go down, she won't be making the big bucks. Back to walking the streets." She shook her head. Naw, don't sound good ta me."

Greasy straightened. "Open your ears. She wouldn't need the money. We'd make a ton of money from the book. More than enough for all of us." He lowered to a whisper in an empty restaurant. "I'd make sure you girls were protected. You know I have connections in the police department. If we give them big enough names, they'd be happy to let you skate on any charges. You'd both be big stars as far as the cops are concerned."

Sugar gasped, "Do you really think so?"

"This is our chance to make it big. Set up a meeting with your friend, Lizzie, let me talk to her. If she says no, that's the end of it. But I'm telling you, Sugar, we could be rich. Rich and famous."

Greasy's eyes glimmered with greed while Sugar's welled with hope.

He'd dropped Sugar off and started dialing. On the fourth call, he discovered 'Hudson' was the well known businessman, Lars Hudson. Car salesman was an understatement. He was one of the damn owners of Oceanview Mercedes.

A pot of gold had dropped into his lap.

***

He'd followed Hudson home from work for the first time, just two weeks ago.

Calling Lar's work number, he's charmed his way past an assistant and made contact with the big man himself. Greasy had whispered through the line that he knew the truth behind running expensive girls.

Hudson hung up on him.

Tightening the noose, Greasy called his home and left messages with the wife. As added pressure, he'd parked in front of the man's home, just to disturb him. If the rich jerk had thought he could brush him off, he was in for a surprise. Greasy wanted nothing more than to tumble the snotty rich boy from his high perch.

Just his kind of luck. The biggest story of his life and the lousy bastard had up and died on him.

He needed a new angle, and fast.

8

Tom sat through the morning department meeting, listening to reports of what was going on in the city, far different than the exploited stories papers and television offered. His father worked as a printer in the newspaper business for thirty-eight years and his belief was passed to Tom as gospel truth.

"Son, if the newsman don't know the facts, they just make'em up."

Back at his desk, Tom leaned back in his chair, rubbing tired eyes. Prior to the Hudson mess, Tom and Ruby had been working nights, chasing hookers out of one area of the city, only to find the same girls the next night on a different corner. A grown-up game of hide-n-seek. With the popularity of Craigslist, there were fewer women trolling the old fashioned way. In this day of instant communication, they were setting up websites and taking credit cards for payment. An entire division of vice dealt only with the internet and its myriad offers of sex.

If Hudson's operation panned out, he should be awarded for his creative approach.

Last night, returning from the garage graffiti incident, Tom had put in another two hours looking over what little information he had, trying to find a thread to follow.

The painted garage door was one more piece of the puzzle. Who wanted Bygie Hudson to keep her mouth shut? Shut about what? Or did she paint the message herself?

According to her, hubby was afraid of headlines saying he'd shacked up with a woman other than his wife, but Hudson had been doing a whole lot more than spending cozy time with prostitutes. He set them up.

The high-class escort case was less than twenty-four hours old when Tom had been notified that his main suspect, Lars Hudson, was killed in a car accident. How could a man be running a tidy little escort service on the side and his wife be oblivious to it? At first glance, he figured she was one of the main players. He'd met plenty of kinky couples in his line of work.

The trouble was, she wasn't kinky at all.

Why the hell would a nice woman, one who appeared to have a brain, stay with a man like Hudson? His conclusion so far?

She was staying for the money.

She may not have agreed with how the extra money was earned, but she wasn't above enjoying it. There were plenty of women who turned a blind eye to illegal money, as long as they got to spend it.

He needed to find out where that money came from.

When he'd gone to bed, he tossed and turned most of the night from too much caffeine. This case had him breaking his personal rules. Number one rule was to never, ever, under any circumstance, accept food or drink from a suspect. It's a self-preservation thing.

A shake of rat poison in your coffee, officer?

He blamed his restless night on caffeine, but the new widow shared credit. She came across cool, hard to rattle. When she did 'rattle', her emotions were extreme. Laughing, then crying. A lady on the edge. Was it because she knew more than she was telling?

Even her home was a contradiction. Walking through it last night, most of the rooms felt warm and inviting. They looked lived in and comfortable, until you entered the god-awful living room. He was no expert on antiques, but the furniture in there looked to be a hundred years old and un-comfortable as hell. To Tom, it was ugly as shit.

He wondered why rich people had such bad taste.

When Tom made the initial death notice, he remem-bered watching Bygie take a seat on the only sturdy piece of furniture in the room, what he called a footstool. Years ago, a wealthy man suspected of murdering his wife informed Tom the proper term was ottoman.

Looked like a damn footstool to him.

He used to enjoy unwrapping a case. Peeling back each layer of an investigation, never knowing exactly how the parts would fit. Ten years spent in homicide had earned him and his partner, Mike, the reputation of the go-to team for solving cold cases . . . until Mike up and quit.

Tom requested his transfer to vice and all he'd been doing was coasting. Doing a boring job keeping the city safe from hookers. Not exactly a thought-provoking occupation.

This was the first case he'd found stimulating in awhile, one that kept him awake late into the night It got the juices flowing, as his old partner used to say. Mike used to feel the same way. They had worked together like a veteran quarterback and his favorite receiver. Once they bit into a case, they didn't let go. Their partnership had netted a damn impressive record of cases solved.

When Mike found out his wife Annie had breast cancer, he immediately resigned.

Just like that.

No questioning the decision. No discussing it with Tom.

Mike's only priority was his wife.

Without so much as a backward glance, they packed belongings and moved to South Dakota to be near Annie's extended family. They needed all the help they could muster. Tom felt he was losing a brother and had reacted like an ass. He pushed the line when he called Mike an awful name. It made him sick to think about it.

"Jesus, Mike, slow down. You can't make a decision this big overnight. Take time to think before you rush headlong into a choice you can't undo."

"Back off, Hall. You wouldn't understand." Mike glared. *"I gave this job all I had . . ."* He studied Tom. *"Aww, never mind, it's useless."* He turned back to cleaning out his locker. *"You don't get it. Probably never will. The only reason I could do this job and stay sane, is because of Annie."* Mike carelessly threw his belongings into a box.

"I'm sorry Annie is sick, but I'm telling you, you're moving too fast. Annie will be fine."

Mike spun around, jabbing a finger into Tom's chest. "Annie's the one that didn't question long hours when we were on a case." Another sharp jab. "She's the one who propped me up when I came home from vicious crime scenes." Jab, jab. "She's the one who gave me a normal life when my job required me to deal with blood and guts. Human depravity."

Tom slapped Mike's finger away and pushed him hard into the locker. "Don't ever get in my face buddy. You're acting pussy-whipped. Doing whatever Annie's telling you."

Mike's face hardened as he stared at Tom. His voice growled, "Don't ever speak about Annie that way, you lousy bastard. I'm doing it because I love her, not because she asked me too." He grabbed his box and pushed his way past Tom, stopping at the door for the last word, "If you'd put as much energy into your marriage, as you did this fucking job, Gloria wouldn't have had to go looking elsewhere." The door slammed shut behind him.

Tom knuckled his eyes, wishing he could erase the awful words.

Even though they were true.

Instead of investing any emotion into his own personal wreck of domestic bliss, he'd examined Mike's marriage, like a science experiment. As if the results would rub off.

He'd been too dumb to figure out Mike was happy *because* he put Annie first. Tom always put Gloria second. His big time important job was nùmero uno.

How many times had he canceled plans? Gloria understood last minute changes were a side effect of dating a cop. Once they married, he'd quit bothering to call when work interfered with their plans. In his self important smugness, he hadn't had the decency to let his wife know he'd be a no-show. She'd sat through too many movies alone. Dinner dates were the same. Why should he phone? She knew his job came first.

Saving society rested on his shoulders.

Gloria had been up front and honest with Tom at the end. She'd met someone new, a man she wanted to raise a family with.

He placed the blame on her, called her a cheater, a gold-digging bitch.

In the end, he'd bought her a truck. A damn truck.

He knew he had a share in how bad their marriage turned out. He treated Gloria like nothing more than a considerate roommate. His career and his marriage had become a big velvet rut. Not bad enough to leave, not good enough to inspire, comfortable enough to stick around.

Tom stretched his arms over his head, clenching and unclenching his fists, trying to shake off the past.

He leaned forward, focusing on the file on his desk. Ruby had been in for the routine, early meeting, surprised to see him sitting there. She'd expected him to be at the Hudson home for the morning interview. He'd have to fill her in on the garage door message when she got back with the autopsy report. The one she'd forgotten to pick up on her way to work.

He'd probably have to stomach ten apologies.

He'd also have to fill her in on the action at Hudson's the previous night. Another failure on his part for not including her. It sucked to be saddled with a greenhorn.

Last night, no matter how hard he pushed, Bygie stuck to her story. She claimed ignorance on the subject of an escort service. Her husband had only told her he'd been caught in the company of a hooker and was afraid of bad press. Tom had to figure out a way to unwrap the damn layers, peel each piece back until he found the truth.

Before leaving her home, he'd waited for Bygie to calm down, get her crying under control. Mike had been better at consoling over-wrought people; he knew how to show kindness, without losing authority. Tom failed miserably, and came across as uncaring and cold. He was at a loss on what to do.

Maybe Goldilocks could pick up his slack, that's what good partners did for each other.

What partners didn't do was apologize for every little damn thing.

His desk phone rang and he grabbed it on the second ring.

"Hall."

"Hi, Tom, this is Amanda, from Chief Pope's office. He would like to see you. The sooner, the better."

Groaning, Tom said he would be right up. This case had the Chief keeping tabs.

"Mark," he yelled over his cubicle wall, "Would ya tell, Ruby, I've gone up to see The Pope?"

"Write her a damn note, I'm not your errand boy."

"Aww, come on. If you don't, I'll tell Pope you're hiding doughnuts." Walking by the cubicle on the way to the elevator, he saw the one finger answer. Tom smiled.

He knew his message would get passed on.

9

Nathan Pope had been chief of San Diego Police for eight years. His law enforcement career started with a college degree in criminal justice and two years of street patrol. From there, he steadily shot up. He was, not so secretly, referred to as "The Pope." A stand-up guy, a real cop's-cop and most of the force had mad respect for him.

Nathan Pope hadn't changed into what they called a "suit," the derogatory term rank and file cops used to describe higher up power players. Power players that forgot they ever wore a uniform and only goal was to grab the next rung of the ladder. They didn't care who they stepped on in the process.

Pope still cared. He wore a uniform to work and was damn proud of it. He made hard decisions based on his strong moral code, not on what would make the political jokesters happy. He played the political game close to his chest and the only person he placed absolute trust in was his wife, Elyse. Tom Hall was a close second; they shared a history going back to their rookie days. They used to spend their patrol time discussing the merits needed in a good chief and The Pope never forgot. He fought hard for what he believed was best for the force: better pay, better hours, and recognition for a hard job done well.

Past San Diego chiefs were accused of being publicity hounds, something Pope's adversaries couldn't use against him. Rarely taking control of press briefings, Pope would introduce whatever officer was most closely connected with the case at hand and have him, or her, speak for the department.

His enemies still found a way to use that approach against him. Opponents claimed he stepped back to avoid being caught in anything that could look bad on his record.

Pope's handling of the press came solely from giving credit where credit was due. It didn't make sense to have an officer tell him what he needed to tell the press. His uniforms understood the stakes and handled the press just fine. It may be the only reward they got, if you could call it a reward. His men were the ones in the trenches and at least their families got to see them in the spotlight being recognized for a tough job.

Nathan Pope knew the toll law-enforcement careers took on marriages; the job caused break-ups of too many families. His first marriage had suffered and ended in divorce but Pope straightened out his priorities and his second marriage was in the double decades.

He watched over his force like a mother hawk watching its baby. He had a keen intuition when one of his men or women needed a break, when they needed to step back from the job. Known to demand time-off when he sensed instability, he rarely made a wrong judgment. Officers forced to take leave, or take unplanned vacation time, didn't appreciate his efforts, but most came back acknowledging the good call. The ones who didn't return? It proved his point. They were too burned out to do the job required of them.

With the city's financial crisis and ensuing budget cuts, they were short-handed, making it difficult to take a well-earned vacation, much less for Pope to demand time off.

Pope's office wasn't set up as a shrine. He didn't follow in the steps of his predecessors by putting up an array of photos showing him shaking hands with dignitaries. He possessed the photos, that's for sure, but Pope told his wife she could use them at his damn funeral. He didn't want them cluttering up his office. He didn't need them on display to bolster his sense of self-worth. His ego was doing fine.

"Send him in, Amanda."

Sitting behind an immensely scarred, old oak desk of his father's, the only thing he insisted on having in his office, Pope stayed seated when Hall gave a tap on the half-open door. He didn't stand, use his size to appear imposing, but he wasn't above using it if a situation needed it. He was 235 pounds of muscle packed into a six-foot, six-inch body. He towered over most men but was on even footing with Hall.

Pope was a health fanatic and never missed his time at the gym. He preached exercising the body was a way to exercise the mind. According to The Pope, if you exercised your body, the mind would free itself of clutter. A clear mind was needed to stay on top of a demanding job. Doughnuts and chips were hastily shoved into desk drawers when the Chief made visits to the lower floors. When an officer was caught in the act of wiping off traces of a jelly-filled doughnut, he'd better be ready to hear a lecture on artery-clogging fat and how exercise could change his life.

"Hello, Chief. Amanda said you needed to see me?" Tom crossed the open space, taking one of the two seats in front of the desk, happy to see the chief stayed seated. It offered a subtle clue that he wasn't in for a reprimand. Tom veered to the chair on his left, leaving the right-hand one empty.

The chief chuckled a greeting. "It's good to see you never lose your edge, Hall."

"Sir?"

"Right down to the seat you choose, always keeping your right side clear. Angling the chair so you can keep an eye on the door behind you. Most people automatically take a chair to their right, unless they're lefties, and you're not a lefty. You choose a seat to your left because it keeps your right side open to action, in case you need to draw. Something I hope you won't do in my office."

Tom relaxed, grinning. "No, that wasn't on my mind. At least not today."

"Thanks for coming straight up." Foreplay over, Pope questioned, "How's it working out with Ruby Wilson?"

"Fine. She's fine."

"Don't give me that crap. I know it's a major adjustment after partnering with Mike for half your career. I wouldn't put a rookie with you if you couldn't handle it, but I need honesty, Tom. I'm never thrilled with the 'straight from the academy' hires. How green is she?"

"Chartreuse. She picks up quick, no problem there. Not afraid to work hard either. I'm sure her, ahhh, politeness, will wear off after spending time with me."

Pope sat back in his chair. "I'm sure you're right. Yes sir, I'm real sure about that." Picking up a pencil, Pope began a one-handed circus act, rolling and flipping the pencil over his fingers.

Tom thought he was probably exercising his damn digits.

"Catch me up with the Mercedes escort case. I've got everyone from the Mayor down, pushing for answers. And the damn Tribune reporter, Tucker?"

"Yeah, good old Greasy Tucker. Excuse me, I mean Robert Tucker."

"Well, we need to keep a lid on Greasy. He's spewing innuendo, insinuating higher-ups used this 'Mercedes' escort service, threatening he's ready to run with the story. It's beyond me how the bastard stays one step ahead of us. We find out a judge is playing hanky and the damn reporter finds out before the judge has his privates tucked away and his pants zipped."

"He can't prove a damn thing. He's fishing."

"No, he doesn't know much, yet, but he sure can use our favorite 'sources say.' The public eats that shit up. When I used 'judge' and 'hooker' in one sentence, the Mayor went ballistic. He doesn't want bad press, nothing new there, but particularly important when it's an election year." The pencil flipped and rolled faster.

Tom smiled. "It makes my day picturing the look on the Judge's face when we tapped on his car window. He was arrogant and damn mad we interrupted the action. That changed quick enough when he realized I was still booking him for solicitation. The great Judge Lockner, being treated like a common criminal." Tom looked down, rubbing his neck. "When Ruby and I were asked to go get a cup of coffee after bringing him in, told to forget who we had sitting in the backseat of our patrol car, I figured his arrest would disappear."

Pope scowled, "It would have been fine with me to see him spending time in the county lock-up. When your watch commander reported you'd detained Judge Lockner, as the situation unfolded, I handled it correctly."

"Yep, another big important guy, skating on a charge."

Pope growled an answer. "You know as well as I do that we needed to offer him a deal to see how far this escort case goes. The good old Judge was the one to open the can of worms and now it's our problem. I didn't ask to step into the mess. I'm glad you have such faith in me, Hall." The pencil Pope was twirling snapped in half. He stared at Tom. "I haven't forgotten my pledge to treat everyone the same, fair and square, regardless of an idiot's high-falutin' occupation. You know as well as I do that the little guy on the pole isn't charged if he leads us to the bigger fish. That's all this was."

"So how did you get him to resign from the bench?"

"When he realized I was the one climbing into the front seat, he started talking faster than I could whistle Dixie. I tilted the rearview mirror down to get a good look and let him spew. When he finished with his tale of how he got lined up with the girl, he'd all but implicated every power player in San Diego who drives a Mercedes. I let him sweat in silence, then made him an offer he couldn't refuse. Resign, or be booked." The chief picked up two more pencils, now he had both hands flipping and rolling the damn things.

Hall widened his eyes, "No one was more surprised than me when the morning papers announced his decision to step down."

"Ye of little faith."

Tom threw both hands up in surrender. "Yeah, well, chalk it up to past experience."

Pope shook his head. "A judge being caught with a hooker? I don't know what the hell he was thinking. At least we got him where it hurt and forced him off the bench. He gave up his throne, but he got to keep his good name out of the tabloids. The man's ego was out of control." Pope locked eyes with Tom, a smile playing around his lips. "That statement doesn't leave this room."

Tom arched his brows. "Your secrets are safe with me."

Pope threw both pencils down. "Who the hell thought a time would come where you'd buy a damn expensive car and get a hooker with it? That's if the Judge's story is true and not what his twisted little mind made up as a cover. If Hudson did set him up with a hooker, he probably wasn't running the escort business on his own. How far have you gotten with the partners?" asked Pope.

"We're on it."

"Damn it, lean on them and lean on the little shit reporter. Find out what he knows and how the hell he knows it."

"Not much I can do to lean on him. You know the courts don't give a crap." Tom scowled. "Unless he knows where and when a murder is going to happen, I can't do a thing to make Greasy talk. A little matter of the constitution getting in my way."

Pope pushed his glasses up to rest above his brow, and locked eyes with Hall. "I agree with the mayor. We don't need another scandal, another damn vulture feed. I want the lid kept tight on this until we know what we're dealing with. Greasy could be our only ticket into the show. Promise him an exclusive if you have to. Until we find out who's feeding the little shit information, I want this case locked down tight." Pope's face looked as if he'd been sucking on lemons. He didn't much care for reporters. Mocking a lazy drawl he added, "Old Greasy is so busy dreamin' of winnin' the great Putt-zer prize for investigative journalism, I'm afraid he'll jump in without a plug for his ass. We'd be left trying to clean up the mess."

Tom shrugged. "It didn't help to have my investigation start with the main player doing a swan dive off the highway in his SUV. The Judge drops Hudson's name as the man hooking up dignitaries, and before I can turn around, Hudson is killed in an accident. He oughta get a friggin' refund on that big expensive SUV. They should protect you, not crumple like a tin can."

"Any questions surrounding the accident? Anything off?"

"Not anything up front. It's damn lucky I'd even man-aged to get a BOLO filed on Hudson. At least I was one of the first to be notified. So far, it's the only thing that's gone right."

Tom had filed the routine paperwork, a Be On Look-Out for, as a first step in finding out what Hudson was up to. The BOLO meant Tom would be notified if Hudson was involved in an incident with law enforcement. The most he'd had been hoping to get out of the BOLO had been notification of a rou-tine traffic stop. With luck on his side, the stop would have involved Hudson and a hooker.

Turned out it was far worse than a traffic violation.

By the time Hall arrived at the site of the accident, the ambulance had been canceled. A transport team from the Medical Examiner's office was on scene, ready to take custo-dy of the body. It was routine for death notification to come from the ME's office, but after a quick conference, the duty was handed to Tom. In delivering the news, Tom and Ruby had gained immediate access to the Hudson household.

"Ruby's picking up the autopsy report right now, but I'm not counting on it for help. As it stands, we don't have enough to get a search warrant for his house or enough in-formation to involve the dealership." Tom shrugged. "Until we shake someone loose, we're dead in the water."

"Any sign of the girl Lockner was caught with?"

Tom scowled, "Nope. Once she was driven to Del Mar and booted, she disappeared."

"Jesus, Hall. I hope you're kidding with the Del Mar crack."

When Judge Lockner was given the opportunity to re-sign, it turned into a lucky day for the hooker. Instead of booking her, Hall gave her free ride to Del Mar, thirty miles up the coast. He dropped her off, warning her not to come back to his jurisdiction, a dirty little trick police departments in neighboring cities did to one another. Get the bad seeds out of town and make them someone else's problem. In do-ing that, the line between legal or not was frequently blurred. There were laws against coercing someone into the free ride.

Tom looked down. "Nah, you know, just an old saying." He swiped at his neck. "I've got guys working the streets, trying to find her, but she wasn't the average street hooker. All the information she gave us was false. Wrong address, wrong phone number, false SSN, fake name. Of course, if we'd booked her, that would have been checked. As it is, we're looking for a ghost."

"If she was the average, run-of-the mill, girl gone wild, I wouldn't be so concerned. But a Judge? With Greasy Tucker foaming at the mouth for a big story . . . ." The chief's jaw clenched. "It concerns me. Our missing hooker could have a rolodex of big names."

"Not to mention that some scumbag is feeding Tucker information."

The muscle in Pope's jaw turned to steel. "Hudson's wife? Any idea if she was involved?"

Tom frowned, staring at a scar on the old wooden desk. "Not sure. She's one hard lady to figure out. One of the strangest death notices I've been involved with. When we told her hubby was killed in a traffic accident, she started laughing."

"Laughing?" Pope's eyebrows traveled up, carrying his glasses with it. "That would play well in court."

"Either she's one hell of an actress, or it's time for me to hang up my shield. I haven't got a clear read on her yet." He looked up. "She wasn't laughing over something funny, more like something . . . ." Hall looked down, then glanced back to Pope. "Maybe the word I'm looking for is ironic."

"Ironic? It'd be pretty damn ironic if she was involved in her husband's activities and you caught up to her that fast."

Hall shook his head, "I've done preliminary background searches on the couple. So far nothing pops. It doesn't fit. The Mrs. looks squeaky clean, the Mr. showed nothing more than a coupla speeding tickets." Tom ran both hands through his hair in frustration, creating digit-sized rows down his scalp. "Talking to her last night, I have the feeling she thought her husband was stepping out on her, but nothing to the magnitude Lockner reported. She's coming in this afternoon to pick-up her husband's personal property recovered at the scene. I'll have Ruby take a crack at her. Maybe she can get her to loosen up and something will slip." Hall stared at the floor, picturing the tormented crying from the night before. "One more thing. Mrs. Hudson had an incident at her home last night. A creative graffiti message was left on her garage door."

Pope raised his eyebrows again, waiting for him to continue. Tom lost concentration for a second, wondering how the hell Pope's glasses rode up and down without falling.

Maybe he exercised his forehead too.

Tom regained his focus. "She was out shopping when her garage door was painted with big red letters, Whore Keep Your Mouth Shut. I take it as a juvenile attempt to distract us. If she's in on the escort business, she could have painted the cryptic message herself. She's an artist so it's not a big stretch. Nothing else was messed with."

"Did she report it?"

"She phoned me when she came home to the happy greeting. I guess my calling card was handy."

"Work on her. We need to find out who was involved. If Hudson was alone on hooking up a coupla big names for a twist in the sheets, case closed. But, and it's a big 'but' at this point, if this thing runs as deep as Greasy Tucker is hinting, or as deep as honorable Judge Lockner would have us believe, we may have others involved. Others that'll do most anything to keep their names out of the mess."

The chief nodded his chin hard and his glasses fell smoothly to the bridge of his nose.

As far as Tom was concerned, the glasses trick was better than a carnival act.

He also knew it meant the meeting was coming to a close.

"Keep me posted," Pope said. "I want to know what you get from Hudson's wife this afternoon. The sooner we close this, the better."

Tom rose to leave, but was stopped half-way out of the chair.

"Made a phone call yet?" Pope glared through his glasses.

Tom sat back down. "Sir?"

"Have you talked to Mike since he left? Changing partners is worse than divorce."

"No, I haven't. I've been meaning to check and see how Annie's doing. I haven't got around to it."

"It's been months. Get it done. I hear he's got good news." Before Hall could speak, Pope put up a hand, "No. I won't tell you what it is. Call him yourself. It's no good to leave bad feelings on the table. Deal with it."

"Yeah, I hear you. I'll try to call tonight."

The chief pulled a scrap of paper from under his desk blotter, pushed it across to Tom. "Here's his number in Dakota. No excuses. Clean up your table, Tom."

With a cursory nod, Tom indicated he'd received the message and left the office. He held back on slamming the door.

With all of his clogged artery speeches, the damn guy sure used a lot of table analogies. Probably dreamt of Krispy Kremes at night.

10

No time had been wasted in divesting themselves of Lars Hudson. His old partners followed up their offer with paper work to complete the sale, four days after his death. They were probably shaking in their collective Gucci shoes, afraid she wouldn't sign. She had the right to march in and take over her husband's spot as co-owner. The look on their faces, if she showed up to take over Lars responsibilities, put a grim smile on her face.

The dealership had grown dramatically over the four years Lars and Bygie had been part owners. Lars had found his niche. He could take credit for enlisting Hollywood's "B" list of celebrities to appear in television ads touting the good principles of Oceanview Mercedes.

Using a celebrity for endorsement opened a new source of revenue. Those same celebrities regularly sent their family and friends to buy vehicles from Oceanview, and once that happened, business soared. They were now the largest Mercedes dealer in the U.S. At least Lars hadn't done anything to screw that up. The prestige of turning around a struggling dealership did wonders for his sense of well being . . . at first. With the success, Lars became more demanding, a know-it-all.

He'd been brushed by fame and the brush had bristles of greed.

It left Bygie cold.

When an Oceanview commercial was nominated for a Telly award, an honor bestowed on the best advertisements, they disagreed on her needs for the award ceremony.

"Lars, I don't want to go buy a damn dress for the award dinner. I have a closet full that I hardly wear." She threw her arms up in frustration, "I'm not competing with Mitzi and Bitzi, I don't need to wear a dress from their designer." She rolled her eyes, "never thought I'd hear that word come out of my mouth." She smiled, inviting him to play, as she used her fingers as quotes. "Designer. Who would've imagined the two of us arguing over a designer dress?"

Lars considered her with cold eyes. "I can't do anything right, can I? I want my wife to buy a pretty dress. Shame on me for being so stupid. I work around the clock to buy you nice things and instead of being proud, you're so damn disdainful." He turned to walk out.

Bygie touched the back of his arm to stop him, lightly holding on. "Lars, I am proud of you. I am. I'm proud of what you've accomplished." She stood her ground, speaking to his back. "But I want us to remain the same people we were before the success. Don't you remember? We made fun of people who thought camping was done in a motor home while we slept in a tent. People who had to have name-brand everything," she joked, "I agreed to drink bottled water, what more could you want?"

His back remained unyielding. She dropped his arm and snuggled tight against him, stretching to wrap her arms around his neck. "Life was easy. We were two beach bums."

Without turning, Lars unlaced her arms and stepped away from her embrace. "Grow up, Bygie." He stalked out of the room.

Lars attended the Telly awards alone.

What Bygie wanted to do was close the deal with the partners, get it over with. Carefully read the documents and sign them. But she put the brakes on. Along with the major satisfaction of causing the men to worry, she refused to rush headlong into a decision that couldn't be rendered null and void when completed. It had nothing to do with the money, more money than she'd ever had, or could have dreamt of having. The zeros tacked on to the offer made her wonder if she needed glasses.

She didn't want one damn cent of it.

Seeing the offer on paper, the large number in writing, increased her anger — the only feeling she could deal with. Why on earth had the bastard tried earning more money with an escort service? Could the police be wrong? Her body temperature rose with humiliation. Lars had admitted to an indiscretion, his word, not hers, but nothing more. But running an escort service? It didn't make sense, they were doing fine. They didn't need the money.

The bastard.

Preferring to think Lars had been motivated by greed was the only way she could deal with it. Shaking her head to clear the disturbing image of Lars with other women, she attempted to focus on the project laid out on her work table.

Before the accident, she'd been spending long hours in her studio, getting ready for an outdoor show in La Jolla. This would be her third year at the popular event and in the two previous years, she'd completely soldout. The orders from that show alone kept her busy for months. Right now, work was keeping her from falling apart.

She looked at the mirror she was working on, hands trembling with the sudden urge to smash it.

Bygie had a hard time titling herself an artist. Like the detective asking about red paint, most people assumed she painted.

Ass-u-me Mr. Detective. I don't paint.

When she explained to others what her form of art was, she'd get a fake smile in return, followed with a 'how nice for you' remark.

The brief comment sounded like Bygie created silly Girl Scout projects by gluing shells onto old jars and cigar boxes. She'd started decorating small mirrors with seashells, making gifts for family and friends. Her finished pieces were complex. When a beach shop owner in North Carolina happened to see one Bygie had made, she ordered them for her store. At first, she didn't make a huge profit, but the work was satisfying. It melded two of her favorite things into a paying craft.

Seashells and sand.

Not long before moving to California, she began using antique mirrors. Mirrors of varied sizes and shapes that she picked up at flea markets or found combing through second hand stores. Ones with blemishes in the silver backing were her favorites. They showed character and had a history. Her sales skyrocketed when she added the term "recycled" to her work.

Recycled Beach Reflections was her baby.

There was irony in the fact that she lived minutes from the beaches in San Diego, but her shells came from North Carolina. The beaches on her part of the West coast didn't have much to offer, mostly uninteresting mussels or clams. She'd read that the west coast's Pacific Ocean was as full of shells as the Atlantic, but the colder water temperatures on the west coast destroyed the shells before they made it to land.

The warmer Atlantic ocean of her childhood offered a wide selection of shells in different sizes and hues. A trip home meant bringing back more shells than she could fit in her luggage. She'd carefully pack her find in layers of bubble wrap and ship the boxes to San Diego.

On visits to the North Carolina beaches she'd grown up on, Topsail Island and Atlantic Beach, she could find a wide selection of shells. Calico scallops with a slightly pink color, or Noble scallops with a range from orange-yellow to a beautiful purple hue. A delicate shell, the Lion's Paw, was a rare treasure as they rarely made it through the surf intact. Finding one unmarred was a thrill. The elegant Dosina, what folks referred to as an Egg Cockle, worked great in her designs. Their iridescence added a natural shine. She used large Van Hyning cockles to anchor the corners on big projects.

Bygie placed each shell on a mirror with careful consideration. Forming a pattern of color was important. She produced mirrors that started with light colored shells at the top, graduating to darker hues at the bottom, creating a soft flow of color. Or, she may choose shells that had a mad variety of color from deep purple to orange to white, colors that demanded attention by the boldness.

Her method of attaching shells to the mirror had taken months of experimentation. She'd finally found satisfaction in working with mortar. She placed shells around the outside edge of the mirror first, working her way in until creating a two to three inch border, leaving the inside edge random and curvy.

Once the shells were placed in the bed of mortar, she bent stainless steel wire around the undulating inside edge for sharp definition. Next, she tediously used a sand-glue mixture to fill in space left between the shells, leaving the impression they were buried on the beach. The final step was masking off the mirror and coating with polyurethane sealer.

Over the years, Bygie had tried applying shells to anything stationary, attempts that produced disastrous results. She smiled, remembering how her mother wouldn't let her throw anything away. On visits home to her parents, she'd find long-forgotten, dusty shell projects her mother kept on display.

Her parent's objectivity had been pretty biased.

She focused mainly on mirrors, but at the art festival in La Jolla, last year, she'd introduced a line of lamps. The lamps were cast-offs as well. Yard sales yielded a treasure trove of ugly lamps to choose from. Sometimes, the ugliest lamps had the greatest shape, perfect for her projects.

She smiled when other bargain shoppers noticed the pitiful lamps she carried away. Most of them needed new wiring and halos, so she taught herself the basic techniques for upgrading old wire and switches. The final results were wonderful. The soft glow from the lamps, highlighting colorful shells that looked buried in sand, were a huge hit. She sold out at her first showing.

Her workspace above the garage consisted of a large airy room surrounded on two sides with windows, filling the space with natural light. A half-counter separated a small, open, kitchen area where Bygie used the sink to mix mortar and wash shells. The bathroom was separated by a wall with a sliding pocket door where she'd shower off sand and dried mortar before heading to the house. She enjoyed her time under the relaxing warmth without hearing the water lecture.

The corners of her studio space were filled with sad looking lamps in need of repair. Two large work tables held mirrors she was currently working on and more mirrors were stacked against the walls . . . each facing in. She'd scared herself numerous times seeing a reflection of movement only to realize it was her own image.

The only seating, besides her padded work chair, were a couple of wooden counter stools and a droopy couch shoved against the wall, one that had made the move with Bygie and Lars from North Carolina. Lars had urged her to get rid of it and buy a new one, but she wanted to flop down with dirty clothes and not worry.

Besides, the sofa was sentimental.

It was the first piece of furniture they'd purchased as a couple.

11
LARS and BYGIE

The Beginning

The typical fish house restaurant in Myrtle Beach, SC. was packed with sunburned bodies. Tourists lined up outside in the humid air, waiting for tables to open. Inside, customers ordered fresh flounder, local shrimp, and baskets of steaming hushpuppies served with butter. Most of the tables were eight-toppers and tips were good.

Wiping down a scarred, wooden table top, Bygie stood waiting for it to dry before putting down new placemats. She was reading the ads covering the thin paper mats, wondering who shopped for an insurance agent while out eating fish. Her eyes shifted to a crumpled, used placemat, lying in the cart alongside dirty plates and glasses.

Bygie thought you could tell a lot about a person by what they doodled on a placemat. Once, a guy had left a crude drawing of his idea of mating shrimp. No stretch to figure out what'd been on his mind. Young couples giggled as they drew hearts with their initials in the middle. Older couples kept their eyes glued to the print or quietly worked the maze, one designed to keep pre-schoolers occupied.

The placemat from the last table she cleared had a handwritten slogan in the corner.

Before you Burn it Down — Shop Around!
Brought to you by: Giveashit Insurance Co.

Intent was left to the reader's imagination. A penchant for starting fires? A frustrated agent? She smiled and turned back to cleaning her last table. She laid out new placemats and added sets of cheap silverware wrapped in white paper napkins.

She hurried through sweeping, anxious to get home and shower off the cloying scent of fried food. It would be after ten by the time she got to the beach club, but at least they wouldn't smell her before she got to the door. Her best friend and roommate, Anita, was supposed to meet her outside the front door of the club. She promised Bygie she would be there, waiting for her.

There was nothing worse than walking into their favorite hang-out alone. It didn't seem to faze Anita, but Bygie's stomach turned into a knotted mess. She'd stand outside and wait before she'd force herself to open the door and walk in alone. All those eyes, turning to look when the front door of the club opened? No way.

***

Anita was one of the most exciting people Bygie knew. They'd met while taking a pottery class at a community college near Raleigh–Durham, both right out of high-school.

Bygie came from Burlington, a town located fifty minutes from Raleigh. A middle class upbringing put her dead center in her group of high-school peers. Her friends varied from lower socio-economic backgrounds, to classmates with wealthy parents.

With either group, she felt awkward. Instead of feeling comfortable in the middle, most of the time she felt out of place. Better off than some, but poor by other's standards.

Her parents couldn't afford a new Trans Am for her sweet sixteen birthday, like a number of friends received. On the other hand, they did provide her with a used, bucket-seat family Dodge, more than other friends would ever dream of getting. Bygie alternated between feeling embarrassed for not having a good enough car and ashamed for not feeling blessed at having one at all. Stuck in the middle.

Anita grew up on a tobacco farm, one that provided her family a hard-earned income. There were good years and bad; it depended on Mother Nature. Anita picked tobacco each summer to earn her own spending money and from a young age, she learned the value of a dollar. A used Dodge would have been treasured.

The two girls bonded due to Anita's persistent good cheer. She included Bygie in spur of the moment adventures and introduced her to a vast group of friends. Life was fun with Anita around.

The first summer break from community college, they both returned home. Anita picked tobacco and Bygie went back to her high school job at a hamburger joint. They vowed to spend the next summer differently. They schemed, planned and saved over the next year.

Driving to the beach in the old Dodge one spring week-end, they found a small, furnished, walk-up apartment that would be available in June. After paying the deposit, they announced the plan to their respective parents. Bygie expected her parents to put up a fight, but was surprised when they took it in stride. She was, after all, turning twenty.

They moved to Myrtle Beach, SC the summer of their second year in college, the old car loaded with swimsuits, beach chairs and books they would never get around to reading.

The furniture in their beach rental consisted of nothing more than plastic lawn chairs around an old mesh patio table and matching twin beds sitting on squeaky metal frames.

Never there for more than a quick shower or much needed sleep, furnishings were unimportant. Both girls worked waitress jobs to pay bills, spending free time together on the beach. Most nights, they hit the 'beer only' clubs for people under twenty-one.

A carefree life, one Bygie thought she should be enjoying more than she was.

Most of the time, she maintained the familiar ache of being lost, adrift among people her age. A lot of kids she met knew exactly what they wanted to do in life and were going after it with gusto, sure of their place in the world. Others were the complete opposite. They partied all summer, drifting from job to job during off-season, content with the direction life was taking them. Bygie felt the awkward split of not exactly identifying with either group.

Exactly the same as high school.

Anita easily managed to straddle both lifestyles with gusto; she liked to party, but was driven to succeed. She handled both with a casualness that made Bygie envious. Her roommate made it look easy, with her open, confident manner. Always ready for an adventure, Anita drew people to her like a magnet. The few who weren't charmed by her big smile and friendly acceptance didn't faze her. A driving need to have people like her wasn't a blip on her radar. She rolled through life, ready for fun, but never losing sight of her goals.

Bygie was much less trusting. Driven by shyness, her self-consciousness came across as a cool reserve. She was cautious in warming up to others. Anita told her two of their new friends described Bygie as stuck-up. It stunned her. How could anyone say that? She tried so hard to be friendly. What little self-confidence she'd developed was setback by the casual remark.

Anita felt comfortable discussing sex and referred to her intentions regarding a man with great innuendo and humor. She said drummers have the best rhythm in bed and Bygie wasn't sure if Anita was joking or dead serious. Bygie felt naive and clueless. Sexual encounters of her own felt shady and left her feeling empty. Making the appropriate sounds and moving her hips in a way that excited her partner, she felt awkward and foolish. She wasn't sure of the timing. What should you touch? How hard should you touch it? In worrying about doing it right, her mind was too occupied to enjoy it. Sex was a mystery and she wondered if she'd ever be brave enough to solve it. She imagined Anita had sex with joyful abandon and couldn't see her hiding under the sheets to pull off her underwear, embarrassed by her nakedness.

Walking into any room, Anita could head straight to a guy she thought was cute and strike up a conversation and they'd end up becoming fast friends. At the beach clubs, guys

she didn't know would grab her, heading to the dance floor.
With a laugh, Anita would go along for the ride.

Bygie never found it easy.

Only the inebriated made staggering attempts at flirting
and Bygie became expert at brushing them off with sarcasm.
Other men stayed back, cautious of the serious, dark haired
girl, and she never understood why, she felt like she smiled
all of the time. Her insecurities took a firmer hold each time
she watched Anita interact with playful abandon.

Bygie would sit at the table, smiling, always smiling, trying to look comfortable sitting alone while her best friend
danced or played pool. Anita put their differences with men
down to the basics of hair color. She would pose with one
hand on her hip, the other tousling her blonde hair,

"Ya know what they say, shu-gah" She'd swivel her hips
to punctuate each word, "Men take blondes to bed," switching to fluttering eyes, with both hands covering her crotch
she'd add, "But take brunettes home to their mama. That's a
whole lotta' serious business when you're talkin' mommas."

Bygie didn't believe hair color made a difference, but
something in her manner kept guys from moving in too
close. No matter how much she smiled.

Until she met Lars.

***

After work, Anita met her in front of the beach club as
promised. Walking into the noisy bar, Bygie scanned the
crowd, looking for the cute bouncer. Anita referred to him as
Bygie's secret crush, but even Anita didn't know how occupied she was with the lanky blonde. In her fantasy, they
would be the couple who doodled hearts on paper placemats,
with their initials written in permanent ink.

They were past pretending not to notice each other, had
moved to locking eyes across the crowded room with shared
smiles. Two nights ago, when she stood watching two guys
square off in anger, the bouncer, her bouncer, passed behind
her, lightly touching a hand to her shoulder, warning her to

move back. To Bygie, the protective touch spoke louder than his smiles. It was a jolt of electricity.

Anita found out his name was Lars and he didn't have a girlfriend, at least not one the beach-club waitress had seen. Bygie was ecstatic, but found it highly improbable. He was so good-looking. His long, bleach blonde hair was pulled straight back into a neat ponytail, and she'd catch him running his hand down the length, smoothing any strays. Dressed in jeans, with a button-down white shirt under a black, chest-hugging vest, his appearance was sharp.

Bygie knew what he wore each night was a uniform. All of the bouncers wore vests and white shirts, but they all looked shabby. With wrinkled shirts tucked into grubby looking jeans, they were surf bums by day, bouncers by night. Only Lars looked right. His crisp shirt and jeans were clean, as if he belonged in a white shirt crowd of business men.

The deciding factor? While the other guys wore beach sandals, or a beat-up pair of tennis shoes, Lars had on a great pair of boots. The boots were icing on the cake. They showed real class.

Anita encouraged Bygie to talk to him. She didn't understand putting off the obvious.

"Come on. Ya know ya want to," Anita teased. "Go over and say hey. Want me to do it for you?"

"Don't say a word Anita, I mean it!" Reminiscent of high school, she grabbed Anita's arm, "I mean it! I will go talk to him, maybe. Well, maybe . . . eventually."

"He's gotta' great set a buns."

"Is that always on your mind?" Bygie playfully punched Anita's arm.

Heading out at closing time, Lars spoke to her.

Perched on a stool by the front door, he was watching people leave in clustered groups, checking to make sure no one snuck out a can of beer. Walking by Lars on her way out, Bygie kept her eyes down, sneaking a look at the last minute.

He reached over, gently grabbing her arm, pulling her so close she was forced to stand between his legs. At the last minute, Bygie spun so her back was to him more than her front.

She felt breathless.

"Where do you think you're sneaking off too, Smiley?" Lars asked.

Not daring to turn and make direct eye contact, she looked at Anita with big questioning eyes. His closeness left her speechless.

Coming to her rescue, Anita said, "We're going to breakfast. Wanna' come with us?"

Simple as that, Anita set it up.

"I'll be awhile yet." He playfully jiggled Bygie's arms. "Hey you, Smiley, wanna' wait with me?"

Bygie turned enough to look at him and nodded yes.

12

Within a week, Bygie moved her few belongings out of the apartment she shared with Anita, and in with Lars. She put her things away in a drawer he emptied and tiptoed around, fearful of intruding too much into his space. She played a role, never sure of the lines. She could only dart short glances into his eyes, nervous of losing herself completely. She squirmed when he studied her up close, fearful he'd see something he didn't like.

Uncomfortable yes, but oh, so exciting.

They were hardly ever home. Life together happened after the bar closed. Whatever plans Lars made, she cheerfully accepted. At after hour parties, she began opening up to people quicker than she ever had. His arm casually draped across her shoulders felt like a blanket of security. Before long, when they showed up for an impromptu party, their names were shouted in a communal greeting.

They were recognized as a pair. A couple. She belonged.

Being with Lars gave her confidence a boost. Her dry, sarcastic, sense of humor kept their friends laughing. She'd catch him watching her through hooded eyes, motioning for her to come back to his side if she strayed very far. Melting into him, he told her he'd never felt so loved, nothing in his life had felt this good. Goose-bumps traveled her arms at the thought of making this perfect man so happy.

She was fulfilled. No longer in the middle, she was flying straight to the top.

Each night, when they returned to the apartment they would make love. Lars would pull down her shorts and shove his way into her. She wasn't ready, but understood it as his desperate need of her. Sometimes they didn't go home right away and made impulsive love under the darkness of the pier. She was willing to try most anything Lars wanted and he patiently taught her what to touch and when to touch. Lars enjoyed being the teacher.

Bygie was positive they were the only couple who'd ever felt this close. She felt adored when he laughed at her theory that paper placemats dictated how long couples had been together. Her fascination with seashells amused him and he bought her a used book identifying each cherished find. Soon, Bygie knew most of the shells by name.

"Lars, look! A Lion's Paw. Do you know how hard it is to find these? Look at the colors. This one's a treasure."

"You're the only treasure I need." The sentiments rolled out easy and nonchalant.

"That's 'cause I bring you left-over fish from the restaurant."

"Yeah, that too," he'd tease.

She collected jars of shark's teeth and jars of olive shells. The apartment soon filled with baskets of shells and Bygie lined the outdoor steps with piles waiting to be rinsed off. When Lars told her to quit dragging them home, she was crushed, but didn't say a word. From time to time she noticed the restless way his eyes moved around a room and she worried he was getting tired of her.

She worked harder at loving him.

Waking late in the day, Bygie rushed to get ready for work, her restaurant shift started at two. She'd spend her time at work, eagerly looking forward to seeing him at the bar. She didn't ask Anita to meet her at the door anymore. With trepidation muted, she walked in alone.

Her relationship with Lars put a huge strain on her friendship with Anita. To ease her guilt over abandoning their plans, Bygie found a girl to move in with Anita and take over her share of the rent. But the easy camaraderie between them was damaged.

Two months with Lars passed in a blur and time for Bygie's return to school arrived in a flash. Tearful and edgy, she avoided making plans with Anita on returning to Raleigh. She tried to steer clear of facing the awful truth of leaving Lars. More than anything, she wanted Lars to step in and plead for her to stay. He didn't ask her to stay, or ask her to go. He left her fumbling with the decision, not knowing what he wanted.

When he asked what was wrong, why she was upset, she let tears flow unchecked.

"School starts next week. I need to go, but I don't want to leave you." Saying the words out loud hurt. She sat down and cried, covering her face with her hands. She wanted Lars to implore her to stay, beg her to stay. Say he couldn't live without her.

He only grabbed her, hugged her tight. "I don't want you to go either but you need to do whatever's best for you." Lars remained calm, in control.

Bygie could only wonder at his strength. His sturdy arms and simple words told her he was being strong for her sake, doing what was best for her.

"You could move to Raleigh. Come with me?"

"I thought you shared an apartment with Anita?"

"You know Anita. She won't care." Bygie said words she knew weren't true. She'd hurt Anita once by moving in with Lars, a second time would be the death of their friendship.

"And your parents? Won't they be mad, shacking up with a guy?"

"Yeah, but I don't have to tell them you've moved in with us. I'm sure Anita will cover for me." She felt sick for putting Anita in a lousy situation and wasn't sure she would agree to any such thing. "Once they get to know you, we'll be fine."

But what was she to do? This wonderful man felt loved. By her.

They moved to Raleigh. Anita, Bygie and Lars. The damage to the girl's friendship was critical, as Bygie thought it would be. Anita found a new roommate and another apartment within a week of returning to Raleigh.

Bygie spent all of her time with Lars. She was consumed with showing him how much she adored him. She planned her days around him, going out of her way to make his life easy.

He found work at a college bar and graduated from bouncer to a bartender. On the nights he worked, she'd watch from a corner stool at the popular hangout. Pretty girls flirted with the good-looking bartender and she looked away when Lars flirted back. Each night, in the comfort of his arms, Bygie was assured the stupid girls didn't matter; he only flirted for the tips. Besides, he'd say, I always come home to you.

She ignored the tone of resentment that snaked through his words.

Treating her classes as intrusions, she only attended enough to get through. Her grades were hanging on by a thread, and phone calls to her parents were filled with half-truths. They sensed something was going on and wanted her to come home for a visit. Face to face with her parents, she couldn't keep up the pretense of living with Anita. She let them in on her new roommate, looking up only to plead her love for Lars. She tried to make it better by saying they were practically engaged.

It didn't help.

Her father demanded the hooligan be put out. "A bartender for Christ's sakes. What's gotten into you? I'm not footing the bill for a freeloader you picked up at the beach." "He works, Dad," Bygie defended him. "He's even thinking about selling cars. One of the guys that comes into the, ahhh," she avoided the word bar, "the place Lars works, is doing great selling cars. He offered to set Lars up for an interview. He'd be a terrific salesman."

Her dad snorted. "It's obvious what a good salesman he is. He's selling you a bill of goods."

Her mom interrupted. "Bygie, honey." She tried to smooth things over, calm down her ill-tempered dad. "We only want what's best. You're too young. You need to finish school."

"Mom, Dad, he's a good guy. He loves me. Isn't that what counts? You need to get to know him, that's all. Give him a chance."

Her dad refused to back down. He wanted Lars out of the apartment he was paying for.

"We'll move then, or pay for it ourselves. You don't understand. I love him. He loves me."

Her father stood up, slashing his arm sideways, putting an end to the discussion. "Go do it then. You two can pay next month's rent on your own. Shack up with whoever you want, but it's not going to happen on my dime. I didn't raise you to be a tramp."

"No, Jack, stop it. That's not fair. Bygie's in school, she's a good girl."

"Mom. That's fine, we'll be fine." Bygie stormed out of the house, wondering for the first time how come she'd never noticed how dumb her parents were.

"Jack, that's not right. Catch her. Tell her you didn't mean it."

"I did mean it. Let her see how far her knight in shining armor gets her. She'll be back asking for help soon enough."

Bygie and Lars got married the next week.

***

They struggled, but made ends meet. Bygie finished another year at the community college, earning a piece of paper with an associate's degree in graphic art, and no idea what she wanted to do. Lars landed a job selling cars and was making enough to keep their heads above water.

Bygie never told him exactly what her father said, but he knew her parents disapproved. Her mom and dad drove to Raleigh once a month for dinner with the 'kids', and the first few years were rough. Lars worked hard to impress her dad. While Bygie would have appreciated the effort on her behalf, she began to doubt his motivation. She felt she was merely a sideline benefactor. His driving force was proving his worth to her father.

According to Lars, his childhood was a mess. He was an only child whose father had abandoned him and his mother shortly after his birth. Lars believed he was dead. His mother wasn't much better. She took off when he was six months old, leaving him with her only sister. He never saw her again. He was raised by his stern aunt who made it a point to let him know it was his fault she'd never marry and have a family of her own. Who'd want an extra brat?

Lars told Bygie he never felt loved until he met her. She responded to his need and put aside disturbing questions. Forgave him for not putting her needs first. How could he? He'd been forced to look out for his own well-being at a young age. It made her love for him stronger and she vowed to give him the family he deserved. Her life revolved around making him happy. It never crossed her mind that Lars was as much in love with the idea of a 'normal' family, as he was with her.

They talked of having children, someday, a mythical day in the future. Lars struggled with the idea of having a baby; he didn't think he could be a good parent. He made up excuses. He wanted enough money to provide his children all that he'd lacked as a child. Bygie told him children didn't need possessions, they needed unconditional love.

He'd smile and answer they needed to wait.

Lars worked long, hard hours. Weekends and holidays were spent at car sale blowouts and he jumped from one dealership to another, always chasing the golden goose. They disagreed bitterly each time he announced a move. She wanted him to stay in one place long enough to work his way up, but when it came to telling her parents he'd switched dealerships, again, she spoke in optimistic terms. She hated telling them anything that would reflect poorly.

His hard work paid off. He became one of the top salesman in the Raleigh–Durham area, but the satisfaction didn't last long. He dreamt of buying into a dealership, but the amount of money to do that was beyond their means. Lars had proved his worth and her parents may have helped, but she refused to ask. Her father's hurtful words, all the years before, had lodged in her psyche. They held a firm grip on her. She tried to make it up to Lars by being the perfect wife.

Four years into their marriage, a week shy of her twenty-fourth birthday, Bygie found out she was pregnant. Nervous how Lars would receive the news, she made herself believe he would be overjoyed. Once the shock wore off. Spending time cleaning their apartment, she fixed his favorite meal, a roast beef dinner. She put on a skirt that Lars once told her looked sexy. She lit candles, pacing off anxiety, waiting for him to come home.

Lars was surprised when he walked in. "Who's the lucky guy? I hope you weren't expecting someone else. What's the occasion?"

"I wanted to do something special, no big deal. You can treat me to dinner, next week, for my birthday. Tonight it's my turn." Bygie missed the look of relief that washed over Lars face. She didn't realize he thought he'd forgotten her birthday or anniversary.

He scooped her into his arms, lifting her up for a kiss.

"You're the best, Bygie. Something smells wonderful, and I don't mean what's cooking." He nuzzled her neck, his intent clear.

Overwhelmed with the secret, she forgot her plan to wine and dine Lars before sharing the good news. She couldn't believe how nervous she'd been about telling him they were going to have a baby. This was her husband.

"Lars, wait, I have a surprise." She struggled to get down, laughing.

"I hope it involves what you have on under your skirt," his hands traveled the length of her body as he eased her down.

She playfully swatted him away. "Hold off buster. That's how I ended up in my condition."

Lars looked bewildered.

"I'm pregnant, silly." She studied his face, beaming, and reached out to touch him.

Lars froze, then stepped back, removing himself from Bygie's touch. "You're pregnant? Now? How did that happen?"

"It must have been the last time I fixed your favorite dinner." She leaned back into him, rubbing suggestively, needing to feel his arms around her.

He pushed her back, held her at arm's length. "So that's what you're dolled up for? Thought you could soften the news?"

"Lars, of course not. I know it's not what we planned, but it happened. You'll be such a good dad."

"No."

"What? What do you mean 'no.' I'm pregnant."

"No Bygie, we're not having a kid now."

"I think we're beyond that, don't you?"

"You don't need to be sarcastic. We'll have to take care of it."

It took a minute to register. When it did, the meaning of his words shocked her. "Take care of it? You mean take care of our child? What the hell do you mean? I'm not taking care of anything. You don't mean it." His cold words chilled her. Did he mean an abortion?

"I do, Bygie. I'm not ready for a kid. I've told you that over and over, you never listened."

"Lars, I didn't do this on purpose. The doctor said the birth control pill is not perfect. I don't know how it happened, but don't you dare tell me to 'take care of it.' The 'it' you're referring to is our baby."

"This isn't open for discussion Bygie. I do not want children, not now, maybe never."

"We talked about having one of each, a boy and a girl. You can't always plan for it." She was angry and hurt. "This is it. Our dream of a family."

"We didn't discuss children, Bygie. You talked, I listened. The dream was yours, not mine. You never wanted to hear my feelings." He threw his arms out in anger and frustration.

Bygie flinched, stepped back.

"What was that? Did you think I was going to hit you? What the hell's wrong with you?" Lars stormed to the door, "I'm not staying here. Call your sister, call your parents, tell them what a bastard I am. I don't care. Tell them they were right about me. Maybe you can hear me now." Lars put both hands to his face, cupping them like a megaphone and yelled. "I don't want kids. Ever."

He left, slamming the door hard.

Bygie sank to her knees, too shocked to cry. She protectively wrapped her arms around her middle, rocking back and forth. Who was that man?

The next weeks of their marriage were hard to endure. Used to protecting the good image of her husband, she was too ashamed to talk to her mother or sister. She walked around, dazed, wondering how she would raise a child by herself, never questioning doing anything different. She lost weight and felt queasy most of the time, not sure if the root cause was pregnancy or her marriage.

She waited, praying Lars would change his mind. They hardly spoke. He came home late, never explaining why or where he'd been, rewriting the path of their marriage. She ignored him and pretended not to notice if he was home or not. She flatly refused to discuss abortion.

She was dying inside.

One month after telling Lars she was pregnant, Bygie was carrying groceries into their apartment when she halted mid-step, seized by a wave of ferocious cramps. Dropping the groceries to the walkway, she clutched her middle protectively, panting. When she rose, she felt a weird sensation of moisture between her legs.

It was over.

13

They spent a total of nine years in the Raleigh–Durham area. Bygie worked an odd assortment of jobs before landing in the graphic arts department of the largest newspaper in the region, the *Raleigh News and Observer*. She hated it. She left there to work as a museum guide. She never stopped playing with shells and started producing small, shell encrusted mirrors. A tourist shop in Myrtle Beach scooped them up as fast as she turned them out. A big boost to her ego and sense of pride, but not to their bank account. The pay was minimal.

Lars took to introducing her as an artist.

He was at work more than he was home, but Bygie was busy, too. Their marriage changed when Bygie had the miscarriage. She'd questioned staying with him, many times, but in the end, she just stayed. She strengthened the wall between herself and her family, putting a happy spin on their lives. When the subject of children was brought up, she stayed silent.

They started looking for a house to buy, her husband's way of apologizing. Finding a cottage-type fixer-upper, in a quiet cul-de-sac, they made the big decision and moved into a house of their own. Life moved on.

They both changed after the miscarriage, but "sameness" in marriage didn't always mean good. At least that's what Bygie told herself. She had a hard time trusting Lars with her feelings, but over time, justified it by calling it maturing. Maybe this was growing up. She was content, but not happy.

Something in her life was missing, but she didn't dare scratch the fragile surface.

It never crossed her mind Lars would cheat on her.

She found out by showing up at the car lot to surprise him.

The surprise was on her. She walked into his office unannounced, only to see him untangling himself from a nineteen-year-old blonde office clerk.

Lars begged her not to leave him, swore nothing had happened.

"I was feeling lonely, you've been so cold to me. I don't feel loved anymore. Please, please, forgive me. Don't ruin what we've built together."

His words pierced her with unseen wounds.

I'm responsible for the mess our marriage is in? He showered her with attention, coming home early to spend time with her. Holding her tight in the night, whispering he needed her. Needing her didn't have the powerful pull it once had, but she thawed under warm breath on her neck. She ended up feeling at fault, guilty for not living up to his expectations. She'd let him down by not telling him how she was feeling. How was he to know she was lonely too? Forgiveness was her role, strengthening the foundation their relationship was based on.

His need to feel love and acceptance and her willingness to fulfill it.

She didn't discuss his cheating with anyone, stuffing the hurt inside, following the pattern set by her pregnancy and miscarriage. If she tarnished his image, wouldn't that tarnish her as well? She still never wanted to give her parents, her dad, a reason to say I told you so.

In the weeks following her husband's betrayal, she drifted from day to day, not yet on solid ground, still shaky with the uncertainty of her marriage, when her sister made an unexpected visit.

They lived less than two hours from each other, but with busy lives, impromptu visits seldom occurred. She ran out the door to greet her.

"Jane, what on earth are you doing here?" Bygie smiled from ear to ear, looking in the backseat. "Where are the kids?"

"Hey sis, I'm glad you're home." Her sister's face looked pinched, her smile forced as she stepped from the car.

Giving, Jane a hug, Bygie felt her stiff tension. "What's up? Are the kids okay?"

"Yeah, yeah they're fine. Let's go in." Jane looped her arm through Bygies, heading toward the door. Bygie resisted.

"You're scaring me. What's wrong? You never drive over without a reason. Is it Bob?"

"What? No, he's fine. Let's go in. Come on, I've been driving awhile and want to use your bathroom. I could use a cup of coffee, too." They walked arm in arm up the front steps "Where's Lars today? I phoned Oceanview, they said he wasn't in."

"What? That's news to me." Bygie's stomach turned. Had he mentioned being out of the office today? "Why were you trying to find Lars?"

"Go make coffee, I'm headin' to the bathroom. We'll talk in a minute."

Bygie ground fresh beans, then spilled most of them trying to dump them in the filter. Her hands were shaking. Something was wrong.

"Here Biggie, let me finish," Jane teased, using her sister's name the way others did. Her voice sounded weary behind the mask of humor. She took over and within minutes the aroma of fresh coffee filled the room.

Bygie sat at the counter while her sister made coffee, pressing the heels of her hands into her eyes. "You haven't called me Biggie in a long time. Did I ever tell you I thought my name was Biggie until I was six? Mom and Dad were light-years ahead of the curve in the made-up name department. Uncle Byron plus Aunt Margie, equals Bygie. How simple. Until they realized no-one could pronounce it. I always wondered if we had an Aunt Penelope and Uncle Morris, would we have a brother named Penis?"

Jane laughed. "You're a nut."

She continued to rub her eyes, refusing to look at Jane, talking non-stop to avoid hearing the news. "I read the other day a baby girl was named Shi-thade. Not so bad, but they spelled it Shithead."

Jane walked around the counter and put her arm around Bygie's shoulders.

"What is it Jane? Tell me, it's Lars isn't it? Tell me, I can handle it."

"No, not Lars. Why would you think that? Bygie, look at me." Jane perched on the stool next to her, trying to keep control of her emotions. She was the big sister. "You have to know, we'll be okay and we have each other. It's Mom and Dad. They were in an accident." Jane broke down, couldn't continue talking.

In the arms of her sister she gave in to the feeling of a ship going down.

Their parents were killed when a big-rig jack-knifed in front of them while trying to avoid hitting a dog.

***

The next weeks were a fog of numbness. The sisters referred to the truck driver as "Shithead," using the new Shi-thade pronunciation in front of Jane's children. They got through it because each sister wanted to be strong for the other. For weeks after the double funeral, Bygie felt nauseous when she smelled fresh brewed coffee.

Lars apologized for not being there when Jane arrived, Bygie didn't bother to ask where he'd been. It hardly mattered in the face of losing both parents. When he fell apart, she comforted him, as was the norm, thinking, they were *my* parents. They struggled through, feeling adrift but seldom discussing feelings. She had lost her anchor in the world and Lars had lost his biggest motivation for success.

In the months following the tragic loss, Lars regained his footing, his success driven traits fully engrained. Bygie remained lost. There were days she found it hard to get out of bed. Lars was becoming impatient with what he deemed moping. He found a new drive to succeed when he discovered a struggling Mercedes dealership in San Diego, looking for a new partner. Bygie sat in their little family room, listening as he painted a picture of the beautiful life they could have on the west coast.

"Bygie, honey, this is it. It's what we've been looking for. A chance like this may never come again. We can buy in cheap and I know I can turn the sales around." Lar's eyes were dancing with excitement. He sat on the floor at her feet, "Can't you feel it? We can find a beautiful house that looks out over the ocean."

"There's an ocean here, Lars, only three hours away. What makes you think we could afford an ocean view in San Diego if we can't afford one here? The cost of a house out there must be quadruple what it costs here." Bygie's voice was flat.

Lars jumped up, "Damn it Bygie, why do you always have to be so snide? I know what the houses cost, I'm not as stupid as you think."

"I didn't say you were stupid. I said houses cost a lot more. Take it however you want." She leaned her head back against the chair, closing her eyes, refusing to argue. She sensed Lars pacing, then he returned to his spot on the floor in front of her.

"Will you please consider the idea? I know I've messed up, I want to make that up to you. Once we're settled and know where the business is going, let's start a family."

Her eyes flew open. "What? You don't want children, remember?"

"Come on, you've said things you didn't mean when you were mad. I was scared. What do I know about being a dad? After losing your parents, I wondered how I ever thought I didn't want children. Their accident forced me to stop and take a look at our lives. I decided we should start planning for a family of our own."

Bygie studied his eyes, looking for a sign of honesty. What she saw was vivid blue and the reflection of a woman hanging on to hope.

"Don't tell me this if you don't mean it, Lars, it would tear my heart out. You knew I wanted a baby from the beginning, you're the one who didn't have the nerve to tell me up front you weren't interested in having them. You conveniently left that out and implied the time had to be right, the bank account big enough." She closed her eyes again, shutting him out, recalling the pain of miscarriage as if it were yesterday, not seven years ago. "You may not have agreed with wanting children, but you didn't tell me to stop dreaming. Not until I got pregnant. You let me dream, then shattered it."

"I've told you how sorry I was. I know I was wrong. I reacted like a scared kid. I've done a lot of growing up since then. This dealership could be the answer to our security. I promise I can make it a success." Lars grabbed her hands, "Please, please don't give up on me. All I ever wanted to do was make you proud."

Bygie listened to his words, wanting to believe him. She sat up, pulling her hands away. "I've always been proud of you, Lars, you chose not to believe it."

"I don't deserve you, Bygie, I love you so much. Let's go and start over, build a new life together. Please, Bygie."

He promised it would be a second chance at doing things right, a new life, in a new place. The promise of a baby. Bygie jumped on the ride, holding on for dear life to the only anchor she had left. The man she'd fought so hard for. Her husband.

The money from her parent's estate allowed them to buy in as partners at Oceanview Mercedes, in San Diego. Lars threw himself into their new life on the west coast with a renewed zest. He worked hard to become a success. Lars fit into the crisp white shirt club of businessmen she'd envisioned so long ago.

Her opinion now? He was an arrogant ass.

Bygie found her own success in San Diego. Her shell art was sold through an exclusive shop in the wealthy area of La Jolla and she'd built a website that boosted her sales. She never lost sight of the irony of using shells from the east coast to sell on the west coast.

Lars was home less and less. She worked in her studio until she dropped into an exhausted sleep, only to rise and do it all again. Working at home kept her isolated; it didn't give her a chance to bond with other women or make any close personal friends.

Talks of having a baby trudged the same tired circle. The time was never right. Lars wanted to wait a little longer. Let him get a grasp on sales first. The timing would never be right for Lars. Their new life in California was exactly the same as their old. It followed the well-worn rut of their marriage. Without close friends or family to turn to, Bygie slogged through each day, using work to keep her mind occupied.

She turned away from centering her days on making Lars feel loved, to wondering why she didn't feel loved at all. No longer insecure, no longer anxiety ridden.

She was empty.

14

"Son-of-a-bitch!" Tom read Hudson's autopsy report. He rolled his chair out of his cubicle, yelling into the room, "Anyone seen Goldi . . . I mean Ruby?"

A voice floated an answer. "She left. Said she'd be right back."

"Stupidity, that's what's up." Tom muttered as he rolled back over to his desk. He'd come down from meeting with The Pope to find the autopsy report lying on his desk. It sat there, laying in a non-descript manila envelope for a good half hour before he'd opened it. He grabbed his cell phone and punched in Ruby's number.

"Where the hell are you?"

"I'm on my way to get a real coffee instead of the crap at the station. I thought I'd be back before you came down from the visit above. Sorry. What's up?"

"Did you read the autopsy?"

"No, sorry, not yet. When I picked it up, the girl at the desk said the M.E. wanted us to call him this afternoon. He was in a meeting. Sorry, sir, errr, Tom, did I do something wrong?"

Tom blew out a breath, rotating stiff shoulders. "Meet me at *Zach's*, we've got a mess. I'll fill ya in when you get there." He hung up, and shuffled through the report again. Lars Hudson had indeed lost control of his fancy SUV but not due to wet roads. This case was turning into one of the fun ones, surprises under each layer. Now he was probably

going to be kicked from it altogether. It would become someone else's problem.

It seems Lars Hudson had a bullet in his head.

***

Ruby was waiting at *Zach's*, the local diner owned by a
cop's brother, when Tom arrived. Too early for the lunch
crowd meant they had a back booth to themselves. Hungry,
Tom ordered one of the specialties, a cheeseburger with a
fried egg in place of a clump of pickles. He'd count it as
breakfast and lunch rolled into one. Ruby ordered a glass of
iced tea to go with the five dollar coffee she carried in.

When the waitress walked away, Ruby said, "Disgusting.
I can't believe you eat burgers with an undercooked egg for
dressing. It sounds gross and looks worse."

"Don't knock it 'til you try it. It's one of their best."

"No thanks. I'll stick with pickles on mine. What did The
Pope want?

"He's keeping tabs on the investigation. I told him we
had nothing new to report." Tom paused, aiming a hard look
at Ruby. "We do now."

Ruby looked puzzled. "What's up?"

"We're going to lose the case, that's what's up. Turns out
Hudson had a nice size hole in his head. He was shot." Tom
watched Ruby's face, looking to see if she would recognize
where the file would be headed. He impatiently waited for
the information to sink in.

She was slow to understand, but the meaning dawned.
"Oh shit. Does that mean the file will be turned over to homicide?"

"Yep, you get an A+. It'll be moved out of vice so fast it'll
make your head spin." Tom pinned her with an angry look,
"How long did the autopsy report lie around on my desk?"

"Not long. You called right after I dropped it off."

"Not true, Ruby. I worked on the computer for a good
half hour before I even opened the damn envelope. You were
gone all that time." Tom struggled for control. "How long
was it there? Anyone could have looked at it."

"I swear. I put it on your desk right before I left. I checked my messages, booted up my computer and headed out for a decent cup of coffee. My phone rang before I reached the street." Ruby was sick of his holier-than-thou attitude. "Who would look at it anyway? You're acting like I left it on a table in this crummy restaurant and walked away."

"Don't ever leave a document lying around, especially one you haven't taken time to read. How can we keep a lid on anything, if we're the ones guilty of leaving shit out in the open?"

"I put it on your desk damn it, not in the break room." Ruby lost any semblance of innocence. She glared right back at Big Tom.

The waitress arrived with iced tea for Ruby and a diet soda for Tom. She beat a hasty retreat, sensing the tension at the table. It gave Tom enough time to simmer down. He scrubbed his forehead with his fingertips, then combed his fingers back through his hair, following the path of previous trips.

"Ruby, you can't trust anyone. Why do ya think the Pope is so concerned? It'd be nice to know what we're dealing with *before* it's on the five o'clock news." Tom's lip curled. "Aww, shit. Guess it won't be our problem for long anyway."

"We've put a lot of work into it, won't that count?"

He shrugged, "Not too sure why, we were doing our job." Tom smiled. "Parts of it have been fun, though. The judge was pissin' in his pants scared when we busted him. He knew he was in deep shit, caught with his tighty whities down around his ankles." Tom scowled again, "If Pope wasn't the chief, the judge would've walked. I guarantee that the good-ol'-boy network would have saved his ass. As it is, he still got to protect his good name by agreeing to resign from the bench. Way more than I would have given him."

"Yeah, but you're the one who insisted on bringing him in. Other cops would have let him walk and added a pat on his back." Ruby sounded resentful. "We wouldn't know how he hooked-up through the Mercedes dealer if it weren't for you."

"That was dumb luck. Being such an upstanding citizen, I thought he should pay for the consequences of his side lovin' from a happy hooker. Pope's the one who got Lockner to spill the beans on Hudson playing pimp. Hell of a full-service dealer. No wonder they're the biggest car lot in town. Buy a car, get a blow . . . ." Tom's face reddened. "Well, you know what they get." He missed Mike; he wouldn't have had to watch his words.

Ruby laughed. "Maybe that could be the new slogan for the dealership? I can picture the artwork, 'No snow job, just a blow-job. Satisfaction guaranteed.' Or something like that."

Tom grinned, seeing the waitress stop dead in her tracks behind Ruby when she overheard "blowjob." She put his burger on the table without a word and walked away.

Ruby laughed.

They were quiet as Tom ate a few bites, then wiped egg yolk from his chin. Ruby swirled her tea hard and turned away to hide her look of disgust. "Will we be able to get a search warrant? With the main player shot?" She turned to face Tom, wincing as he used his burger to smear gooey egg yolk off his plate.

"Won't matter to us anymore, it'll be a homicide case now. It'll become their problem."

"Can't you talk to The Pope? He was adamant about keeping this under wraps. Moving it means more eyes."

"I'll try. In the meantime, it changes things for the laughing widow. Maybe she can laugh on her way to the bank."

"What?"

"Don't ya find it handy he turned up dead right after she finds out he was busy lining up new car buyers with happy hookers?"

Ruby looked skeptical.

"Why not? I've seen worse." Tom said. "The little wife was home alone. No alibi. She says she didn't know a thing, but it wouldn't be the first time I was lied to. Maybe she found out and was royally pissed." He shrugged. "Sometimes it doesn't take more than that. I need you to find out if Mr. Hudson had a nice fat insurance policy. If he did, it'll be no surprise who the beneficiary is."

"You think she's involved in his murder? I don't know. It doesn't feel right. That would be one hell of a shot to pull off. Shooting someone while driving down the road would be pretty hard. Maybe he shot himself? Realized what he gotten himself involved in and took the easy way out."

Tom tapped the envelope lying on the table. "The coroner's report pretty much ruled that out. Angle of the shot was wrong for self-inflicted. Whoever shot Hudson wanted to make sure the damage was maximized. Not much left of the slug, they used a hollow point."

A hollow point was what the name implied; the tip of the bullet was hollowed out. When it entered a body, it expanded, creating tissue damage far greater than a regular bullet. It was the type of bullet hunters used to increase their chance of taking down prey quickly. Whoever shot Hudson was intent on taking him out.

Tom polished off his burger, but not before using it to mop up egg left on his plate. "There was activity at the Hudson residence last night."

"What?"

"I got a call from the lady. Seems someone thought it important to warn her to keep her mouth shut. I phoned you when I got home, to give you a heads up."

Ruby fumbled her cell phone from the clip at her waist. "Damn phone. I got a new one and they promised my messages would be forwarded." She pushed buttons on the face of the cell, "nothing. No messages."

"Make sure it's working. We need to be able to stay in touch."

"Sorry."

Tom ignored the apology, one of a hundred. He filled her in on the Hudson garage door artwork. "I chalked it up to a lame attempt to distract us, but maybe there's something to it. Pretty damn convenient, don't you think? Her husband is under investigation for pimping, and he turns up dead. Who has the most to gain?"

"I know. Follow the money, right?" Ruby said. "The guilty party is generally a pissed off spouse."

"It's a damn fine place to start." Tom stopped. He was still treating the case as if he owned it. "I'll try to get in to see The Pope right away, see where the case is going to land. Go ahead and follow the paper trail until we hear different." Tom snapped his fingers, then pointed an index finger at Ruby. "Put the widow on hold. We don't want her coming after her husband's property. We need to get a search warrant for items in the property room, along with what's left of Hudson's vehicle. Stall her somehow. Once we have the warrant, there won't be anything to hand over to her."

"Got it."

Leaning in, Tom sternly reminded Ruby, "Keep the damn autopsy quiet. All we need is for 'ole Greasy to get hold of that information If he gets wind of anything, he wouldn't hold back. The murder would be splashed across the headlines by morning. I still don't know how he connected the judge. We've got a leak, but it's not going to be repeated, not if I can help it."

They left the diner together only to split up at headquarters. Ruby headed to her desk while Tom walked straight to the elevator. He impatiently slapped the envelope against his hip, waiting for a door to open and deliver him to The Pope.

15

Tom's second meeting with Pope went better than he could have hoped. The case was still his. With the same foolish reasoning he used his entire career, he felt like he'd been handed a gift, instead of a job. When the chief found out Hudson had help driving off the side of a cliff, he wanted the file to stay with Tom and Ruby. He decided not to move it from vice to homicide. The fewer people involved the better. An unusual move, but with Tom's homicide experience, Pope wanted him to stay on the case.

Someone higher up must be riding the chief's ass hard.

As far as anyone else was concerned, Ruby and Tom were working a straightforward prostitution case. Lars Hudson died in a car accident, nothing more. It amounted to a gag order. It would be up to Tom to make sure Ruby understood the edict and towed the line. Pope had faith in him to do things right.

When Hall and The Pope were rookies, they got together for weekend barbecues, but their seven year age difference put them out of step. Pope was married, Tom was single. They didn't get together anymore and hadn't for a long time. It stopped early in their careers as they moved in different directions with their respective climbs up the law enforcement ladder. The chief chose a path directly into the political swamp, while Tom wanted nothing to do with it. The only remnant of their earlier shared years was a deep-seated trust in one another.

For good reason.

When the Chief was a detective with a rising star, working the streets with Tom, he'd experienced, what the department labeled an accidental discharge of a firearm. It would have been enough of a blunder to derail his career, but Tom stepped up to the plate, covering for him. The incident was never mentioned but they maintained a mutual, unspoken, trust of one another.

Tom headed to his desk, pausing by Ruby's on his way. "Ruby, grab your jacket, we're hitting the road."

"What's up? Are we keeping the . . ."

Tom interrupted, before she could say another word. "We need to go, now." His eyes warned her to stay quiet. "I'll tell you in the car, bring the Hudson file with you." Ruby grabbed a light windbreaker hanging on the back of her chair, scooped up the file from her desk. She was hot on Tom's heels, as they swung by his desk to check messages, then headed to the front door. Juggling to hang on to the file, she bumped into him, hard, when he abruptly came to a stop on the lobby floor.

"Oops, sorry, what's up? Did you forget something?" She moved beside him.

"No, I didn't forget anything, did you?" His eyes were glued to the left of the lobby. Ruby followed his gaze, and flinched. She'd screwed up. Shit. She hadn't called to postpone Bygie's visit to the station. There she was, standing in the lobby looking lost, here to pick up her husband's belongings.

Tom grabbed Ruby's elbow, backing her up, keeping an eye on the laughing widow. They moved around a corner. "Damn it," Tom hissed in anger, "I told you to put her off until tonight. We could be fucked here."

"I know. I know. I'm sorry, I didn't get it done yet. She wasn't supposed to be here until this afternoon. I can go tell her . . . well . . . I can tell her we need to reschedule, we've been called out. Would that work?"

"That's not going to stop her, there isn't a hold on anything. She can mosey right on over and collect it. Shit, let me think." Tom scrubbed his hands over his face.

When an accident occurs, police take into custody the vehicle and contents, primarily for safekeeping. Logged into a report, right down to dirty tissues and packages of gum, it's then checked into the property room. Unless the patrolman responsible for signing it into the property room tags it to be held, the personal property was free to go as soon as a family member requests it. In this case, at the time of the accident, there wasn't reason to believe it had been anything other than a tragic vehicle rollover.

Tom and Ruby had suspicion, but no evidence that Lars was involved in a prostitution ring; they had no legal reason to put a hold on anything. As the widow, Bygie had the right to retrieve the property from the car, and she didn't need their help to do it. She could sign for it and walk. A search warrant was imperative before Hudson's laptop and phone disappeared.

Tom said, "stall her. Take her for coffee, take a tour downtown, I don't care what you do, but don't let her near the property room." Tom's face heated as he tamped his anger. "I'm sure the lady knows how to push a delete button."

"Okay. Okay. I screwed up. But, even if she deletes information it doesn't mean we . . ."

"I know what it means." Tom snapped. "It means we'd have to wait for the forensic computer genius to do his magic and retrieve the information she deleted." The next thought made him sick, "If she's smart enough to destroy the hard drive, nothing can be recovered."

Ruby's face paled, "I'll stall her. Go after the warrant."

Tom turned to walk away, but abruptly turned back, "Don't mention the autopsy. As far as she's concerned, it's an accident." He glared at Ruby, "Got it?"

"Yes. I won't say a word except to ask how's the weather. Is that safe?" Ruby didn't wait for a reply, she pivoted and headed towards the lobby.

Tom took off at a trot, dialing his phone on the way. His first call was to the property room to try and finagle a hold on the evidence.

Not a kosher move, more of a stall.

If Bygie put up a stink, or God forbid, retained a lawyer before the search warrant was in hand, the property could walk.

The wheels of justice moved fast. Tom got the go ahead on his limited warrant, allowing him to confiscate any contents he deemed necessary to the investigation of prostitution, and the big S.U.V. was impounded. He had the laptop and cell phone in his possession.

Tom let Ruby know the coast was clear. He told her to use one of her daily apologies and escort Bygie to his desk.

16

Bygie knew something was up, but couldn't figure out how to get away. After falling apart last night in front of Hall, she didn't relish the idea of seeing him. She had hoped to come in early, take care of business and return home without running into him. Last night's cry fest embarrassed her. Years of grief that'd been bottled under pressure had spewed forth and choked her.

Uncontrollable sobbing was embarrassing enough when alone, but mortifying when done in front of a detective. He'd remained hard as granite, watching as she doubled over in pain, blowing her reddened nose, only to start crying again as he explained the truth as he saw it. Bygie was forced to face the facts Hall had so coldly delivered. Facts much worse than Lars led her to believe. Her husband had been hanging around with prostitutes.

No, not hanging out with them . . . working with them.

According to the police, managing them.

Nothing as mundane as a girlfriend on the side for Lars. He apparently had a slew of women at his disposal.

This morning, she started the day with a grim resolve. Her grief was in check, replaced with a feeling she was accustomed to. Anger. She'd spent time on the phone making sure she could claim Lars' property. She was told she could do so at anytime. So much for needing Hall to baby-sit her. She'd lined up a tow-truck for his SUV and arranged to have it hauled to a junk-yard. Bygie didn't want to see it.

Her last plan for the day was a visit to Oceanview Mercedes, to clean out Lar's desk and office. She drove downtown to the San Diego P.D., on a mission. It felt good to move forward, get something done, but it didn't ease the ache she felt in the pit of her stomach.

Within seconds of her arrival, Ruby appeared, encouraging her to sit and visit, under the pretense of friendly empathy. They sat in the lobby discussing the weather, while Bygie built up a head of steam. She knew a stalling tactic when she felt it, but didn't know why.

Hall had to be behind it.

Bygie was working up the nerve to get up and leave when Ruby's cell phone rang.

"Mrs. Hudson, I need you to come upstairs with me. Detective Hall is waiting." Ruby rose, leading the way without waiting for an answer.

Caught in an unfamiliar world, Bygie followed. She felt like a puppet being pulled by invisible strings.

Getting off the elevator on the second floor, walking past rows of cubicles, each officer looked up, scrutinizing her as they walked by. Like being on a microscope slide. She kept her head down, until she realized it probably made her look guilty. She jerked her head upright to stare back, forgetting she was wearing sunglasses. No one had a clue where she was looking.

Ruby stopped in front of one of the cubicles, a rat's maze of boxy shaped walls.

"Should we head down to the interview room?" Ruby asked.

Tom stood up from his desk, eyeing Bygie, noticing her dark glasses. "Yeah, let's go over to room one." He tipped his chin at Bygie as he walked past, indicating she should follow him.

She stood still for a second, then hurried to catch up with the detective. "Excuse me? I came to collect my husband's property. I was told the Property room was on the first floor."

"You need to come with us Mrs. Hudson." Tom talked quietly, wanting to get her out of the open area filled with big ears.

"I don't understand. What now?" Bygie stood her ground.

Tom stepped away without answering, opening a door, waving Bygie in.

"This won't take long. We believe there are new details you may like to hear in private." He looked at her with eyebrows raised.

Bygie's heart fluttered. With all of her resolve to move forward, Lars and other women was a subject she'd rather avoid. She walked into the cramped room, walking around the table to take the seat indicated. Ruby took a seat directly across from her. Closing the door, Tom kicked out a chair next to Ruby and sat down, shooting a quick look at Ruby, one filled with a silent warning for her to stay quiet.

"What's happened now?" Bygie asked, shoving her sunglasses into her hair like a headband. Her swollen eyes were red-rimmed and bloodshot.

"I'm afraid we have more bad news." Tom considered her red eyes but didn't back down. "The autopsy report came in this morning, it appears your husband's death is not consistent with a car accident." Tom watched her face closely, looking for any reaction.

She looked puzzled. "What do you mean?" She looked from one to the other, waiting for an answer.

They sat silent, watching her grope for understanding. "I thought he died from severe head injuries, or at least that's what you told me. If the accident didn't cause it, then what . . ." realization dawned in her eyes. "Oh my God, did he have a heart attack? Is that what caused the accident?"

"No. There wasn't any sign of a heart attack." Hall's eyes remained locked on her, "It now appears to be a homicide."

The words tangled, they didn't make sense. She locked on Hall's gaze. "Suicide? Lars wouldn't commit suicide. I mean, I know he was upset there could be negative publicity, that's the only reason he admitted anything to me." She gave a short, brittle laugh. "He was being courteous by letting me know before I read it in the paper." She sounded bitter discussing her husband's death, but it was loose and floating before she edited. "But, he wasn't upset enough to commit suicide. No. You don't know Lars, he wouldn't do that."

"Homicide, not suicide. Someone else was involved. Evidence proves it without a doubt."

"You never mentioned another vehicle being involved. It doesn't make sense. You said he lost control on the damp road. Did someone run him off the road and drive away?"

Ruby leaned forward, not looking at Tom for permission. "Is there anyone who would want to hurt your husband? Any enemies, maybe someone he was in business with?"

"Which business do you mean?" Bygie laughed bitterly. "Up until the night he died, I thought he was a hard working car salesman." Her eyes flew between the two detectives. "Are you sure? Couldn't there be a mistake? How did he die?"

"There's no mistake." Hall's gaze never wavered. Bygie had the most to gain from her husband's death. "We'll be going back over the accident report with a fine tooth comb, I'm sure something will pop." Tom knew damn well they weren't likely to find anything new from the reports, but Bygie didn't know that. "Anything you could tell us would help."

"I've told you what little I know. I don't have anything to add. How did he die? I don't understand." Bygie reached up, rubbing her temples out of habit. She closed her eyes, wishing this to go away. She was feeling slightly sick and lightheaded.

"Can I get his belongings?" she asked. "I'd like to go home."

Tom cleared his throat. "I'm sorry, but for now there won't be anything released to take home. The contents, as well as the vehicle itself, will become part of our investigation."

Bygie's face paled further. "When will it be returned? I need his laptop."

The statement surprised the detectives and they exchanged a glance. Could it be so easy? Was there something on the laptop to hide?

"No, it's off limits. Why's it so important to you?"

"Could I at least get the information I need from it?" The question was directed Tom's way. "Lars had the mailing list for my customer base on his laptop, I need it to get ready for a show I have coming up in La Jolla. He used the list to print mailing labels at work." It didn't make sense to mention her show, it looked as if she didn't care. Were they telling her Lars had been murdered? Words rambled before she could reel them back. "Can you give me any idea of when his laptop will be returned?"

"Depends on how long the investigation takes." Tom ran his fingers through his hair. "Mrs. Hudson, we could close this much faster with your co-operation. Are you sure you haven't remembered any names he mentioned? Names you weren't familiar with?"

Bygie slumped in her chair, rubbing her tired eyes. "I've told you so many times it makes me sick to repeat it. I don't know anything. Now you're telling me he was murdered?" She looked up at Tom through tired eyes.

Hall noticed how pale she looked. "Do you have anyone that can verify you were home the night of your husband's accident? Maybe you remembered a phone call, or someone stopping over?"

"What? No." She spit out a derisive laugh, "Don't you hear me? I keep saying the same things over and over. What? No. What? No. What? No. I told you, I was alone, working in my studio." She put an elbow on the table, fingers rubbing her forehead, trying to remember if she had talked to any-one. A fruitless labor. She didn't have casual friends on the west coast. This had all been covered. "No. No one called or came over. What possible difference does that make? What on earth could that have to do with a traffic accident?"

Silence hung in the room.

Ruby fumbled a reply, "We'd need to check, make sure you were home. I mean, we need to know . . ."

"Because," Tom interrupted, "we don't know who killed him."

Their words trickled through, agonizingly slow.

"You don't . . . ?" She jumped up from her chair.

Tom and Ruby stood up in unison, each with a hand resting on their holster.

The look on Hall's face was threatening. Bygie slowly sat back down, never taking her eyes from him.

"I couldn't, I wouldn't . . . you don't believe . . ."

"Would you be willing to take a polygraph?"

"You believe I could do something like this?" Tears pooled, "Hurt my husband?" Her heart was pounding so hard, it hurt. "First you tell me he slid off the road, now he didn't. I don't know what to believe. Please, tell me how he died."

"Sometimes people get pushed to the breaking point. You told me how unconnected you were. His confession of a new business venture may have been the final straw. Take a polygraph to prove your innocence."

Bygie was having a hard time focusing.

Hall's tone softened. "Look, we need your help. I believe you." He jerked a thumb in Ruby's direction. "We believe you." He shrugged his shoulders, "But we need to prove it to our supervisor. The polygraph will let him know we've done our job and you'll be off the hook for good."

Bygie looked at Hall with big eyes, her vision swimming. She blinked hard to remove tears. Her head was pounding and she couldn't seem to catch her breath. Turning her body to the side, she made an attempt to stand and leave the room, crumpling to the floor. Hall and Wilson rushed around the table and helped her back to her feet.

Once she was steady, embarrassed, she refused any offer of further help. She needed to go home and burrow in her bed. Before they let her go, they warned her to keep details of the supposed 'accident' to herself, to discuss their new theory with no one. How could she tell anyone details when she didn't know them herself? They wouldn't answer any of her questions.

Bygie agreed to whatever they said, including taking a polygraph, anything to get away. Hall's last remark stung. Did he really believe she had something to do with her husband's death?

His parting words were not to leave the city for any reason.

Once she was gone, Tom turned to Ruby. "You know the only thing we have going for us? She hasn't hired a bottom feeder."

"What?"

"She hasn't lawyered up."

17

Chief Pope sat with his elbows propped on his desktop, rubbing the back of his neck. The damn Mercedes escort case was turning to shit. Even cars parked in the department lot set off his internal alarm. Divided into sections, an area for patrol and detectives, another for the upper chain of command, the rule was to keep your private wheels out of sight.

With departmental budget cuts, Pope knew employees didn't have extra cash; no one had received a pay raise in two years. He also realized times had changed from when he joined the force. Back then, personal cars belonging to most cops were second-hand beaters. Officers higher up in the feeding pool didn't drive vehicles much fancier than new recruits. Only the top hierarchy had expensive cars when Pope was a rookie.

Not any more.

Unlike the good old days, the Department's tri-level parking garage rarely held second-hand cars that were kept running by cops helping each other out on the weekends. Now, most families had two incomes and could afford newer, more reliable cars. It would be hard to assign a vehicle to any particular level of employee. They all looked expensive to Pope. Why would hard working individuals want to spend so much money on a damn car?

He still drove the one and only truck he'd ever purchased, a half-ton classic '68 Chevy long-bed. At the urging of his wife, he'd had the truck fully restored with the added expense of an aftermarket air conditioning system, which he rarely used. He still preferred driving with the windows down.

This afternoon, after a politics-heavy lunch of chicken coated with something, his casual habit of looking at the variety of cars parked in the lot triggered a warning.

He circled back through each level, checking to see if he'd missed anything. Was it his imagination? Pope would be the last person to claim he kept up on current automobile trends. Maybe what he noticed, plastered on the back end of cars tucked into the department lot, was on a lot of vehicles, regardless of their make or model. He reasoned it could be similar to teenagers putting a BMW emblem on their broken down Ford Fiesta.

No such luck.

Three of the cars, parked in an area designated for department officials only, had a plastic advertising bracket surrounding their license plates.

The brackets boasted the cars came from Oceanview Mercedes.

Did the car owners take advantage of the bonus offered by Hudson with their purchase?

What a fucking mess. He could have far more on his hands than a Judge baring his ass. With the slimeball reporter breathing down their necks, the last thing he needed was for this to become a sensational tabloid story involving his department, be the front page news before they could get a handle on it.

18

Things weren't moving for Greasy at the speed he wanted them to. Sugar's friend Lizzie wasn't willing to come across with the information he needed. Yet. He'd met with her one time, and when she walked into the crappy restaurant he'd taken Sugar too, Greasy couldn't believe she was a friend of Sugar's. The girl was a looker. Fine set of lungs paired with a set of the longest legs Greasy'd seen in a while. Dressed in casual clothes, the woman didn't fit the image of a hooker.

She doled out information in little damn morsels, only hinting at big names involved, and she was uneasy to learn Sugar had mentioned Hudson's name. The only thing he got out of her was confirmation that Lars was involved, more through her glares at Sugar, than through anything she admitted.

Good looking or not, Greasy was ready to choke the livin' daylights out of the whore.

The pressure he'd been applying to Hudson, following him around and staking out his house, had come to zilch. The damn wife wasn't any better. She was one stone cold bitch. Now that the husband was out of the picture, Greasy figured he'd be able to break the wife. She had to know what her hubby was up to; no one could be that stupid. He figured she was more than likely the one responsible for setting up the house, hiring the girls.

So far, she was proving to be another female pain in his ass. She hung up on him when he called and he didn't dare park in front of her house, not with cops coming and going. He'd have to use other means to push her along.

Good reporting was like shooting bullets in the dark, winging it and waiting to see which one would strike gold. As far as Greasy was concerned, if someone innocent was caught in the cross-fire, too bad. Being in the wrong place at the wrong time was their own damn problem. Rotten karma.

He was impatient and wanted the ball rolling. Now.

When Greasy learned from a friend at the department, that a judge was caught with his privates in someone other than his wife, he should have known the department would cover for the prick. Bury the whole episode. When he shopped around the idea of linking the judge to the escort service, he hit pay dirt.

That got the attention of the Chief.

A damn judge!

He knew he hit payday and his plan was to ride this story to fame and fortune.

He'd been holding back from putting a teaser in the paper, but not because Chief Pope warned him to keep his trap shut. Threatening him that he'd be writing for a shit paper in po-dunk Montana didn't scare Greasy, even a tiny little bit. It made him realize how big a story he was sitting on.

At this point, his hands were tied due to nothing more than selfishness. If he published what little information he had, even nothing more substantial than innuendos, the press would swarm like vultures feasting on road-kill. There'd be a mob of reporters in town from across the country, chasing the story. His story.

He didn't want anyone hitching a ride to fame on his coat-tails.

The story was his and his alone.

He needed to know where the damn house was, but Lizzie hadn't told Sugar where it was located. That would change tonight. He'd get the goods from Lizzie come hell or high water. This was his story, and he planned on breaking it well before the cops got off their ass and did their jobs.

19

Tom sat back in the patio chair, listening to the rugrats play around him. The smell of burgers on the grill had him salivating. Becky had thrown them on, while her husband, Joe, changed a diaper on the latest addition to their family. It never ceased to amaze Tom how easy these two were together.

Tom grew up with his father lording over the grill like a drill sergeant and only his mother would've known what to do with a smelly diaper. He had a hard time imagining himself in any role other than master of the grill. Diapers? No way.

He closed his eyes, enjoying the sun on his face. A ball bounced off his head, but he didn't react. He kept his eyes closed, pretending to snore. Another ball bounced, hitting him in the arm, followed by giggles.

"Shhh. I told ya, he's sweepin," said Chrissy, the four-year-old boss. She tossed the ball at Tom again to prove her point. It bounced off his stomach and rolled away. Chrissy and her three-year-old sister, Holly, dared to creep closer, both laughing. When they closed in on his chair, he jumped up with his arms over his head, roaring. Both girls ran away with Tom following like a lumbering bear. Each time he reached out to grab a body, he missed. They ran circles around him until he scooped both of them into his arms and hung them upside down.

"Who's been bothering the bear?" he growled. The girls shrieked with laughter.

"Put us down, Unc' Tom, put us down." Tom gently lowered them to the ground, smiling at their happy faces.

"Come on you two munchkins," Becky said. "Your hotdogs are ready. Time to put food in your stomachs so you can stay strong and fight off bears. Let your Uncle Tom rest a minute."

"Bears don't rest," said Chrissy, "they hiker-nate. Daddy tol' me." The girls climbed up on the picnic table bench.

"Come on Tom, bears can eat too, I don't think its hiker-nating season." Becky laughed as Joe joined his girls at the table. "Joe, your girls are attacking Tom. So much for a peaceful Saturday afternoon, I hope little Jessie is calmer." She bent down to plant a kiss on the baby lying in Joe's arms, giving her husband a kiss on the cheek while she was at it.

Joe growled at each of his daughters. "I'm teaching them to be tough. I want my girls to stand up for themselves. Next year I'll take them hunting, we'll find some real bears."

"There's no bears here, Daddy, it's Unc' Tom pretendin'. Besides, bears aren't real, are they Holly?"

Holly shook her head, always agreeing with anything her older sister said. They both dug into the food on their plates.

Tom stood off to the side, watching the family. Becky and Joe made it look simple. Much like Mike and Annie had.

"Come on, Tom, grab a seat before the baby bears eat all the food. Here, I brought you a beer." Joe reached into the baby seat he'd set on the bench beside him, transferring two beers out and a baby in. Tom took a seat beside Holly.

She squealed, "Look 'Rissy, Unc' Tom seat's by me."

"Eat up little girl or I'll eat your food too." Tom ruffled her hair. Her little body snuggled in close, keeping contact with her favorite uncle. Tom swallowed hard, choking back emotion the only way he knew how. He ignored it.

They ate in silence for awhile, enjoying the warm day of early spring.

"How's work going?" Joe asked "Anything exciting you're not allowed to discuss?"

"Yes and yes. Yes, I have a stinker of a case and yes, my lips are sealed." Tom paused, using his fork to idly stir the beans on his plate. "Becky, I've got a question." He glanced at the girls, checking his language before he opened his mouth.

"Why would a woman stay married to someone she doesn't like?"

"My daddy and mommy are married, that's how the baby happened," offered Chrissy.

So much for little ears not hearing.

Becky smiled, "You're so right sweetie, that's how your sister happened." She reached over and wiped ketchup from Chrissy's face. "Let the grown-ups talk, okay?"

"Boring." Chrissy rolled her eyes at Tom.

"You two may be in trouble when she hits her teens. She's not afraid to tell it like it is." Frankly, the thought of raising a daughter scared him. Lots of bad guys out there.

Conversation drifted until the girls left the table to play in a sandbox.

"Okay, Tom, what were you trying to ask me? You can use adult terms now, Jessie's the only kid left at the table. I know she's a freakishly smart baby, but she won't understand much."

Tom grinned. "Joe's still here. How much will he understand?"

"Don't be gettin' mean now Mr. Copper, I'll sic' the girls on you again." Joe shot back.

Tom dragged his hands through his hair, contemplating how to ask the question. "Let's say there's a woman who doesn't like her husband, yet remains married to him. I don't get it. Why would an intelligent woman stick around?" Tom's face flushed. The way he worded it, it sounded like his marriage. "She makes a fair living in her own right. She's not staying for the money."

"That's not a simple question, Tom." Becky locked eyes with Joe. "Sometimes you stay because you hope it'll get better. Have you ever heard the saying, 'Hope is the feeling you have, that the feeling you have isn't permanent?'"

He shook his head, wondering where she pulled this crap from.

"You believe enough in the person you're married to and hope it will get better."

Tom squashed the urge to squirm. It felt like Becky was talking to Joe, not him.

"Well, I don't get it. She claims it's been this way for a long time. Hope or not, I'm not talking a couple of months. It sounds like it's been a couple years, maybe longer."

"Tom, people stay married for a whole list of reasons. Financial maybe, or for their children . . ."

"This couple doesn't have children. That's not the reason."

"Maybe for security then. I don't know." She shrugged. "It's not the same answer for any two people. Some can't cope with the turmoil of divorce, or maybe they're too depressed to call it quits. The mystery woman may not know herself why she's stuck around."

Tom looked at Becky, then Joe. "Could you ever imagine getting mad enough at one another, I mean the final straw, whatever that would be, and pulling a gun?"

Instead of being offended, they both laughed.

Tom's face took on a red hue. That's not how he intended the question to come out.

"Come on, Tom." Joe said, "no matter how pissed I was, I couldn't imagine doing anything like that. Uhh-uhh. No way. I've seen Bec pretty darn pissed at me, but I know she'd never threaten me with a gun."

"I'd use a baseball bat, but never a gun." Becky playfully punched Joe's shoulder, before turning back to Tom. "You must be dealing with something heavy. Remember, you work with the dregs of society. Don't lose sight of the fact that there are a millions of decent, honest people out there. People you never get to meet in your line of work."

"Most of those millions wouldn't even think of spitting in a cop's food," teased Joe.

"Yeah, yeah. I hear you." Tom studied the top of the table. "This particular woman has me puzzled. She doesn't come from the dregs of society, not even close. A pretty normal childhood, best we can tell, but she's unique, she doesn't fit the stereotype of a wealthy woman. She doesn't react to situations the way I'd expect. Laughs instead of crying, faints instead of demanding a lawyer." Tom ran his fingers through his hair again.

Becky started laughing. "I swear Tom, if you keep dragging those fingers through your hair, you'll have permanent wind-rows. You've been doing that since junior high. I'm surprised you haven't ripped it out . . ." Becky stopped, leaning back and crossing her arms. "Oh, ho. I see."

"See what?" Tom frowned, "I'm all ears."

"Is this a case you're working, or is there something else going on you'd like to share?"

"Care to enlighten me, Bec? I see your lips moving but what's coming out doesn't make sense."

"This married woman, the one who won't leave her husband? She wouldn't happen to be slim, pretty, intelligent, and in the same age bracket would she?" Becky quizzed.

"What? Why would that matter? Joe help me out here, translate for me. What's she talking about?"

"I'm staying out of this one. This is Becky's department. In fact, I'll go change another diaper . . . or something." He rose from the table, carrying the sleeping baby with him.

"Spit it out, Becky, what am I missing?"

"Geez, you can be dense. I know you well enough to see through your story. The part where someone's mad enough to shoot bothers me, yet I'm oddly intrigued."

"I feel like I've landed on another planet. Intrigued?" Tom's frown deepened.

"This mysterious, unhappily married woman. You like her, huh?"

"What the hell? Of course not, she's a suspect in a case I'm working." He stood up and hit his knees on the table edge. "That's the stupidest thing to come out of your mouth, and you've let some big ones escape. You know I wouldn't get involved with someone I'm investigating. That wouldn't be stupid, it'd be fucking idiotic." He avoided her eyes, bending down to rub his knees.

"Me think you doth protest too much."

"Quit talking like fucking Shakespeare. I thought you could add insight, forget I asked."

"I never said you were seeing her, Tom. I know you wouldn't cross that line. Maybe you're attracted to her? I thought her being involved in a case was a cover. You didn't want me to be nosy."

"Fat chance of you not being nosy."

Becky laughed. "You've mentioned that before."

"Well, it's stupid, me being attracted to her is a figment of your imagination."

"How old is she then? Is she involved in the 'trade' as you professionals say?"

"Her age has nothing to do with it and she's not involved in the trade. I mean, I don't think so anymore, that she was ever involved in it, I mean she never was . . . I don't think ." His hands headed for his hair before he could stop himself. "Change the damn subject. I'm sorry I asked anything."

Becky raised a brow, questioning his rambling, but knew Tom well enough not to push it. She stood up, gathering paper plates for the trash. "Come on, let's go in and get dessert. Joe's probably scooping ice cream as we speak." She reached out to put a hand on Tom's arm, "one more thing. We don't want you to be alone so much. It'd be great if you met someone, we'd be happy for you."

Tom protested, but Becky talked over him.

"You're welcome here anytime, with anyone and I promise not to tease you. Okay? Peace?"

Tom blew out a breath. "It's a deal, I'm sorry it took me so long to get over and meet Jessie. I'll make it back before the girls are in college. I promise."

They headed to the house, hearing the squeal of little girls well before they reached the door. Tom had a fleeting thought about how lonely the noise made him feel. He put it out of his mind, replaced it with thoughts of the widow who laughed.

20

Clawing across the night stand, she found the cordless phone but knocked it to the floor. Scrambling out of bed, not awake enough to stand, she sank to the floor, resting her back against the bed frame.

"Hello?"

"Hey, did I wake you up?" Lizzie asked. "I was hoping you hadn't gone to sleep yet. Want me to call back tomorrow?"

"That's okay, what time is it? I'm too tired to open my eyes and look."

"It's almost eleven thirty. I figured you'd be watching late night television."

"Naw, I'm too pooped. What's up?"

"I was wondering what you found out. Should I be worried? I'm going stir crazy cooped up in the house."

"You need to stay out of sight until this thing calms down." She arched her back, trying to wake up. "So far, no one knows a thing and I aim to keep it that way."

"Listen, I need to talk to you." Lizzie hesitated, her jangled nerves flowed along the path of the phone line. "I don't know what to do. I've got a friend who wants me to talk to a guy who wants to write a book. Name the big guys we service."

"What? Who?" She sat up straight, instantly alert and wide awake. "Lizzie, tell me you haven't been talking to anyone."

"No, not yet. That's why I wanted to discuss it with you." She rushed ahead, "this might be an answer for us, a way to get out for good. If I'm willing to talk, there's a promise of big money. Your name would never be mentioned. I promise."

"Who's offering money?"

"A guy who wants to write a book on escort services in San Diego."

"Are you kidding me? You think he'd take what you have to say and let it go?" Her laugh had a sharp edge. "Give me a break. Any writer worth a shit would dig for incriminating information. Who's trying to get you to talk?"

"Never mind, it's nothing. I thought I should run it by you, in case you thought it could work out for us."

"Lizzie, tell me." The tone demanded an answer. "Who the fuck is trying to get you to talk?"

"Remember my friend, Sugar? It's a guy she introduced me to. It's not a big deal, really, it isn't." Lizzie was backpedaling as fast as she could, the conversation was not promising. "He told Sugar he wanted to write a book, it's no big deal. The only reason I listened to what he had to say was because of the money. Maybe it's a way out?"

"Come on Lizzie, you're being stupid. Who's this guy? Let me check him out."

"He's a reporter for one of the papers, but I don't . . ."

Exploding anger rippled through the phone line. "Oh shit. You fucking idiot. Have you talked to the guy? Skinny fucker with a bad haircut?"

"No. I mean, yes, that sounds like him." Lizzie shifted, uncomfortable. "I met with him, but I only listened, I didn't say a word. I promise. I'm sorry for leaving the house," Lizzie whined, "I was real careful. You don't know what it's like to be stuck sitting around all the time."

"If I hadn't been around to protect your sorry ass all these years, who the hell knows where you would have ended up and this is the way you repay me? I can't believe you could be so stupid.

Of all the stupid shitting things you could do." The voice softened but sounded more threatening. "Do you know how hard I'm working to keep the lid on this? Do you? You haven't got a fucking clue." Now the voice shouted. "How could you be so fucking stupid?"

Lizzie grabbed a pillow off her bed and hugged it to her. "I thought it could help us. I thought I'd listen to what he had to say, then talk to you."

"Can he find you?"

"No. No way. I didn't tell him a thing. He had a lot of questions, but I didn't answer any of them."

"What questions did he ask?"

Lizzie hesitated. "You know, general stuff, like the house we work out of and who set up clients for us, nothing specific."

"How the hell did he know we had a house? Huh? Can you tell me that?"

"I, ahhh . . . Sugar told him." Lizzie squeezed the pillow tighter.

"You told Sugar?"

"No, not really." Lizzie's stomach turned. "You told me to look for a couple more girls, so I talked to Sugar. I didn't tell her where the house is, nothing like that. I told her maybe she could get off the streets, but you had to meet her first."

"You moron." Now the voice was screaming. "Can Sugar tell the reporter how to find you?"

"No." Lizzie was crying. "I never told Sugar where I was living." Lizzie steadied her breathing, she hadn't done anything wrong. "The only reason I was in contact with Sugar is because of you. You wanted more girls. I was doing what you asked me to do."

"I asked you to stay low, out of sight, remember that part? What if they track you down, then what? Don't come running to me for help, or, so help me God, you'll regret the day we met."

"I'm sorry. You don't have to worry, they don't know where I'm at. There's no way for Sugar or the reporter dude to find me. I'm telling you, I didn't talk, I listened."

"You better hope you didn't give anything away. I've got enough on my plate without you causing more trouble. I can't believe you left the fucking house. How hard is that to follow? Huh?"

"I know, I know, I was stupid. With Lars' accident, I know you must be upset."

"Lars." She mumbled. "He got what he had coming."

"What do you mean by that? He was a pretty nice guy." Lizzie was puzzled by her friend's reaction to his death, but was too nervous to question the response.

"Right, he was a real nice guy. I love cheaters, that's why I'm so rich now." The laugh was abrupt, more like a dagger thrown.

"Lars was okay." Lizzie released her grip on the pillow, running her hand across the top of it, smoothing the wrinkles.

"You mind your own business and stay the hell out of sight. This will blow over. Then we'll decide what to do. I'm warning you, don't mess this up."

"Yeah, okay. I hope it's soon, I can't stand sitting in the house."

"Give me a couple days. Maybe you can come over here, take a break from those walls, and stare at mine for awhile."

"Okay. Call as soon as you can. I can't stand not knowing what's going on."

"Stay out of sight, I mean it. I'll be in touch." The phone was forcefully disconnected.

Lizzie sighed, wondering what she'd gotten into this time.

21

Her house felt like a prison, but she hated leaving. On Friday, after her disastrous fainting performance at the police station, she put aside her plan to clean out Lars' office and headed to the sanctuary of home. She spent most of the day Saturday accomplishing nothing, but not for the lack of trying. Focusing on a specific task was a joke. She'd catch herself staring at a wall. Trying to take a nap amounted to lying on the couch in her studio, staring at a ceiling instead.

She got up and filled a bucket with soapy water, grabbed assorted bottles of cleanser and headed out to clean the nasty message off her garage door. Scrubbing until dusk, only a faint outline of the words remained. She hoped the outdoor work would help her sleep. In bed, she nodded off with the TV on and woke early to the grating sound of a chirpy broadcaster.

Sunday morning, determined to accomplish something, she phoned Jim Sprague, one of the partners at Oceanview. She asked him to pack up Lar's office and have his belongings sent to her at home. Jim readily agreed, then smoothly questioned whether or not she'd found time to study their proposal.

"No, not yet Jim. I've been busy dealing with my husband. You know, the dead one."

"Oh, no hurry, no hurry for us. You don't need to worry your pretty little head over the business at a time like this. Let me know if I can do anything to help. We feel real bad for you, Bygie. Such a nice couple, it's a crying shame."

His insincerity rankled. "Haven't you noticed, Jim? I'm not nice. Why do you think Lars picked up a side job." She gave a low chuckle, "I'm sure he allowed you to check out the merchandise, or were you pimping with my husband? Betcha' your little wifey would love hearing details."

"Uhhh, now Bygie, I have no idea what you're talking about, but it has nothing to do with me, with us here at Oceanview. I'm sure this is a stressful time for you."

She wasn't backing down this time. "I bet you knew exactly what Lars was doing and I'm sure sooner or later, the police will be knocking on your door." She paused, letting the silence build. "Make sure you have your story straight, Jim."

"Now wait a minute, Bygie, hold up there little girl." His voice changed from smarmy sympathy to cold steel. "We already talked to the police, they talked to all of us right after the accident. If Lars was into his own thing, it didn't have a thing to do with the rest of us. There's no need for you to direct the police our way."

"You believe I have the power to sic detectives on you?" Remembering Hall's accusation of her being involved in her husband's death made her want to hurt someone. "They're not going to drop this you know, they're determined to follow the trail to the end. I hope for your sake, it doesn't end on your doorstep."

It felt good to scare the mighty Jim Sprague. The power to make him squirm was intoxicating. "I've gotten to know the detectives. They don't impress me as the type to let something go. Would it be better if I gave them your home number? You wouldn't have to worry your pretty little head about them showing up, unannounced, during business hours."

"You ungrateful little bitch," he snarled. "After all we've done for you . . . ."

"You're kidding, right? You had a losing business before we bought in. Lars is the one who turned it around. We both know it. He may have been a cheating bastard, but you can't take that away from him. I won't let you." *Why am I sticking up for the serial cheater?*

"I'm warning you. Don't involve us in this mess of your husband's. Maybe if you'd been a better wife, he wouldn't have gone looking elsewhere."

"Yeah, too bad I didn't pay attention when I could have. I could have taken free lessons from your wife, huh, Jim? I would have learned from the best. Go shopping and keep my mouth shut. Right?"

"This conversation is done. I'll have his personal belongings sent over to you, but I'm warning you, little girl, don't go making trouble where there isn't any."

"Nothing to concern you then, is there Jimbo? You can tell the detectives what you know, I mean what you don't know, when they come to talk." She overheard a Mitzi-Bitzi voice asking questions in the background when Sprague hung up on her. Bygie slammed her end down with enough force to open a seam on the handset.

Why the hell had she done that?

The feeling of empowerment was gone. She immediately felt ashamed. She must be losing it. No wonder the detectives thought she was crazy enough to shoot her husband.

Right now, she did feel like shooting something.

She walked from the house to her studio, intending to finish a mirror, but once she was there, she wasn't able to focus. She walked back to the house, poured another cup of coffee and picked up a book to read. Sitting at the counter, she tried concentrating, but gave up after reading the same page for twenty minutes. She closed the cover in disgust and stood up to stretch.

Walking into the formal living room, she sat down on the footstool, putting her head in her hands. *I guess that's what being accused of murder does, makes you lose focus. Go crazy.* She lifted her head, gazing around the room, looking at it as if she was seeing it for the first time. This was the only room in the house that was done by a decorator, someone Lars hired. He assured Bygie the young woman came highly recommended.

Bygie never cared for the room, or the lady who did the job.

At the time, she chalked up her dislike of the woman, a girl really, to resentment and the old feeling of jealousy. She felt old around the young, fresh-faced decorator. Bygie believed Lars found the woman through his partners, that he'd hired her on the advice of Mitzi, or was it Bitzi? Now, she wasn't so sure.

Was the young decorator a woman Lars knew? On a personal level?

Her stomach churned. She suffered the same roaring in her ears she experienced before fainting. She closed her eyes, leaning forward to put her head between her knees.

Could this room have been decorated by one of his escorts?

Was this the design of a hooker?

Maybe that's why Bygie so viscerally hated it. Sitting up, her vision cleared, and she knew. She just knew. If Lars was standing in front of her, admitting another one of his mistakes, it wouldn't be clearer. He had hired one of his damn girls to work in their home . . . *my home.* The bastard!

The damn young decorator was one of his hookers.

She flew to the fireplace, picking up the largest brass candlestick. The candle fell off, knocking over the others in a game of dominoes. She started swinging. She smashed it into the dreadful Victorian chair, over and over, watching the frail wood give way. Turning, she clawed the brass weapon into a framed print, jarring her shoulder as the wood frame resisted then splintered. Ramming the end of the candlestick into the canvas, she destroyed the pretentious artwork.

Spinning around, she made a sweeping motion, clearing a side table of knick-knacks. Feeling crazed, she swung her makeshift bat at a Tiffany lamp, pleased with sound of breaking glass. Dropping the candlestick, she spun to the draperies flanking the floor to ceiling window and pulled with her body weight behind it. The anchors holding the rod in place ripped out, squealing like nails on chalkboard. She jumped back as the entire length of the rod crashed to the floor. The loud sound penetrated, stopping her dead. Gasping, covered with sweat, she sank to the floor, broken shards of glass puncturing her knees.

She felt alive . . . and she felt nothing.

This must be what going crazy feels like.

***

Bygie didn't know how long she sat in the mess, but when she tried to stand, the stiffness in her legs indicated she'd been there for awhile. Looking at the destruction, instead of feeling ashamed at her lack of control, she wanted to do more.

Keep destroying.

She stumbled up the steps, heading to the bathroom, where she sat on the toilet and inspected her knees. What a mess. Getting up again, she reached under the bathroom sink for a box of band-aids, snatching a bottle of peroxide she found sitting beside them. She dug in a vanity drawer for tweezers and sat back down. This was going to hurt, but the pain felt good. At least she was feeling something.

22

Bygie hung up the phone, feeling exceedingly satisfied. She remembered reading that stress can be triggered by indecision. Now she understood what it meant. The indecision with her marriage, either to fix it or end it, had left her in limbo for far too many wasted years.

So clear. So late.

Viewing the mess she'd left in the living room, she made a determination to get rid of anything left, every last piece of furniture and decorator doo-dad in the room. Advertisements on television made it look simple. Dial the number, schedule a time and they'd pick up the items. Whatever she donated would be sold at a second hand store, with the proceeds going to a worthy cause. Like supporting abused women and children. How fitting. Bygie felt abused, even though she'd done the abuse to herself.

Her first bit of luck was having her call answered on a Sunday. The calm voice from the store didn't question why she was giving away a room full of furniture. They assured her the men driving the truck would be more than happy to do the heavy lifting. They would be there Monday afternoon, sometime between one and five.

Grabbing a broom and dustpan, she cleaned up broken glass, hardly noticing the pain radiating from her cut knees. She hauled the broken painting to the trash. Finding boxes in the garage, she carefully packed what wasn't damaged during her rampage. When she finished, the only items left in the room were heavy pieces of furniture, including the damaged Victorian chair.

Feeling energized, she headed to their bedroom, no, *her* bedroom and surveyed the mess. Her dirty clothes were strewn across the floor. In her other life, life before the death of her husband, she'd been manic in her housecleaning duties. If she kept the environment nice and tidy, maybe her marriage would follow suit. It backfired. Lars only commented when something wasn't up to standard.

"Why is the vacuum sitting in the bedroom?"

Reproached, she'd jump to get it done.

In the mornings, not fully awake and her mind drifting, she kept her eyes closed, planning a layout of shells for a mirror she was working on; moments of relief from reality. Then she'd remember the awful truth. When she opened her eyes, bad memories rushed.

Morning anger is what drove her to throwing back the covers and getting up and out of the room.

Shaking her head to clear the vision, resolute, she grabbed a laundry basket and began picking up the dirty clothes. Remembering that police had trooped through her house, she felt embarrassed. At the time, she hadn't given a thought to dirty underwear on her bedroom floor.

In hindsight, she hated anyone thinking she was such a slob.

Finding a shirt of Lars, one thrown over the back of a chair, she raised it to her face, smelling his cologne. Had he ever loved her? Tears welled. She flung the shirt into the laundry basket, not willing to give in. Would there be a time that felt right to go through his clothes? Hard to imagine the day would come. For now, she straightened his drawers, hung up his clothes, feeling soft after the rage.

She decided to vacuum, her form of therapy. The loud sound and rhythmic push and pull action kept troubling thoughts at bay. Lugging the vacuum up two flights of steps, she stopped in the kitchen to catch her breath. Feeling light-headed, she parked the vacuum to pour a cup of left-over coffee. Waiting for it to heat in the microwave, alongside one she discovered in there, she massaged her aching shoulder.

Real nice move. Cut knees and what feels like a torn muscle in my shoulder. My swing was pretty good though. Maybe I should try out for a girl's baseball team. When they ask, if I've ever played before, I can say, no, but once I took on a lamp and a really ugly chair. She smiled, but for the life of her, couldn't figure out why. *Maybe because I'm moving instead of pacing?*

Forgetting the coffee in the microwave, she walked to the bedroom and stripped sheets off the bed. Putting on a clean set felt satisfying. Starting over. Retrieving the vacuum, she plugged it in and got started. What began as normal housework soon became a compulsion. She put the brakes on when she realized she'd spent the better part of an hour trying to vacuum a pattern into her bedroom carpet.

One she'd seen years ago at a swanky hotel.

Bygie and Lars had gone on vacation to a ritzy resort at Hilton Head, South Carolina. They were young, and the trip was way beyond their means, but Lars had won a sales contest at work. An all expense paid glimpse into how the wealthy relaxed; an incentive for the sales force to work eighty hours a week instead of a measly sixty.

Checking into their suite, the first thing Bygie had noticed was a checkerboard pattern vacuumed into the plush carpet. She'd never seen anything like it. How long would it take for a maid to vacuum her way out of a room, leaving behind carpet cut up into perfect squares?

She'd put out her arm, blocking Lars entrance. "Wait, Lars, don't walk on it. Let me figure out how the heck this was done."

"Huh? How was what done?"

"The carpet, look at it. Someone vacuumed a pattern into it. Maybe one of the staff does nothing but this. Vacuum. Someone else cleans the toilet or makes the beds, but this person only vacuums. A vacuuming artist." She'd laughed.

Lars had grabbed her from behind, carrying her to the bed. "Forget the floor, Biggie. We're here for something else, I'll show you an artist." He'd playfully tickled her before leaning over her for a kiss. "One day, I'll hire you your very own vacuuming artist, stick around and see."

Overwhelmed with the memory, Bygie sat down on her bed, tears flooding her cheeks. He must have loved her, hadn't he? How could he act so loving one minute and be so uncaring the next? Were all her good memories wrapped around having sex? *Was I so dumb that I thought sex equated love?*

She yelled out loud, to the empty room, "How could I be so stupid?" Tears pooled. "I'm a stupid, effing idiot. Why did you do this, Lars? Why?" Her crying intensified into deep sobbing and she slid to the floor. "Why?"

She froze, her breath jerky, listening.

Was that the doorbell?

It rang again.

Hugging herself, she rocked back and forth. *Go away. Go away.*

"Bygie, honey. Open the door."

She flew down the steps, crying harder, flinging the door open.

Without looking, she knew who was standing on the other side.

23

The arms reaching out supported her and Bygie clung for dear life, calming down with each reassuring pat on her back. She listened to the steady crooning.

"It's all right, I'm here. Shhh."

Jane. Her sister.

Bygie swiped at her eyes with her sleeve, "How did you get here? Why didn't you call?"

"Here, help me get this bag. I didn't let you know because I didn't want you trying to talk me out of coming. I used a car service. I'm so sorry I wasn't here sooner, little sis. Let's go in."

Jane herded her inside the front door, much as she'd done when their parents died. Closing the door behind her, they walked up the steps and into the kitchen.

"I couldn't let you go through this by yourself. You're so damn stubborn. I would have been here sooner, but at first, I listened to you. By then, Bob was out of town, gone for three whole days, days I should have been spending with you. As soon as he got home, I made arrangements for the kids and here I am. All yours, for awhile anyway."

She held Bygie at arm's length, studying her face. Her eyes were swollen from crying, dark circles smudged beneath them. Jane's eyes watered. Her sister looked haggard.

"Looks like you could use me." She cradled her sister's face, using her thumbs to wipe away tears. "What made you want to deal with Lars death alone? Why would you even think that? This is exactly what family is for." She put her arm around Bygie, "Come on girl, coffee time. I'll even make it for you, if I remember where you keep it. I can't believe I haven't been out to see you in over a year."

Bygie sat down on a stool at the counter, relieved to give over control. She watched her sister dump out the old coffee, offering a nod when Jane pointed out the cabinet that held new filters. "I'm so glad to see you Jane. I know how hard it is for you to get away, leaving three kids at home isn't easy."

"It's good for Bob. He can see what I deal with during the day. Nothing like time alone with the kids to bring him back to earth." She glanced at Bygie over her shoulder, noticing her raised brow. "He wants another baby. Can you imagine? I'm pushing forty." She turned back to the coffee pot, sifting grounds into the filter.

The simple statement opened a floodgate of memories. Her voice flat, Bygie clasped her hands hard enough to turn her knuckles white. "I never told you, Jane. I was pregnant once, when we still lived in Raleigh."

Jane turned around, her mouth open in surprise. "What? Why didn't you tell me?" She couldn't hide the hurt from her voice. "What happened?" She held the canister of coffee grounds in her hand.

"I miscarried."

"Oh my God, Bygie. Did mom know?"

"No, I didn't tell anyone." Her lips firmed. "Well, that's not exactly true, I did tell my husband." This time, when the tears fell, she angrily wiped them off.

Jane walked around the counter, perching on a stool beside Bygie. "Oh Bygie, that must have been a terrible time for you. What happened? Why didn't you tell me? Or Mom?"

"Lars wanted me to have an abortion."

Jane stared, her mouth forming a perfect circle. "Oh shit. You're kidding me, right? The bast ... I'm sorry. What the hell was he thinking?"

"That's all right," Bygie wryly chuckled. "Call him a bastard. I've been doing a lot of that lately. You ain't heard nothin' yet. I have a whopper of a story to tell you." She took the coffee canister from Jane, "Here, let me finish the coffee." She stood up, laughing again as she headed around the counter. Walking to the microwave, she opened the door, waving her arm like a game show hostess. Sitting side by side, were two cups of forgotten coffee. "I've been easily distracted."

"Hate to say it sis, you need to eat. You're looking way thin, or as Mom used to say, you look downright gaunt."

Bygie's smile was weak. "Yeah, well, I haven't been able to keep much down. This is a bitch of a way to lose weight."

"Well, exercise your finger. Order a pizza with the works. Let me wash up, get the airplane crud off. Should I use the same bedroom downstairs? Then, little sis, we'll sit down and have us a chat." Jane's eyes, shiny with tears, brightened, "Forget the coffee. I've got a feeling your story begs for something stronger. Crack open a bottle of wine."

Bygie laughed, "It's only three o'clock."

"You need to listen to country music. You know? Five o'clock somewhere? Which reminds me, I better let my family know I arrived in one piece. Get moving. I'm hungry." Jane headed downstairs to the guest room, glancing through the opening between the pocket doors into the front living room. "We have a lot to catch . . ." her voice trailed off. She pushed the doors aside. "What's going on in the living room? What's in the boxes?"

Bygie stood at the top of the stairs, "Part of the story, Jane." She smiled a real smile. "Hurry, I can't wait to tell you. I'll have a lot of apologizing to do for not filling you in sooner. Go. Take time to put on sweats, we're in for a long night. Pizza and wine coming up."

***

They didn't stay up as late as they would have when they were young; both hit the sack by midnight. Two bottles of wine helped make the decision to turn in easy. Bygie slept through the night and woke in the morning, instantly aware why Lars was missing from his side of the bed.

Feeling clear-headed, less burdened and slightly hungover, she threw on jeans and a t-shirt, quietly heading out to make coffee. She smelled the aroma before rounding the corner. Jane had beaten her to it. Listening, she could hear water running in the downstairs shower. What a comforting sound. Someone in the house.

She knew her sister's feelings were terribly hurt.

Bygie had purged fifteen years of marriage and tried to explain her lack of sharing. It had nothing to do with love, or trust, it was her own feeling of inadequacy that kept her mute.

Her fear of admitting failure.

Polishing off a bottle of wine bolstered her bravado and Bygie told Jane the police now associated Lars death with the word murder. Opening a second bottle of courage, she told her sister that her husband may have been involved in an escort business and that the police were questioning her involvement with both.

Today was a new day.

Bygie turned back to her room for a shower, deciding to treat Jane for breakfast.

Somewhere else. Out of the house.

***

"Listen, I know you didn't want to hear it last night, but you need to get a lawyer."

"I don't. I didn't do anything wrong."

"Don't you ever watch television? It happens all the time. Totally innocent people are put on trial. Remember the girl accused of poisoning her husband? They lived out here in California. It was all over the news. Turns out he died of a heart attack and she spent two years in jail for a crime she didn't commit." She grabbed her sister's hands, "Listen to me, please. Let's find a lawyer, get some advice."

Bygie shook her head. "I wouldn't know who to call. Besides, they aren't going to give out free advice. You know that. It would be 'sign on the dotted line.'" She frowned, stubborn. "No, I don't need a lawyer, it would make me look guilty and I didn't do anything."

"Maybe someone from Oceanview could recommend a lawyer? Who did you guys use when you bought into the dealership?"

Bygie removed her hands from Jane's grip, sitting back.

"Jane, I promise, if anything else happens, I'll go straight to a lawyer. I'm not dumb. I know police suspect the spouse first. Okay, I understand that and will deal with it, but they'll move on. I didn't do anything."

"I know you didn't kill your husband, but I want you to protect yourself. My God, Bygie, someone came to your house and painted your garage door. Who knows what could happen next? I'm worried." Jane's voice had risen, causing the couple at the table seated next to them to stare.

Bygie smiled brightly at them. "Let's get out of here. The people from the thrift store should be there in a couple of hours and I can't wait to show you the studio and my new pieces."

Relenting, Jane laughed. "I guess I don't have to worry. You still have your marbles."

"What'd I do to reassure you of that?"

"Made a plan to get rid of that ugly-ass furniture."

They both laughed, walking out of the restaurant arm in arm, heading down the sidewalk, but the laughter was weak and short lived. They covered a block in mutual silence.

"Jane, thank you."

"For what?"

Bumping her hip into her sisters, "Thanks for coming out. I was falling apart. I have a lot of soul-searching to do. Why I stayed married so long, or at least, didn't work harder at fixing it, will be on the top of the list. I'll work on those issues, as soon as I get out from under this murder rap." She bumped hips with her sister again. "How do you and Bob manage to make marriage look easy? Mom and Dad did the same thing, made it look simple."

"Ha! That's a joke."

"What do you mean? You've been married twenty years, have three great kids."

"Bygie, get real. There've been times I'd rather shoot Bob as . . . ahhh, sorry. Bad tasting joke." She looked at Bygie.

"Let me start over." She linked her arm through her sister's. "I guess I can't come up with any wise-older-sister words. It boils down to the person you marry. It takes a big commitment, from both people. There's no way only one person in the marriage can hold it together. When two people are committed to making it work, it's like a teeter-totter. One person is strong, while the other is down and vice versa. Mom and Dad certainly had their share of arguments over the years."

"Get out of here. No they didn't. I thought I was the only one that made Dad steamed. I remember Mom getting pretty mad at him, but I never heard her cuss, or threaten to leave him. In fact, I don't remember ever hearing either of them swear. When Dad was beyond mad, the most he'd say was "Gol darn it all anyway." Bygie swallowed a lump, remembering the hurtful words her Dad said when he found out she was living with Lars. "I can't recall Mom ever raising her voice, she was so kind."

"That's what being five years younger than me means. You were too young to remember. They had fights, believe me. Thing is, they always worked it out. I guess by the time you were old enough to remember, they had most of the finer points of arguing down. Most couples that make it over the long haul have figured out how to fight fair."

"That was one of our problems, Lars and I. We never worked anything out. He'd talk circles around me until I agreed with his point of view. Not because I agreed, because I was sick of arguing. I always caved. I stood my ground once, when I told him I was pregnant and refused to discuss abortion. Look how well that turned out. I had a miscarriage."

"I'm so sorry that happened, Biggie." She hesitated. "I used to talk to Mom about you guys."

What did she mean they talked about her?

Jane felt Bygie's arm stiffen. "Come on, sometimes I worried." She gave her sister's arm a gentle pat. "I wanted you to be happy, so did Mom. You always felt you needed to support decisions Lars made, no matter how they affected you. I suppose it was because of the way Dad reacted so many years ago."

The truth hurt. She'd always championed each choice Lars made. She wouldn't listen when Jane declared choices should be based on a mutual agreement. Or her mom would mention compromise, the preferred word for welding a successful union.

"So, none of you, Mom, Dad, Bob, none of you, liked Lars?" Bygie stopped walking and faced her sister.

"He became part of our family the minute you married him, you know that. Maybe from the outside looking in, flaws are more apparent. We all have them, Bygie, everyone does . . . except me." Jane joked, but then her face clouded. "I never thought for a minute he would be involved in anything like this. He fooled all of us. Don't be so hard on yourself, learn to talk to me."

"I'm a gonna' talk til' ya turn blue. Ya'll won't be able to get me to hush up." Laughing as they reached the car, Bygie looked at Jane across the roof. "Did I tell you about my little episode at the police station? I fell out, right there, in front of God and the cops."

"I'm sorry that happened. It's a good thing I'm here to help you."

"I'm okay."

"Nope, afraid not. That lousy accent needs work. Anybody hearin' you 'fell out' would assume you showed your goods to the police, like Janet Jackson at the Superbowl. Fell-out my ass. You sound like a hillbilly. No one in this here family has 'fell out' in years. We just plain old faint."

Bygie laughed.

They put the top down on the car for the trip back to the house, enjoying each other's company.

A brief respite.

24

Tom made a cold call on good ol' Judge Lockner, who was less than thrilled to see the detective standing on his porch, bright and early on a Monday morning.

"Howdy there, Judge. Is that you? In case you don't remember me, I'm Detective Hall, with San Diego P.D."

The judge stepped out onto the porch, holding his bathrobe closed with one hand and pulling the front door shut with the other. "What the hell do you want? Come to gloat? Get the hell out of here. My wife's home."

The Judge's pencil-thin mustache quivered, like a living slug stuck to his upper lip.

Tom disliked the cocky little S.O.B. He'd been in front of him in court too many times to be ill at ease. Especially after catching him with his pants down.

"I didn't recognize you, with the change in robe color and all. I'm used to seeing you in black." Tom rocked back on his heels, continuing to put on the good ol' boy country charm.

"It's a right fine day here in Southern California, don't ya think? Much too nice to have to be rushin' off to work . . . but I guess you don't have to rush anywhere now, do ya, Judge?" Lockner scowled, and Tom smiled wider. The scowl would have been threatening when delivered from a bench, but then again, the bench is what gave the little toad some height. He stood five-foot-four and had the 'short-guy' temperament to go with it.

Tom stepped in close, forcing the judge to look up at him.

"I have questions for ya, Judge. I'm sure you wouldn't mind going over a few things, would ya? I mean, being a law-abiding person such as yourself, you'd want to help us put away scum. Am I right, or am I right?"

"You'll have to come back. I'm not talking to you while my wife's home. She doesn't need to . . ." Lockner stumbled back as the front door handle flew out of his hand. His much younger wife stood on the other side, smiling.

Tom looked, then glanced away. Her skimpy pajama style left nothing to the imagination.

"I didn't know you were expecting anyone, Pauly. Where are your manners? Invite the young man in." Sleazy charm oozed from the nipped and tucked wife. Her lips didn't move as she spoke, they looked like fattened night crawlers after a good rain.

"He's not staying, Hon. I'll be right back in." He patted her behind. "Go ahead and pour yourself coffee. I'll be right along."

She tried to form a pout but failed, looking more like a scum-sucking fish. She'd need a straw to drink her morning coffee. Turning to head back in, she attempted to blow a kiss towards, Tom.

He grimaced at the fish lip pucker and waited for the door to close before continuing. "We can do this now, get it over with, or I'll be demanding a visit to the station. Your choice."

Lockner pulled the door tight. "Let's go sit in your car, get this over with." The Judge marched down the steps towards Tom's van with as much dignity as a man can muster while wearing bedroom scuffs and a bathrobe.

Tom smiled. Now this was fun. He walked to the driver's side and climbed in.

"Why does your van smell like a bakery, officer? Need a side job to make ends meet?"

Tom could have taken a nice car from work, one that had been seized in an asset forfeiture or drug bust, but he rarely bothered. He ignored the slight directed at his shitty-van and fired back, "How'd you explain your sudden resignation to the wife? Tell her you wanted to spend quality time with her?

Bet that made her real happy." He felt confident the judge's wife would be happier if left to find her own entertainment.

By the look on the Judge's face, Tom's remark hit the bulls-eye.

Lockner bristled. "What do you want?"

"When we arrested you, you said . . ."

"I was not arrested."

"When we detained you . . ."

"I was not . . ."

Tom knocked his fist onto the dash. "Stop the bullshit. We know the truth. My pants were up, where the hell were yours?"

The judge muttered, but held his tongue.

"You said you met the girl through Lars Hudson, at Oceanview Mercedes, correct?"

"Yes, I already told Pope all of this." Lockner glared.

"You're gonna' be telling *me* this time, as many times as I want, until I don't want to hear it anymore." Tom glared right back. "Tell me again, how was it set up?"

"When I traded in my Mercedes, as I do each year, Lars offered something extra for being a faithful customer. A bonus of sorts."

"Tell me how that happens. I mean, I've been a damn fine customer at my local burger joint, but I haven't ever been offered anything more than an apple pie. How does it go when a car salesman offers you a prostitute?"

The judge's face turned red, "It wasn't like that."

"I'm not following you. Not like what?"

"Like picking up a prostitute."

"You paid a girl for sex. What'd I miss?"

"I didn't go out and solicit the girl, damn it. It was a straight forward business transaction."

Tom laughed. "Let's start over, Judge. If you've managed to tell yourself it's normal business, let's go have a sit-down with your wife. Maybe the two of you can figure out how to deduct the business transaction from your taxes."

"For Christ sake. Haven't you got a heart?"

"Now, that's funny coming from the hanging judge. Wasn't that the nickname you worked so hard to earn?" Most cops would like a hanging judge, figuring he'd be one to rule in their favor. Not so with Lockner. His arrogance made him detestable.

The Judge straightened his bathrobe, running his hand down the folds as if he was wearing an expensive suit. "Look, you're a guy. Let's talk man to man. You probably would've done the same thing. The man offered some relaxation and I took him up on the offer. No harm in that. We're all adults."

"Keep talking." Tom drummed his fingers on the dash.

"I don't know how Hudson knew the girl. While we were completing paperwork on the new car, I mentioned how cute the girls were around the sales office. One was wearing a short . . . ."

He stopped short when Tom reached over and thumped his arm with his middle finger. Hard."I don't want to hear any bullshit fantasy. Tell me how you got set up with the girl."

The judge rubbed his arm, veins in his neck bulging. "Hudson said if I thought that girl was cute, he had something I may be interested in. He offered me a visit to a house, one that guaranteed to delight my senses." He waggled unruly eyebrows. "If you catch my drift."

Tom's eyes snapped to the judge. "You never mentioned a damn house. What house? We caught you doing the dirty deed in the hotel parking lot."

"Well, that's what Hudson said." Lockner's cheeks flamed, "I didn't have time for a house visit. I'm a busy man." He held up his hand to ward off the next question. "I don't know what house he meant. It could have been his own damn house."

"Hence, the quickie in the car that got you caught."

"Why the hell are you hassling me? Go ask the damn girl I was with. She knows more than I do." He leered. "I'm sure I wasn't her first. She was a real pro."

"What's her name? The pro you were caught with?"

"I never asked. We skipped the formality. Ask her yourself."

"We'd love to ask her, but she disappeared. Looks like you're my answer man until she turns up." Tom grinned wide. "You're practically my new best friend."

"I don't have anything else to tell you." Lockner tried to hide his gloating, "Guess it didn't help your investigation to have Mr. Hudson crack up in a car accident, did it? With the girl gone, you don't have much of a case, do you?"

"Oh, I'll have a case, judge, no matter how long it takes." He stared hard at Lockner. "People like you make me sick. Someone the public trusts to make wise decisions deserves to have their face plastered on the front page of the paper. The headline could read, 'Hanging Judge Lockner . . . Gets Hung by His Own Dick.'"

"My career's over. I'm sure that makes you happy, ya piss-ant." He leaned in towards Tom, "I used to tear up people like you for a living . . . ." Lockner's face was beet-red, veins in the side of his neck bulging.

Tom leaned in closer, a hair's space from touching nose to nose. "You may have worked a sweet deal by resigning, but that doesn't mean things don't have a way of leaking out. Bigger men than you have tried to cover something up and failed. Don't push me."

Refusing to back down, Lockner said, "Are you threatening me, officer? I could have your badge for that."

"Not any more Judge, not any more. I've seen what you've got, and it ain't much," Tom wiggled his eyebrows, holding his thumb and forefinger spread apart an inch, "if ya catch my drift."

Lockner slammed the door on his way out of the van, scampering back to the arms of his plastic wife.

Hall leaned forward with his elbows on the steering wheel, cupping his chin. Damn, that was fun. He gave the horn a couple celebratory toots. Too bad his old partner wasn't here to enjoy it; he sure did miss working with Mike.

25

Driving to the station, Tom speed dialed Ruby's cell. She answered on the first ring, sounding chirpy for a Monday morning.

"Hey, how'd it go with the Judge? Anything new?"

"Yep. We've got new info to chase down." He looked in the side mirror, checking out his big stupid grin. "I do have to say, I enjoyed the hell out of that. Anything I need to know from the morning meeting?"

"Same old drill there, but I've been rocking and rolling myself. You're gonna' like what I turned up."

"Don't tell me 'til I get in. No, better yet, lets meet at Zach's, my kitchen away from home. I'm feeling real hungry. I guess telling off a Judge increases my appetite. See ya in fifteen."

When Tom arrived, he ordered the biggest breakfast on the menu and was eating pancakes before Ruby slid onto the bench.

"Hey, I guess you weren't kidding. Looks like you ordered enough for two."

"Sit down, I got an extra plate for you."

"Uhhh, no, thanks. Not for me. After I eat pancakes, all I'll want to do is go to bed." Ruby's face colored, "I mean, I'd be so full, I'd want to take a nap."

"Wondered what you were trying to tell me, kiddo." Seeing her face color deepen, Tom was embarrassed. After Ruby's improved slogan for Oceanview Mercedes, he'd thought they were comfortable enough to throw a joke. "I'm kidding, don't be so sensitive. What ya got for me? You sounded excited on the phone," Tom asked around a mouthful of pancakes.

"I found a gun," she blurted.

Tom put his fork down. "You did what?"

"I mean I found out Lars Hudson had a gun. He bought it four years ago, in North Carolina." Ruby grinned. "It didn't take long to find his permit, once I decided to try his home state. It's legal, but he neglected to register it when they moved to California. I copied the dealer's record of sale for you." She opened a folder, handing Tom the sheet.

He processed the information. "Good work. A Smith and Wesson would be capable of putting the hollow point in Hudson." He sat back, frowning. The eggs and pancakes he'd woofed down felt like dead weight.

"This could change things. If we can place the gun in the laughing widow's hand, bingo," Ruby snapped her fingers, "we've got a murder case wrapped up."

"Not so fast, Ruby, there's the little matter of proof."

"I figure you were right, I've been dragging my heels," Ruby shrugged. "It's hard to believe the lady pulled the trigger, but I'm coming around. Big time." She gave a huge grin, breaking off a piece of Tom's muffin and eating it. "I found out more." Ruby looked like a smug cat with a mouse. "You know your motto? Follow the money? Well, I did. She stands to inherit a big chunk of dough."

"You found a life-insurance policy?"

"I sure did." She slid a second piece of paper over to Tom. "A nice fat check to the tune of a half a-mil." Her grin widened. "The money won't be released until after the investigation is over, you know how insurance companies operate. If they can find a way to deny benefits, they will." She picked at the muffin Tom slid in front of her. "I also got the unofficial word on how much her share of Oceanview Mercedes is worth."

Tom whistled. "You spent the weekend working? Are they buying her out?" He wasn't impressed, he was concerned. She'd done it without talking to him. *Or am I being an ass? I relaxed at a barbecue while the rookie made headway.*

"Well, mind you, it's based on office gossip. On Sunday, I went to the dealership and test drove a car. Best way to get a captive audience." At the blank look on Tom's face, Ruby clarified, "I told him I was ready to purchase my dream car. No way they let one of those babies off the lot for a joyride; the salesman rides with you. I asked if the death of one of the partners meant they were going out of business. It got the guy talking. Word around the office is they sent a generous buy-out to Mrs. Hudson. He didn't know the actual number, but overheard 'millions'. Plural." She sat back with a satisfied smile. "How'd I do?"

"Damn good work, Ruby."

"What'd you find out from the Judge?" She continued to peck at the muffin.

"The old bastard let it slip Hudson offered him a trip to a house. A trip that would 'delight his senses.' Lockner's words, not mine." His tone was clipped.

Her head shot up. "Not following you. What house?"

"I guess Hudson must have had a real class operation going. Lockner said Hudson threw in the offer of a visit to a fancy house, but the good ol' Judge was too busy. He couldn't take time away from handing down justice, so he opted for a quickie in the parking lot. Hudson set it up. Anything the customer wants, right?" He pushed the plate of food away. "The judge denies knowing where this so-called house is."

Tom motioned for the waitress to bring the bill. "We better send someone over to canvas Hudson's neighborhood. It'd be nice to cross his residence off the list of possible houses. Neighbors, even ones spread as far apart as they are in Stony Point, would notice traffic at odd hours." He threw money on the table for the bill. "We can search county records to see if Hudson owned another property and forgot to inform his wife."

"Or she knew the property existed. She's acting too innocent. No one is as nice as she looks on paper. Most people have something to hide."

"You're not supposed to be so cynical. Not yet anyway. You haven't been on the job long enough. Did you get a chance to run down anything new on our missing hooker? The one caught in the act with his honor?"

"Another dead-end. No sign of her. Her information was fabricated. Too bad we let her go before running her."

"I have a feeling we'll never see that broad again. They probably paid her off, sent her packing. Whoever the hell 'they' are."

"Are you up for another 'crime-scene' walk through? I'd like to go out and look again." Seeing Tom's expression, Ruby added, "I know, I know. It's over-kill. I can go out alone. I'd like to see it in the daylight for myself. See what I can learn. It's not like I think the traffic accident investigator missed anything but . . ."

"As soon as we had the autopsy results, Crime Scene investigators reworked the site and vehicle. Nothing, nada, zilch. The original traffic report stated the skid marks were dark to light, so he was accelerating when he flew over the side. When they returned Friday, they couldn't even find any evidence of skids one way or the other; too much rain and too many other tires scrubbing away the evidence. What are you hoping to see?"

"I'm not sure, but I'd like to go walk it myself."

"Off with you then. Make it a short commune. I'll need you close if something pops with Hudson's laptop. I'm headed over to see what our computer guru Noah's found, if anything. Let's hope our Mr. Hudson was a dumb-ass criminal who kept a black book downloaded. We need a break."

Ruby grinned. "I'll check in as soon as I get back. I won't be long."

26

Ruby shot down the on-ramp to the freeway, her mind racing. She drove through heavy mid-morning traffic, wishing she could put on a siren and move faster. The conversation with Hall had gone better than she imagined. Most cops trusted their gut, trusted it to tell them when danger was around the corner, or when a suspect was telling the truth. She'd kept her fingers crossed, hoping Tom would let her follow her instinct. She'd worked her ass off all weekend to impress him.

Exiting off Interstate Eight, Ruby merged onto the four lanes of Highway sixty-seven. Lost in thought, hers eyes drifted to watch a plane land at the local Gillespie airport. Traffic steadily thinned as she moved north, starting a gradual climb into craggy landscape. Forty minutes from the beach, and the change in topography was dramatic. It reminded Ruby of pictures of the moon. Boulders of all sizes were scattered randomly across the hills, like giants had played a game of marbles and left a mess.

The right-hand side of the road, protected intermittently by a guardrail, dropped off at a steep angle. She continued climbing until reaching Sycamore, then swung into the left hand turn lane to make a u-turn. Heading back down, she carefully slowed, approaching the scene of the accident.

The shoulder of the road was narrow and the drop-off on this side was as steep as the opposite. An area without protection of steel railing.

She parked, looking carefully over her shoulder for on-coming traffic before opening her door. Wouldn't do any good to get nailed by a speeding driver.

Ruby studied the scene, trying to visualize how it could have played out. Tom figured Hudson was driving with the window down, or maybe he rolled it down when he recognized the car pulling up alongside him. The shooter took dead aim through the open window. The bullet entered his cheekbone and traveled upwards to enter his brain, causing instant death. From the position of the shot, the ME guessed he may have been glancing over at his attacker.

Once the bullet struck, he lost control of the big, heavy SUV, and it took a hard right, straight down the slope. The vehicle over-turned several times, and Hudson's body was slammed around like a rag doll. The open window allowed his head to hit the ground, more than once, causing so much damage he was unrecognizable. A small fire had started from leaking fuel, mutilating him further.

When there was a break in the traffic, she crossed the two lanes, studying the scene from the center of the road, standing tight to the center divider. Walking downhill, she swung her eyes from side to side, studying the concrete, trying to picture how it would've worked. The shooter would have been in the left-hand lane at the time of the incident. Walking down the center of the road, with her back to traffic from one direction and facing the oncoming traffic from the other, was making her uncomfortable. What the hell was wrong with drivers? Her hair fluttered as vehicles blew past at high rates of speed, none of them moving away to an empty lane. Her heartrate accelerated.

She continued walking down the center, traveling downhill from the scene of the accident, the same direction the shooter would have been driving. Even though the crime scene crew had been here, she was amazed at the amount of garbage.

Items, from cigarette butts to soda cans, would have been picked up and tagged as possible evidence, so all this crap was new. Garbage people tossed out their windows. Unreal.

After running possibilities through her head, she scuttled back across the highway, turning to walk back uphill. Halfway back to her car, Ruby stopped. She bent down and studied the tall foxtail grass. Hastily, with the toe of her boot, she pushed together a mound of rocks and hightailed it back to the car to tell Tom.

27

After Ruby took off on her wild goose chase, Tom headed straight to the computer lab, hoping Hudson's salvaged laptop would come through with information. The news was good . . . and bad.

Good news was that Noah, the expert of microchips, had removed the hard drive from the heavily damaged shell and was able to retrieve information. Bad news was he hadn't found anything of interest.

"Looks to me like your guy was the average user, no hidden codes, nothing tricky. Only took me minutes to break his passwords. For a big-time pimp player . . . I mean, 'alleged' pimp player, he used dumb security. I always try the easy guesses first. You know, birth date, address, whatever. This guy was a real idiot. He used the word 'password' on his accounts. Don't people read? That's like leaving a key in the front door, inviting strangers in." Noah shook his head, amazed at the rookie mistake.

Tom was glad Noah was intently staring at the computer screen. He didn't want the whiz kid to see it written on his face that he needed to change the password on his bank account. Who had time to read techie magazines and find this shit out? Tom cleared his throat, "Did he do any banking online?"

"Yep, one guess on his password, what an idio . . . ."

Tom interrupted the speech, "Yeah, I get the idea."

"I printed out the statements for the past twelve months. That's as far back as I can go. His savings account held a meager balance of nearly seventy-five grand. Sheesh, chump change for you and me. You'll need to have the bank release anything older than that."

"Did you get a chance to look through them? Anything look off?"

"Nothing jumped out, but I'm a low-level computer hacker, not a super-duper detective." Noah turned to Tom grinning, secure in the knowledge that most of the detectives would be lost without his help.

"No sign of an address book?"

"Now that's where it gets interesting. He's got one, and it's much bigger than an average run of the mill address book. There's a file with over two hundred names and addresses and lots of email contacts too. Some of the names are recognizable, a list of real 'who's who' in San Diego. Maybe it's his dream list of people to sell cars to." Noah moved the mouse around and brought up the file.

Tom's cell phone rang, but, not wanting a disruption, he reached into his pocket and hit the mute button. He was excited to see the address file on Hudson's computer. He leaned over Noah's shoulder, scanning down the row of names with a sinking feeling. "It looks like more women are listed than men. Hudson would have been damn prolific to have an escort service with this many girls."

"Yeah, well, maybe it's a wish list." Noah gave Tom the standard eyebrow waggle that eerily reminded him of the Judge. "The name on the file is Reflections. Maybe he was reflecting on getting lucky."

It took a minute for Tom to figure out why the name sounded familiar. When he made the connection, his face fell. He scrubbed over his face, feeling tired. This must be the file Bygie Hudson was looking for, her list of customers. "Did you print it out?"

"In the stack." Noah motioned to a side table covered with carefully arranged piles.

"Is that for me?"

"Yep, your night time reading."

"Thanks for getting right on this, Noah. I appreciate you jumping it ahead of other work." Tom walked over to pick up the neatly stacked paper trail.

"No problem. This was an easy job. Next time, bring me a challenge."

"I'll get right on it. I got a feeling we'll be bringing in a couple more computers to look at real soon." Subpoenas for Hudson's household and work computer were in progress. He was waiting for approval. "Did you get cell phone records?"

"In the pile kemo sabe. The cell phone records will take awhile to check. Best you can hope for is no one was smart enough to use a throw-away phone."

Pay as you go phones, or throw-away phones, couldn't be traced.

"Thanks again, Noah. I appreciate you getting this done."

Tom hefted the pile back to his cubicle. He pushed aside other stacks to make a clear spot on his desk and dumped the paperwork from Noah. Remembering to check his phone for messages, he listened to a playback of Ruby's excited voice.

"I found something near the accident scene. It could be important, I mean, it might not, but I thought you should know. It's a shell casing." Sounding like an eager kid on Christmas morning, she said she would bag it, tag it and bring it in.

He snapped his phone shut when Ruby started apologizing for interrupting him. Finding a shell casing was information that only soured his already foul mood. A rookie in the vice squad, finding possible evidence in a homicide? It made his blood boil. How could the crime scene tech miss a casing? He hoped to hell she knew the protocol for bag and tag, or the evidence, if it turned out to be anything, would be useless. She probably picked the damn thing up without thinking.

He pushed back from his desk, disgusted, his eyes rolling up to stare at the water stained ceiling. Making a decision, he rolled forward and reached for the phone on his desk.

He'd make the call before he started slogging his way through the information from Noah. He picked up the desk phone and then put it down again. Walking back out of his cubby, he headed down the hall, searching for privacy. Last thing he needed were big ears listening to his request for a polygraph. He used his cell phone.

"Hey there Stu, Tom here. I'm needing a poly on a subject. She agreed to it on Friday, and I'm hoping she hasn't changed her mind over the weekend. How soon can you get her in?"

"A month from never would be the soonest opening. What ya got going on?"

"We had a car roll-over last Tuesday, one adult male fatality. It looked to be an accident. Turns out the guy had help from a 9mm, before going off a cliff. I'd like to get the spouse down here for you to work with."

"Is she in custody?" If she was they'd need to move fast to get the polygraph done before the arraignment.

"No, she's not, but we've got a sensitive issue here. I'm afraid she'll lawyer up if we don't move quickly. In fact, it's unbelievably lucky she hasn't hired a hotshot already."

"How soon can you get her here? I had someone lawyer up, so I'm free if you can get her here right away."

"Let me track her down. I'll call you right back."

Hanging up, Tom scrolled through his cell phone, looking for Bygie's cell number. It should still be there from the night she reported her spray painted message.

He listened to several rings.

"Hello?"

Her voice sounded different. More relaxed. Tom could hear a hollow noise whistling in the background. "Mrs. Hudson? This is Tom Hall with . . ."

She interrupted, "Detective?"

"I need you to come down to the police station. As soon as possible."

"Hang on a sec, I can hardly hear you. Hang on."

Tom waited, listening to the whistling roar through the phone line, along with the muted sound of voices.

"Are you still there, Detective? I'm sorry. I was driving and needed to pull over. I can't hear anything when the top's down on my car. What did you say?"

That explained the noise, but not the second voice. "I'm glad I caught you, it's perfect timing, you're already out. I need you to come down to the police station."

"Now? For what? Have you found out something new?"

Her voice lost the relaxed sound."I have a polygraph examiner lined up. We can get it over and done with right away."

"Ahhh, okay. I mean, I didn't know you were serious about a lie detector test."

"This is nothing more than a tool we use to rule out your involvement. I'm sure you'd like to get it behind you. Relax, tell the truth, it should go fine."

"Relax, right, I'll make sure I do that. Where do I go? This is the first time for something like this. I've never done anything that required a lie detector test. I don't know if I'm ready, I mean, what do I have to do?"

"You don't have to do anything except answer questions. Nothing to get ready, it's not a test you can study for. How long will it take you to get here?"

"Hold on a minute."

Tom could still hear the muffled sound of another voice and it sounded like an argument, but he couldn't make out the words. Someone was definitely with her in the car. A new boyfriend?

"I'll be there in twenty to twenty-five minutes. Where should I go?"

"Take the elevator down to the bottom floor and follow the signs to the polygraph office. The Examiner's name is Stu Pond. He'll be waiting for you."

"You aren't doing it?" She sounded surprised.

"No, we have specific officers trained to do polygraphs. I'll let him know you're on your way."

He phoned the examiner to discuss in detail what he was looking for. A polygraphist for twenty-plus years, Stu helped train new examiners and had been called in to assist the F.B.I.. He grasped what Tom needed right away.

"You want to know if she had any role in hubby's death, and you haven't enlightened her on the autopsy results."

"That's between you, me and a short list of others."

"You believe she's the doer?"

"It'd be hard to pull off shooting him while driving down the road, but let's see if she knows anything. Then I'll know whether or not I'm beating a dead horse or if I need to look for an accomplice." Tom wondered who'd been in the car with her.

"Okay, I'll find out what the lady knows. You coming down to watch?"

"Yes, but I'll watch from the closed circuit viewing room. I tend to make the lady pretty nervous." He closed his cell. It immediately rang.

"Hall."

"Sorry for bothering you, again. Did you get my message?" Ruby was talking fast, "it's pretty mangled, could have been driven over hundreds times, or it could be from something entirely different. It's a 9mm Luger, it's kind of hard to read but . . ."

"Yeah, got it. Take it straight to the lab when you get in."

Each gun leaves a distinctive mark on a casing, from the firing pin hitting it, to the scratches left behind when it slides back and forth in the chamber. If heavily damaged, it was probably too far gone for ballistics to get a good comparison to gun type. They probably couldn't get a clear read even if they had the actual weapon used in the shooting.

Then again, the slug found in Hudson's head was a 9mm, so it needed to be checked.

"Okay." At his abrupt tone, her voice lost enthusiasm.

"I'll be down watching a poly. We've got Hudson's wife coming in."

"Whoa, that's great. Now?"

"She's on her way. I also got the info off Hudson's laptop in the car. He was smart enough not to put anything incriminating on there, but we have big piles to wade through. Lots of homework. See you soon." Hesitating, Tom added, "Good work, Ruby."

28

Greasy slumped over his desk, trying to keep his mind centered on the article he was writing. He picked his way across the keyboard, backspacing to erase most of what he'd written. The story of two teen-age boys going on a shooting spree with B.B. guns was of little interest to him. The whole damn thing was just boys being boys. He'd done the same thing when he was young, but wasn't stupid enough to get caught.

Of course, they didn't have security cameras on corners when Greasy was young. Thank God for small favors.

Greasy had bigger fish to fry. Why waste time writing a story on juvenile delinquents when he had the biggest story of his life hanging in limbo. Lizzie remained silent. She had some smarts about her. His luck sucked. Running into a damn hooker with a brain? Had to be one in a million.

Their planned second meeting never happened. Lizzie didn't show. Sugar was supposed to be setting up another sit down. If Lizzie knew what was good for her, she'd be there on time and ready to tango. Greasy needed to be clear on what he'd do if she didn't start squealing on the johns.

Instead of looking like an innocent woman taken advantage of by men with money, she'd be painted as the instigator. If he didn't have the goods, he'd fabricate her guilt through insinuation and splash it across the headlines. Lizzie, the woman who gave up names for pocket change. Not even low-life pimps would trust her.

To top it off, he had to avoid meeting with the asshole detective. The voice message from Hall lacked any form of professional courtesy. He didn't request a meeting, he demanded one. No way Greasy was walking into that trap until he was good and ready. If they wanted to play hardball with him they'd be in for a surprise. He'd demand an exclusive.

At least they were taking him seriously. When Greasy initially floated escort service rumors, he was treated like a joke. Even the dirty cop willing to give up info for cash snickered.

"Whatcha' got Greasy? Big time hooker story? You can hang out on the El if you want to see live action." The typical pause before the punch line. "Oh that's right, you already do. Careful you don't get to itchin' in your privates. We'd have to change your name to Scratchy."

Lousy bastard thought he was so much better. Greasy would have the last laugh, come hell or high water. He'd show them. He was capable of more than handing out greenbacks to get tidbits of information thrown his way.

Times like this, when his frustration level was high, he needed Sugarlips. He grabbed a tweed coat from the back of his chair, in a hurry to find salvation. He'd avoid the detectives as long as possible.

With visions of Sugarlip's finely honed skills running through his mind, his low-throated chuckle brought a look from the blonde reporter at the desk next to his. Licking his lips, giving her a once-over from head to toe, Greasy had her turning back to her desk real fast.

Yeah, Greasy had it going on. He was unstoppable.

29

"Bygie, you've got to listen to me," Jane yelled over the high-way noise. "Don't go in and take a lie detector test without a lawyer. At least talk to one first."

"I don't have anything to hide. I'm not getting a lawyer. Leave it alone, Jane." She was happy to have her sister here with her, but she wanted her off the lawyer kick. She was in-nocent of any wrongdoing, and pushing to get a lawyer only made her feel guilty. Of something.

"Once this is done, I'll be cleared. I told you what the de-tective said, they're doing it to rule me out." Hall's reassur-ance spiked her confidence.

"I've read enough to know that's what they'd tell anyone, even ax wielding Lizzie Borden." Jane knew she wouldn't get Bygie to change her mind. She was damn stubborn. Discuss-ing a lawyer was adding another layer of stress and Jane backed down. She reached over, laying a hand on her sister's leg, "Okay, okay. I'll drop it for now."

They pulled into a parking lot, the front tires rocked up against a cement divider. Before the car was done moving, Bygie jumped out to put the top up. Jane clipped her side down, watching her sister do the same with shaking hands.

"Hey there little sis, get a grip. Take some deep breaths before you explode. No worries, right? You'll ace it."

They crossed the parking lot, stopping at the corner, waiting for the signal to cross.

"I'm getting worried. What if they ask questions like, 'Have you ever stolen anything?' If I say no, it's a lie. I remember taking gum from a store when I was six. What if they ask if I ever wanted to kill my husband? If I say no, well honestly, the thought did cross my mind, but I wasn't serious."

"You don't have to do this, Bygie. We can turn around and go home."

She squared her shoulders. "I want to get it over with. I can't be the first person who took gum or was pissed enough at their husband to wish, well, wish that he'd go away."

"If you change your mind once you're in there, you can leave, okay? Promise me you will."

Bygie put two fingers above her brow in a salute, "I promise."

"You're such a dork. That's a Boy Scout salute, not a Girl Scout."

They both laughed. Bygie felt better as they crossed the street, entering the front door of the police station.

"You've got to admit, I'm showing you a good time," Bygie whispered.

"I could do with less stress. Next time, let's go to the zoo. Maybe we'll be lucky and get attacked by a gorilla."

They found the door marked Polygraph, half-way down a narrow hall. Opening the door, Bygie was surprised to see a smiling man look up from a desk. She didn't expect a warm greeting.

"Hi." The man looked at each of them, "One of you must be Mrs. Hudson."

"Uhhh, that would be me," Bygie raised her hand, then put it down, feeling like an idiot.

The guy continued to smile, pushing back his chair and standing up. He reached across the desk, holding out a hand, "I'm Stu Pond. I'll be doing your test today."

He had an unthreatening appearance. His silver hair looked windblown and his sunburned nose was peeling. The white shirt he was wearing was wrinkled. He looked about as intimidating as Santa Claus. Bygie was comforted by his warm handshake.

"Who do you have with you?" Pond indicated Jane's presence with a nod.

"Oh, I'm sorry, this is my sister, Jane. She's visiting from North Carolina."

"Well, Jane, from North Carolina, I'll have to ask you to wait here, while I spend time with your sister. We won't be long. The time will fly while you read year old issues of Newsweek or catch up on the latest fly fishing techniques." His chin lifted, indicating a couple of chairs and a battered side table filled with old magazines. "If you get bored, there's a coffee stand back out the front door, to the left."

"Thanks, I'll be fine." Jane smiled.

"Okay then, let's get you started, Mrs. Hudson. I'd call you by your first name, if that's alright with you, but I'm not sure how to pronounce it."

Bygie appreciated his directness. "It's Bye-gee, although I've been known to answer to Biggie. It depends on who's saying it." Her lame attempt at humor felt out of place.

She trailed him back through a door that led into a drab corridor. Opening the first door they came to, he ushered Bygie in. The cubicle of a room contained a standard issue metal desk, and sitting on it was a strange-looking instrument full of knobs. One end had odd, needle-looking darts, poised over graph paper. The only thing Bygie recognized was a blood pressure cuff.

"You can have a seat while I get my old lady here warmed up." He patted the instrument.

Bygie sat down in the chair he'd indicated, a straight-backed, wooden chair, sitting by the desk.

"So, are you from North Carolina, too?" His tone was pleasant and invited conversation.

"Yes, I am. I've been in California about six years."

"You don't have much of a Southern accent."

"I know. I worked at erasing it when we moved out here. Until we moved to California, I didn't think I had an accent."

Stu smiled. "Okay, looks like we're ready."

Her stomach knotted.

"What do you know about polygraphs?"

"Not much, only what I've seen on TV."

He chuckled, "On television they add a lot of drama. Let me tell you what I'll be doing. I'm going to ask you a set of questions, and before we start, I'll go over each question with you. No surprises, you'll know exactly what I plan on asking. Doesn't sound too hard does it?"

"Uhhh, no. It's not what I imagined. I figured you'd be flinging questions at me like a drill sergeant."

"Nope, that's the televised version. We'll go over each question, and I guarantee, those are the only questions I'll be asking. The only thing I need you to do is tell the truth." Stu picked up a two pieces of Velcro with wires dangling from them.

"We'll be putting these on your fingers to measure sweat. When people lie, their fingers sweat. Betcha didn't know that." His blue eyes sparkled.

"That's news to me." Bygie made a half-hearted attempt to smile.

"We'll also have a blood pressure cuff to measure you heart rate. It always tells the truth. Whether it's a big lie, a small lie or something in between, it'll start racing. It sure makes my job easier. Not many people can control their heart beat."

"Mine's racing right now. Won't that look bad?" Bygie was scared. What had she gotten herself into?

"Nope, most people would be nervous. Before we start, I'll know exactly what your heart rate is. Nothing to worry about, as long as you tell the truth." He peered at her from under craggy eyebrows.

She motioned around the room, "That's what I've been doing, telling the truth. It hasn't done me any good so far."

"I don't believe you've done anything, and the polygraph will prove it. Detective Hall told me to take it easy on you."

She relaxed a little. Very little.

"We have these pretty straps to put around your tummy and chest, they'll let me know you're still breathing. The only other thing is to sit absolutely still once the test starts. No wiggling around." He looked at her, "Just remember to tell the . . ."

She interrupted, "I know. Tell the truth."

"You're going to do fine," he patted her arm. "Let's go over the questions, the exact same ones I'll be asking. Ready?"

"As I'll ever be."

Stu Pond patiently covered each question, explaining exactly what information he was referring too.

"When I ask, regarding the death of Lars Hudson, I'm referring to the accident which occurred on Tuesday May 16th. That's different than a bad argument that left you wishing he would go away. Okay? I've been married a long time, we all get mad now and again. That's not the same thing."

Bygie nodded her understanding, relief flooding.

"Good. We're ready to go."

Stu gently attached Velcro wrapped sensors around her ring fingers to measure sweat. He had her lean forward, carefully wrapping the bands around her chest and stomach to measure breathing.

"This is the only uncomfortable part of the test." He picked up the blood pressure cuff, "I'm sure you've had your blood pressure taken before, right?"

She nodded again, offering a bleak smile. Her mouth was too dry to speak.

"Well, then you already know it gets tight. If it gets to be more than you can handle, let me know. Here we go, make sure to sit still and answer the questions truthfully. You'll be fine." He patted her arm again.

The test started with basic questions, her name, age and address. He'd explained the simple questions gave him a good base on his readings to start with. It didn't take him long to get to the gritty questions, ones concerning Lars death.

"Regarding the death of Lars Hudson, do you suspect anyone in particular of directly causing his death?"

"No." Her mind was racing. What if he thought she was lying?

"Regarding the death of Lars Hudson, do you know with certainty, who directly caused his death?"

"No. I don't even know . . ."

"I know it's hard, but we need to stick with one word answers, yes or no."

"Okay. Sorry."

He repeated the question.

"No."

"Regarding the death of, Lars Hudson, did you yourself directly cause his death?"

"No." Pond had explained that even if they'd argued, causing Lars to speed off in anger and wreck, she was not directly responsible.

"Regarding the death of Lars Hudson, is there any information about this investigation that you are intentionally withholding from the police?"

"No." She felt like squirming.

"Regarding the death of Lars Hudson, did you hire someone to directly cause his death?"

Bygie jerked. Pond patiently repeated the question, like he was reading off a grocery list.

Bygie answered. "No."

Pond asked the same questions several times, changing the order each time around.

Her answers remained steadfast.

He released the pressure on the cuff, saying "I bet it feels good to get that cuff off."

"Yes, it does. Is that it? What happens now?"

"I'm going to have you sit back and relax. I need to go over the results, double check we have everything we need. Could I get you a bottled water while you wait?"

"No, I'm fine."

Pond ripped off the printed paper and loosely folded the long sheet. "I'll be right back." He stepped out of the room, closing the door behind him.

Hoping she hadn't made a huge mistake by agreeing to come in for this, Bygie slumped in her chair. Drained.

30

Stu walked into the hall, stepped a few strides and entered an adjacent room. "Hey there, Hall. How ya doing?" Stu reached out to shake hands.

"Good to see you, Stu," Tom grasped his friends hand, his eyes remaining on the monitor. "Been out fishing lately?"

"As often as Carol lets me. How 'bout you? Been fishing for anything besides criminals?"

"Nope, haven't been out since last fall. Guess I have enough fish stories to last me a while." He glanced at Stu then back to the monitor and its picture of Bygie. She was massaging her temples. "How'd it go in there?"

"Pretty good. She was an easy test." He scratched his peeling nose, sending flakes flying. "But . . ."

"I hate the 'buts.' They're never good news."

"She's holding back something. When I asked if she had a suspect in mind, she flagged, but that's no surprise. She hasn't a clue. Like most people would, she's scrambling to figure out if it could be someone she knows." He rocked back on his heels. "Then she went off the mark. When I asked if she was holding back information, she scored negative 15. She's lying, big time." He spread the printed sheet out on the table for Tom to see.

Hall turned to look at the long squiggly lines running down the length of the graph paper. "When are you going to get with it and start using the computer for polygraphs?"

The type of instrument Pond used for Bygie's exam was considered a relic, one that was used long before polygraph instruments entered the digital age.

"Not you, too." Pond rubbed at his nose again. "I use the computer to teach new polygraph examiners at Baxter's, but using my old Stoelting Ultrascribe? Nothing better than the smell of ink and watching the pens do their magic. It's like driving a classic car." He had a reputation for being a regular da Vinci at reading the pen and ink printouts. He pointed out high peaking points on the graph. "See this? You wouldn't have it so sharp and clear on the computerized version. It'd be full of jaggies. Computers are great, but the pixels don't line up exactly . . ." Pond trailed off, noticing Hall was back to staring at Mrs. Hudson on the monitor. He cleared his throat and Tom turned around. "This is where she was lying. The 'holding back information' question got to her. Her reaction to other questions was steady and truthful." His finger traced along the lines.

Tom turned back to the screen, staring hard at Bygie. He knew she'd be wondering what was taking so long. Without looking at Stu, Tom asked, "So. Is she involved? Got anything there to lead one way or the other?"

"She's not the doer, if that's what you're asking. I'm not sure what she's hiding." Stu studied Halls back.

"My new partner called," Hall faced Stu, bracketing the word partner with his fingers. "She went to walk the accident scene and happened to find a 9mm casing on the side of the road. It could represent a whole new scenario." Tom dragged his fingers through his hair. "This has been a mess from the beginning, I told you we assumed a straightforward accident until the autopsy. Working backwards, we figured the shooter pulled up beside him, popped off a lucky shot and got the hell out of there." Tom was pacing the room, talking to himself more than Pond.

He came to a halt and stretched out his arm, his pointed finger taking aim across the room. "If the shooter was driving, he'd have to stretch across the seat to fire and the casing would likely eject somewhere in the car." His arm dropped. "At least that was our assumption. Finding a casing outside of the car could mean two people were involved. One for driving, one for shooting. If the casing has anything to do with Hudson's murder, it could change the direction."

"Ahhh, I see. You're wondering if the little lady sitting in there has played you for a fool. You're wondering if she was in the car when the shooting happened."

"Yes."

"I'll give you an easy, tentative, answer. No. She doesn't know who directly caused his death and she wasn't in the car. I also asked if she hired someone to cause his death, she said no and passed with flying colors."

Tom's eyes pulled back to the monitor. "What's she holding back on then?"

"Want me to go back in and find out or do you want the honor? You could always use the old wet-rope torture trick if you're not trusting my antique polygraph instrument." Pond said.

Tom turned, inhaling deeply. He'd been holding his breath. He ignored Stu's attempted humor. "No, I'll let you do it. The lady's not exactly a big fan of mine."

Nothing much got by the sharp-eyed examiner. He'd known Tom for a long time, they'd spent many an hour together chasing fish. "Any wonder why? Hard to show concern after bringing her in for a polygraph."

"Concern? I'm no more concerned than you are. She seems like a decent person who was married to a creep." Tom's voice had a hard edge.

"I thought maybe you wanted me to treat her with kid gloves out of respect . . ." Stu looked up in the nick of time, seeing a black look on Tom's face. He blew out a breath and didn't finish the thought. "Okay, then. I'll go back in. I have another set of questions I'd like to run."

***

Bygie was on edge. Her sister's list of people, ones wrongfully accused of a crime, raced through her mind. She was startled when the door opened. She smiled timidly at the examiner, hoping to leave. Seeing his face, her heart sank. Pond's hangdog expression could only preface bad news.

"Is something wrong? How did I do?" She clasped her hands tight to calm down.

Stu scrubbed his hands over his face, pausing to pick at his sunburned nose. "Well, there's no easy way to say it, Mrs. Hudson." He shook his head, "I can tell you haven't been completely honest with me." He watched her color blanch. "I'm not sure what you're holding back, but this would be a good time to tell me."

"I told you everything. How could this happen? I'm not lying to you. I promise."

Stu bit back a smile. The woman was engaging. "I'd like to run another test, it may help clear up my confusion."

"Are you sure it won't get me into more trouble? If the first test says I'm lying, and I'm not, I swear, how is another one going to help?"

"This one will have different questions. I'm sure it will clear up any uncertainty I have. I'll go over the questions first, exactly as before. If you're not comfortable telling the truth, when you hear what I'm going to ask, we'll quit. How's that?"

She didn't like it, but couldn't see a trap. "What are the questions?"

"It's really one question and a pretty easy one. I'd like to go through a list of possible ways your husband could have died." He watched the color drain from Bygie's face.

"I don't know how . . . he died. No one has told me. I thought it was a car accident."

"Well then, the truth will be simple and this will be quick." Stu was good at putting people at ease, one of the reasons he was good at his job.

She shrugged her shoulders, giving up. "Let's go for it." She wasn't involved, wasn't guilty of anything, end of story. She'd say that as many times as necessary until someone sat up and listened.

Like the first time, Stu ran through the set of questions.

Bygie flinched at the harshness of the words.

When Pond was sure she understood what he was looking for, he re-attached the straps, put on the blood pressure cuff, and inserted her fingers into the sweat testers.

"Ready? Sit still, tell the truth, simple as that. Here we go." His eyes were glued to the lines running down the paper. "Regarding the death of Lars Hudson, if you caused his death, did you do it by poison?"

"No."

"Regarding the death of Lars Hudson, if you caused his death, did you do it by strangulation?"

"No,"

"Regarding the death of Lars Hudson, if you caused his death, did you do it by disabling his brakes?"

Bygie jerked, he died in a traffic accident. It could have been the brakes, couldn't it? What were they holding back from her?

Stu looked over, "Sit as still as you can. Let me ask you that question again. Regarding the death of Lars Hudson, if you caused his death, did you do it by disabling his brakes?"

"No."

"Regarding the death of Lars Hudson, if you caused his death, did you stab him?"

It took all her control to be still. The questions were torture. "No."

"Regarding the death of Lars Hudson, if you caused his death, did you do so with a gun?"

"No." She choked out the answer, tears were flowing.

He asked his list of ten questions, each one as gruesome as the next. Again, he switched the order around and questioned her a second time.

Bygie felt drained.

"That's it, we're done. Let's get you un-hooked."

"Can I go now?"

"I won't be gone long, I promise. Let me do another quick check." He walked out of the room, heading straight to Tom.

"Anything new?" Tom asked the second Stu stepped into the room. Time for small talk and tales of catching big fish was long gone.

"Naw. She wasn't involved in his death. No reaction when I mentioned a gun. If she was responsible, I'd know. I'm telling you, the girl can't lie. I don't know what she's holding back, but she's not the shooter and she wasn't driving the vehicle. She was not in the car."

Tom tamped down the feeling of relief. "Thanks for getting this done so fast. At least I can move on with the investigation. What do you think she's not telling us?"

Stu rubbed the back of his neck, "Not sure. If I had to guess, it'd be something she finds embarrassing, but not relevant to his death. Maybe she knew hubby was playing around but didn't want to admit it. What I do know, and I'm positive, she didn't kill him with a gun in the parlor or a candlestick in the library."

Silence from Tom.

"Forget it. I was quoting a kids game. She didn't kill him, wasn't involved. I'll stake my reputation on that. I'm telling you, the girl can't lie."

31

Bygie was surprised she hadn't seen Hall during the polygraph. She figured he'd be hanging around, waiting for the results. She felt let down that he wasn't there to find out how she done. The feeling surprised her.

Guess I'm experiencing the Stockholm syndrome, identifying with my attacker.

On their way out of the station, Bygie grabbed Jane's arm, jerking her to a stop.

"What's up? Did you forget something?" Jane asked.

"Shhh, look. Over there. I'd swear that's the reporter who was watching our house. I'm sure of it. Sometimes he would stand outside his car and stare."

Jane followed Bygie's eyes, coming to rest on a man scurrying through the lobby. "That guy? He looks like one of those troll dolls we used to play with as kids. Are you sure?"

"Yes. I'm pretty sure. I don't want to see him. Wait until he's gone."

They watched him exit through the front door. Bygie didn't release her grip on Jane's arm until he was out of sight. "Let's wait. I don't want to run into him outside." She pushed her sister to get her moving. "No, go look, see where he's going. Hurry."

Jane walked to the doors, stepping out to the sidewalk. She scanned both sides of the street for a short man in an ugly tweed coat. He was gone. Stepping back in the station, she motioned to Bygie the coast was clear.

She hurried over, "Did you see him? I don't want to run into him. You can't imagine how many times he called our house. At least I'm pretty sure he was the caller. He's spooky." She let out a sardonic laugh. "Maybe I should be thanking him."

"Thanking him? What on earth for?"

"Without him, Lars never would have told me what was going on. Not that I know, even now, what was going on. Lar's version? He'd been caught with a hooker and the reporter was ready to do a story on him. 'Big Time Car Dealer Caught in the Act' or something. The police are saying it's a whole lot worse than that." Her jaw clenched tight. "He was a regular pimp according to them."

"The police could have it wrong. What if it was a car accident, nothing more? They aren't telling you a dang thing besides his death looks suspicious. What a load. You need to . . ."

"I know, I know. Get a lawyer." Bygie gritted her teeth, "I told you, I'm not getting a lawyer. At least not yet. I didn't do anything."

They walked across to the parking lot, Bygie never stopped looking for the reporter.

"The polygraph guy said my test looked good. I guess that means I passed. He told me the detective, Hall, would follow up." Bygie came to a halt, slapping her forehead, "Oh crap, I forgot."

"What?'

"We were supposed to be at the house when the guys from the thrift store came for the furniture. What time is it? I bet we missed them."

Jane looked at her watch, "It's after three. I forgot too. Maybe they're still there. You said sometime between one and five. Maybe you'll be lucky."

Bygie snorted, "Have you noticed my luck lately?"

"I'd say, sucks big time, pretty much covers it."

Driving home, Bygie caught herself picturing Hall. *Wonder what his story is?*

She wasn't sure what she thought of his partner, Ruby Wilson. The woman appeared caring when she delivered news of the accident, but there was something off.

It's probably because she's younger, and I'm feeling old and tired.

Tears threatened. Behind her sunglasses, she stretched her eyes wide to ward them off, afraid she wouldn't stop if she started. Pulling into her driveway, she was heartened to see a big truck, one emblazoned with the thrift store logo and two men sitting inside.

"Looks like they waited. Probably wish they hadn't after they see what's going in the truck." Jane said.

"Hey now. Don't make fun of my designer furniture."

"That's not furniture, it qualifies as artifacts. Those chairs belong in a museum."

They stepped out to greet the men. It took Jane a minute to realize the smiling men spoke only a smattering of English. They nodded and continued smiling, no matter what either woman said.

Bygie laughed when Jane raised her voice. "Even when you yell at them they won't understand English."

"I wasn't yelling . . ." Jane stopped. Turning back to the men she put on a big smile, motioning for the men to follow. "Like three blind mice. You lead, Biggie, and we'll follow."

They trooped in a line to the front door, pausing while Bygie dug through her purse for a key. One of the men stepped around her, motioning to the door. He pantomimed opening it. Bygie nodded, making a turning motion with her hand, trying to tell him she was searching for the key.

The stocky man criss-crossed both hands, waving them in front of Bygie, the universal symbol for no. He motioned to the door again.

"La puerta está abierta."

Bygie groaned. "I think he said something-something-open, did I forget to lock the door? Maybe they already loaded everything."

"No. You locked it. You waited for me to go back and grab a sweater."

With a sinking feeling, Bygie grabbed the knob and twisted. The door opened. "Shit. I must not have, I didn't set the alarm either. I haven't been worried with you here."

"Right. Like, I'm a bodyguard and would know what to do."

Entering the house, Bygie immediately noticed the packed boxes were opened. The contents had been moved around, bubble wrapped items had been lifted out. She turned to the smiling men. "You came into mi casa?"

They shook their heads, but their eyes looked frightened.

One spoke up, "No, no. No entramos en la casa."

"You came in. It's all right." Bygie insisted.

They vigorously denied it. "No, no. Entreabierto, ahhh, es open?"

What little Bygie could understand of their Spanish became clear through their gesturing.

"Bygie, what's up? Did they come in?" Jane looked from the men, to Bygie, then back, trying to follow what was being said.

"He might be saying the door was already open. I'm a space cadet, but I'm sure I at least shut the door. Didn't I?" Lately, she questioned whatever she did.

"I'm positive you locked it. Call your detective. I don't like the looks of this." Jane's eyes traveled around the room. "Call him. Now. Let's go outside. Maybe someone's in the house."

Bygie didn't believe the men had done anything wrong and she hated to get them in trouble if they were in the U.S. illegally. Then again, someone had painted her garage door. Maybe the person had returned?

"I guess you're right. Should I call him? Detective Hall?"

"Heck yeah. Come on." Jane took Bygie's arm, shuffling around the nervous men and stepping back out onto the deck. The men followed, bug-eyed when Bygie used her cell phone.

"No, no. No entrar, si?" One man wildly pointed at their truck. "Siesta, mi camion."

"Si, si. I know." She did her best to calm them down with her limited Spanish by smiling and repeating 'si.' To the men's credit, they didn't try to leave.

Scrolling through the numbers on her phone, she found the detectives number and pushed send. He answered on the second ring.

"Hall."

"Detective Hall? This is Bygie Hudson. I'm sorry to bother you . . ." she hesitated. "I guess I have another problem at my house. I mean, I might. I'm not sure. It's probably nothing but a misunderstanding."

"Are you home now?"

"Yes, I returned from the polygraph to find someone's been in my house. Maybe." She smiled brightly at the two men to reassure them.

"Did you go in?"

"Only into the front entry. Someone went through boxes I'd packed . . ."

"Packed? For what? Were you going somewhere?"

"No, nothing like that, it's for donation. It looks like someone dug through boxes. It could be the two men here with me. I'm not sure."

The more she talked, the more confused Tom became. "Two men are there? Fill me in when I get there. I'm on my way. I won't be long. I'm, ahhh, in the neighborhood."

"Fine, yes. Thank you." Bygie snapped the phone shut. "He's on his way, he said he was nearby." She smiled again at the two men, motioning for them to take a seat. They nervously squatted on the edge of outdoor chairs. Both looked ready to bolt but to their credit, they stayed put.

The spokesperson tried again, "No entrar, si?"

"Si, I believe you." She sincerely hoped the detective understood Spanish. The whole scenario puzzled her. Why would anyone go through the boxes? If the men had been wanting to line their pockets with treasures before delivering it to the store, they wouldn't have left the boxes open. Would they? That'd be dumb. She didn't believe it.

Help arrived as panic was taking root. Tom pulled into the driveway, followed by two patrol cars with lights flashing.

32

"Whoa, looks like the cavalry arrived" Jane was amazed. "That was a fast response. Were they waiting around the corner?"

"He must have been real close." She only had a minute to wonder if Hall was following them, before he strode up the front steps.

With rigid attention, other officers stepped out of patrol cars, like dogs on point.

What had he told them? Why were they even here?

Tom studied the men, asking Bygie, "What's up?"

"I'm sure it's nothing. We're having trouble communicating."

"You called me over to translate?"

Bygie blushed under his scrutiny. "No. I mean these guys were here to pick up furniture I was getting rid of. They were sitting in their truck when we arrived home from the polygraph. I was happy to see they waited, because we were running late." Bygie gestured towards the door. "When I went to unlock the door, the shorter man said 'Entreabierto'. I think it means open." She was talking too fast, waving her arms around.

"Did you go in? Together?" Hall's eyes looked grim.

"Well, yes, enough to see the boxes had been opened. I'm sure they were checking to see if they were supposed to take them, then decided to wait."

Tom kept an eye on the men, "Were you two together?" He waggled a finger at Jane. She was standing off to the side, silent.

"Oh, yes, I'm sorry. Jane, this is Detective Hall. This is my sister, Jane."

Tom darted a look, wondering why he hadn't noticed the similarities. This must have been who was in the car with her. His feeling of relief pissed him off. He snapped to one of the officers, "Loll, come here would you? You speak Spanish don't you?"

One of the officers stepped away from the group, advancing to the porch.

"Sir?"

"Seems Mrs. Hudson here, came home and found these two waiting. They were here to pick up some furniture and packed boxes. Problem is, when she went to unlock the door, they told her the door was open. Not unlocked, but open, or half open. Inside, she discovered packed boxes had been disturbed, the contents sorted through. Is that right so far?" Tom's eyes fastened on Bygie.

"Yes, but," she hastened to add "I don't believe these two men did anything wrong. They stayed here instead of running off. If they did go in, it was probably a lack of understanding."

"You don't need to speak English to understand it's illegal to enter someone else's property." Tom sounded harsh. "Get their story, Loll. I'll have the others do a walk around."

Jane watched, wide-eyed. Her only involvement with law enforcement was the death of her parents. Feeling shaky herself, she put an arm around her sister's shoulders.

Bygie leaned on Jane's shoulder, taking in reinforcement.

"Can you believe any of this?" Bygie asked, keeping her voice low.

"Nope. I swear, you're the best entertainer ever." Jane eyed Hall, "You forgot to mention the detective belongs on a television show."

Lifting her head, Bygie looked at her sister, questioning the statement.

"He's the epitome of a handsome television detective."

Bygie laughed softly. "You watch too much TV. He looks scary to me."

"You must be blind." Jane whispered. "That's one good-lookin' drink of water standin' there."

The exaggerated southern drawl had Bygie smiling as her gaze traveled over Tom. He turned to look at her. Her cheeks colored.

Tom averted his eyes. "Let's have you ladies wait in one of the patrol cars while we take a look inside."

Bygie tugged Jane along. "It's where they had me wait last time." She felt like an old pro. Yeah, yeah, cops again. No big deal.

They were ushered into the back seat.

Jane asked, "How can you act so calm? I feel trapped and guilty of something."

"I'm not calm. I guess I've been shocked so much that I'm becoming immune. I feel stupid. What if I did leave the door open?"

"Unlocked and open are two different things, and you're forgetting someone opened the boxes." Jane shivered. "I'm creeped out thinking someone could have been in the house.

"I know. That's how I felt when I came home to a message painted on my door. I was jumpy for days. I still am."

"You need to come home with me. I'm not leaving you in California by yourself."

"I can't."

"What do you mean you can't? Of course you can. You can stay with us for awhile."

"I really can't. That good-looking TV detective of yours? He told me I had to stay in the city; I can't leave until this is settled."

"That's ridiculous. It's not like they wouldn't know where you were. Talk to him. You can't stay here alone, not with this going on."

"We don't know if anything weird is going on or not. Those guys . . ."

Jane interrupted, "What do you mean you don't know if anything weird is going on? Have you lost it? We're sitting in the back of a patrol car. Your husband was murdered, and someone left a nasty message for you. How much worse does it have to get? Come on Bygie, you're not thinking straight."

She wasn't listening to Jane. Bygie's eyes were glued on the men coming out of her house. *At least my house was clean this time, no dirty clothes lying around.* She shook her head at the thought. Her sister's words broke through. Maybe she wasn't thinking straight. Clothes on the floor were the least of her concerns.

One of the officers walked over to the car, opening the door to let them out. His face was stern, not giving anything away.

"No one was in there, right?" Bygie questioned.

"Ma'am. Detective Hall is waiting. He'll fill you in. You can go up to the house." He trailed behind the women, as they headed to the door. Officer Loll was still sitting on the porch interviewing the two men. Bygie smiled weakly. Both men were wide-eyed and trembling. She felt awful.

Standing in the entry foyer, Tom turned to greet them. "All clear. I need you to look around, see if anything has been taken. It looks like someone searched your home."

Bygie looked stung. "Searched? For what?"

"I'm not sure. My guess is the moving guys startled someone and they left through the patio door off the kitchen. The moving men are saying pretty much what you understood. When they knocked on the door, it swung open. They called out and when no one answered, they shut the door. Headed to their truck and had a nice little siesta on the clock. Plenty of time for someone to sneak away." He dragged both hands across his scalp, then self-consciously let them drop.

"I'm positive they didn't do anything wrong." She shivered. "Was anything taken?"

"We don't know. You'll need to tell us that."

Her eyes narrowed. Instead of his usual penetrating gaze while he spoke, he avoided eye contact. For the first time since meeting him, she could clearly read he was uncomfortable. "What aren't you telling me?"

Hall reached into his coat pocket and withdrew papers, handing them to her. "We're here to execute a search warrant."

"What?" Bygie took the papers, reading fast. "It says you're here to search the residence located at . . . ." her voice trailed off. Her eyes jerked up to lock on Tom, "A gun? We don't have a gun." Reading more. "You're taking my computer? For what?" She was trembling, not from fright, but because she was angry. "Is this why you were here so fast? You were on your way to take property from me? I don't believe this. I took the stupid polygraph."

"It's not you. It's your husband. We need to find out what he was involved in. Someone took his life, Mrs. Hudson. Murdered him. I'm doing my job, investigating."

Bygie felt as if she was down a rabbit hole. Her vision narrowed, she rocked unsteadily.

Tom reached out to support her, fearful of her fainting again.

She shoved his hand away. "Don't touch me."

Jane put her hand on Bygie's arm, patting it to calm her down. She jerked her arm away, not wanting to be soothed.

"First, you accuse me of killing my husband, but don't bother to tell my how he died. Then you put me through a stupid lie detector test." She laughed harshly. "Now you're here to go through my house? What next? Want to lock me up in case you've forgotten something?" She noticed the other officers, hovering in the door with hands on their holsters.

"Come on in, help yourself." She waved her arms. "Take whatever you want."

"We'd like your co-operation." Tom's voice was back to its normal, inhospitable tone. "I'd like to walk you through each room, check to see if anything has been taken."

Bygie stomped past him, up the steps to the kitchen. She looked around carelessly, not bothering to open anything, "Nope, nothings been taken from here."

"Slow down." Tom's hands were clenched as Bygie marched into her bedroom without answering. She stopped abruptly at the doorway.

Her room had been torn apart.

Drawers were hanging open; clothes were thrown around the room. She spun on Hall, "Looks like someone beat you to it." She viciously kicked clothes out of her way as she walked to the open closet. She tried to slam it shut, but it swung back, hitting her in the face.

"Bygie, slow down. You're going to get hurt. Stop." Jane reached out, gently touching her sister's back.

Bygie jerked away, twisting to face her sister, a red lump forming on her forehead. Tears running down Jane's face stopped her cold. She sank down on the foot of the bed, covering her face with her hands. "I'm sorry Jane. I don't know what's wrong with me."

Tom cleared his throat, "No one wants their privacy invaded. I'm sorry it has to be done. We'll do what we need and get out of your way."

For the first time, Bygie heard a hint of compassion in his voice. She dropped her hands, silently studying him. "Let me look around to see if anything is missing." She slowly rose, then stood ramrod straight, her hand flying to her heart.

"My studio, oh no. What if someone got in there?" Pushing by Tom, Bygie headed to the steps.

Hall reached out and grabbed her wrist.

"Whoa. I had the officer's check. It didn't look like the door had been tampered with." He could feel her rapid pulse underneath his fingers, he quickly dropped her arm. "Let's go look to make sure." He led the way, motioning with his chin for one of the uniforms to come with them.

Bygie unlocked the studio door. She looked in, breathing a sigh of relief. "It's okay."

Tom stepped through the door, not sure how she could tell. "How can you be sure with a quick glance? It looks, well, like a lot of stuff."

He took in the two work tables covered with mounds of shells. Underneath the tables, sitting on the floor were baskets, packed full of shells. A fine layer of dust coated surfaces. Old lamps were standing haphazardly in a corner, butting up against stacks of old mirrors of vastly different shapes and sizes. A couple of large wooden transport frames leaned underneath a back wall of windows.

Tom took in the muddle of bits and pieces, bewildered. "You work with this? Mirrors and old lamps? Seashells?"

"That's right, no red paint in sight. No paint of any color." She smiled wryly at Hall.

He rubbed his neck, changing the subject. "Do you wire the lamps yourself or do you have an employee that helps?"

"I do it. I'm an expert. At old lamps, anyway. Don't ask me to wire anything more complicated." She looked around the room as if she hadn't seen it for a long time. Walking over to a mirror, trailing her hand along the shells, "This is why I needed the mailing list off Lars laptop. I've got a big show in La Jolla coming up, and it pays for me to send a flyer to people that purchased in the past. They usually bring someone new with them."

Jane was walking around the room, admiring Bygie's work. "You've gotten a lot done. These are beautiful. This is some of your best work." She squatted eye-level with a finished lamp sitting on the floor. "The pictures you sent of the lamps didn't do them justice." She smiled, looking up at Bygie over the edge of the table. "You know I'm not leaving without . . ." her voice trailed off, remembering there was a Detective watching, she felt foolish.

"You can have whatever you want, after the show." Abruptly, anxious to get the search warrant done and have her house back, she turned to Tom. "Let's get this over with."

33

Walking back to the house, Bygie observed the two men walking towards their truck. "Will they be okay?"

Hall looked at her with raised brows. "Excuse me?"

"Were they illegals?"

"I'd have to check with, Officer Loll, but since they're headed to their truck, I'm assuming not."

"Well, Detective Hall, I don't want to hurt your feelings, but I'm not real comfortable trusting your assumptions."

Tom bit back a retort when he realized she was teasing him. Uncomfortable, he brushed his hand down the center of his head, keeping his eyes glued to the ground.

"What were you planning on having the moving guys haul away?" Hall questioned as they stepped into the entry.

"They weren't moving guys. I wasn't skipping out on you. I was donating to a second-hand store. I had the urge to re-decorate the living room."

The sister's eyes met. The shared identical, wry smiles.

Tom was puzzled. He was missing the joke.

"I decided I didn't like the decorator." Bygie glanced at Jane, then back to Hall. "A pretty female my husband hired."

Tom's interest sharpened. "You didn't know her?"

"No. I was told a partner at Oceanview recommended her." She locked eyes with Hall. "Now? I'm not so sure. I'm trying to look on the bright side. I always hated that room."

Hall made an effort not to smile, remembering the ugly furniture. "Do you know where I can get in touch with this, ahhh, decorator?"

"I have a card around here, somewhere."

"Do you remember who she worked for? What the business was called?"

"No." Her forehead creased, "It only had her name and number. Suzie? No, that's not right." Bygie brightened. "It's on my laptop. Lars forwarded designs for me to look at."

"Where's your laptop?"

"It's in the . . ." her face fell. "Oh no." She sprinted up the steps to the kitchen. The table was empty. "It's gone. I'm sure I left it there." Twisting towards her sister, "Do you remember, Jane?"

"That's the last place I saw it. Unless you took it into your bedroom last night."

"Are you kidding? I barely made it there myself." She groaned, "I better call my bank, notify my credit cards."

"As long as you didn't use the word 'password' as your password, you may be okay. I hear that's a dumb thing to do." Tom added.

Bygie rolled her eyes, "I'm not *that* ignorant."

Tom brushed his neck again. "Was it the only computer in the house?"

"Yes. Lars and I each had laptops. He had a desktop at work."

"My partner should have it by now. A second warrant was issued for Oceanview." He'd hated sending Ruby out to do her first execution of a search warrant without him. The officers going with her knew more than she did. Since the business warrant focused only on Hudson's personal office space, it should be foolproof.

Bygie snorted, remembering Lars' partner telling her to keep the police away. Tom and Jane were both staring at her. "Sorry. I spoke to one of the partners, Jim Sprague, yesterday. I bet he's one upset man."

"Detective Hall?" A uniformed officer was walking up the kitchen steps. He stopped mid-way when Tom turned to him. "Sorry to interrupt, sir. We have something you're going to want to see."

Tom followed the man back down, stopping at one of the boxes in the entry way. He glanced in, then looked back up at

Bygie standing at the top of the steps. His eyes were hard, black discs of stone.

She frowned. What now?

"Could you come down here, Mrs. Hudson? I'd like you to see this." Hall was back to being formal.

Bygie knew it had to be bad. What were they looking at? The stupid designer twig balls she'd tossed into the box wouldn't garner attention. She moved slowly down the steps, approaching the box with caution. Maybe an ugly bug. Or a snake. Chills followed the length of her spine. She hated snakes. Peering over the side, her eyes widened and flew to Hall's face.

"Oh my God. Where did that come from? Is it real?"

"What Bygie? What is it?" Alarmed, Jane leaned around to look. She squinted into the box and parroted the question. "Is that thing real?

Lying in the bottom of the box was a gun.

A dull, black, 9mm Glock.

34

The grueling day left Tom drained. He'd briefly touched base with Ruby. Following the retrieval of Lars' computer from the dealership, she'd delivered it to Noah in the computer lab. She was back at her desk, filling out reports. He should be doing paperwork himself, but was troubled by the gun showing up at Bygie's house.

Too damn convenient.

If someone was trying to hide evidence, they wouldn't pack it in a box headed to a second hand store. With the amount of time he'd spent in the presence of Mrs. Hudson, he didn't see her doing something that stupid. Or that reckless.

Worst news? The numbers on the gun had been filed off.

Ruby's search of Lars' office at Oceanview had been successful as well. A second gun was found locked in Hudson's office desk drawer, with the serial numbers intact. The weapon registered to Hudson in North Carolina. Good news for the laughing widow; she didn't steal his gun and use it to shoot him.

Finding a gun at their home, put her right back in the hot seat.

He stood up from his desk, needing a break.

Walking over to Ruby's cubicle, he leaned against the flimsy frame, "Getting the reports done?"

She looked up, surprised to see him. "Yep. Crossing my 'T's' and dotting my I's.' She pushed back from her desk, stretching her arms out to the side. "Feels like this day has lasted forever, and I'm only halfway through the paperwork."

"Did you get the gun down to the lab?"

"Yep. How long will it take for them to do a ballistics test?"

"Not long. Couple of days at the most, depends on how backed up they are. How'd it feel to execute a search warrant?"

She smiled. "I wish you could've seen the expression on Sprague's face. When one of the officers pried Hudson's locked desk drawer open, I thought he was going to have a coronary."

"Maybe the shell casing you found will match." Tom's smile was casual, friendly.

She shrugged. "Thanks, but we won't know anything until the report is back. For all I know, the casing blew out of a truck bed. It's so mangled, I can't imagine it will help. I'm surprised you found a gun at Hudson's home. Maybe it'll match the casing or slug."

"Depends if there's enough left of either one for a decent test. I'm going to ask the lab to run an acid test on the gun from the residence. Maybe they can raise a trace of the numbers that were filed off, and we'll find out where it came from."

Ruby stood up to fiddle with a plant sitting on her filing cabinet, asking over her shoulder, "When did an acid test become routine?"

"It's not routine, but if you know who to ask, it's possible to get one done. Pope wants this solved and is willing to spend funds to do it."

"How does it work? It was only mentioned in basic training." She picked dead leaves off the plant.

"Where the stamp is located on a gun, the metal is denser, more compressed from pounding the serial number into it."

Tom watched the back of Ruby's head cock to one side, questioning.

"Did you ever push a finger into soft bread when you were a kid? The finger spot stays flat, denser than the surrounding bread. It's the same type of deal when numbers are stamped. If someone filed off the numbers, but stopped as soon as it looked smooth, it doesn't mean they're completely gone. The acid solution will eat away the metal, but the dense material where the numbers were stamped is slower to disintegrate, because it's more compacted. The serial number, if it's still there, will briefly be visible and appear raised. If we're lucky, which we haven't been."

She turned to face him. "So you're saying, the deeper they were filed off, the less chance of seeing the number?"

"That's how it works. Let's hope we had someone lazy doing the filing."

"How long will the test take?"

"We should know soon enough. The casing, the recovered slug, the gun, they'll do what they can to match 'em. I asked Noah to work fast magic on Hudson's computer. He'll do what he can, as soon as he can." He pushed off the wall. "The casing, if it's connected, could put a new spin on how Hudson was shot."

"How's that?"

"We could be looking for two suspects, a driver as well as a shooter."

"The casing could also bounce off a headrest and out the window." Ruby's v-neck shirt gave away a tinge of red creeping up the front of her neck. "I thought that's what you told the crime scene crew."

He shrugged, too tired to get into it. "Another one of the mysteries to solve."

"Not looking good for the laughing widow is it?" Ruby said. "Looks like the deck is stacking against her. Pretty much a textbook case, wife kills cheating husband and inherits the dough. Maybe she was the driver?"

"We still have a lot of evidence to wade through before that claim can be made." Tom turned to leave, "I'm checking out for the night. Call if anything new turns up."

"Sure will. I'm going to finish these reports and head out myself. Anything else you want me to do?"

Tom pivoted back, "Wade through the reading material from Noah. Make a note if anything, and I mean anything, doesn't look kosher. I'll do the same. Maybe with two sets of eyes we'll find something. You've been doing good work here, keep it up." He rapped his knuckles against the wood.

Ruby nodded, looking down, trying to hide how much his approval meant to her. She glanced over, hesitating. "Want to grab something to eat before you head home?"

"Thanks, but I'll pass. I need sleep. I'd be lousy company tonight." Tom didn't notice her cheeks flush.

"Okay, see you in the morning then." Ruby forced a bright smile.

***

The television was on, and Tom was stretched out on the couch, ignoring the program on Discovery channel. He hit the mute button, killing the noise. Swinging his legs to the floor, he sat up, carelessly tossing the remote to the coffee table. He reached for his cordless phone. He glanced at the clock and calculated the time difference. Kids should be in bed, but not too late to call.

Digging the scrap of paper out of his billfold, he dialed the number before he could talk himself out of it. Listening to the ring on the other end, he halfway hoped no one would be home so he could be a chicken shit and leave a message.

"Hello?" The voice was soft, a whisper.

The awkward softness of the voice made his stomach hurt. "Hi, Annie, this is, Tom." He felt like a fool. He abruptly stood up to pace.

More whispering, "Oh! Tom! Hang on a second."

He could hear the rustling sound of fabric against the receiver. Annie was probably motioning for her husband to get the phone so she wouldn't have to talk to him. He heard a hollow sound followed by the click of a phone hanging up.

"Hello? Are you there?" Hall said.

Annie responded, in a normal tone. "Tom. It's so good to hear your voice."

Intense relief washed through him. His knees gave way as he sank back to the couch. He swallowed hard before answering. "Annie, how are you? I'm sorry I haven't called before now. For a minute there, I thought you'd hung up on me."

"What? Oh, Tom, I'm sorry. I was putting baby Gabe to sleep and I didn't want to wake him. I ran and grabbed the phone in the kitchen, so I wouldn't be trapped on the upstairs phone whispering to you. How are you, Tom? We sure have missed you."

Tom squeezed his eyes shut. "I wasn't so sure you'd want to talk to me. I was such an ass when you left. I'm so sorry, Annie."

She laughed, "Tom, you and Mike are two of the most hard-headed men I know. I'll be happy to rub it in my husband's face that you were the first one big enough to pick up a phone. I've been after him to call you."

"You sound good, Annie. How are you? The Pope mentioned he'd talked to Mike, but he wouldn't share any news. How are the treatments going?

"Can you believe I miss hearing you and Mike discuss The Pope?" Her laugh quieted. "It's looking real good, Tom. I survived chemo and radiation. You'd swear they were trying to kill you with the medicine they pump in. Thank God that's over. I'm bald as a cue ball, but done." She paused. "Right now, things are looking up. I'm starting to feel human again. Want the best news, or should I go find Mike?"

"No, keep going. What's the best news? I want to hear it from you."

"The latest test shows I'm cancer free, for now, but it's a good prognosis. As long as I keep on top of it, get regular check-ups, I should live to be a hundred." Her voice lowered into a cautious tone. "One thing seriously concerns me."

His heart sank; he didn't like the sound of that. "Oh no, Annie, is something else wrong?"

"You better believe it. When they told me I'd live to be a hundred, I told them I wasn't so sure I could handle Mike that long." She made a sound between a laugh and a whoop. Mike must have been standing beside her.

"Okay, I give up, I'm being tickled. It sure is good to hear from you. I hope you can visit us, either here in South Dakota or in . . ." her voice trailed off as Mike grabbed the phone before she could finish.

"I had to stop Annie from telling you all the news."

Just like that, the two men were speaking.

"From the way Annie sounds, you guys are doing okay, huh?"

"We're pretty good."

Silence hung, long enough for Tom to feel uncomfortable.

Mike cleared his throat, "I'm glad you called, Hall. I felt bad leaving things the way they were. With Annie's cancer and . . ."

Tom interrupted, "Are you kidding me? I'm surprised you're still talking to me and real sorry it took me this long to say, well, to say, I'm really sorry, Mike. I acted like an ass."

"Yeah, but you always acted like an ass. I should've been used to it." Mike said.

"Hey now, careful there. You never know what dirt I have tucked away."

Both men gave a half-hearted chuckle at the lame joke.

"Got time to talk shop?" Tom said.

"Oh, now I get it. You didn't call because you miss my pretty face. You called because you need a real detective. Run it by me, brother. I'll solve it before we hang up."

Tom blinked hard, wondering why his emotions were out of whack. It was damn good to hear Mike's voice again. "This one starts out routine, with happy hooker shit, but veers left. I need an outside opinion, but if Pope finds out we talked, I may as well hang up my shield."

Mike's tone changed, the disgust in his voice was apparent. "I can't believe The Pope let you transfer to vice."

Silence hung as Tom groped for an answer. "Yeah, well, I begged and pleaded to be put back in Vice. I wanted back in the action. Ha, ha."

"Action, my ass. Homicide back to vice? You must be going stir crazy rounding up hookers and johns." Mike's voice took on a hard edge. "It's a waste of your talent. You know it, I know it and sure as hell The Pope knows it."

Tom didn't know what to say. "Uhhh, thanks for the support, I guess."

Mike laughed. "You're such a hard-headed ass. Whatcha got for me? Let me dust off my rusty detecting skills and solve it for you." He laughed again. "Shit brother, maybe that's what we should be doing."

"What's that?"

"Let's start a business. 1-800 solve a crime. One call to us, and we'd solve a crime over the phone from the comfort of a couch. Sitting in our boxers, sipping a cold one."

"Living out there in the sticks hasn't dulled your intelligence one bit, that's good to know."

"We don't have much for sticks in our part of South Dakota. More like amber waves of grain."

"Well, let's see if the amber waves can blow the cobwebs out of what little brain you have left. That little thing has probably shriveled to nothing." Joking with Mike felt wrong. Tom was the one who needed cobwebs blown out. He'd been worse than an ass to his best friend. Six months and he hadn't checked to see how Annie was doing.

Tom cleared his throat, "Mike, I really am sorry. It's such a relief to hear Annie's good news. I'm sorry I haven't called. I don't know why I haven't picked up the phone. There's no excuse."

"Yeah, well, I had some pretty harsh words for you too. We were both under so much damn stress. It's water under the bridge." Mike was quiet and then added, "in a funny way, Annie getting sick has turned out to be one of the best things that could have happened to us."

"Don't let Annie hear you say that."

"It's okay, it's not a secret. We're closer than we've ever been. She says it's because I've seen the light, gotten my priorities straight."

"What's that?"

"The job. You know what I mean. We busted our asses for The Job. We were damn good at what we did, but it put our families on the backburner."

"You handled it well enough. I'm the one who let my marriage fall to shit."

"We were both doing the same thing, Hall. You know that. All that mattered was getting the next lead, but the thing is, being away from it, I can see how I had it backwards. The cases we closed gave me a tremendous high, but I missed other highs along the way. Family, friends, my kids. Life celebrated around me while I played macho boy."

"You did a pretty good job of it from my viewpoint. You and Annie . . ." he didn't know how to finish what he was feeling.

"Yeah, me and Annie. You always put us on a pedestal, but we had our share of struggles. She didn't like sitting home alone anymore than Gloria did. I'd be there for family barbecues on the weekend, play with the kids, laugh, drink a few beers, but you know damn well we were waiting for the phone to ring with the next tantalizing clue. The next high." Mike blew out a breath. "I was nothing more than a bystander, always waiting for the next big crack in a case. There's a lot more to life and I was missing most of it.

"Don't you miss it? The action?"

"Not so much, at least not anymore. I thought I'd go stir-crazy, but I was way too busy to miss much of anything. Annie was going through chemo and radiation, and I became more of a parent than I'd ever been. The kids became my total responsibility." He laughed again. "Being a decent parent? It's a much harder job than what you and I were doing. But the reward of watching who your children are turning out to be is far greater than putting any homicide case to rest."

"Sounds like you have a good handle on it."

Mike picked up the bitterness in Tom's voice, a telling clue of Tom's struggle to find personal satisfaction. "Don't get me wrong. There are parts that I do miss. Not quite ready to hang it up and be Suzy homemaker." He paused, "As a matter of fact, I'm going back in."

Tom let the information sink in. Is this what Pope was referring to when he announced Mike had news? "What the hell. You're coming back?"

"Nope. I'm afraid you'll have to slog through on your own. I'm not returning to SDPD."

Tom was puzzled.

"I took a job in South Carolina . . . they snatched me up quick." Mike laughed. "Who wouldn't? They're getting one of the best."

Tom snorted. "Good to hear your ego is intact." The news was surprising. More than surprising, it was hard to believe. "South Carolina? How the hell did you end up looking for a job down there?"

"Annie's parents would like to retire someplace warm and when Annie was well enough to travel, we headed south to check out some places. South Dakota is a great place to live, but man, oh man, you wouldn't believe how cold the winters are. That's the only reason I'd want out of here. The cold winters, along with snow as high as the roof. Shit, that's enough to put even a stout man in the grave."

"Why don't you come back here? What you need is sunny San Diego. The in-laws could thaw out on the beach. You could probably step right back into your old job."

"I want back in, Tom, but not that big, ya know? It'd be too hard coming back to SDPD. My priorities have changed. I'm looking to slow down, not go back to twenty-four-seven."

"I guess." Tom didn't get it.

"While we were on vacation, we stopped for breakfast in this little town, and I mean little, like population of twelve thousand. There were a couple of local cops sitting at the counter, and get this, drinking coffee and eating doughnuts in public." He laughed. "I talked shop with them, you know, I wanted to show brotherly love from a big city detective. Next thing I know, they're telling me the town is looking for a new Chief."

Tom's jaw dropped. "You're going to the dark side? A Chief? No frickin' way."

Mike's voice was excited. "Hard to believe, isn't it? I never thought I'd wade into any kind of management swamp, but it's a small town. Counting the dog catcher, there's a total of seven full-timers on the force. But hey, that means I'll really look good."

Tom stood up, treading a familiar path around his coffee table. "And your new awakening? I thought staying home and baking cookies was a job description you were happy with."

"That's exactly the point. Baking cookies with my kids? Sounds all right to me. It doesn't mean I'm brain dead. My intention is to do it right this time around. I'll work my job, and work it hard, but family and friends? That's my priority." He remained silent for a length of time. "This time around, I don't plan on forgetting it."

"Annie's okay with this?"

"Yep. She understands my 'passion', her goofy word, not mine. She's relieved I'm not heading into a big swamp, only keeping my feet wet in a small one. The last homicide in town was during the civil war."

Tom's head was spinning. "When are you heading out?"

"Not for a couple months. In the meantime, how 'bout you let me get to the bottom of whatever little dilemma you have going on. I'll solve it while I put in another batch of cookies. In my Scoobie Doo underwear."

"What?"

"Never mind. It's a kid thing."

Tom laughed. "Damn. It's good talking to you, Mike."

"I can't wait for you to get off your lazy ass and come visit us. When we're settled in Carolina, you can come down and check it out. You may like our new and improved, laid back life. It'd be good to see you partner."

Tom snorted. "Partner. Yeah, right, that's another story. You wouldn't believe the partner they stuck me with in vice. A female rookie. Not even a rookie, rookie. She came straight out of the academy and into vice." He winced before admitting the worst of it. "I'm her FTO."

"You got to be kidding? No shit?" Mike laughed, hard. "A field training officer? That's rich. The Pope's way of punishing you for the transfer?" He was laughing so hard he had a hard time catching his breath. Mike moved the phone away, still laughing, as he tried explaining to Annie what was so damn hilarious.

Tom could hear then both laughing now. "Hey, it's not that funny."

"Oh, yes it is. That's the best thing I've heard in a long time. I bet you're on pins and needles trying to clean up your language." Mike tried to catch his breath. "Let me ask Annie to grab me a beer. Sounds like we'll be talking awhile."

***

Tom stretched out in bed, his arms crossed behind his head. Talking with Mike felt damn good. The conversation had lifted a heavy burden, one far heavier than he realized he'd been carrying. Maybe the Pope was on to something. Keep your table clean.

Discussing the case with his old partner brought back why they worked so well together. Ideas bounced across the phone line, cementing the direction Tom's gut was taking with the case.

If his gut proved correct, there was going to be one hell of a mess at the San Diego PD.

35

Morning again, at least Hall thought it was morning. He was feeling old, and switching between nightshift and dayshift was a bitch. When his alarm buzzed, he'd thought it was six at night instead of breaking dawn.

At work, he sipped coffee as he sat outside Pope's office, waiting for him to return. He was late in getting the chief caught up-to-date and his tardiness would not be appreciated. When Pope's secretary offered him coffee, it didn't bode well and this morning she was overly solicitous of his needs. Hall likened it to fattening the calf before slaughter. It meant the Pope was in a prickly mood. Catching him up on what they'd been doing would not improve his day. If Pope's temper was sour before Tom talked to him, it would likely worsen.

He had few hard facts to report in the Hudson murder investigation. The man was still a damn mystery. No straight line in the investigation.

Tom heard the sound of the The Pope's footsteps echoing down the hall. Each footfall resounded with a determined plunk on the tile floor, like a boogie man moving in on his mark. When Pope turned the corner into his office atrium, he strode past Tom, straight into his office without as much as a nod.

Uh oh.

The open door was the only indication Tom was to follow him in. Rising from his chair, he headed into the lion's den, wishing he hadn't noticed the look of pity from Pope's secretary.

"Hall. I thought I'd be talking to you right after Hudson's wife came in to pick up the personal property. I hope to hell you got that stopped before it walked. Shut the door."

Tom shut the door and took his usual seat. This time, the chief didn't comment or bother with lighthearted talk.

"Tell me some good news." The Pope sat back with his hands behind his neck, lifting the front of his chair off the floor and balancing on the back wheels.

He may have a casual look, but Tom knew different; he was winding up to pounce. The tilted chair would propel him forward with alarming velocity.

"We got Hudson's property and vehicle secured. Nothing new from the wife when we talked to her, but I requested she take a polygraph to help prove innocence. Pond worked her in right away."

Pope nodded, encouraging Tom to continue.

"Based on Pond's opinion, the wife passed the polygraph. He believes she's an innocent in this. She flagged on one issue, but Stu thought it wasn't connected to her husband's murder." Tom tried to pass over a folder containing the polygraph results and updated reports.

Using his elbow as a pointer, Pope indicated Tom should put the report on his desk. "I respect Ponds professional opinion, but at this point I'd be willing to take any flag and run with it. What'd the widow flag on?"

"When he asked if she was intentionally holding back information, she scored a big time negative. He felt whatever information she wasn't sharing with us was probably more of an embarrassment to her, not a sign of involvement. In his opinion, she passed everything else with flying colors."

Pope's chair snapped forward with a loud bang. "So all we're doing here is chasing our damn tails, running after the wife."

Tom massaged the back of his neck. "We turned up a couple of guns, but only one fits. It's a 9mm, the weapon of choice."

"Where'd they turn up?"

"During the search at Hudson's office, Ruby rounded up a Smith and Wesson from the locked drawer of his office desk. Registered in the state of North Carolina, it was under lock and key when Hudson was popped, but we'll let ballistics figure it out." Nervous energy had Tom bouncing one of his knees. "The other gun came from the Hudson residence."

The chief leaned back again, rocking a chair that wasn't made to rock. "This gets more damn annoying each time we speak. I suppose it's another 9mm?"

Hall nodded and filled The Pope in on the details of the two men from the charity. "When she called, I was on my way over with the search warrant. How's that for timing? The gun was in the bottom of one of the boxes. It's in the report."

"That's pretty damn convenient." Pope leaned forward, picking up the folder. "What's your take on it?"

"You're right, it's too convenient. She's not an ignorant woman. I can't see her leaving a gun in the bottom of a box heading to charity. She denies knowing how it got there, denies ever shooting a gun. Whoever took out Hudson was a crack shot. Moving down a highway? I'm not saying it can't be done by a lucky amateur, but it looks like a professional hit. Someone is setting up Mrs. Hudson for the fall."

Pope used the folder to slap his desktop. "That's all we need. If a pro took the shot, we've got a cover-up on our hands.

"The gun from the Hudson home had the numbers filed off."

"Damn it." The folder slapped harder. "Sounding more professional all the time."

"Nothing else to report with the warrants. We didn't find shit." Tom paused, locking eyes with Pope. "Our rookie managed to stumble across a 9mm Luger casing on the side of the road. It may have been missed during the initial sweep. Who the hell knows? No one looked for anything until after the autopsy results came back."

Pope only grunted, staring hard at Tom. "Go back to the damn dealership. Someone there has to know more than they're telling us. If they knew Hudson was stepping out on his wife, they get high honors for keeping it quiet out of respect for her, but that's over. Go back, push hard."

Tom nodded. "I'll also try to meet with Greasy Tucker today. He's been avoiding me. I'll be pushing him hard too"

"Again, I'll caution you on that one. We don't want him running with a half-baked story." Pope threw the report on his desk and flexed his fingers, bending them up and down. "Did you get around to visiting with Judge Lockner?"

Tom couldn't help himself, he smiled. "Yes. He stuck to the same story, but this time threw in that Hudson first offered him quality time with a girl . . . at a house."

Pope's eyes flashed. "The little prick. What house?"

"Swears he doesn't know. He ended up in a car with the girl because he didn't have time to take Hudson up on the offer. He was a busy man, dispensing justice and wisdom. Anyway, Hudson probably knew, once the Judge got a quickie sample, he'd be back asking for more."

"Anything turn up on the computers?"

"Dead end on the laptop from Hudson's car. Same with the cell phone, although we're still cross checking numbers. The laptop from the home, one that belonged to Mrs. Hudson? Disappeared before we got to it. Could be whoever planted the gun, took the computer." Tom motioned to the folder on the desk. "It's in the report. The garage door message is starting to make sense. A big red arrow aimed straight at her. If someone is framing her, they're going for overkill."

Pope's voice was forceful, his words evenly spaced. "I can't stress enough how much I want this wrapped up, quietly and quickly . . ." He took a deep breath. "Our own damn parking lot has me seeing signs of involvement."

"Huh?"

"Go out and take a look. Pay particular attention to license plate brackets with Oceanview Mercedes stamped across the top."

"Jesus." Tom scrubbed his face, the implications enormous. "Do you know who the cars belong to?"

"Not yet." He handed Tom a list with a total of nine plate numbers and the type of vehicles they were on. He'd spent more time circling the lot than he had at his desk, even coming down over the weekend to take a look. "Find out who they belong to without raising anyone's suspicion. If I'd requested information, it would've been all over the station."

"I'll get on it."

"This is between you and me. Got it? Don't even bring the rookie in."

"Yes sir." Tom looked down, studied the floor. "I talked to Mike."

It took Pope a second to follow the change in the conversation. "Glad you did."

"Yeah. I, uhhh, ran some things by him."

His fist slammed the desk. "Damn it, Hall. I meant it when I said quiet. I don't think Mike is anything but a stand-up guy, but we can't take any chances."

"Give me a break. You think he cooked up Annie's cancer and ran? He's the safest one to discuss this with. I needed to see if he'd follow my line of thought.

"And?"

"He did, and you're not going to like it."

"There hasn't been one damn thing I've liked since the judge was caught with his hairy ass in the air. Where you heading with this?"

Mike had agreed wholeheartedly with Tom.

One of their own was doing more than passing information to Greasy Tucker; they were involved up to their ears.

36

It was time for Jane to return to her family. Bygie knew it, she certainly understood it, but at the airport, she clung to her sister.

"Bygie, it's not too late. Call the detective and ask if you can come home with me. I could stay over another day, Bob and the kids will survive."

"No, I'm okay." She pushed off her sister. "I couldn't go with you even if they said yes. I need to do the art festival in La Jolla. I want to do it. Getting ready for it will keep me sane, or at least help keep me sane."

Jane's eyes pooled. "I could try and come out, work the show with you. That would be fun, right?"

Bygie shook her head. "Go back and take care of your family. Come hell or high water, I promise I'll be there after the show. We need to plan a memorial for Lars."

She looked hard into Bygie's eyes. "You know, Bob has been worried. So far, I've avoided filling him in on the details over the phone. Don't panic if he shows up on your front step when he finds out what's been going on."

"He better not. Don't you dare let him. I'll be fine. I'll be so busy time will fly by. I already promised to give you a daily call."

"That's a promise I'm holding you too. If I don't hear from you, I won't hesitate phoning the good-looking detective."

"No way. I'll call you, I promise. You better go before you miss your flight. Let me know as soon as you get home, okay?"

"I will. I love ya, sis." Jane turned to go, then turned back to face her. "You know what Bob will say."

She cocked her head.

"Call a lawyer."

Bygie shook her head as she waved good-bye.

***

At home, Bygie changed into work clothes. Spending time in her studio was more comforting then being in the big echoing house alone. Besides, she had a lot of projects to catch up on. Heading back out the front door, she paused, then double stepped back to the kitchen table and retrieved her keys. She set the alarm and locked the front door. No more running between the studio and house without locking up.

The realization hit her like a blow, made her jerk to a halt. This was to be the new pattern of her life. Checking locks and closing windows; a ritual needed to feel safe inside her own home.

Anger at Lars threatened to boil over, followed by shame and humiliation so great that her knees weakened. How did she end up in this mess? She stiffened. Not today. Not again.

Marching to her studio, she slammed the door shut and twisted the lock. A virtual prisoner. Grabbing the coffeepot, she rinsed out stale coffee and put fresh grounds into the basket. Damn it. All she could do was try to work. Turning from the counter, she looked around the room, her eyes landing on the mirror lying on the worktable.

Without enthusiasm, she crossed over to it and wondered where to start. She glanced at a stack of mirrors along the wall. She went to them and started turning them around to face into the room. Her pace became frenetic. She supported one against the corner of another and onto the back of her chair, continuing around against the legs of her worktable. She built a cocoon of images. She sank to the floor amidst the chaos of reflections and studied her offset image bouncing from one mirror to another. *Who am I? What do others see when they look at me?* She felt like smashing them all, one reflection at a time. She stilled herself and stared, until the distorted vision blurred into an unrecognizable mass of eyes and noses, an amorphous lump of body parts.

She rose to her feet, and walked to the coffeepot, before doing something stupid, like practicing her swing.

She sipped at the fresh cup of coffee, and regained a semblance of control before starting on her unfinished project. At first, the motions of her work were routine, but soon the rhythm of finding the right colors and placing each shell occupied her mind. It temporarily chased the demons away. She kept a notepad handy to write down reminders of what she needed to do before the show. The list was long.

With little time left to prepare, she'd have to put in long hours. Fine with her. Anything to occupy her time, until . . . until . . . what? Until she heard from the police? Until she knew what happened to Lars?

Then what?

She had no idea what was going on with the police, but was damned if she'd call to find out. During the search warrant, they'd left without taking much from the house, but not from a lack of probing each nook and cranny of her home. Cupboards, drawers, closets and filing cabinets were examined. One of the officers even walked around, knocking on walls and floors, and when she asked what he was doing, no one gave her an answer.

Then there was the gun. Bygie shuddered. Who did that belong to? How did it get into her house, into the boxes she'd packed? No wonder she didn't feel safe without double checking windows and doors, making sure they were locked.

Encouraging Jane to return to her waiting family had been hard. Bygie had put on a brave face. The same fake face she'd been wearing her entire marriage. In reality, she was afraid to be alone. She didn't tell Jane how bad her nightmares were. The constant dream of Lars in the arms of other women left her drained. Each time it repeated, instead of intensifying her anger at Lars, with definite precision, it carved out another chunk of her self-esteem. She felt worthless. And stupid.

She needed to face the whole truth.

Be brutally honest with herself.

Disgusted, she rose from the work table, striding to a dust covered radio. If she couldn't turn off her thoughts, maybe she could dull them with music.

She picked up a pencil to add a note to the growing list. She'd have to rent a van, or truck, to get her artwork to the show area in La Jolla. Her Miata wouldn't cut it. Normally, Lars would have borrowed a vehicle for the weekend from the dealership, along with hiring a couple of the service department guys to help load and unload. She refused to reach out to anyone there, but without assistance she couldn't manage loading big mirrors.

Another thing to add to her list . . . help. Renting a truck was a no-brainer, but she'd still need help loading it. *Maybe the guys from the used store? Right. They'd run if they ever set eyes on me again.*

They could have driven off, taken whatever they wanted from her home. When talking to the police, the men stuck to their story. The door swung open when they knocked. The police must've believed it, or they wouldn't have let them go.

Could she track the men down by going to the store and asking? Worth a try. She was out of better ideas. She could pay them well, try to make up for the trouble she caused. The more she thought about it, the better it sounded. She needed the help.

With the decision made, Bygie settled down to work.

37

Hall solved crimes by applying pressure in the right place. He'd keep twisting until someone buckled and came through with the next lead to follow. A major problem in the Hudson murder was not having enough players to twist. One hooker, a wife and a less than honorable judge. No new names on the list to put the screws too.

He wasn't forgetting Greasy Tucker. The piss-ant reporter was avoiding him. He would be the number one priority this afternoon, but right now, Ruby and Tom were headed to the dealership. Tom hoped to add a new name or two to play with, and they were playing hardball.

Ruby was driving the unmarked car and Tom was riding shotgun, and uncomfortable. When partnered with Mike, Tom drove. They bantered ideas with ease. The camaraderie was missing with Ruby. When she hooked the keys, Tom opened his mouth, then shut it. The newer, nicer, gentler Tom, the one letting Ruby drive, was barking out orders. "When we get there, let's isolate the partners first. You take one, I'll take the other, and then we can switch."

"Good cop, bad cop?"

"Nothing so obvious. I figure if they were playing in Hudson's game, they might open up to a woman faster. You know, turn on your charm."

"Jesus." She shook her head. "Yeah, send me in to be a hooker for information instead of a cop."

"That's not what I meant."

"What did you mean?"

Tom growled. "It's the truth, that's it. You're a woman and some men open up faster to a female. Some *women* open up faster to a female. It's not sexist, it's the truth." Tom rattled nervous fingers on his armrest. "Are you going to be able to do this?"

"Yes sir. I'll apply the charm so thick they won't be able to resist."

"That's all I'm saying." Tom knew when to quit.

"For the record, I don't think this is necessary. I've been to the dealership twice."

"What? You have a better idea?"

"If you like applying pressure so much, let's push on Mrs. Hudson. You know, the lady who laughed when she found out her husband was dead? You found a gun at her house and didn't do a thing."

"What was supposed to happen? I should have arrested her?"

"That'd be a good place to start."

"There's a matter of proof, Ruby. What would we charge her with?"

"She had a gun. That's got to mean something."

"It's not illegal to have a gun. If ballistics comes back with a match, we'll put her in cuffs. Right now, we're going to chase down any lead we can get out of the partners. Or any employee for that matter. If Hudson was running a prostitution service for his customers, someone noticed."

They pulled into the lot, both getting out and slamming their doors too hard. Ruby stalked ahead of Tom.

She slowed as she entered, waiting for Tom to catch up.

"Sorry. Guess I'm having a bad day."

"S'okay." Tom muttered. "Put on your game face," he motioned at a salesman heading their way.

"Good morning folks. My name is Mark, how can I help you?"

"We'd like to speak with Jim Sprague and Niles Harris."

"Do you have an appointment?"

"No, not exactly. Tell them Detectives Hall and Wilson are here to see them and to open their schedules."

Color blanched from the salesman face. "Uh, yes. Let me get them for you. You're welcome to take a seat in the waiting area."

"We're fine. Let them know we're here."

He trotted off down a hallway.

They stood, looking at cars they couldn't afford. Other employees gave them a wide berth. Word traveled fast in the hushed environment that police were on the floor. Impatient, Tom waited only a short time before motioning to Ruby with his chin.

"Come on."

She followed Tom to a hallway lined with offices.

"What now?" Ruby asked.

"Do you know which office space belongs to the partners?"

Ruby pointed to the set of double doors at the end. She picked up her step to keep up with Tom as he headed straight towards it. She looked back to see heads peeking out of other offices, but no one stepped out to impede their progress.

Tom didn't hesitate. He opened the set of twin wood doors with a flourish, and walked in.

They caught the partners with their mouths open, but Sprague recovered quickly enough. He stood up. "Detectives. We're sorry to keep you waiting." He turned to the salesman, "You can go now, Mark."

When the doors whispered shut, Tom said, "I sure hope you weren't giving Mark a hard time. You know, killing the messenger."

Sprague's smile didn't reach his eyes. "Not at all. What can we do for you?"

Without being invited, Tom sat down on a white couch facing the desk. Ruby joined him.

Harris hadn't said a word. He was standing off to the side when they barged in. He took a seat in the chair next to Tom. Sprague remained standing behind his desk with his arms folded across his chest.

Tom looked around. "Nice office. Do you share?" He motioned between Sprague and Harris.

Sprague answered with a smirk. "No. Definitely not. Niles' office is in the east wing."

Tom whistled. "Pretty impressive place. You have wings. Who'd of thought." He would have reached over to high-five Harris, but the man's eyes were glued to the floor.

"What can we do for you? Does this have something to do with Lars?"

"Yes, sir. That's exactly why we're here. We'd like to talk to your employees."

"What? I'm afraid that's impossible. My sales staff is busy and I can't pull them away from customers. I'm sure you understand. We feel bad about the accident and wish the best for the little Mrs., but we've been inconvenienced enough. We've fully cooperated, but this is beginning to feel like harassment."

Tom bristled. "Get ready for more harassment, gentle-man." He turned to Ruby, "Why don't you have Mr. Harris show you his office."

Ruby stood up. Niles Harris looked at Sprague, then shrugged his shoulders and walked out of the office, with Ruby following.

"Well, that was easy. I'm happy you're both so willing to cooperate." Tom smiled.

Sprague glared, but took a seat. "I have a busy day, so let's get this over with. What do you want?"

"Information on Hudson's side business."

"I already told your partner. This is a waste of time. Whatever Hudson was doing, it had nothing to do with this company." He reached and tugged at his tie.

"You knew what he was doing?"

"Not until your partner questioned me. When I last spoke to Mrs. Hudson, the poor thing, she confirmed the atrocious behavior. I certainly wasn't involved."

Tom's hand clenched to a fist when Sprague referred to Bygie as a 'thing.' "Yes. You certainly did say you weren't in-volved." He let the silence hang long enough to make Spra-gue uncomfortable. "Problem is, I don't believe you, and when I don't believe something, I stick to it like dog shit on a shoe." Tom grinned. "I'll keep coming back and talking to you until I'm satisfied, one way or the other, you weren't in-volved." He looked around, taking in the big windows facing the distant ocean. "That's fine with me. Your office is a lot nicer than my desk at the station. I wouldn't mind spending quality time, right here." He patted the couch cushion.

Sprague tugged at his tie as if he were choking. "What do you want?"

"I am going to chat with the members of your staff. If you try to stop me, I'll arrest you for impeding an investigation."

Sprague leaned forward. "Just try it. You don't know who you're messing with, officer. We're one of the biggest con-tributors to all that *is* San Diego." He sat back with a causal air and crossed his legs. His fingers continued to fiddle with his tie. "No one is likely to take kindly to you threatening us."

"When murder is involved, people tend to back off."

"Murder?" He raised his brow. "Are you threatening me?"

"No, I'm stating a fact. Your partner, Mr. Hudson? He was murdered."

"Ridiculous. He was killed in an unfortunate accident." Sprague appeared calm, but sweat beaded along his plugged hairline.

Tom shrugged. "Well, the autopsy proved otherwise, but, I guess we're done here." He slapped both hands on his knees, making to get up. "I'll go through the courts to tie up your business. Courts don't look kindly on murder. It'll take time, but I'll get it done. Remember? Dog shit on a shoe."

"Hold up. This business, Oceanview, has nothing to do with Hudson. Not anymore. His wife signed the papers and delivered them. You can't tie up our business. We had noth-ing to do with his accident."

News that Bygie had signed over her share so fast star-tled him. Could it be as simple as it looked? Murder for mon-ey?

Tom barked back his reply, "Murder. Not accident. Hud-son was a big part of this business at the time of his *murder*. Maybe your little dealership will come out squeaky clean, but that's what a lengthy investigation is for." Tom smiled. "Rest assured, Mr. Sprague, we'll leave no stone unturned in proving your innocence. No matter how long it takes." Hall snapped his fingers. "We'll do you one better. We'll keep the public aware of each step. Let them know how our investigation proceeds. Your adoring customers can form a prayer circle. At the end? Maybe you're right. We'll all know you weren't involved in prostitution."

Sprague's face looked gray. "What do you want to know?"

"Did you condone Hudson's creative approach to an incentive program or were you a paying participant?"

"This stays between us?"

"No deals."

Sprague locked eyes with Hall, considering his options. God knows, he'd donated enough money to create a strong foothold in the politics of San Diego. His reputation wasn't a concern, but protecting the business was a priority. Money opened doors, and he couldn't afford to have his sales suffer by a naïve public. He cleared his throat, "None of us had anything to do with the, ahhh, rumored operation of Hudson's, but . . . ahhh . . . some of us used the service."

"He hooked you up."

"Nothing as trashy as you're implying."

"He set you up with hookers. How is that not trashy?"

"These women were adults and got what they wanted." He leaned back, palms behind his head. "Nothing but a straight forward business transaction."

Tom barked out a laugh. "It's funny how you rich guys believe twisting with a hooker is different when there's big dollars involved. That's a good one. A business transaction. Where did the business take place? In the backseat of one of the demo models?"

"Of course not."

"At a house?"

"No."

"Where?"

"Here." Sprague's eyes lingered where Tom was sitting.

Tom looked at the white couch. "Here?"

Sprague nodded, the smug look returning.

Tom resisted the urge to move. "Numerous girls?"

Sprague waggled his index finger. "Only one."

"What's her name?"

"Lizzie. That's how I was introduced to her."

"You don't know her last name?"

"No. She wasn't going to be added to my Christmas list. I didn't ask."

"Would you recognize her?" At his faint nod, Tom flipped a picture on to the desk. "Is this the girl?" The picture was blurry, but it would do. Noah had cut a still from the video of Tom's dash mounted camera, of the woman picked up with Judge Lockner. The name she'd given at the time was Linda.

Sprague glanced at it, his eyes widened. The girl was standing, cuffed, in front of a police car. "Yes, that's her. Lizzie."

"Are you surprised she's in trouble? Hooking is against the law. People do get arrested. Or maybe you already knew she'd been detained and you're helping her out. Have you seen her lately?"

"No. The last time I saw her was a week or two before Hudson's accident." His hands dropped to the desktop; he shifted uncomfortably. "Look, I let Hudson set me up. That's it. I don't even know how he met her. Are we done? I have a business to run."

"Your partner, Mr. Harris. Did he use the service too?"

Sprague snorted. "Not likely. His nuts are in his wife's pocket."

"Unlike you."

His face reddened. "Are we done?"

"I still want to talk to your employees."

"The only girl I've ever seen in here is this one." He flicked the picture across the desk, back towards Tom. "She came after hours when no one was around. It's a waste of time to talk to anyone else."

Tom studied him, and then nodded. "Give me a list of employees. I want names and addresses for every last one." He knew they'd been interviewed previously, and it could be a waste of time, but he wanted to press the point.

Tom left the office with the list of employees, and an urgent need to wash hands that had touched the white sofa. He found Ruby walking around the sales floor.

She shook her head when she saw Tom. "Nothing new for me. Do you still want to talk to Harris yourself?"

"I'll tell you in the car. Let's go. I need a shower."

Ruby frowned. "A shower? You want to skip the employees?"

"Forget it. I got what we needed. A name. Part of one, anyway."

38

His dreams were within reach. Greasy smacked the steering wheel with both hands in a parody of a high five. His hard work was going to pay off, but not through Sugar's hooker friend. That woman, Lizzie, could take a dive. He looked forward to meeting with her later tonight, telling her the deal was off. Poor baby. Turns out he wouldn't need her. *Ya snooze, ya lose.*

He folded his arms behind his neck, remembering the phone call. The hints, dropped by the unfamiliar voice on the phone, had him stoked. Definitely someone with knowledge and willing to share. Greasy was going to get straight-up details. If what the mystery caller said was true, he'd have more than enough to put some rich bastards through the grinder.

Who his new informant was remained to be seen.

Another dirty cop, maybe? He snorted. If the public knew how many cops were willing to take a slice for themselves, they wouldn't be in such a rush to glorify the bastards. Skim a little dope here, trade a little bit there, they lined their blue pockets when opportunity knocked.

He'd have to play this one right. Play it cool.

Avoiding Detective Hall had been a pain in the ass, but worth the trouble. Once he had the goods, he'd tell Hall to stick it, right alongside Lizzie.

A judge caught with a hooker? That was nothing. The mysterious caller promised more than a judge. The angelic voice guaranteed dirt on players from the top hierarchy of the San Diego PD.

He brought his hands down from the steering wheel and held them out in front. They shook with excitement. What he needed was a nice smooth shot of Jack to calm his nerves. Reaching over to the passenger seat, intending to finish eating a sandwich, he put it back down. His stomach was too nervous. Between avoiding the detectives and his lust for the big story, he was probably developing an ulcer.

The only time he could forget the stress was when he was with Sugar. He shook his head to clear the image. This was not a time to be sidetracked. He needed to be on his toes.

The plan was to meet his new informant at dark, not long now. He arrived at the agreed upon meeting spot plenty early, afraid he'd get lost trying to find his way after sunset. Hard enough to find your way during daylight, Greasy found it next to impossible to figure out the twisted, confusing roads in the dark.

Following the edge of the coast, by La Jolla, the street he used would end abruptly, only to start again after winding through cramped residential areas. Street names changed without warning. He could have laid it out better than a high-paid, jackass, city planner. The snotty people who lived in the area treated the confusion as if it added charm to the over-priced real estate.

If you asked a local for directions, they'd vaguely wave you down another path. They were probably lost as well. Poor locals, shuffling around in high priced loafers, trapped into buying expensive coffee while looking for their own homes. When Greasy reached the parking lot of a remote, scenic overlook, he sat in his car to wait. No way was he getting out to check the view. The cliff edges were known to crumble, and the fall was straight into the icy Pacific. Greasy shivered, watching as the last carload of tourists left.

He impatiently marked time, rhythmically tapping his fingers on the steering wheel.

Once in a while, car lights would brighten the area, but instead of pulling in, they'd sweep on around the curve. Trying to relax, he leaned his seat back, placing his arms across his stomach. He closed his eyes, picturing the next week unfolding; his byline on the front page next to a huge breaking story. Probably a CNN interview to cap it off.

His eyes popped open at the sound of a car turning into the lot. It parked a few spaces from him.

This was it.

He snapped the seat straight up, but waited until the other car's engine quieted and the headlights were extinguished, before stepping out. He turned back to his car, grabbing a beat-up, soft-sided briefcase from the passenger seat, one that held his laptop and working notes. Greasy walked towards the parked car. It could be his contact, or a tourist out for a late night viewing.

When the driver stepped out, his jaw dropped. He covered his surprise with a big smile and walked forward with a swagger. "Right on time. I like that." His eyes traveled up and down his informant's body.

A nervous look around by his informant before the eyes swiveled back to Greasy. "I can't take a chance on you being wired. Mind if I check?"

"Wired? Who'd wire me? Go ahead and check if it makes you comfortable." He lifted his arms, his smile widening. "Don't go touching anything inappropriate."

The pat down was brief. "Let's move away from the cars."

"Sure, sure. Afraid they're bugged too?" He slowly followed his angel of information to the low guard rail.

A hand patted for him to take a seat on the edge of the rail.

Greasy sat down and tried to ignore the yawning emptiness of the steep drop behind him. He clenched the handle on his briefcase.

His informant's voice was low, nervous. "I'm not used to doing this. You've got to promise you'll keep my name out of it."

He leaned forward, closing the distance between them. The low voice was hard to hear over the loud noise of the ocean. "Whatever you want. You treat me square and I'll protect your good name."

"Did you bring your notes? Whatever you have? Let's go over them. I'm sure I can add a lot of information, point out where you've gone wrong."

Greasy held up the satchel. "I keep this with me at all times. Wouldn't want someone nosing around and stealing my thunder. I have a nose for it. A natural instinct. I know when I'm on to something great."

"What I've got for you is better than great. It's killer."

39

The little shittin' reporter was hiding. No one had seen him for a couple of days. Tom tracked down an address for Greasy and yesterday, Ruby had stopped by his home to bang on the door. No answer. On his way home tonight, Tom planned to drive by again. If lights were on, he'd stop. He wanted face time with the weasel reporter. Find out who was feeding him information.

Television cops had it much easier. Bada bing, bada boom, bad guy caught.

Or bad girl.

Someone was doing their damn best to make Bygie look like the bad girl. Motivation was the key factor in solving any murder and the motivation for her to kill her offending spouse was pretty damning. A cheating bastard and a boat-load of money. Bada-bing.

Tom didn't believe it.

Ruby was another burr in his hide. Needing to clear a backlog of routine cases, along with keeping the Hudson investigation under wraps, was wearing them both down. She was hell bent for arresting Bygie, the sooner the better. Close the case and move on.

Following their conversations with the partners at Oceanview Mercedes, they doubled their efforts in tracking down the woman Sprague knew as Lizzie. They worked the streets, showing her picture and asking if anyone recognized her. If the girl had walked the streets before becoming a high-class call girl, no one was talking. No surprise. Memories on the street were short when fogged with drugs or alcohol.

Copies of Lizzie's mug shot were handed out at a morning briefing. They wanted her to come in for routine questioning. Nothing out of the ordinary in the request, a normal daily occurrence in the life of a cop. Tom or Ruby would be notified if the woman was picked up.

So far? Dead end. No sign of the woman.

While Ruby was occupied with paperwork, Tom decided to make a trip to the Hudson residence. He had an idea and wanted to follow up on it — alone. He didn't want another argument with Ruby. Time to check on Mrs. Hudson anyway. Make sure she wasn't packing up more than goodwill boxes.

When Jim Sprague dropped the bomb that Bygie had signed the deal selling her share, he'd experienced a momentary falter in his belief of her innocence. Ruby's gossip mill informant believed it to be a huge chunk of money, and Bygie wouldn't be the first person to commit a desperate act in the name of greed. There'd been plenty before her and sure as the sun would rise, there'd be plenty after.

The hitch was he didn't believe she murdered her husband. His gut again.

He drove out of the city and into the foothills of Stony Point. Not wanting a record of this errand, he didn't check a car out of the department pool. He was driving his own van. It felt sneaky and covert.

He hadn't called ahead to see if Bygie was home and when he pulled into the driveway, it was empty. Plenty of garage space now that the big SUV was gone. Maybe better parking was the motive to kill.

Grabbing a folder off the seat, he climbed out of the van, heading to the front door. A warning niggle ran down his neck as he reached for the doorbell. He glanced around.

Nothing in sight. He depressed the button and heard a distant chime ring inside the house, but no one came to the door. He was ready to push the button a second time, when he heard muted tapping.

Shielding his eyes, he looked up. In the window above the garage he could see the vague image of a hand poking between the blinds. The blinds snapped up and Bygie was in the window, a startled look on her face. She was in her studio, motioning him to come up.

Tom walked around to the opposite side of the garage and up the steps to her studio door.

When Bygie came to the door, he took notice that she unlocked it to let him in.

"Hi. Where's the cavalry?" Bygie voice was tense. "Not here to arrest me?"

"No. Should I be?" Her nervous humor made him uncomfortable.

"No." She reached up to push stray strands of hair away from her face. "I'm not sure how this works. I didn't know if there'd be a knock on the door one day with you coming to cart me away."

Tom slapped the folder against his leg. "I'm alone today. I wasn't planning on taking you anywhere." He cleared his throat. "Am I interrupting your work?"

"No. Well, yes, but come in if you can stand the mess."

She pulled out a stool at the counter, swiping the seat off with her sleeve to remove dust. "Sorry, it's a side effect of my trade."

"That's okay. I won't take much of your time." He stood still, taking in the room. "Looks like you've been busy," If the room had looked crowded and chaotic the first time he was in it, now it looked jam-packed.

Bygie looked around, her face brightened. "I've gotten a lot done. The show is this weekend." Her enthusiasm with her work was unmistakable. Enjoying human contact, she walked over and pivoted a huge mirror. "This is one of my favorites, and the biggest one I've ever done. Do you like it?" She went on, not waiting for his answer. "One of my customers called.

She wants me to do a huge mirror in the entryway of her beach house. Beach mansion would be an apt description." She laughed. "It's not like any beach house I spent summer vacations in. I'll have to do the project on-site."

Her enthusiasm was contagious. She was wearing a stained shirt over jeans with holes big enough to put his fist through. Her hair was twisted into a messy knot at the nape of her neck, the shine dulled by a fine layer of dust. As she reached up to brush at the errant strands, he noticed her hands were red and dry.

Tom rubbed his neck, frowning.

Bygie turned with a smile, going still at his serious expression. The light drained from her eyes as she walked around him to pull out a second stool. She made a half-hearted attempt to brush off the settled dust. "The mortar I use to attach the shells makes a mess, I send up a powder cloud whenever I'm mixing."

She dampened a wad of paper towels at the sink to wipe off the stools. "That's better. They're safe to sit on."

"That's fine. I've sat in worse places." His neck reddened as he pictured the white couch in Sprague's office. "I have a couple things to go over with you." His smile was fleeting. "Is your sister still here?"

"No. She left a couple days ago. She has a family to get back to. I'd like to go home and visit as soon as the show in La Jolla is over. Will I be able to go? I'll give you the phone number and address of my sister's place, that's where I'd be."

"Unless something changes, I think we can work it out."

"How long will I have to do this? Check in before I go on a trip?" She didn't look up for the answer. She was using damp paper towels to muddy the dust on the counter.

"I can't give you a definite answer." He reached into the file, removing several sheets of paper. "I, uhhh, brought you these. Thought you could use them, but it's probably too late." Tom had printed out the names and addresses of her clients from Lars' laptop. Although he'd gone through the list carefully, he felt uncomfortable handing them over. He'd made the decision to give her the names without mentioning it to Ruby. Or the Pope.

Bygie took the sheets and balanced them on her raised knees, avoiding the wet, dirty counter. "Thank you."

"Yeah, sure. No problem."

"I forgot. I was going to call you. Would it be possible to get the names of the two men that were here to take my furniture to the used store? I wanted to talk to them."

Tom's interest sharpened. He looked at her with an odd expression. "Why would you need to do that?"

She indicated the mirrors and lamps. "I need help getting everything to the show. Lars used to line up guys from Oceanview to help." She looked up to meet Tom's gaze. "Not going to happen this year."

"I talked to Jim Sprague yesterday."

A smile flickered across her face. "Bet that was fun."

He responded by looking down at the folder. "I have a picture to show you. See if it's anyone you recognize." He opened the folder and laid a Polaroid shot on the counter.

She tentatively reached for it, not sure what to expect. Was it a picture of, Lars? The face in the photograph caused her to flinch, knocking the sheets containing her customer names to the floor between them.

Automatically, Tom reached down to pick them up, brushing against her arm as she did the same. He jerked back with the sheets in his hand. His voice was rough. "Here."

She didn't reach out to take them. Her eyes were riveted on the picture. "It's her. Our decorator." Her voice was flat. "How cozy was she with Lars?"

"We haven't talked to her yet. She's been hard to find." He rolled the sheets of paper and drummed them against his leg. "I'm sure she'll turn up. She was using the name Lizzie. Does that sound familiar?"

"Lizzie." Bygie laughed, "Yep, that's it. My highly recommended decorator." She poked at the blurry photo. "Is this a mug shot?"

"No. She was, ahhh, detained." He tapped the papers faster, dreading the follow up next question.

"What was she detained for?" Her eyes never left the grainy photograph.

"Prostitution." The one word answer hung in the air.

She swung her eyes to Tom without moving her head. "With who? Lars?"

"I'm not at liberty to discuss it."

Bygie exploded off the chair. "What?"

Tom didn't react to her fast movement. He would have done the same thing in her shoes. "We're looking for her."

"That's a load of crap. You won't even tell me how my husband died. Was he shot? Strangled? Did his brakes fail? Which one fits your best assumption?" She jerked the stool further away from Tom and sat back down. "Tell me. I'm tired of guessing."

He wasn't free to tell her what she wanted know. He answered through a clenched jaw. "We're working on it."

She sagged. "Yeah, right. Working on it. Does this 'Lizzie' have something to do with Lars' death?"

Hall's eyes were stony.

"Got it. You're not at liberty to discuss it."

The muffled sound of a ringing phone had her looking around to see where she'd left her cell. She zeroed in on Tom's pocket as he dug for his.

Hall stood up, paced to look out the door as he answered the call.

"Hall." His face turned to stone. "Where?" Listening to the answer, he turned to stare at Bygie, his eyes harsh. "I'm on my way." He snapped the phone off, returning it to his pocket.

Bygie questioned, "What is it?"

He reached for the mug shot on the counter and replaced it with a crumpled list of her of clients. "I'll be in touch."

40

The torso was bloated and swollen, distended into a malformed shape. Even in open air, the smell was horrendous. It caused hardened officers to gag. Having been attacked as a food source, flesh was shredded or missing. Eye sockets were empty.

Floaters were the worst. They no longer resembled a human being.

Tom and Ruby took in the scene. The cordoned off area was useless against the unrelenting ocean and they'd have to retreat as soon as the tide rose. The body was discovered by a group of tourists from Minnesota, who were now standing in front of the store talking to TV cameras. Their great vacation to sunny San Diego was turning into more of an attraction than they bargained for, but they were flattered with the attention.

From streetside, the store appeared to be a large, flat-roofed one story building, but that was deceptive. It sat on a cliff and had a full bottom walkout basement that opened onto a private seaside cove completely surrounded by steep, jutting walls. From inside the souvenir shop, you could purchase a five dollar trip down through a "pirates" tunnel that led to the private beach. A gloomy set of concrete steps, winding down to the lower level of the building, was decorated with lit niches of pirate treasure and platoons of fake skulls. Tourists could go down through the tunnel to check out tidal pools in hopes of finding buried treasure, like starfish and shells.

You could search tidal pools for free, up and down the coast, but you didn't get the five dollar thrill of going through a pirate's tunnel.

The normal routine would be to have an employee, dressed as a pirate, lead the tourists through the dimly lit passageway, explaining how pirates used the warren for hiding stolen treasure. On this bright morning, someone had called in sick, leaving a single employee to man the store. When the group came in, she pointed out the steps and let them find their way to the cove, without aid of a canned speech. Lucky for them.

The tourists had exited the dim tunnel into the blinding sunlight of the cove. Shading their eyes, looking in purses and pockets for sunglasses, they were disorientated after the darkened stairwell. The body, laying in plain view on dry, hard-packed sand, was off to their right. When first noticed, being a pirate tunnel and all, they thought it was a distasteful prop.

Then the smell hit.

"They won't find a thing here." Tom muttered to Ruby. "Any evidence on that body is long gone. He's been in the water for awhile."

The captain in charge of the scene walked by. "What are you doing here, Hall? Sick of chasing pretty little hookers already?"

Tom's face darkened at the ribbing. "Yeah, something like that. What's it looking like?"

"It's looking real mushy." He shrugged. "That's all I can say right now. Judging by the decomposition, the coroner's guess is the body has been in the water for a coupla' days. Won't know more until after the autopsy."

As the captain walked on, Ruby looked at Tom, her face slightly green. "I don't know how anyone can work a scene like this. The smell is killing me."

"They won't be working it for long. The tide will have them out of here pretty quick."

"Can you tell if it's him? I'm not sure."

"Size fits. Not much else left to identify him. How'd you find out?"

"It spread around the station like wildfire. I called you right away." She glanced over at Tom. "Where were you anyway? Took you long enough to get here."

"Out." He'd be damned if he was going to explain his moves to, Ruby. "Looks like we found our missing reporter. First Hudson, now we can add Robert 'Greasy' Tucker to the list."

"They don't know if it's him, not for sure. Maybe that's not who it is."

"Generally speaking, a driver's license in the billfold is correct."

"What a way to go. Yuck. What now?"

"Another wait and see. The autopsy will shed light on how he died. If he drowned, they'll have to question family and co-workers to see if he'd be a jumper." He shrugged. "For all they know right now, he could have been dumped."

"We need to find out if Mrs. Hudson has visited the area."

"Why?" His hard tone returned.

"She'd probably want Tucker gone. Maybe she blames him for the whole cheating husband thing coming to light. If it weren't for Greasy hassling her husband, maybe she'd still be enjoying her happy little pampered life."

Tom looked away to hide his anger. Bygie was far from a pampered wife. "We would have gotten around to questioning her sooner or later, with or without Tucker. Judge Lockner, remember him? That's why we were looking for Hudson in the first place." He turned to look at her, his arms crossed tightly. "Or maybe she hasn't gotten around to knocking off the Judge yet? Watch your back. Maybe we're next on her list."

Ruby's face flushed.

Tom squinted, "Why do you have such a bone with her?"

She scuffed sand with her boot. "I don't." She dug her boot toe into the sand, pushing hard. "You've got blinders on. That's all."

He stiffened. "What do you mean by that?"

"The lady has motive, means and opportunity. She probably sold her share of the dealership. Who does something like that so fast? Someone who's after the money, that's who." Her eyes spit fire. "You find a gun in her possession and don't do a damn thing."

"The ballistics didn't match."

"I thought they couldn't prove it either way. They couldn't say for certain."

"You don't arrest people for murder because *maybe* they did it. Didn't they teach you about solid evidence?" His voice rose, sounding harsh. "We've been over this. Tie the gun to her, Ruby. Find a prosecutor willing to charge her with murder based on a gun in the bottom of a box, one without fingerprints. Anybody could have put it there. Once you do that, I'll lead the way with the arrest warrant." He was conscious of other people on the scene looking at them. He took a breath. "In the meantime, if the body over there is Greasy Tucker, we'll follow up. See what the word is on cause of death."

"Yes sir."

Without another word, Tom turned and stomped back to his van. Damn rookie know-it-all. She would never amount to much of an investigator if she only followed one train of thought.

Tom was certain Bygie wasn't involved. She was as straightforward as they came. He found it hard to remember why he thought she was difficult to get a handle on. Why he tagged her the laughing widow. When he was around her now, he found it easy to decipher her sardonic laughs from real ones.

Bygie had few good reasons for a real laugh, but when one came, he noticed how her entire face lit up. He slammed his van door with too much force.

Bygie? When did he start thinking of murder suspects by first name?

41

She'd fixated on the idea of tracking down the men from the charity store. Detective Hall hadn't called to give her the information on the men and she was damned if she'd contact him to ask again.

The night Hall dropped off her customer list, she'd penciled out a flyer to email to whatever customers she could. With only three days until the show, she didn't have time to send them out using snail mail. She'd have to settle on handing out copies at the show, if she could get them finished in time. Squeezing it in added to the long hours, but she didn't mind. It kept her mind busy and off Lars. Off her life.

Then she remembered she didn't have a computer to finalize her layout. It had been stolen. Her list of errands grew.

The next morning, she purchased a laptop at a big-box store, insisting the battery be charged before she left. She went to a local copy store, where she used her new computer to create a flyer and email the finished product. She lugged out a box of colorful copies.

The hardest part of her list was all that remained. Taking a gamble on finding the men, she entered the thrift store with her fingers crossed. Walking to the counter, she asked if drivers had a specific time when they were in. The language barrier reared its ugly head; the clerk understood little of what she was asking. Bygie hardly understood it herself. This was a wild goose chase she didn't have time for. She asked for a manager.

Describing the two men she was searching for was easier the second time. The manager stood behind the counter and rocked back on her heels, smiling at Bygie. She rattled off a stream of Spanish that caused the other clerks to laugh.

"Do you know them? Would it be possible to speak to them? They were at my house to gather some stuff and . . . well, we had a bit of confusion." She looked from the manager then back to the laughing girls.

Recognition flitted across the manger's face. "Si. I know them. It's my husband and his brother. You shook them up good."

Bygie flushed, "Ahhh, yeah. I wanted to apologize to them and uhhh . . . see if I could hire them." This was one of her stupidest ideas.

The manager's eyes lit up. "Hire? How much you pay them? You got more furniture?"

Bygie left the store without talking to the men. The savvy agent/wife did the negotiating for them, pinning down when Bygie needed them and how much money would they make. She guaranteed her husband and brother would be at her house by six a.m., and ready to go. She was slightly hostile when Bygie asked if they would be able to drive the rental truck.

"They are professional drivers. Si, they can handle it."

What Bygie had been attempting to confirm was if they had driver's licenses, but she was afraid to push for an answer.

***

Opening day of the big La Jolla art show.

The alarm rang at five a.m. but Bygie was already awake, staring at dots in the ceiling texture. This morning the dots vaguely resembled a horse. Yesterday, a flower. Grabbing a pillow, she pulled it over her face. She was losing it. Seeing shit in her ceiling texture. She needed to get moving, it would be a busy day. She was exhausted, but sleep would have to wait until after the weekend was over.

She stayed in bed, running a list through her head. Everything was ready to go ... almost. Her booth area at the park would need to be organized and ready for business by noon today, and she'd left the most important element of the weekend hanging by a thread. She had her work done and ready to go. Lamps were cushioned in bubble wrap; mirrors were in rough wood frames and ready for transport. The rental truck had been delivered and was sitting in the driveway.

The only thing missing was help.

She crawled out of bed and headed for a shower. Sticking to her guns, she waited for the water to heat up before stepping in. *Better late than never.*

Dressed, she was finishing her second cup of coffee when an old vehicle wheezed into the driveway. She stepped on to the deck and smiled, motioning the men to come up. They hesitantly stepped forward, but refused to go further when she opened the front door to go in. She didn't blame them. She welcomed them with an even brighter smile. "Would you like a cup of coffee?"

"No, no café. Gracias."

"Well, let's get to it then."

They followed her to the garage, their eyes nervously looking around. Bygie hoped they would calm down before the day was over. Communicating through motions and rudimentary words, Bygie was pleased to see they were hard workers. She had them get a metal rack out of the garage and into the truck. They wrestled the heavy piece into place without complaining.

They secured the large rack in place using heavy cargo straps and started sliding mirrors, upright, into the rack. She'd learned the hard way to never travel with mirrors lying flat, they were too fragile. On one of her first attempt in delivering a big, finished mirror, she'd put it flat on the floor of borrowed pick-up. When she went to unload, it had cracked into tiny pieces.

Loading the last of the lamps, Bygie was startled by the amount of work she'd gotten done. With the wooden display easels for mirrors, painted blocks to display lamps on, and a box of miscellaneous items, the truck was nearly full.

They followed Bygie in her Miata to the park at La Jolla. Winding their way across the grass to her designated spot, they parked and jumped out to start unloading. This wasn't her first rodeo, and she directed them with precision. Within a short time, they had a semblance of order.

Her mirrors were placed on their easels; they only needed a touch-up with glass cleaner. Each lamp had a multicolored block under it, raising it to eye level. Spread out on the table were the brochures touting Recycled Beach Reflections list of satisfied customers. Huge baskets of seashells filled in empty gaps. She sank into one of the two chairs each booth was given. The men perched on the back edge of the open truck.

"I suppose we better get the truck moved before they have to come and warn us." She wasn't sure the men understood they were done for the day. Her plan was to have them take the rental truck, then come back with it on Sunday to help her load. The possibility of never seeing the men again, along with an expensive rental truck, crossed her mind.

"The show ends, gets over on, Sunday, Domingo, Si? You come back at three, tres, on Sunday?"

"Si, si. Domingo."

"On Sunday, si?"

"Si. Sunday."

She watched them drive away, crossing her fingers they'd return. Shaking off her anxiety, she turned to look at her booth area. It looked pleasing in the bright sun. The reflection from the mirrors made her spot stand out. It looked much larger than the neighboring booths with the same square footage.

The grassy park was on a high bluff that looked out over the ocean. Her mirrors reflected rolling waves, green grass and a bright blue sky. Bygie took a deep breath of the sea air and settled. It smelled like home. She smiled as another vendor walked over to admire her mirrors.

Before the show officially opened, vendors liked to walk through the park to check out displays and competing talent.

This year, Bygie would have to skip her walkthrough. Her view of the art and artists would be limited to what she could see from her area. She was alone.

Lars had looked at the event as a golden opportunity to press the flesh with potential customers. His presence gave her time to walk around the festival.

Her confidence wavered.

There would be people attending the show that knew both of them. She should have canceled. She wanted to hide, but forced her chin up.

42

Lizzie sat in the back booth, watching Sugarlips wipe her nose with a cheap napkin, adding it to the growing pile. "It's awful Lizzie, I can't believe he's dead."

"I know, Sugar, I was shocked when I found out." Lizzie was more than shocked, she was scared. First, Lars died in an accident, now the reporter. Who was next? She shivered. "Do you think he jumped?"

Sugar's eyes flashed. "Of course not, we were planning a future together." She grabbed another napkin from the holder on the table and swiped at the mess on her face. Dark trails of mascara snaked down her cheeks. When she caught her reflection in the restaurant window, the black trails looked like proof of desperate grief over Greasy. She left them in place. "He must have slipped or something."

Lizzie reached out to pat her hand. "I'm sure his death is real hard for you. I know the two of you had become close."

Sugar's face brightened. "Did you see the story in the paper? His death made front page news. My Greasy was pretty famous ya know."

Lizzie resisted the urge to roll her eyes. "Has anyone else talked to you about the story Greasy wanted to write?"

Sugar moaned loud enough to cause the few customers to turn and stare. "I can hardly bear to hear his name. After we wrote the book, we would've been famous. I'd be Mrs. Robert Tucker." Her voice rose, "why did this happen to me?"

Lizzie bit her lip. "It was worse for Greasy, Sugar."

Sugar's chin lifted. "Well it's my life that's messed up now. He can rest in peace, but I'm left all alone."

"Sugar, listen. This is serious. I need to know if you've talked to anyone else about what Greasy was working on."

"No." Her eyes lit. "Is someone new interested in doing it?"

"No, not at all. I'm asking if you've told anyone"

"Of course not." Her cheeks flushed at the lie. "Well, I told girls on the corner I'd be leaving the street soon, that I found a man who wanted to take care of me. I might have mentioned I found a better job."

Lizzie's gut tightened. "Do you know if he'd started writing the book yet?"

"How could he?" Sugar straightened her shoulders. "You were always leading him on but not bothering to show up. I wasn't even sure you'd be here now. I couldn't tell him what he needed to know." Sugar sobbed loudly, but her eyes were dry. "What am I going to do now? I should have gone off the cliff with Greasy. My life is over."

This time, Lizzie did roll her eyes. "It'll work out Sugar. We've been through tough times together, and you'll get through this, too."

"That's easy for you to say. You have a nice cushy job, making great money. Me? Without Greasy, I have nothing." Sugar lowered her eyes, then looked up through her lashes at her friend. "Unless you can help me? You told me you'd hook me some good work."

Lizzie's smile was weak. "I'll see what I can do. You hang in there, and promise to let me know if anyone comes around asking questions, okay?" She reached across the table, grabbing Sugar's hand. "Are you listening? This is real important. Don't talk to anyone, and whatever you do, don't mention my name. Okay?"

"Yeah, I heard you. I won't say anything to anyone."

"You stay quiet while I work at getting you off the street. I have to go. I'll be in touch real soon."

Lizzie left the restaurant, carefully checking out the parking lot. It wouldn't go over well if a certain someone found out she'd left the house again, but Lizzie had needed to speak with Sugar. She had to make sure the she didn't go yapping her big mouth. This was the end for Lizzie. She wanted out for good. She never should have gotten involved.

Maybe she could take up decorating.

43

Weekends were still hard for Tom. When Gloria first moved out, Tom slouched around the empty house never settling on a task. Giving in to the urge to flee the empty house, he'd go back to the station. He'd fill his time off work with more work. There was always something that needed to be followed up on, reports to write.

It took up empty time.

He'd quit going in on weekends when the good natured teasing from co-workers took on a hard edge. Tom was working seven days a week in an attempt to avoid his empty house. He sure didn't do it to set an example of dedication to the job, but others in the department saw it that way. Instead of staying home, relaxing with their families, dedicated investigators started showing up on days off, putting in extra time.

***

Most employers would be ecstatic to see free overtime being put in, but not The Pope. He met with Tom and told him to knock it off.

"Get the hell out of here on your time off, Hall. I can't afford to have my officers making mistakes, exhausted from trying to keep up with your ridiculous hours. Stay out of the station. Take up volleyball. The exercise would do you good."

"Volleyball? Is that even played past grade school?"

"Tennis, racquet ball, golf. Go fishing, I don't care what it is, but take your damn days off. It's not healthy to be on the job twenty-four-seven, and I'll be damned if I'm going to sit and watch it become a competition between my men to see who can put in the most time."

Tom's face turned to stone. "I'm doing my job."

Pope locked his gaze. "I don't want you to burn out. A divorce takes a toll."

Tom crossed his arms across his chest. "Move me then."

Hard to surprise, the statement stunned Pope. "Move you?"

"Take me out of homicide." He watched as surprise spread across the chief's face. "I've put in enough years. Transfer me to another division."

For once, Pope was still. No finger stretching or pencil twirling. "How long have you been planning this?"

"It's time. I'm already burned. Put me on a desk job."

"Does this have anything to do with Mike leaving?"

"No . . . and yes."

Pope leaned forward, reaching out to Tom. "Look, I've been there. Divorced, I mean. It takes awhile to get solid ground under you. Don't go making a rash decision. With Mike leaving so suddenly, it surprised all of us. Give it time, you'll find another partner."

Tom appreciated Pope's intent, but wasn't sure if he meant a partner, as in a woman, or partner, as in Mike. Dragging his hands through his hair, Tom let down his defense. "I need a change. It's getting old, I'm getting old. I'm done chasing down murderers. I need something new to do."

"I'm not moving you anywhere. Not yet. You need to put more thought into it before going off half-cocked."

Two months later, Tom had left homicide and returned to Vice. No one questioned why he'd made such a downward career move. The circulating rumor was he'd got into trouble and was forced into the backward step. Other vice detectives avoided him like the plague, afraid his bad luck would rub off on them. No one stepped forward to partner with him, which was fine with Tom. Then, he was 'asked' to be Ruby's field training officer. Pope's way of punishing him for wanting something different.

***

Now he willingly stayed away from work on his time off. But old habits die a slow death, and he wanted answers. With the death of the reporter, no one was pushing hard for Hudson's murder to be solved. It had been ruled a drowning. The investigation into suicide was a dead end. With Greasy gone and the threat of a front page story removed, the escort business twined with murder, was pushed aside.

Tom couldn't step away from the case. He found it impossible to let it go and wind up in the unsolved file. Let Bygie live under a threat of suspicion. Two guns, one destroyed casing, a damaged hollow point, it all led to nothing. No match. Nada. Zip. The only thing he was waiting on were the results of the acid test on the gun taken from the Hudson residence. He wanted answers, even if solving it turned into bad news for the department.

The list of vehicle plate numbers from the department lot were registered to some of the highest ranking officials at the station, and Tom was holding on to the information. The names were too close to Pope for comfort. He rubbed the back of his neck. What was he imagining? That Pope was dirty? Oceanview advertising didn't mean the owners accepted a bonus from Hudson.

It didn't mean they'd refused either.

Hudson had big balls to be offering women in the first place. Would he have had the cojones to make the same proposal to known police officers? Probably. So far, the man screamed slimeball.

Tom was spending his Sunday on the couch in sweats, trying to focus on the television. The distraction wasn't working. He kept muting the sound to follow a train of thought, but as soon as the noise cut off, so was the thought. Like his brain was hardwired to the channel changer.

He punched the buttons on the remote, determined to occupy his mind with a good show. A loud commercial snatched his attention. It was about the art festival La Jolla.

He sat up.

Indecisive, he brooded through several more commercials. Coming to a conclusion, he stood up, heading to the shower. What would it hurt? If he hurried, he could get there before the art festival was over.

***

As usual, traffic around La Jolla was jammed up. Lucky for Tom, there were more cars trying to escape the logjam then there were trying to get in. It still didn't help the parking situation. Frustrated, he left mini-shitty next to a fire hydrant. Against rules, he put a card on the dash of his shitty-van, identifying the vehicle as one driven by an officer on the job. He seemed hell-bent on breaking rules lately.

He was following up, sort of.

Tom walked through the dwindling crowd. What did he hope to see? He didn't plan on talking to Bygie. He wanted to take in the flavor of what was going on around her, see how she operated outside the presence of police.

He walked past paintings and sculptures and hand-woven rugs without seeing them. He was looking for mirrors. Some booths were being packed. The show was over at three and it was two forty-five. He was cutting it close. Running a hand through his hair, he stood still, feeling awkward. Wearing jeans and a tucked in polo shirt, he blended with the crowd, but felt out of his element. The last of the crowd were mostly couples, strolling hand in hand, laughing as they juggled their purchases, heading towards their cars. Tom tugged at his collar. He cut through the first row of booths, heading to a second row that sat closer to the ocean.

The breeze felt good. The air was humid and heavy, filled with the scent of the sea. Scowling, he pictured what was left of Greasy lying on the hard-packed sand, his feet brushed by the waves, giving them an eerie look of movement.

He snapped his head to clear his focus, and looked up to see Bygie staring at him.

She was standing not ten feet away, still as a statue. Wary.

His plan was to observe, not be observed. Damn.

He nodded a greeting as he walked towards her. She tentatively offered a hint of a smile.

"I'm not here on, ahhh, business. Thought I'd get out of the house and do some shopping." He tugged his shirt collar again.

She visibly relaxed. "Oh. Well, then." She studied him. He looked different. Dressed in something outside his detective blazer, he looked, well, more normal. Not as threatening. "Have you purchased anything?"

Caught in a lie, he rubbed his neck. "No. I've been looking around. Nice day, huh?"

Bygie laughed. "I'm glad you weren't coming down to see me . . ." she trailed off, embarrassed.

"How has the weekend been for you? Sell lots of mirrors?" He looked past her shoulder in the direction of her booth. It looked empty.

"I did. It's been a good weekend. Long, but good. I don't have nearly as much to haul home as I did coming down. That's always a good sign." She turned back to her area, pointing out two big mirrors sitting on short easels. "The big ones are sold too; I'll make arrangements to have them delivered." She looked around at neighboring booths. "I guess I'm done. I can start packing." She arched her back, working out a kink. "I'm ready to go home. After this weekend, maybe I'll be able to stay in bed . . ." She stopped.

"Do you have help?" He averted his eyes, his neck flushed. "I mean, how did you get everything down here? I've seen the car you drive. It wouldn't hold much."

"I have help on the way." She glanced at her watch. "They're supposed to be here." Her eyes darted through the dwindling crowd. "I guess they're running late."

He picked up her sudden tension. Was it someone she preferred he didn't see? "Can I help?"

She looked at him, surprised by the proposal. "Uhhh . . . Sure. I guess. I can't do much until the truck gets here. I have to tack wood frames around the leftover mirrors and bubble wrap the lamps, but what I need is in the truck." She muttered, "It better be here soon."

"Trouble?"

"Compared to what's happened in my life lately, this is nothing." Lifting her hair off her neck, she mumbled, "I'm hoping they didn't steal the truck."

Tom homed in on one word. "Something was stolen?"

"I hope not." She picked out a lumbering yellow Ryder truck heading their way, and blew out a breath. "It's okay. I see it."

When the truck pulled up, two men jumped out, immediately running around to open the back drop-down ramp. They looked slightly familiar to Tom, but he couldn't place them. He followed Bygie as she walked over to greet them.

"Hey guys, I was getting worried." She made a show of ringing her hands for emphasis.

"Si, si. El camión está mal, no arranca." They pantomimed jump-starting the truck.

She groaned. "Oh no. I'm sorry for your trouble."

Tom cleared his throat. "Ask them to try and start it again."

Bygie looked at him and laughed. "They can hear you fine."

She motioned for them to try and start the truck.

One of the men jumped into the cab and turned the key. He looked puzzled when there was no reaction. He tried again, then frowned. Nothing. He looked at Bygie, smiled tentatively and shrugged his shoulders, refusing to make eye contact with Tom.

Tom's mouth fell open. Now he knew why the men looked familiar. The last time he'd seen them, they were on the front deck of Bygie's house, being interviewed. He turned a stony look in her direction. "Did you give them keys to your house, too?"

Distracted by the truck refusing to start, she was slow to recognize his meaning. "What?"

Understanding crossed her features. "Oh, no. Of course not. These guys? They've been great."

"How did you track them down?" He never intended to give her contact information for the men. For all he knew they were career criminals who hadn't been caught.

"They were the talk of the thrift shop after relaying their experience at my house. Pretty easy detective work." She introduced him to Jose and Emanuel as Tom Hall. She purposely left off the detective tag, not wanting to make the men nervous. She gave Tom a self-satisfied smile. It slowly left her face at his hard look of dissatisfaction.

"What?" She looked between Tom and the men. She took his arm and led him away. "Is there something I should know?"

"I don't have information on them. That's the point. It's reckless to spend the weekend with men you don't know."

"Spend the weekend? I had them help load for the show and drive the truck I rented. That's it."

"You rented? You mean they're driving around in a truck you rented? They could have driven it to Tijuana and sold it. Have you lost your mind?"

Bygie's voice was frigid. "Why, yes. I guess I have." She should have stopped with that but she continued without regard. "I'm too tired to deal with your 'assumed' suspicions. I've known you to be wrong a time or two." She spun and walked away.

Shit. Hall, you're an idiot. You could have handled that better. He watched as she tried to figure out what the men thought was wrong with the truck. They had brought along a portable battery charger, but the truck refused to turn over.

One of them was clearly communicating 'fatal' by slicing a hand across his throat. He pointed at the battery.

Bygie sank down on the ramp, so tired she didn't know what to do next.

Tom walked over and cleared his throat. "Won't start?"

"No." She refused to look at him. "We'll figure it out."

"Phone the rental company. They should be able to bring another truck down."

She brightened, marginally. "Good idea. I'll do that." She rose to get her cell phone.

Tom took her place on the ramp, sitting next to her helpers, making firm eye contact with each man. They quickly looked away from the cold eyes. No one said a word. They paid strict attention to Bygie as she paced and talked.

44

She hung up, dissatisfaction written on her face. "Bad news. They said leave the truck and they'll have it taken care of, but bringing down a replacement is out of the question. They don't have a truck left on the lot to bring us." She rubbed her eyes, dropping her arms to her sides. "I guess I'll take one of the guys back to my house to get their truck. I'm assuming they left it there."

Tom met her eyes, raising his brow at her word choice. "You assume?"

Bygie's chin tilted up. "The rental was in my driveway when I left this morning. I assume they drove over to switch trucks. Assuming I'm right, their truck is at my house." She pinched her lips together in a smile that looked more like a grimace, "but you know how assumptions can be wrong."

She snapped her fingers, "Here's a great idea. I'll ask them."

Tom's face was dark. "Is this all you have?" He motioned to her booth area. "If it is, it will probably fit in my van. It doesn't have any back seats in it."

"You'd do that?" She met his eyes, looking for an ulterior motive. Her gaze darted away, uncomfortable with the contact. "Do you think everything would fit?" She looked over what was left to cart home. "The only problem is the two big mirrors. They need to stand upright; they can't lay flat."

"My van has racks in the back. We'll use them to anchor the mirrors in place."

"The big rack in the back of the rental truck is mine. I know that wouldn't fit in your van."

"Call the truck company again, tell them to deliver it. It's the least they can do for the inconvenience."

Bygie wasn't sure how to take the detective's helpfulness. She was too tired figure out if he had a hidden agenda. She wanted to go home, take a shower and go to bed. "You're right. I'll call them."

"Give me the number. I'll call for you. You can get the guys to start packing."

She was happy to let Tom take charge. She wasn't sure she'd get the rental company to follow through on delivering her mirror rack, but was pretty confident they'd listen to him. *Having a cop for a friend . . . .* She shut down the thought. *Where the hell did that come from? The last thing we'll ever be is friends.*

Tom pulled up in his mini-shitty-van and opened the back hatch. Along one side wall was a sturdy metal rack, similar to what was used in bakeries.

"Do you do a lot of baking, Detective?"

"No." The response was short, it didn't invite conversation.

"Ohhhkay." He was back to true form, one she was familiar with. Probably regretting his offer of transport. With her work secured in the back of the van, Jose opted to ride with Bygie and cheerfully volunteered his brother, Emanuel, to ride with the detective. Emanuel looked as if he'd rather walk. He entered Tom's van akin to facing a firing squad.

She was no longer intimidated by the big, surly detective. She brooded as she drove. *Maybe I'm getting a backbone. It's about time . . . even if it's fourteen years too late.*

***

Although she was feeling too worn out to measure grounds into a filter, after Hall's van was unloaded, she invited the men in for coffee. Jose and Emanuel declined the offer a shade behind Tom's acceptance. Finding his face easier to read, she recognized he said yes because he thought the other men would. Now he was stuck.

He watched as she handed each man an envelope and instead of shaking hands, she gave them each a light hug.

She turned around, noticing his frown. *What now?* "I promised you a cup of coffee. If you're nice I'll spring for pizza as a big thank-you."

"Uhhh, no need. You look tired. I can always take a rain check on the coffee."

"It would have been a mess without your help. Thank you." He'd saved her butt today, it wouldn't hurt to be nice. The tired smile returned, "I'd like to have a cup of coffee, no, make that I *need* a cup of coffee. I couldn't leave my booth to go get one, and I've been in La Jolla since seven this morning."

"You worked it alone? The entire weekend?"

"Yep." She turned and led the way back to the house and into the kitchen. She motioned towards stools at the counter, "Have a seat. I'll make coffee." She walked around the counter, washed out the pot, added grounds and water to start a fresh one brewing. Grabbing two mugs, she faced Tom as she waited for it to finish.

"Seriously, thank you for the help. Did you get the rental company to agree with delivering my mirror rack?" Her lips curved.

"No problem. They promised to have it to you first thing in the morning."

"I bet they will, especially if you introduced yourself as Detective Tom Hall." Her face clouded, and she lowered her eyes. "I'm sorry I gave you grief over 'assuming'. That's not like me. I respect what you do. It's a hard job." She closed her eyes, wanting to avoid the subject but had to ask. She opened her eyes, "Any news on, Lars?"

"Nothing new, but I'm working it," he rubbed his neck. "With the death of the reporter, Robert Tucker, some of the . . ." He saw a look of shock on her face.

"What reporter? The one bugging us all the time?"

"It's been all over the news. His body washed into a narrow cove on Friday. He drowned."

She walked around the counter, sinking to a stool, still holding two coffee mugs. "Do you . . . I mean does it . . . what happened to him? Was he . . ."

"It's been ruled an accidental drowning, possibility of suicide. I'm sorry, I thought you knew. The local coverage has been non-stop." He took the mugs from her.

She rubbed her hands over her face. "I haven't had the television on in days. I've been working the show, home only long enough to sleep. I never turn on the radio in the car, it's too hard to hear." Dropping her hands, she took a deep breath, "Could it be related to what happened to Lars?"

"We'll keep checking, but there's not much to go on. Probably not." His smile looked lopsided. "Same old drill."

He moved towards the coffee, her gaze tracking him. He filled the two mugs and put one down on the counter, in front of Bygie.

"Drink up. You look like you need it." Walking back around, he hesitated, then pulled out a stool, taking a seat beside her.

She wrapped her hands around the steaming mug, the rest of her body rigid. "What I wanted was sleep, but I doubt I'll be getting much now." She threw a look his way. "Are you wondering if I had something to with the reporter drowning? Is that why you came to the festival today?"

His answer was unequivocal. "No."

"So, why were you there? Making sure I hadn't skipped out?"

He fumbled, stalling by taking a drink of coffee. "I wanted to see the show. It was too nice to sit inside."

"My lucky day when you showed up." She lifted her mug, but set it down rapidly, sloshing liquid over the rim. "Do you know if there's something wrong with Emanuel or Jose? They're nice guys. They did a great job for me."

He handed her a napkin from the holder on the counter. "They seem fine, but with what's been going on around you, it's not the time to take chances. It's too trusting."

"Is there more to the reporter's drowning? Should I be scared?"

His answer was indirect. "Be cautious."

Bygie gave a derisive laugh. "I've been locking the doors and double checking the alarm, sometimes two or three times a night. I still find it hard to sleep with Lars gone." She played with the paper napkin, tearing off tiny bits and letting them drift to the counter. Quietly, with her gaze locked on the torn pieces of napkin, she said, "One time, I followed him."

The meaning was lost on Tom. "Followed who? Robert Tucker?"

She exhaled loudly. "No, not the reporter. My husband."

"You followed him? Where?" Tom froze.

"It's nothing. I was being stupid." She balled up the pieces of napkin. "I don't know why it took me so long to admit that Lars was having an affair." Feeling ashamed, feeling less than a whole woman, a desirable woman, she added, "He stepped out on me before."

"You knew he'd cheated on you before? And you stayed?"

The question struck like a knife, she could hear his disgust behind the accusation. The humiliation flooding her was not new. Why was she admitting this to a virtual stranger when she hadn't to her own family?

Maybe that made it easier.

"I didn't know for sure, but the signs were there." Her smile was bitter. "Of course, he denied it. He credited me with an active imagination." With careful control, she balanced the mug on little balled pieces of napkin. "I had one constant thought. If I knew for sure, without a doubt, that he was cheating, I would leave him. Does that make any sense? I should have left the first time." She looked straight at Tom.

"Thing is, deep down, I did know he was cheating. I followed him one night when he left. I still thought I needed proof. What a joke." She set the mug on the counter and leaned forward on her elbows, hands covering her face. She pressed hard to hold the ugly images at bay.

"How long ago? When did you follow him?" He held his breath waiting for the answer.

Her voice was muffled behind her hands. "A couple months before he died. I wasn't cut out to sneak around and follow him. Instead of wondering where he was headed, I worried what I'd say if he caught me trailing him." She dropped her hands and pivoted to face Tom. "How twisted is that? I was sick over what *he'd* think of me." She didn't wait for an answer. "I turned around and headed home when he entered a residential area. What was I going to do? Go peek in the windows?"

"Can you find it again?"

"The area? Probably. Why?"

"Do you know how important this could be?" His pulse quickened.

"I don't see how it matters. I don't know if he went to a house, and if he did, I have no way of knowing which one. He could have been driving around or making a u-turn. I told you, I didn't stick around to watch. I didn't want him to see me."

"It's my job to determine what's important or not." He stood up. "Let's go."

"What? Where?"

"I need you to show me the neighborhood he drove into."

"Now? Can't it wait? I'm not sure I can find the road in the dark. It's up off highway sixty-seven somewhere."

Tom's face turned red, his fingers pushed through his hair. "You followed him to a neighborhood near the scene of the accident, but didn't mention it? You thought, what, it was a coincidence?"

Her face paled. "I didn't believe the two were connected. Admitting I felt the need to the follow my husband?" Her voice broke. "I was mortified that I'd stooped so low."

"Let's go."

Bygie stood up and woodenly followed Tom to the front door. With slow, controlled movements, she set the alarm and locked the door.

She felt as if she would break into a million pieces if she moved too fast.

45

Tom left work early on the pretense of a dentist appointment. The little, harmless white lie was a huge dividing line in his mind. It incisively split his twenty-plus years in law enforcement into separate divisions. Time before the lie and the time after. He worried the stain of falsehood would be permanent.

He wasn't sure why he lied. Gut instinct? Self-preservation?

Last Sunday night, Tom had driven Bygie up the dark winding road of highway sixty-seven, in silence. She'd hunched in on herself, sitting as close to her door as possible. Her answers were monosyllabic. It took three passes on the highway before she was confident of the road Lars had chosen the night she'd played investigator.

Tom had turned right off the highway and wound up the sharply rising strip of asphalt. On the first pass, he followed the road, finding out it looped back on to itself and straight to the highway. They drove through a second time, slower than the first. A total of eight relatively new houses sat amongst the boulders. The acreage between them was spacious. Nothing obvious caused one to stand out from another.

He'd taken Bygie home, the van silent as they wound their way back to Stony Point. Tom was busy planning the next step. Distracted, he'd dropped her off with a promise of an update — his only attempt at conversation. She'd nodded as she climbed out of the van.

He'd waited for her lights to switch on before leaving.

In the week following, he discussed the possible lead on a house with one person: Mike. Their lengthy phone conversation cemented Tom's determination to work alone. He didn't mention it to Ruby. They didn't work together like a well oiled machine the way Tom thought partners should. He wasn't bothered by keeping her in the dark. But the fact that he didn't discuss it with The Pope could end his career.

He was following up this lead on his own time. He put in his normal hours during the work day, but began tacking on a self-imposed second shift at night, watching the neighborhood Bygie had directed him to. Tracking cars and the people driving them.

The lack of sleep was taking a toll, and today he left work early to go home and rest. He'd laugh if he didn't feel so guilty. Sneaking out of work, not to play golf or goof off, he was going home to take a nap.

Tom stretched out on his couch and rubbed his eyes. The action brought an image of Bygie doing the same thing. He pictured her hunched over her counter, face buried in her hands. He thought she would cry and was frantically crafting words to shut down the tears.

But she didn't cry.

Instead, she'd lost her spirit. Her face was haunted, humiliated. Her eyes vacant.

Tom felt a churning. The look on her face was familiar.

It was the same face he saw in his own mirror during his divorce.

Her grief was a perfect reflection of his pain. Her humiliation was recognizable. He didn't have the right to question why she stayed with her husband. He wasn't condemning her for not leaving Lars; he was using her to understand his own scorching embarrassment of being left for another man.

In hindsight, Tom too had known Gloria was seeing someone. He couldn't answer why he didn't pack up and leave anymore than Bygie could. What kind of man believes his wife is cheating and does nothing?

He wasn't entitled to examine why Bygie stuck with Lars.

He punched the couch pillow into a new shape with more force than necessary. He was craving sleep, but unable to find it. He'd originally thought men spending time with a call girl on a weeknight would be easier to write off as a business dinner, but nothing had materialized. His Friday night plans demanded he stay awake. He was hoping to catch some bump and grind action at the house in the hills.

Most of the homes contained families with children, and he'd observed nothing but routine activities. Parents leaving for work, only to arrive home and shuttle children to soccer and dance. Pulling county property records helped narrow down his choices. Only two of the houses were listed as non-owner occupied.

It appeared one of the rentals had two guys living in it, and Tom had thought he was on to something. Two men, with Hudson as a partner, would fit what he was looking for. He checked the renters' backgrounds using car license numbers. They came up squeaky clean, and when he saw them holding hands, he crossed them off the list.

Tonight, his focus would be on the last house on the list. The only occupant he'd spotted was a woman. The only glimpse he'd gotten was when a shadowed female figure crossed the room to pull the drapes shut. In five nights of watching, Tom had yet to see her leave home. If she had a vehicle, she kept it garaged. No way of knowing what type of car she drove, or if she owned one. If she left the house during the day, she was home before Tom arrived to watch.

He turned to his side and drifted into a deep, hard sleep. When he woke, the sky was pitch black. Disorientated, not sure of the time, he pushed himself up and stumbled to the kitchen and checked the time. Crap. Past seven, later then he intended. He scrubbed his face to wake, wondering why the hell he was doing this.

Atonement? Making up for being a rotten husband?

Whatever the motivation, he'd better get moving. He made a fresh thermos of coffee, a couple of sandwiches and grabbed a dark sweatshirt on his way out. If something didn't pop over the weekend, he'd have to give up working it alone.

He couldn't keep up the pace. He'd be forced to bring in Ruby and notify The Pope, conversations he'd like to avoid.

His last choice? Let the investigation die a natural death.

When he was on the highway, Tom chugged a cup of coffee and kept the window rolled down, trying to revive after the hard nap. Friday night traffic was heavier than during the week.Countless cars filled with happy couples leading normal lives, heading out for a late dinner or movie. He couldn't remember the last time he'd gone out on a weekend for fun. Or a weeknight. Barbecues in Becky and Joe's backyard, were the extent of his outside entertainment.

It was no wonder Gloria had looked elsewhere for companionship.

Tom pulled off the highway and headed up the looped road. The posted 'neighborhood watch' signs were a joke. He'd considered the idea of renting a vehicle, but decided his shitty-van fit the family neighborhood. He passed the same people more than once and had taken to waving. They waved back. In five days he'd become an accepted member of the neighborhood.

He chose to settle in behind a grove of citrus trees. There was enough clearance to see traffic on the road, and it offered a direct line of sight to his main target for the night. Using high-powered binoculars, Tom would be able to see a pimple on the chin of anyone coming in and out of the house. At least lights were on in the home. Raising the field glasses, he checked to see if any of the windows offered a glimpse inside. Even with cracks between the window blinds, his sight was blocked by the backside of draperies.

Settling in to wait, Tom leaned his seat back and refilled his coffee. This is where patience was a virtue . . . and staying awake was hard.

46

Bygie leaned into the mirror, pulling her skin back, forcing it tight over her cheekbones to erase sleep lines. She looked awful and the eyes reflected in the mirror were dead. Flat. No spark.

No wonder she looked so bad. Nightmares were haunting her. When she had tried to sleep, she'd pictured Lars in the arms of other women. Daytime hadn't been any better. Her daily chant had remained the same. Lars is dead. Lars is dead. Lars is dead. Doing laundry, making something to eat, running an errand, the mantra circled on a loop.

She'd faithfully reported in to Jane each day. The success of the show, the reorganizing of her studio, the sorting and cleaning of her house were all details she used as conversation filler. Avoiding other topics, she rambled on to her sister in a bright voice.

It didn't fool either of them.

It's what she'd done most of her married life.

Avoid. Avoid. Avoid. The words kept coming in groups of three.

Assume, assume, assume.

Lars, Lars, Lars.

She felt hollow. Waking each morning to stare at the ceiling and wonder how she let her life get to this. Was it pride? Embarrassment? Love? The questions changed and evolved. Bygie had spent many years of her marriage questioning whether or not Lars loved her. It had finally come full circle. Now, she questioned her feelings for him.

Had she loved Lars? Did she even know what love was?

Growing up, Bygie had been surrounded by love from her family. Her parents, her sister, her grandparents — they all loved her. She knew they loved her through caring actions and kind words. Soft pats on the back from her dad, the note of pride in her mother's voice.

The truth was hard to face. She had been too young when she married, not old enough to have developed any self-assurance. Not old enough to understand she needed to love herself before committing to another person.

Hindsight arrived with crystal clarity. She'd expected Lars to fill her need to be loved, but it was a bottomless well. An impossible task for a husband to fulfill. Her well was a dry, yawning pit of emptiness and she'd placed total responsibility for her happiness in Lars' lap. She'd been looking for him to give her confidence, assurance and self-respect, instead of looking for it in herself.

Lars had felt so loved, and Bygie reveled in it. She'd waited for the same warm feeling to envelop her, but it never happened. The more she worked at showing Lars how much she loved him, the more the ante raised on her own needs. She made him her entire world and wasn't satisfied when his efforts weren't the same. She became angry, a bitter and resentful person because he acted so damn important.

But wasn't that partially her fault?

For years, she'd worked hard at making him the most important person on the planet. Why wouldn't he act as if he were? She'd helped form him into what he was, what he'd become.

She pushed away from the mirror, disgusted with her self-pity.

Getting ready to head out, she pulled on jeans and a tee shirt. Making a phone call was put on the backburner. Sick of being nervous in her own house, she promised Jane she would contact Hall to see when she could schedule a visit home. *Avoid, avoid, avoid.*

Admitting she'd followed her husband hurt, but Hall questioning why she stayed with him hurt worse. His tone of repugnance was apparent. The simple words cracked the final shard of pride she'd been hanging on to.

No, she wouldn't be asking him for anything.

Each morning dawned with a big schedule of emptiness. Her studio was as clean as it needed to be. The house was spotless. She wasn't inspired enough to start a new project. So she made a choice based solely on her own needs. There wasn't another person to consider in the decision. For the first time since the accident, her loneliness brought a sense of freedom. Her anger was displaced, for a time, by simple joy.

She was going to get a dog.

Her family had always had a dog, a mutt to chase in the yard and sleep at the foot of her bed. The day their parents gave in to their daughters pleas for the last of the family pets was one Bygie remembered with clarity. With two daughters begging for an expensive white ball of fur, her parents came up with the money. The terrier they named Fuzzer became another member of their family.

And yet, she'd married a man that didn't care for animals of any kind in the house.

She had been naive enough to believe he'd change his mind when he understood the importance of a pet. Early in their relationship, she'd drag home abandoned kittens from the restaurant, or lost dogs she found on the beach and each time the results were the same.

"You can't keep it, Bygie. I don't want a smelly dog in my house."

"I know, but it's so cute. Look at the poor thing. What if I keep it outside?"

That never worked. Bygie couldn't leave an animal tied to a tree. She'd end up taking it to the shelter or finding a good home.

That was then. This is now.

The house would be inhabited by a dog.

Bygie glanced into the empty front room on her way out. When the police finished with the search warrant, she had been ordered to let the boxes sit until they were cleared to go. When word came she could clear it out, her two friends from the charity carted it all away. Time had not changed her mind.

The only thing left in the bare living room was a black lacquered box on the fireplace mantel. Lars' ashes. She had moved it to different locations throughout the house: a closet shelf, the studio, downstairs in a guest room. One sleepless night she had marched them out to the garage, only to wake up feeling guilty, so she brought the ashes back in. The black box containing the urn dressed the empty room better than anything chosen by the decorator Lars had hired.

Bygie set the alarm and locked the door on her way out, the habit fully entrenched. Greeted daily by the faint lettering of "Whore, Keep Your Mouth Shut," she thought to change the "Wh" to "Sn". It would proclaim she'd lost her mind over snoring.

Right.

She should pick out a great big dog, one mean enough to scare people away, but that wasn't how choosing a pet worked. There is more to it than picking one out of the crowd. The right dog would find her. There would be an instant bond and she would have to be patient enough to wait for it.

***

Her little car had never felt so cramped. No matter which end was facing her, she was assaulted by fur. She had two choices, a wagging tail or wet kisses and dog breath. Both made her laugh.

"Sit down ya big lump, I can hardly see around you."

The dog sat, but his back end quivered with excitement all the way to touchdown.

"Good boy. You're a good listener." She reached over to pet him.

The good boy jumped up again to stick his entire head out the window, leaving Bygie with a slap of a tail. She laughed.

"Sit down. I can't see. We need to watch the road."

The dog sat again, and when she risked a glance, she saw his tongue hanging out the side of his mouth. He was staring straight ahead, navigating them home.

Home. The word didn't sound so bad.

She knew she'd found the right companion. He was around two years old and had been abandoned. His former owners had moved out of their house and left him chained to a post in the backyard without food or water. How could anyone leave their dog of two years?

She'd had him for less than an hour and couldn't imagine letting him go. When she'd first spotted him in the back of the cage, he offered a tail thump without raising his head. When Bygie squatted down to talk to him through the barrier of the cage, she was shaken at how thin the poor dog looked. His ribs were poking through, and his head looked too big for his body.

"Come here buddy. You've had it rough, haven't you?"

He remained curled up in the back of the cage but his tail twitched fast at the sound of her voice. She rose to ask if she could walk him around.

When the cage door was opened, the dog still didn't move. Bygie squatted down again.

"Come here big boy. Let's go for a walk."

She watched as he stood up, his head held down as he approached her yet his tail was wagging a mile a minute. When she reached out to pet him, he quivered.

"It's okay. You're scared aren't you? It's okay big boy, I am too."

Reacting to her calm voice, he leaned into her, knocking her to a sitting position. Bygie laughed. When he tried to climb in her lap, the deal was sealed. Her dog had found her.

He was medium sized, and the best guess from a volunteer vet was a shepherd/terrier mix. Bygie paid the fees, bought a collar and a leash, and walked him out the front door, both ready to start a new chapter in their lives.

When they arrived home, she opened the car door to let the dog out, expecting him to jump out and run, but he remained glued to the seat.

"Come on. You can get out. It's okay." The dog jumped out. "You're pretty dang smart, you know that?" He rewarded her by trying to jump on her chest.

"Down." He immediately dropped and slunk away.

Bygie softly reached out to pet behind both ears. "Come here, buddy. It's okay. You need to stay down. You're too big to jump on me. Okay?" The dog sighed; she felt the tension release from his body. He leaned into her hand, begging for more pets.

"We're going to get along fine. I think we both have a lot of love to give. Come on, let me show you around."

They walked around outside, the dog never venturing more than a few steps from her. Once inside, he didn't run through the house to investigate, he stuck to her side. His presence made the house feel like a home.

Her home.

47

Hall sat up straight, snapping the seat forward, the ratcheting sound loud after hours of silence. *Here we go.* The garage door lifted and a sports car backed out into the driveway. He twisted a knob until he brought the back of the car into focus. *Hot damn.* It had a shiny insignia on the rear of the trunk. A Mercedes emblem. The now familiar license plate border was also in place, one boasting an Oceanview Mercedes purchase. Without removing his eyes from the binoculars, he jotted down the plate number on a notepad resting on the console. He refocused on the back of the head in the driver's seat.

Come on, drive by me. Let me see who you are.

He watched taillights as the vehicle backed out and headed away from him. Tom tossed the binoculars on the seat in disgust. Hours of waiting only to see the rear end of a sports car. He made a sweeping turn between the trees and bumped back over a curb onto the street. He drove away from the house in the opposite direction, planning to intersect with the car where the road looped back on itself. If he made it fast enough, his headlights would highlight the driver.

He sped through the neighborhood, praying he would make it to the intersection ahead of the other car. The stop sign was on his portion of the road, and he was hoping whoever passed in front of him would glance over long enough for him to get a look.

His timing was perfect. The face looking out the window was framed in his lights.

Holy shit.

He recognized the face without a moment's hesitation. He didn't wonder where he knew her from, or question why she looked familiar. It snapped into place at an instant.

What now? Should I stop her? In my shitty-van? Right. Shit.

He hooked a left and stayed well behind the car as it snaked the rest of way back to the highway. Traffic on sixty-seven was minimal again and the Mercedes performed a rolling stop before turning on to the highway and heading towards the city.

Where's a cop when you need one?

Tom waited for another car to pass before pulling out to follow. He memorized the taillights as they swung in and out of view around the curves. Unless he ran into a Mercedes car club, he'd have no problem picking out the rear of the car.

At the intersection of Freeway Eight, the Mercedes merged over to the westbound lane, heading towards the coast and downtown San Diego area. Tom narrowed the gap. There was plenty of Friday night traffic to hide in. His mind was racing to catch up. He'd stumbled across the woman all of San Diego's finest were on the lookout for.

Lizzie. The prostitute caught with Judge Lockner. The bad decorator.

He smacked the wheel with both palms. Damn. This sure got the adrenaline flowing. Driving with one hand, he fumbled around for his cell phone. He wanted to call in the license plate number, find out who the car was registered too. Driving his van felt awkward. If he'd taken a car from the station, he could have radioed in a request for information. Instead, he was stuck using old-school technology.

Punching number one on his phone, he speed dialed the teletype operator at the station. He read off the plate numbers. The information came fast enough.

The car was leased from Oceanview Mercedes, registered in the name of Elizabeth Knox.

Elizabeth? Lizzie? Made sense.

The address listed on the registration was the house she'd backed away from.

He followed the car up the exit ramp for Severin/Fuerte, still plenty of other vehicles exiting between them. Traffic thinned as the Mercedes turned left onto Fuerte Drive, right onto Lemon Avenue, then another left. He followed the car as it wound its way up through the residential hilltop of Mount Helix. The climbing road was narrow and without streetlights or sidewalks. The curves were sharp, with driveways leading off into blackness; a reminder that the area was once considered the boonies. What he was driving on was not much better than an asphalt covered horse trail.

The area looked vaguely familiar, but Tom was having a hard time remembering the last time he had been in the vicinity. The houses weren't the typical over built McMansions. Most were well tended older homes of modest proportions. Location dictated price, which made this an expensive neighborhood to live in.

With few cars in the neighborhood, he was forced to fall back even further when he was left without a distraction between him and the Mercedes. He reached up, dragging a one-handed furrow through his hair, feeling the sweaty dampness of his scalp. Swinging around a curve in the road, he had enough time to catch a glimpse of taillights disappearing around the next bend.

Near the crest of the hill, brake lights ahead of him punched on, slowing down. A sudden left turn had Lizzie pulling into a driveway and out of sight. Tom turned into the first sign of a driveway on the opposite side, killing his lights before finishing the turn. He was sitting in front of a home, hoping an alert homeowner wouldn't come out to greet an unexpected guest. Tom's eyes twitched between the dark house in front of him and his rearview mirror, looking for any sign of movement.

Backing out of the driveway, keeping his lights off, he headed in the opposite direction for half a block, pulling over to park on the side of the road. Without a berm, his van was still blocking half a lane, the best he could do. Grabbing his dark sweatshirt, he pulled it over his head as his stepped out, quickly walking back towards the driveway the Mercedes had pulled into. His step slowed as he neared the house. He leaned around the leafy branches of an Oleander to see the house.

Sticking next to the shrubbery, he ducked down and scuttled up the driveway. The only sound was the ticking of the Mercedes engine cooling down. Wary of motion lights, he squatted down, crab walking closer to the house. With his back pressed against the garage door, he covered his options.

Try to look in a window or get the hell out?

He opted for the first plan.

Hugging the side of the garage, he headed for the back-side of the home. On his left, he heard a dog yapping behind a neighbor's fence. The constant stream of abuse from the animal made him nervous. Someone was bound to look.

A backyard light came on, followed by the loud squeal of a sliding glass door, forcing Tom to retreat.

"Shut up, you stupid mutt. I'd like to shoot that damn . . ." The door slid back into place with a loud thump, cutting off the rest of the complaint from the female's voice.

A voice he recognized.

Crouching, he again went around to the backside of the garage. It stuck out further than the back of the house, giving a brick patio a semblance of privacy. Above the sliding glass doors sat a twin set of spotlights, but they'd been switched off. He'd have to take a chance.

Staying low, Tom crept in a straight line to the back of the yard, angling to his right enough to see through the door. If the lights came on now, he'd be trapped. Fenced in with no place to hide.

Blinds covering the sliding glass door were twisted shut, but only pulled halfway across the big door. Two women were in the kitchen, one on each side of a breakfast bar coun-ter. Lizzie, the missing prostitute, was sitting on a stool and appeared to be crying. She used the napkin from under a glass of wine to wipe at tears and blot her nose. Looking up at the woman standing on the other side of the counter, she shrugged.

Tom watched as the other woman walked out of the shadow and around the counter, leaning down to give Lizzie a hug.

His partner, Ruby.

48

Untangling herself from Ruby's embrace, Lizzie reached for her wine glass.

"You're right, Ruby. I know you are. I can't help worrying. When Lars was killed in the accident, well, I took it hard. He was a friend." She sipped her wine, avoiding Ruby's intense stare. "Now you're telling me Lars was murdered? It makes me sick." Her hand shook as she set the goblet on the counter. "When I heard the reporter jumped off a cliff, I needed to see you. I'm scared. What's going on?"

Ruby laughed. "You've always been one to make a big deal out of nothing." Leaning against the counter beside Lizzie, she reached out, touching her friend's shoulder, feeling the muscles tense under her palm. She squeezed hard, then let go. "Hey girl, no worries, okay? I've got us covered. Haven't I always protected you? Hudson must have pissed off the wrong person. He wasn't exactly a stand-up guy." Ruby's tone had the quality of a sneer. "You would've been meat in the foster home if I hadn't stepped in. This is the same sorta deal. Do what I say, and it'll work out."

"I know Ruby, you've always had my back, but this is different. People are dying."

"That shit doesn't have anything to do with us. We'll lay low for awhile and then go back to business as usual."

"What? Are you kidding? I want out. I'm done. I shouldn't have gotten involved again. I had my life straightened out. I can't do this anymore."

"Who are you kidding? You were living in a dump, working your ass off at a crummy job and unable to pay rent. When I put you up in a nice house you were happy enough. Now you want out?"

"It was a postage stamp apartment, but I owned it. No one around to tell me what to do and when to do it . . ." Lizzie saw the look on Ruby's face. She backed down. "I was doing okay." She rubbed her arms, feeling chilled. "I guess I'm tired. I'll be better tomorrow." She smiled at Ruby.

Ruby's face remained hard, her tone harsh. "That's exactly what we're going to do. Get some rest and let it blow over. Then we'll continue like nothing happened. It took me a long time to set up this gravy train and we're staying on it. If you hadn't been stupid enough to get caught doing a damn judge in broad daylight, none of this would be happening." Turning away from Lizzie, rolling her shoulders, she turned back with a softer tone. "You're sure the judge doesn't know your name?"

"I'm positive. He didn't give a shit what my name was. He was in a hurry. I did exactly what you told me to do."

"Have you shared the reporter's great book idea with anyone else?"

"No, of course not. I told you I didn't. At first, I thought it was a good idea, but after I talked to you, I changed my mind." Briefly holding Ruby's gaze, she ended up dropping her eyes, tracing a finger along the bottom of the wine glass.

"Will your friend Sugar keep quiet, or is that another problem for me to deal with?"

Lizzie tried to meet Ruby's gaze and read her intent, but looked away at contact. "She'll keep quiet."

"Tell me again. How did the reporter find you?"

Lizzie's neck flushed, "I told you. He was one of her regulars, and Sugar told him high dollar guys may be rolling her way."

"Sounds pretty simple."

The silence hung. Lizzie twisted her glass around by the stem, eyes glued to the hypnotic movement.

"But that puzzles me," Ruby said. "Why would a reporter be interested in a sorry-ass street hooker nailing rich guys?"

When Lizzie didn't look up, Ruby snapped, "Look at me, Lizzie."

Lizzie complied but struggled to hold eye contact.

"What did Sugar know? Tell me the truth."

"Nothing. All I told her was I'd try to get her off the streets and into a safer place."

"I hope that's true." Ruby stepped behind Lizzie, massaging her shoulders again, her grip strong enough to leave prints. "Go back to the house and relax. We'll talk again soon. It's not safe for you to be out. Every cop in the city is on lookout for you."

"What do you mean? You said no one knew who I was."

Ruby stepped behind her, gathering Lizzie's hair into a ponytail, pulling it up hard enough to force Lizzie's chin down. "No worries. I told you, I've got it covered. My old fart of a partner managed to have a print made from his dash board camera, from the night you were caught with the judge."

"Why didn't you tell me?" She groaned when her hair was twisted tighter in Ruby's hand.

"I told you to stay at the house, didn't I?"

"I only wanted to . . ."

Ruby reached around and placed a finger on Lizzie's lips. "Shhh, it'll be alright. Trust me, I'll take care of you." She bent down and trailed a line of kisses up the back of Lizzie's exposed neck.

***

Feeling a wave of relief when she was in her car, with the doors locked, Lizzie turned the key with shaking hands. Despite their long tangled history, it was the first time she'd felt afraid in her friend's presence.

Ruby was the smarter of the two. When they met on the street at fourteen, she'd set up a system of watching each other's back while they turned tricks. The money was good and the two formerly homeless teens did well. By the time they turned twenty, they had a rental house and a thriving business.

Ruby was able to leverage one of her regulars into helping her finance a house in Mt. Helix. She was vague on details of how she managed the deal. Lizzie had often wondered if she'd blackmailed one of her regulars.

Lizzie opted for a box called a condo and stepped out of the trade to try a different path.

Ruby never pulled back, she'd geared up. Like a benevolent dictator, she'd rounded up stray girls and hustled to keep them busy. She'd kept in touch with Lizzie, mostly to brag on her success, and taunt her decision to quit. When Ruby mentioned attending the police academy, Lizzie thought she was joking.

Ruby made it through the police training, earning a living running an escort service. Thumbing her nose at the establishment.

Lizzie struggled to make ends meet working a nine-to-five job, and when the bank foreclosed, Ruby reached out to save her. Lizzie was uncomfortable with turning tricks again, until Ruby paid for rent on a house and bribed her with a Mercedes. That's how Lars Hudson became involved, and Lizzie went back to work.

Lizzie and Lars hit it off.

At first, he visited her at the rented house once a week, but soon, he was sending a high caliber client list her way. Lizzie lived in the house alone, but five other girls helped meet the needs of the lofty clientele.

Now Lars was dead.

She also knew Ruby still lived life on the wild side. She tempted fate by showing up at the house to turn tricks herself. She called it stress relief. Dressed in black leather, wearing a wig and stilettos, she was unrecognizable.

Lizzie shuddered. How far would Ruby go to protect her investment?

She followed the half circle driveway back to the street, taking the circuitous route to the interstate.

Occupied with troubling thought concerning Ruby, she didn't notice a vehicle pulling out to follow.

49

She kept one hand on her dog as she listened to the phone ring. Voicemail, exactly what she wanted. She'd waited until Sunday to phone, hoping he wouldn't answer.

"Hi, Detective Hall? This is Bygie, ahhh, Hudson. If you could call me back, it's not an emergency or anything, I wondered about traveling to North Carolina, for a visit. Anyway, just let me know. I'd appreciate it. I mean, when you can. Thanks. Oh, did I say this was Bygie Hudson? Anyway, thanks."

Could I have sounded any dumber?

She closed her cell, burying her face in dog fur that smelled of her shampoo. The poor mutt had been tortured with two baths, the first one was with Lars' shampoo. When she'd pet her dog, she was left with a lingering reminder of Lars and wanted to cry, so she'd bathed him a second time to get rid of the scent.

She'd put off speaking to Hall, dreaded fumbling around in a conversation with him. Leaving a message only put off the inevitable discussion. She ruffled her dog's ears.

"Got it done, buddy. Thanks."

Bygie had taken to calling her dog Big Moose on the Loose and the quirky name stuck.

Moose.

The bouncing, sad-eyed dog made her feel human and appreciated. If she so much as moved, Moose was at her side with a questioning look. He wasn't taking a chance on being left behind and she didn't blame him. Soon enough, Moose would settle down and begin to trust her, at least she hoped he would. But for right now, his behavior was exactly what Bygie needed.

Moose was doing a great job of filling an empty spot in her life. Adopting a dog had re-awakened a dead zone. She had someone to nurture, someone to love that gave as good as he got.

She plopped down on the floor, eye level with Moose. "You're worried I'm going to leave you? Not a chance buddy. You're the best thing that's happened to me in a long time. Who knew a stinky dog could fix so much."

Moose tried his hardest to lick her face but gave up when Bygie blocked his attempts. He flipped onto his back, offering her a wider area to scratch.

She rubbed his belly. "Let's go outside Moose. Go for a walk."

The dog flipped to his feet effortlessly and stood waiting for Bygie to make the first move.

She used him to leverage herself off the floor. "I swear you understand whatever I say."

Moose gave his coat a shake, his rear end staying in motion. He waggled back and forth, simply happy to hear her voice.

"You're not going to appreciate being caged and put on a plane, but I'm not going on a trip without you. Got that?" She patted his head. "That is, if the big bad wolf will even let us go."

Hopefully, Hall would leave her a message while she was out.

Avoid, avoid, avoid.

50

Tom was operating on so little sleep he should have been falling asleep at the wheel, but adrenaline was still pumping hard and strong. His call to The Pope early this morning, asking to meet with him on a Sunday, was greeted with questions that Hall flat out refused to answer over the phone. His only response to the barrage was 'I'll explain when I see you.' The puzzle pieces were dropping into place and Tom dreaded delivering the news to The Pope.

Pulling into the driveway of Pope's house, he parked behind the chief's old Chevy pickup. Sitting for a minute, delaying the need to deliver news that would rock the department, he scrubbed his face with both hands, then slid out of his van. Walking up the brick pathway, he cringed when the front door opened before he reached it.

"I wasn't sure you were going to get out." Pope looked him over. "You look like shit."

"Yeah, well, good morning to you too, Chief. Got any coffee?"

"Elyse put out on a fresh pot before leaving for church. That's where I should be. I hope this is worth missing a good service. Come in."

He followed Pope through the house and into a bright, spotless, kitchen. Grabbing two mugs and the pot of coffee, Pope elbowed open the sliding door, heading out to a patio. Filling the mugs, he handed one to Tom. "Have a seat cowboy. Let's get this over with. What's the mystery?"

Tom remained standing as he picked up his mug, breathing the aroma. His eyes met Pope's over the rim. "I know who murdered Hudson."

Pope jerked, spilling hot coffee on his hand. "Damn it." He set the cup down, wiping his hand on the leg of his pants. "By the look on your face, I have the feeling this isn't going to be good news." Scraping a chair out from the table, he sat down, waving his hand to cool it down.

"It's the 'who did it' part of the equation that'll be causing you grief."

Pope's hand froze. He leaned forward, elbows on the table, tenting his fingers. "Spit it out, Hall."

"My new partner."

"Your new partner what?" Impatient, his index fingers tapped against his upper lip.

Hall let the silence hang, until The Pope grasped the meaning of the statement.

"Let me get this straight. You're saying Ruby Wilson killed Hudson?" He squeezed out words through a clenched jaw. "Tell me how you came to that conclusion. I can't wait to hear it."

"I've been working the case on my own time."

"Without talking to me? Why?"

Tom shrugged. "I'm not sure, I couldn't let this one go. Bored maybe?"

"You asked for vice, remember? I was against it from the beginning."

Tom took the high road, ignoring the invitation to rehash the old argument. "I talked to, Byg ... Mrs. Hudson again, last weekend." He saw Pope's eyebrows rise at the word weekend, but let it pass without an explanation. "She admitted to playing amateur sleuth. She followed her husband one night when he left on the pretense of a meeting. She was embarrassed, so she never mentioned it. I'm sure that's what Pond picked up on during her polygraph." Tom sipped his coffee, avoiding the next inevitable reaction. "The area she followed him to is a ranch-style housing development off Highway 67."

"She didn't think it had anything to do with his death? For Christ sakes, someone snagged him with a hollow point coming down that highway."

"Yeah, well, for whatever reason, she didn't put two and two together."

Pope's eyes narrowed. "Sounds as if she wanted to hide it."

Tom's face darkened. "I've been spending my nights staking out a couple of the houses in the subdivision."

"Alone? You didn't feel the need to discuss it with me, let anyone else in on the loop? What's up with you, Hall? That goes against every single departmental rule on the books."

"The whole investigation has been against departmental rules. No one was supposed to be 'in the loop'."

"Since when did that include me?" Pope leaned back in his chair, crossing his arms. His biceps strained against his shirt. "Get to the point. Your partner. Murder."

"The hooker we've been looking for, Lizzie? The one caught with the judge? On Friday night, she came walking out of one of the houses I was watching. When she left, I followed her, straight to Ruby's house in Mt. Helix. They had a nice long, rather intimate, conversation." Tom shrugged. "When she left, I detained her."

"Friday night? This is Sunday. Why is this the first I'm hearing of it?"

Tom fiddled with his cup, avoiding direct eye contact with his boss. "I didn't take her in. I have her tucked away at a no-tell-motel.

Pope exploded out of his chair, towering over Tom. "Let me get this straight. You've got a witness sitting in a damn motel, telling you Ruby killed Hudson? Have you lost your mind? She needs to be brought in."

Hall looked up at Pope, meeting his eyes dead on. "No sir, not until I'm sure who to trust."

"Are you questioning my trustworthiness? Is that why you're hiding a witness?"

Tom stood up, pacing to the edge of the brick patio. "It's not you. It's anyone in the department who's driving a car advertising Oceanview Mercedes. I couldn't take a chance."

"Is there something else you haven't bothered to let me in on?"

Tom spun to face him head on. "The case was dead. You said to let it go. How would you take that if you were in my shoes?" Tom reached into a pocket, coming out with a crumpled piece of paper, the names written in black ink. Handing it to Pope he said, "Have a look for yourself."

Pope scanned the list of plate numbers he'd compiled from the department lot. His broad shoulders sagged as he read the names associated with the vehicles. He sank back down to his chair. "Holy shit. I don't . . . I'm not sure how to take this. It doesn't automatically mean they had anything to do with Hudson."

"But some of them did. Certain names were familiar to Lizzie. Although Ruby insisted no one use real names, people slipped up."

Pope's gaze was riveted on the listed names. "Who's with Lizzie now? You didn't let her walk did you? If this gets out before we get a handle on it . . . well I don't know what would happen. Shit hitting the fan would be the understatement of the year." Two of the names were departmental chiefs; one was the Lieutenant in charge of public relations.

"I've got someone sitting on her."

He glanced up, "Who garnered that much of your confidence?"

Tom stopped pacing, facing the chief. "Mike."

"Son-of-a bitch." Pope shook his head. "How the hell did he get involved in this?"

"I spoke to him late Friday night. He caught a plane out Saturday morning."

"No one else you could trust? That it?"

"Pretty much." Hall glared right back at Pope. "The girl was scared shitless. There've been cops through her front door looking for services. She was freaked out I'd send one of them to protect her."

Pope took a drink of his cold coffee. "What did Lizzie have to say about Ruby?"

Tom filled him in on the lengthy relationship between the two women. "I guess they were pretty damn successful long before Craigslist." Tom sat down, his energy zapped. "Lizzie got out for a while, but not our Ruby. She continued honing her skills. She set up a house and started running girls herself. A big time madam cop, working vice. Kinda ironic isn't it?"

Pope scowled. "How does Hudson fit into the story?"

"Lizzie was having a hard time making ends meet walking the straight and narrow. When her condo went into foreclosure, Ruby put her back to work. She even paid for the lease on a Mercedes." Tom shook his head. "I guess they needed a classy car to do on-site blowjobs. It wouldn't do for moneyed boys to have their bare ass touch naugahyde. Maybe they couldn't reach an orgasm in a Honda, who the hell knows."

Pope didn't even blink. He circled a finger in the air to get on with it.

"Lizzie met Hudson when she leased the car. Within a short time, he was using her services. He wasn't the money man. The business was in place long before he took a roll in the sheets. Hudson's only part was bringing in big spenders by adding it as a bonus to certain Mercedes customers." Tom's hands followed the comforting path down his scalp. "It gets worse."

Pope's face slackened. "Don't tell me."

"Afraid so. According to Lizzie, Ruby serviced clients herself."

"God damn it." The veins in his neck bulged. "We've got one of our own, not only managing an escort service, she's turning tricks herself? Son of a bitch. She should have been vetted long before being accepted into the academy."

"For what? I checked. Ruby has a clean record. She admitted to a prostitution charge when she was a poor, young, misinformed teen. That's why vice wanted her so bad; she had experience. She doesn't do drugs. She pays her taxes. Why would they kick her?"

Pope growled, "She passed a fucking polygraph as a new recruit."

"She told the truth. Why would she fail? Have you ever been involved in prostitution? Her answer was truthful. Yes. Asked and answered."

"She. Is. A. God. Damn. Madam. Running an escort service." Pope struggled to contain his fury. "God damn it." He kicked a patio chair from under the table and watched as it toppled on its side. "God damn it."

"Don't kill the messenger." Tom waited for Pope to get a grip on his temper. "This can't be kept quiet, like Judge Lockner. As far as I'm concerned, the whole bunch of them can rot in cell hell. Lockner can lead the way while we go after others in the department. All of the bastards with Oceanview advertising on their car need to be questioned."

Pope's temper increased. He leaned across the table, barking in Tom's face. "Slow down, Hall. You're not running off half-baked and bringing down the entire department. You started this conversation stating you knew who murdered Hudson. Tie that up for me, before you go off half-cocked. You've been working this solo. You're too close."

"Hudson charmed Lizzie with pillow talk. He told her Greasy Tucker was breathing down his neck. Lizzie told Ruby."

"That's a reason to kill him? Where's your proof? Got any?" Pope's eyes lost focus, listening to an internal dialogue. "If this comes to light, it will end my career. Someone's head will be on the chopping block, and mine would look real good to plenty of the power players I've pissed off over the years."

Tom's eyebrows shot up. "That's why you're worried? Your career? Give me a break. You've got one of your detectives running an escort service, committing murder, and you're worried about your damn survival?" Tom snorted, "Maybe you've become more of a suit than I thought."

Pope rose halfway out of his chair, clenched fists held stiffly at his sides. "How dare you question my intent. You think because you bailed me out when we were rookies, you have the right to question my integrity?"

Tom held his ground and yelled back. "If you push to cover this up, I'll sure as hell question it."

"I didn't say a damn word about covering anything up, you self-righteous bastard." Pope was shouting too, the veins in his neck standing out. "As far as I'm concerned, anyone involved can rot, but I want it done right and tight. Got it? When sneaky ass, cheating, slime-ball, sons-a-bitchin' reporters put shit in the paper, they twist and turn it so god damn much no one knows the truth. I don't want innocent bastards who bought a Mercedes caught in the crossfire."

Someone a yard or two over started a mower. The sound broke the tension and Pope sat back down.

Tom leaned forward, his elbows on his knees, running his hands back and forth over his scalp. He looked up at Pope and smiled. "Welcome back from nowhere, I was afraid I'd lost you. I owe you an apology."

Pope grunted.

"Do you want to hear my plan?" Hall asked.

"I'm not surprised you have one. Finish telling me how Hudson fits into this. You sure he wasn't the money man?"

"Nope. His only involvement was bringing in rich referrals. Lizzie was the first one to meet him." Tom cupped his chin, remembering Bygie's tormented face. "According to Lizzie, she and Hudson developed a friendly relationship, enough of one for the bastard to pay her to decorate his home. I'm sure she serviced him well. According to Lizzie, Hudson was trying to help her get out of the business."

"Did Mrs. Hudson know her husband's hand-picked decorator did more than pick out paint chips and fabric?"

"No. She was as much a victim in this as anyone."

"I'm following you, but I'm waiting for you to get around to murder."

"Ruby did it."

"You come here, making a big announcement that a member of SDPD murdered someone and now you're telling me, what, exactly? You're guessing?"

"I'm telling you it adds up. Lizzie said Hudson was backing off. He told her he was going to try to work on his marriage. Lizzie repeated the bedside conversations to Ruby. Ruby was well aware they would be losing their biggest advertising, but a far bigger concern was that Hudson was a weak link that needed to be removed. When Ruby realized Greasy Tucker was after a story, she must have been concerned enough to take him out of the equation, too."

Pope jumped to the same conclusion as Tom. His questions were rapid fire. "Was Tucker shot before cliff diving? Anything suspicious from his autopsy? Something else you've neglected to fill me in on?"

Hall shook his head. "The autopsy report says death due to severe head trauma. A 150 foot drop, bouncing off sandstone on the way down will do that to a person. No water in his lungs. He was dead before hitting the surf. But Greasy was homing in on the truth and I'd bet he was pushed."

"I suppose he happened to be one of Ruby's clients."

"Nope. He wasn't that classy. He had a regular girl he picked up from the El, a girl Lizzie knows, who uses the name Sugarlips."

"This is more convoluted than a god damn back road map."

"It makes sense. Greasy found out about Hudson from Sugarlips. She knew about him from Lizzie. Ruby panicked. She figured if Lars was forced into a corner, he'd whistle Dixie real fast."

"Can you prove anything? This is coming from a hooker who has as much to lose as Ruby. Maybe it's nothing more than getting back at her friend for getting out, becoming a cop and making something of herself."

"If anyone caved under pressure, it would have been Hudson. He was in over his head. Ruby couldn't take that risk. Her carefully crafted life could go down with him."

"There's the little matter of proof."

"Don't worry. I plan on getting plenty of proof." He smiled at Pope, "I'll even deliver it with a bow on it."

51

Tom spent Sunday evening, holed up in motel with Lizzie and Mike. The old partners covered details with Lizzie until they were confident she had the drill down pat. When they released Lizzie from practice, she took a shower and fell asleep as soon as she lay down. Tom and Mike stepped through the door to the adjoining room to lay out the final plan.

"I'm not sure she can do this without breaking." Hall sagged to the corner of the bed, sinking low on the old mattress.

"What else can we do? It's the best plan to wrap it up fast. She'll do okay."

"I'm not sure. Ruby's had her in the palm of her hand for years. If she figures out Lizzie's wired, we're screwed. This could go all ways of wrong."

"We got it covered. Go home. You brought me in to babysit. I can handle it. You need to be on your toes tomorrow." Mike grinned, "I sure wish I could have seen the look on The Pope's face when you told him I was here. Did he use his 'I just sucked on lemons' look or the famous glare over his glasses?"

Tom pinched his face tight, speaking through puckered lips. "The lemon look."

Relaxing his face, his fingers walked the trail down his scalp. "I'm beat. I guess I'll go home. You're confident of the guys we got picked out to help?"

"As sure as I can be. We'll be fine."

"Okay, if you're sure. I'll be back tomorrow and we'll get this show over. If you need anything, call."

***

Exhausted as he felt, Tom never fell into a deep, restful sleep. When his alarm burred Monday morning, he was lying flat on his back, mentally clicking off items on a list.

Number one. Crack shot? Bingo. Ruby was more than capable of making the shot from a moving vehicle, especially if Hudson was slowing down when he recognized her pulling alongside him.

Number two. Shell casing on the side of the road? Bingo. Ruby hand delivered it, blaming the crime scene crew for not doing their jobs. It probably came from her back pocket. She couldn't resist the temptation to show off what a great detective she was.

Number three. Gun in a box at the Hudson home? Bingo. Any mall rent-a-cop would have made fast work of picking the house lock, so it was easy enough for Ruby to do. If she'd been caught at the house, she could have talked her way out of it, using a follow-up visit as an excuse. She'd probably been ransacking the house, taking Bygie's laptop, when the lumbering charity truck pulled into the driveway. She tossed the gun in the box before sneaking out the patio door.

Number four. Pushing to arrest Bygie? Bingo. From the beginning she'd directed the game, from painting the garage door with a veiled threat to stashing a weapon.

Ruby had Tom questioning his instincts on this case, and for that alone, he wanted her behind bars. He needed to get through the day with Ruby, treat it like any other normal work day.

But at day's end, the gloves were coming off.

He staggered out of bed, feeling old and tired. A long shower and a full pot of coffee helped, but Tom really felt the adrenaline kick in when he walked into the Monday morning department meeting. Ruby was there ahead of him. She raised her hand in greeting.

He nodded back, with a slight smile.

Game on.

*****

Tom stopped at Ruby's desk around noon. "Want to grab an egg burger at Zach's for lunch?"

She looked up at him and laughed. "Right. I'll eat one of those when pigs fly. I'm up for food, but I'm ordering something better than a gooey egg yolk burger."

"Let's go, I'm starving."

They took a back booth and Tom sat sideways with his legs stretched out on the seat. "So, what'd you do this weekend? Anything fun?"

Ruby raised her eyebrows. "If you think painting is fun. I stayed home and painted the outside of my house."

"Is it a real fixer upper, your house?"

Ruby tilted her head, looking at him. "Yeah, it's in Mt. Helix.

Tom whistled. "A pricey neighborhood. You'll have to invite me over to see it."

Ruby smiled up at the waitress when her iced tea was set in front of her. "I couldn't have done it without my inheritance. I was able to put enough down to make the payments affordable."

"Lost your parents?"

Ruby nodded.

"That's too bad, they must have been pretty young."

"Foster parents."

"Really? You never mentioned that."

"You never asked."

Tom smiled. "They must've thought a lot of you. Proud of you I bet."

"They treated me as if I was theirs. They had other foster kids before me, but when I came to live with them, I was the only foster they had at the time. They were older and ready to slow down, but when I showed up, they said I was a keeper. I stayed with them until I entered the police academy. They were a wonderful couple, my true mom and dad. It's been hard without them." Ruby blinked fast to ward off tears.

Jesus, this girl is good. Or I'm wrong and Lizzie gave us a load of crap.

Tom smiled up at the waitress when their food was delivered.

"What made you want to become a cop? Was your foster dad a cop?"

"No. He was a plumber, and I sure didn't want to follow in those steps. My mom stayed home, took care of the house, and me. You know, cookies and milk after school." Ruby took a bite of her salad. "Why the sudden interest?"

"I know I've been riding you hard. You've been a casualty in the crossfire." Tom's neck flushed. "The partner switch was harder than I thought it would be, but I need to let the old shit go. Start fresh."

"That's good to hear. I was beginning to take it personal."

"Nope, it's old age and a general bad attitude."

"You're not that old."

"I'm forty-one going on sixty, judging by the stiffness in my knees. What are you, mid-twenties? That's still a baby in my eyes."

"Thanks for the compliment. I'm pushing thirty and age doesn't have anything to do with stiffness. I was up and down the ladder so much, every muscle hurts."

"You'll recoup fast enough." Without wanting to, Tom took a big bite of his burger. His appetite was gone. "So, how do you like being a cop? Is it what you thought it would be?"

"It's pretty much what I thought." She forked around in her salad. "Truthfully? My goal is to be a homicide detective." She glanced at Tom to gauge his reaction. "That's what I set my sights on in the beginning, back in the academy."

Hall raised his brows. "You'd be giving up a lot. You think vice has bad hours? Homicide covers the spectrum. Weekends, holidays, birthdays, doesn't matter. You work the scene when it happens." He shook his head. "I'd think real hard about what you'd be giving up before jumping in. It'd be hard to settle down and have a family."

Her lifted fork halted, Ruby turned icy. "You mean, because I'm a woman it would be too hard, but not for a man?"

"Whoa there." Tom put up his hands in mock surrender. "I was speaking from life experience, not because you're a female. Didn't anyone let you in on the divorce rate of a cop? This job can suck the life right out of you and homicide is the worst. Hard to go home, carry on a normal conversation when you finish working the scene of a mutilated three year old."

Ruby leaned forward, "Don't you miss it? The excitement I mean? Pulling hookers off street corners doesn't compare to tracking down who pulled the trigger. Like the Hudson case."

Tom stiffened. "You still been trying to figure that out?" He shook his head. "First thing you need to do is learn to let shit go. That case is a prime example of how frustrating homicide can be. Unlike television, not all whodunit's get solved. The Hudson murder is dead in the water."

"I still think the wife's good for it."

Tom chilled. "You know what Pope said. With Hudson dead, the case is as good as over. He must have been the mastermind."

"You're saying it couldn't be a woman running the business? Maybe the wife was the brains behind it."

"I'm not saying it couldn't be a woman, I'm saying I don't believe it's the truth in the Hudson case." Tom shrugged. "Doesn't matter. It's in the cold case file. We've got enough to do without marching through this again. Eat up, let's get back to work." Tom choked down another bite before pushing his plate to the side. "Guess I wasn't as hungry as I thought."

52

"She's on her way home. Ready on your end?" Tom spoke on his cell, snaking his way through backed up traffic. Inching along at a snail's pace. Christ. He could get out and run faster.

"The guys are here, testing the wire on Lizzie. We'll be ready to roll when you get here." Mike said.

Tom slammed on brakes, nearly rear ending a car. "Traffic's at a dead stop. Damn it."

"No problem. We're not going anywhere. We've got Struble tailing Ruby. Chill."

"Yeah, yeah. On my way." Chinning his phone shut, he tossed it on the passenger seat. "Damn it." Tom wasn't convinced Lizzie could pull it off. She needed to follow their script, but she was a nervous wreck. If she didn't remain calm enough to get the information they needed, the entire set-up would be in jeopardy. Ruby was way too sharp to incriminate herself, and if she became suspicious, it might put Lizzie's life in jeopardy.

Tom's knowledge of mental illness was limited, but in his uneducated opinion, Ruby fit the bill of a sociopath. Superficially charming, manipulative, no sense of remorse and she certainly was authoritarian in her treatment of Lizzie.

Push her into a corner and the true Ruby was likely to explode.

They needed to come at her sideways, lay a trap.

Lizzie had spent a great deal of time in the Hudson home during decorating. Ruby had never been past the front room.

With the right question, they could push Ruby into a corner, get her to comment on interior rooms. Lay the groundwork and move forward. They wanted Lizzie to play up how smart Ruby was; bragging would be her downfall.

Incriminating a cop was tricky.

Traffic inched forward, but Tom didn't move until the car behind him honked. He crept forward, picking up speed until traffic flowed at a normal pace, as if nothing had stopped it in the first place. Tom shot out of his lane, cutting off a neighboring car to get to an off ramp.

Lizzie was stashed at a motel off Interstate Eight. Tom made a beeline for the parking lot, anxious to get the ball rolling.

***

They moved around the claustrophobic room, waiting. Two of the officers that Mike and Tom had handpicked to help, were outside for a smoke break. Waiting.

By far, waiting was hardest on Lizzie. She was unraveling.

Most detectives were used to sitting in their cars on a stakeout, hours at a time, doing nothing more than staring through a windshield. Mike used it for meditation time. He could sit for hours with his eyes half closed, not moving a muscle, but he never missed a thing. Tom, on the other hand, twitched, moved positions, rubbed his head, arched his back, groaned, fiddled with radio knobs, anything to make the time pass. It never worked.

Trapped in the musty motel room, he couldn't pace off his anxiety.

All set up and no place to go.

Two hours ago, Lizzie had spoken with Ruby and asked if they could get together after work. Ruby had responded that she was heading to the gym and would call her back in an hour to make a plan.

She hadn't called back.

Officer Struble, responsible for following Ruby home, reported she made a fast stop by her house, running inside and returning with a backpack, her cell phone glued to her ear. Tom figured she was talking to Lizzie. The time fit. The officer tagged along, well behind Ruby, to a downtown gym. He radioed in that she hadn't left the large fitness center, and that her car was still in the lot.

Tom wasn't comfortable with Ruby out of his sight. It felt off, wrong.

Staring out the motel room window, Tom tossed his cell phone from hand to hand, in a grown-up's game of hot potato. Thinking about Bygie Hudson. He hadn't answered her request for a trip home. If it played out according to plan, he could do a lot more than give her permission. He could tell her she was free to go wherever she wanted, whenever she wanted.

His hands froze. Mumbling under his breath, "No."

Mike stood up from the only chair in the room, walking over to Tom. "What's up, Hall? Talking to yourself again?"

Spinning to face Mike, he asked, "What if we've got this wrong?"

Mike went still. "She did it. Don't go second guessing. If we're barking up the wrong tree, we'll find out soon enough. No harm, no foul. If she's innocent, Ruby will never know what we suspected." Mike didn't believe the words. The gossip mill at the department would spread the news like wildfire. No way could they keep the surveillance of Ruby under wraps. Even working with handpicked officers they trusted, someone would slip up. Bound to happen.

Tom shook his head. "No, no, it's not that. I don't think she murdered Hudson, I know damn well she did. It feels right. What I mean is this," he spread his arms in frustration.

"The waiting game, it's wrong. She's gone." Hall barked, "get Struble on the horn. Now. I want him inside the damn gym to find out if she's there." Reaching around Mike, he yanked open the motel room door, startling the officers standing outside smoking. They crushed cigarette butts under their heels at Hall's expression.

"Get in here, we're moving."

Lizzie came over, plucking at Tom's arm. "What is it? Is she coming here?"

Tom ignored the plea, "You guys stay here with Miss, uhhh, Lizzie. Don't open the door for anyone but us, got it? Mike, let's go." He headed to the parking lot towards the unmarked, not turning around to see if Mike was following. He started the car, putting it in reverse, slamming on brakes long enough for Mike to jump in the passenger side. He gunned it out of the lot, tires squealing on the hot asphalt.

Grabbing for the dash, Mike hung on as Tom hooked a fast left towards the freeway ramp. "What the hell's going on? Mind letting me in on where we're heading?"

"The Hudson home." He opened the window, sticking a magnetic cherry bubble to the top of the roof. Traffic was stop and go. Tom maneuvered onto the shoulder of the freeway, flying past startled drivers. He slapped the steering wheel. "What's the best way to fix Ruby's problem?"

"Ruby? I thought we were heading to Hudson's. I'm afraid you lost me, pal."

"Bygie is her target. She needs to get rid of her. If she can make it look like an accident, I don't know . . . ." Tom jerked the car across two lanes, avoiding the rear end of a beer truck.

Mike looked at Tom. "That was too close for comfort."

Tom didn't comment. In response, he pushed the Crown Vic harder.

Mike tried again. "Why would Ruby have it in for Mrs. Hudson? Sounds off-track to me. The only thing that would accomplish is another murder to cover-up."

"In Ruby's mind, that would be the least of her concerns. Remember? She's the smart one. Damn it." Tom kept one hand on the wheel, dragging the other one through his hair. "She's worked hard to incriminate Bygie. A logical step in her mind would be to set up a suicide. So full of regret for killing her husband, Bygie does herself in. She believes Bygie knows more than she's telling. That's why she warned her, told her to keep her mouth shut."

"Pretty hard to pull that one off. Even a rookie would know it's difficult to make murder look like suicide. It's a lot harder than most people think."

"I'm telling you, Ruby would believe she could pull it off. Here," Tom tossed Mike his cell phone, "call Bygie. See where she is."

Mike caught the phone, "Got her number?"

"It's in there. Look at missed calls, or recent calls. Find it, okay? It'll say Hudson."

Mike found the number and pushed send. "It's ringing. Is it a cell or the house phone?"

"Cell. Has she answered?"

"Straight to voicemail."

"Call again. Maybe she's mixing mortar and didn't get to the phone." He glanced at Mike in time to see his eyebrows raise. "What?"

"Mixing mortar? I thought she was a stay-at-home wife."

"She's an artist. Damn it, call her." Sweat trickled down the back of his neck.

"No answer."

"Shit. Call Struble. See if he found Ruby at the gym."

Tom's cell rang before Mike finished dialing.

"Is it her?"

Mike looked at the screen, "No. It's Struble."

"Answer it."

Mike punched a button. "Give it to me. Did you find her?" He nodded his head listening to the details, turning to stare at Hall. "You're sure? Did you get a description? Let me tell Hall what's going on. I'll get back to you, hang tight." Snapping the phone shut, Mike said, "Looks bad. Our girl snuck out of the gym's back door and left in a borrowed car."

"She's heading for Bygie's." Tom accelerated up an off ramp and through a red light.

"You don't know for sure. She told one of the employees that her car ran out of gas and asked to borrow her car to run to a station. The girl knew Ruby was a cop, figured it was safe to loan her wheels. It's a 2005 Honda Accord, white, four doors. She didn't know her plate number, but Struble's getting it."

Tom slowed, approaching a right turn that wound its way up the granite hillside into Stony Point. Bygie's neighborhood. "Keep your eyes peeled for the car Ruby's driving. I doubt she'd pull into the driveway and announce herself."

Down from the crest of the Hudson driveway, Tom rolled to a stop on the narrow road. He studied the setting sun, worried it'd be dark before they got a handle on Ruby's location. After seven, full on dark would happen fast. "Let's walk the rest of the way. There's not much to cover us. The best we can do is stick to the shadow side of the hill."

Cresting a hill leading into the driveway, they got their first glimpse of the house. The little Miata was sitting in the driveway.

"Looks pretty quiet." Mike said.

"Her art studio is above the garage, maybe she fell asleep over there."

They scuttled their way to the house, Tom heading for steps leading to the studio, motioning for Mike to take the house.

After knocking and using the doorbell, they met back in the driveway. Tom was staring at the house, hoping a light would switch on. Crouching against the granite hillside, Tom stated the obvious. "She's not here."

"Does she have another car? She could be out."

"No other vehicles that I know of. Damn it. Let me call her again." Hitting send on his phone, he listened until voice mail picked up. He flipped it shut against his leg. "No answer."

"What now, boss?"

Tom stood straight and stared back at the house, wondering the same thing.

53

Waiting. Waiting. Waiting.

For what? Detective Hall still hadn't returned her call requesting a trip home to North Carolina. She'd hung around the house most of the day, anticipating his call and dreading it at the same time. In his presence she felt . . . she wasn't sure what she felt. Flustered would be an apt description.

Her day passed quickly enough as she tackled jobs she'd been putting off. The morning was cool and by six a.m., she was up and outside, pulling weeds, trimming outdoor plants, watering a patch of pathetic grass. Thoughts drifting as she worked, she remembered a conversation she'd had with Lars shortly after they moved to California.

He'd come home earlier than usual, and she'd been outside working, much as she was today. Walking up behind her he'd wrapped his arms around her, startling her.

"Who's this gorgeous gardener?" he nuzzled her sweaty neck.

She sank back against him. "Yuck. I stink and I'm dirty."

"Not you. You smell like you've been working hard. What's not to like? I keep telling you we can afford a gardener."

"I know, but I enjoy it." She laughed. "My dad always said there was nothing better than getting your own real estate under your nails." Turning, she held out her hands. "Looks to be about an acre. So much for a manicure."

"Come on." Lars took her arms, walking backwards, pulling her towards the house. "Let me help you clean up. After hugging you, we both need a shower. Last one in is a rotten egg." He spun around, opening the door and running up the kitchen steps. Bygie grabbed his ankle on the top step, causing Lars to tumble to his knees. She climbed over his back, laughing. "All's fair in love and war." When she tried to stand, Lars grabbed her ankles, dragging her back towards him. He crawled on top of her, planting kisses on his way up.

"What's the hurry?"

Could that really have been them? How was it possible to remember such light-hearted moments amongst the drudgery of their marriage?

Using her sleeve to brush away tears, she reached over, rubbing her dog's back. "I'll take you for a walk later. We'll go to the dog park." When Lars and Bygie had moved to California, they'd been surprised by many cultural differences, and one of the biggest was finding parks designated for dogs. "Land of the free, huh, Moose? Unless you're a dog." Standing up, she brushed dirt and leaves from her knees. "Let's go in and work some magic on the house first. I need to do laundry."

Bygie and Moose were on their way to dog park heaven by six. The evening was balmy and Bygie decided they had plenty of time to walk the mile there and back before dark. Moose started the walk full of energy, pulling on the leash and dancing around her feet. She waved to one of the neighbors as they danced by.

Reaching the area designated for dogs, Bygie bent down and unclipped Moose from the leash. "Go for it, Bud. You can run free." She ruffled his fur. "Make me proud and play nice." She glanced around the open area, ringed with trees on all sides. No friends for Moose to play with tonight. The last visitor was headed to the parking lot.

She shadowed along behind Moose, watching him turn every few steps to make sure she was close. Bygie looked down, shuffling her feet through green grass. It made her homesick. North Carolina looked like a rain forest compared to the desert area she lived in. Her head jerked up as Moose took off for the tree line. She whistled, "Moose, wait up." She saw him slow down, but he was on a mission. *Probably a rabbit.*

Moose stopped short of the trees, wagging his tail. A figure was squatted down, in the shadow of the tree. Bygie slowed her step, allowing her dog to meet someone new on his own terms. He inched forward as a hand reached up to pat, but he let out a startled bark, swinging back to face Bygie. She hurried across the field. "Sorry, I'm not sure how he reacts to strangers, I recently adopted him. It's okay Moose." Her dog was struggling to come to her, starting to whine. "It's okay, you can let him go. Moose, come here." The woman stood up, hanging tight to her dog's collar.

The familiarity of the person holding her dog took a minute to register. She recognized the woman holding on to Moose, holding hard enough to hurt him.

"Detective Wilson? Moose, come here, buddy. Detective Wilson? Is that you?" Ruby was wearing gym shorts and a tee shirt and looked different out of uniform.

"In the flesh. Nice night to walk your dog." She was dragging Moose backwards, further into the trees. Claws scrambling for purchase, Moose tried to reach back and bite. Bygie heard his teeth snap. The collar was twisted tight in Ruby's grip. Moose was choking.

"What are you doing? Let go of my dog. You're hurting him."

Ruby pulled a gun from her pocket and pointed it straight at the dog's head.

Bygie's eyes widened. "What are you doing? No, no. Let go of my dog. He's not mean."

"Let's make a deal. A trade. You up for it?"

"I don't know what you mean. Trade for what?"

"I'll trade your mutt . . . for you."

Bygie watched as she tightened the twist on Moose's collar. His air made a wheezing sound as he tried to breathe.

She looked wildly around the deserted park.

"Looks like you're out of options. No one around to help."

"What do you want? I don't understand what you're doing."

"Come over here. Clip that leash back on this mutt and tie him to a tree."

"Okay, okay. Calm down. I don't understand. Moose hasn't hurt anyone. Please, let him breathe." Bygie walked forward, holding both hands up, the clip on the leash clutched in her right hand. "Don't hurt him." She reached Ruby, never taking her eyes off the gun. It stayed locked tight against Moose's head.

"Nice and easy. Get that leash on him. If you let him come after me, I'll shoot him."

Bygie crooned to her dog. "It's okay, Moose. It's okay." She clipped the leash, holding it short and tight. "Okay, let him go."

Ruby let go, quickly backing up a couple steps, her gun still taking aim at the dog. Her voice was harsh. "Tie him up. You let him go and he's dead. Got it?"

"Come on, Moose." She pet him as he coughed, trying to take in air. He looked at Bygie, his warm brown eyes watering. "It's okay, boy. Come on." She walked him further into the shadowed tree line. Holding tight to his collar, she unclipped his leash, looping it around a thin tree trunk. Pulling the end back through the circle, she attached it to her dog's collar. She turned to face Ruby, moving away from Moose, wanting the gun away from her dog. "Okay, he's secured. Put the gun down."

Ruby swung the gun towards Bygie, taking aim between her eyes.

"He's tied up. What are you doing?"

"Taking care of a problem. We're going to go for a ride. Move it." She jerked her head towards Moose. "Don't worry, some kind-hearted little dweeb will rescue your dog. If not?" Ruby shrugged. "The shelters are full of them."

"I'm not going with you. Where's Detective Hall?" Bygie took a step away from Ruby.

"Sorry. Your knight in shining armor won't be around to cover your ass this time." Her eyes narrowed. "Wanna run for it? Go ahead." Without breaking eye contact, Ruby stretched her arm out straight, moving the gun back to

Moose. "Go for it. One thing you need to know. If you do, you'll be sacrificing your mutt."

"Why are you doing this? I don't understand." Bygie continued backing away from her dog with Ruby mirroring each step, swinging the gun back to face her.

Ruby's laugh was wicked. "I bet you don't. What have you ever had to do? Nothing. Sit in that fancy house while Lars busted his ass to take care of you."

She halted. "You knew Lars?"

"Yeah, I knew him. He liked what he saw and wasn't afraid to sample it. Like every other man, he thought about one thing. Himself." She watched Bygie's face drain. "What? You don't think I'm good enough for him? Is that it? Honey, he appreciated me, make no mistake on that. He was nothing but a two bit hustler dressed in fancy clothes. He got what he had coming."

Bygie's knees weakened. "I don't understand. Did you do something to him?"

"You sound surprised. He was a weak, weak man. He started talking about coming clean to his little wife, and I knew he'd be trouble. Another weak bastard I couldn't count on. I wasn't going to let him take down what I've worked my entire life to create." Ruby stepped closer, growling. "Get moving."

Bygie hesitated, looking back at her dog. "Okay. No problem. Don't hurt my dog. He hasn't done anything to you." She inched a couple of steps away from the crazed woman.

***

Tom's phone rang again, disturbing the silence outside the Hudson home. "Hall." His questions were clipped. "What? When? Got it."

Mike watched his old partner's face turn red as a beet. "Who was it? I can tell the news wasn't stellar."

Tom stuffed his phone back in a pocket before answering, freeing both hands to scrub his scalp. "They were calling with the results on the gun we found, from here, the one conveniently tossed into a box headed for Goodwill. I requested an acid test to see if they could raise the numbers that had been filed off. I guess the shit worked."

"Spit it out for God's sake. Did they trace the numbers?"

Hall walked in a tight circle, spitting out the words as Mike requested. "Sure. It only gets better, right? The damn gun came from the station inventory. The fucking bitch had the balls to waltz in and take a gun right out of the property room. I'm telling you, she's fuckin' psycho, and I know she has Bygie."

"Wait, we don't know that for sure."

"She fucking has her." Hall yelled. "It fits. It's the last piece of the puzzle."

Mike knew his partners instincts were something to pay attention to.

Tom whipped out his phone and started dialing.

"Who you calling?"

"I'm sending someone up to check out the love-nest off sixty-seven. Maybe she'd take her . . ." he cut off with a wave of his hand. "Yeah, Struble, redeem yourself for losing Ruby. Get your ass up to 67, right damn now. I'll text directions, get moving. Be discreet. We may have the lady running with a vic in tow. Update me when you get there."

Tom paced a tight circle. "That doesn't feel right. She'd have to set up a suicide somewhere that would make sense. It's more common to find a suicide on their own prop . . ." his eyes looked wild. "Oh shit. Maybe we're too late. Maybe she *can't* answer the door. Could Ruby have been here and gone?" He took off for the front of the house, praying as he ran and feeling strong enough to break down the door on his own.

Mike was hot on his trail, snapping an order. "Go for a window. It'll be faster."

The two men ran around the perimeter of the house, stopping in front of the floor to ceiling windows that fronted the living room.

"Find something." Tom was spinning, looking for anything big enough to break the glass. Mike hefted a log from a covered wood burning pile.

"You want the honor?" He didn't wait or watch for a reply, he lifted the log like a quarterback readying to throw the game ending toss and heaved. It hit the glass and bounced back. A second log was pitched from behind him. The fourth strike was a bulls-eye and they hustled back, shielding themselves from falling glass. There were seconds of mind-numbing noise followed by dead silence.

Tom brushed away shards that were stuck in the window frame and hoisted himself up, with an unlikely pair of hands on his ass trying to help. Once he was in, he turned to help Mike through the window. "I'll check up, you check down, be careful."

They covered the house in short order and came up empty. "We've got to check her work space and the garage, then . . . I don't know where else to look."

"We'll get it, pard, no worries."

They didn't have to break windows to get into Bygie's work space. The blinds on the glass paned door were raised to half mast, allowing a clear view of the one room studio. The only room separated from the whole was the bathroom and it too was in clear view, if only in reflection. One unfinished mirror against the wall gave a birds eye shot of the tiny washroom interior. Empty. The garage was unlocked and cleared as well.

"Now what?" Mike wiped off sweat with his sleeve.

Tom was bent at the waist, hands on his knees, waiting for his heart rate to slow. "Hell, I don't know. Maybe she ran off with one of her boyfriends from the used store."

"You're rambling again. Her boyfriends?"

"Forget it. Let's see if any of the neighbors have seen her, unlikely as that would be."

They hit pay dirt on the third house. The lady who answered, cautiously speaking through a tiny crack of the open door, said she'd seen Bygie walk by with her dog around suppertime.

Dog?

"Are you sure it was Mrs. Hudson? Short, pretty brunette? Your neighbor from up the hill? I'm unaware she owned a dog."

"Yes, it was Mrs. Hudson. She waved to me as they passed. I noticed her another day with her dog. Maybe they were heading to the dog park? It's a ways down, turn left at the bottom of the hill and the next right, you can't miss it."

They thanked her and headed to their vehicle on a run.

"Let's check it out, it will be dark soon. If she has any sense, she'll be on her way home. After that, I'm out of ideas."

They drove to the dog park, but passed without stopping. Tom parked a distance away and both men stepped out, quietly easing their doors shut. They walked back, folding into the trees bordering the open grassy area.

"Hell, I don't think she'd be down here this late, but I wouldn't put it past her either." Hall, speaking in a soft undertone, scanned the area in a regimented sweep.

"You've gotten to know her pretty well, huh?"

"Only well enough to accuse her of murdering her husband." Tom moved to his right.

"Hold it. Stop. I thought I saw something by the trees." Mike motioned to the far side of the park. Only a shadow could be clearly seen, but that shadow was moving.

Tom recognized Bygie's form.

Before he shouted her name, Mike jerked him to a crouch. The single form morphed into two.

Mike whispered, "let's split up."

Tom nodded, heading off to his right while Mike took the left flank. He hustled back to Mike and pulled his cell phone out, reminding Mike to turn his off as well. They separated again with a nod.

Working his way closer, snaking though what little cover there was, the only thing Tom could hear was his heartbeat pounding a fast rhythm. *Get to her, get to her, get to her.* He froze as the figure hunched in the trees stood up, the head swiveling in his direction.

A voice rang out.

"Buddy. Buddy. Come here, Buddy." A shrilling whistle followed.

What the hell was Mike doing?

"Hey! Have you seen my dog? He's brown, about knee-high? He heads over here when he escapes our yard." Mike cupped his mouth and yelled, "Buddy, come boy." Mike headed straight to the women, plastering on a big goofy smile.

Ruby moved fast. She was at Bygie's side, but stepped behind her and shoved the gun into her back.

"Hey. Nope, we haven't seen your dog." She hugged Bygie to her, mimicking a warm embrace. Moose started howling.

"Hey, is that your dog? He looks lonely, can I pet him?" Mike continued towards the dog, noticing Bygie's face, frozen in a grimace of fear.

"No. I wouldn't do that. He's not fond of strangers." Ruby turned to follow Mike's movement, with Bygie's body pressed tight against her.

"That's okay, I'm good with dogs." He continued towards Moose, turning at the last minute towards the women with his hand outstretched. "Sorry, bad manners. I'm Mike. You two live around here?"

If the distraction worked, Mike could close the gap and tackle Ruby, but Tom had doubts. Mike reeked cop. It wouldn't take long for Ruby to catch his scent.

Tom slithered along on his belly, until he was to the right of the women and their grotesque embrace. His attention was located squarely on Bygie's face. He watched her blink and slowly turn her head in his direction. When their eyes met, Tom lifted his hand, then let it drop to the ground.

Please understand.

In one swift movement, Tom rose and shouted. "Freeze."

Moving an arm around Bygie's neck, Ruby lifted the other and pressed the revolver to Bygie's temple. Mike fell to the ground as he pulled his holstered weapon and took aim at Ruby's forehead.

A momentary standoff.

Ruby grunted, and her gun swung up as Bygie went limp and fell to the ground like a wet noodle. Not knowing which way to turn first, her gun swung between Tom and Mike.

What took Ruby out was a painful bite to her leg.

***

While Mike finished cuffing Ruby, Tom lifted Bygie to her feet, brushing at the grass and twigs stuck to her. Her face was pale, but her eyes spit fire. She coughed and gagged, then retched with dry heaves. Standing straight and wiping her chin, she pushed by Tom, taking off in a stiff trot, angling off to the tree line. He stepped after her, squinting in the dark. He watched her kneel in front of a whimpering dog and unclip him from the leash attached to the tree. She buried her face in his fur and sobbed.

Walking to her, Tom leaned down to pat her shoulder, but withdrew his hand, feeling as useless as usual in this type of situation. When she looked up into his face, there was a ghost of a smile forming through dirty tear tracks.

"I can't believe I bit her. Gross. Did it help?"

Ignoring Ruby yelling in the background about suing, Tom answered. "Yes, you did everything just right."

Tom's smile was melancholy as he answered a question that was almost too late to be of any consequence.

"You can go home now."

54

The blow back was strong and fierce, reverberating around the country.

Picked up by major news outlets, the story was covered by a hording mass of Greasy Tuckers, all with the common thread of looking for fame. The duplicate expressions of shock and awe on the faces of reporters came across gleeful. A vice cop running an escort service? Committing murder? They high-fived their camera man on being so fortunate for this to have happened on their watch.

Ruby became the poster child for what was wrong in our country. How the corrupt foster system formed her socio-pathic personality. There was a top ten billboard song rec-orded by an Indie band titled, 'The Day Ruby Blew.' The double entendre wasn't lost on anyone with a brain, but flew over the heads of her fans. She garnered a cult following of society's lost souls; people who used her as a totem for what was wrong with politics, police, and the government in gen-eral.

Their convoluted message had nothing to do with Ruby. They preached of utopia, where people were allowed to live free, and range free. No need to abide by laws designed to propagate a dumbed-down society. Don't let the Big Man Win! No one owned or owed anything to anyone. Societal rules forced Ruby to take the actions she did.

Protesters took to the streets. They wore the weary look of the underfed and under-bathed as a talisman, using it to ask for money in their fight for freedom. Front page news claimed jobs were scarce, why should they bother looking? Employers begging for help were shunned with upturned noses. The job of filling fry baskets was beneath the movement. They needed to awaken the world to the truth.

What a bunch of crap. It didn't matter their new hero was crazy as a bed bug.

Ruby Wilson was sent to live at a psychiatric hospital, albeit temporarily. She would face two murder charges and one attempted murder charge, along with a litany of lesser charges when, and if, she was ever declared fit enough to stand trial.

She admitted to shooting Hudson, she admitted to shoving Greasy Tucker off the cliff, she admitted to harassing Bygie Hudson, calmly stating the facts. Her meticulous record-keeping covered fifteen years. Listed in her personal journal were dates, times and the particular unsettling needs of the men she serviced. She willingly opened her chronicle of sleaze to the tabloids.

Her calmness made her look crazier than ever.

Who knew? Was she crazy or just crazy enough to pull off acting crazy?

Before being locked away from public consumption, Ruby spewed forth enough names to rock San Diego's political, judicial and legal system. She'd been involved in widespread 'business' transactions', including a recently elected senator who'd run on the platform of moral, right wing, Christian conservatism. His denial was aired with his family by his side. They looked shell-shocked, but slightly flattered with the attention.

Denials were countered by offering video of the rendezvous, video that magically found its way to the internet. The top viral clip showed the newly elected senator rolling with more than one body in the frame, some female, but mostly male. Subsequent videos were released with precise timing coordinated by a marketing team of professionals. There were so many hits on the videos, they were encompassed en masse under the heading 'Ruby's Box.' The people, the acts and the talented pornographic positions were the headlining topic of the talk show circuit.

Her team of high priced lawyers worked the case pro-bono, saying they believed in fair justice for the downtrodden of society. They gleefully enjoyed camera time, eagerly bleeding the contents of her dissertation to the public. The lawyers would tie the case up for years, as they actively worked to keep their names in the news.

The network of good old boys tried their best to shut it down. When that didn't work, they switched like a mass of homing bees, declaring they had failed, as great men before them had failed. Press releases were dotted with shots of them attending family functions and sitting in church on Sunday mornings.

"Please forgive my sins," they pleaded. "Who before us hasn't sinned in some manner?"

Their names were at the top of the list in prayer groups, pushing aside cancer stricken children and bereft parents who were deserving of heavenly intervention.

The lone, solid voice of reason amongst them was The Pope. His men stood strong beside him, their trust in him never wavering. If there was someone to lead the way out of the mess, he was the man to handle the job.

Tom just wanted out.

***

With the arrest of Ruby, Bygie became a prisoner in her home. Her confinement following Lars' death had been self-induced, lending itself to a mental healing, or mental breakdown, depending on who told the story.

This was captivity of an entirely different sort.

The last she'd seen of Hall was at the dog park, right before she was hustled to a cruiser and put in the back seat, a pattern she was familiar with but made better by Moose's head resting in her lap. She'd suffered through hours of repeated questions served with bad coffee. They set her free amidst camera flashes and, again, bundled her into the backseat of a cruiser.

The officers in the car were kind as they questioned her. Wouldn't she rather go stay with a family member? Perhaps

a friend? They warned that the next few days would be intense. She insisted on returning home as they pulled away
from the station in a haze of running tripods. If one reporter
hanging around was an annoyance, groups of them were
frightening.

Intense was an understatement.

The floor to ceiling window in the front room had left a
mess when Tom shattered it, but it was already boarded
over. She had to pull Moose away from investigating, pulling
the pocket doors closed to cut off entry. She followed the police around, like a stranger inside her own home. They
checked to make sure her home was tight and secure. When
they left, she felt abandoned.

The narrow road leading to her home and to three houses sitting beyond hers, became a logjam. She shut the rarely
used gate at the end of her driveway, which created a chaos
of vehicles with nowhere to go. Up they came, ignoring signs
below that stated no outlet. With room for just one car to
nose up against her gate, others drove past her drive and
continued up the hill, only to find gates shut at the top.

In an effort to turn around, vehicles became stuck and
spun decomposed granite onto the windshields of the vehicles around them. Fist fights erupted.

Diehard reporters climbed over her gate and walked
down her long driveway to ring the doorbell, cameramen in
tow. She closed window blinds and wished she knew how to
disconnect the doorbell as easily as she did her phone. One of
the neighbors, attempting to get home, notified the police,
only to be told it wasn't their jurisdiction, sorry, you're in the
county. He called the sheriff. The only way the blockage
could clear was to back them down, a slow tedious process
for large news vans backing around blind curves.

When she spotted someone mountaineering the backside
hill in an effort to gain access, Bygie caved. She needed a
lawyer. Opening the yellow pages, she twirled her finger
above the ads, not sure what branch of law practice to contact. She settled on one that stated personal injury; it seemed
to fit. The random choice, even if misguided, was perfect.
The lawyer who showed up was older and wizened, jaded in

the correct way. He ignored cameras shoved into his face and snarled for them to move, get out of the way. On his first visit to her house, he'd brought bagels, a basket of fresh picked blueberries and paper cups of aromatic coffee. His manner was not lawyerly, more fatherly, and she hugged him when he left, wishing he could stay.

She was more than happy to give away what she didn't have. Control. Jane's husband had been on his way to Canada for business, but re-routed to California. By the time he arrived, Bygie had managed to organize help.

Her lawyer recommended hiring security to be present on her property, at least for a short duration. At first she denied the need, then gave in on that as well. She called her friends from the used store. On familiar turf, she brokered a deal with the manager-wife and the men camped on her front porch, taking shifts watching her driveway and hillside. Refusing to sleep inside, they camped in their truck and made use of the studio bathroom. They delighted in playing with Moose and taught him to fetch, speaking to him in rapid Spanish. In a matter of days, her dog was bilingual.

The main question she had for the lawyer was how soon she could pack up and leave.

After five days of hell, he informed her she could go. As long as she left pertinent information on where she could be reached and promised to return on short notice if needed, she was free to go. Some of Lars' hard earned money paid her lawyer, money well spent in hastening her exit. He would also handle selling the house. Her brother-in-law resisted her quick decision in listing the property for sale, but relented at the obvious relief the decision brought Bygie. He pitched in with packing her studio, boxing up mirrors and lamps and shells, but refused to let her box up sand.

Jose and Emanuel were happy to get back to their routine. They helped her pack, carting boxes to the garage that would need to be shipped. With her brother-in-law there, the men now returned home each night, loaded down with a truckload of beds and dressers and other household goods. She made sure they understood she wanted them to have first choice. What they didn't want or need could be donated to the aid organization. They became emotional and called her a princesa when she motioned for them to take an enormous flat screen television. She hoped the manager-wife would let them keep it.

She kept little for herself. She agonized over the couch in her studio, but let it go as well.

She was starting over.

Two weeks to the day after biting Ruby, Bygie's house was listed, the moving van had departed, and her brother-in-law caught a flight home. She insisted on making the drive alone, and headed cross country, with Moose as her navigator, anxious to see California in her rearview mirror. As she crossed the state line into Arizona, she pulled to the side of the freeway, overcome with grief for a life that felt wasted and wrong.

Moose whined and crowded into her lap and attempted to lick her tears. A sharp tap on the passenger window made Bygie jump and Moose growl. She peered around the rump of her dog to see a police officer bent low, looking through. The ridiculousness of her life, a big dog in a tiny car, both of them homeless, brought her from one funk to another. She laid her head against the headrest and started laughing. It'd feel like home if the cop led her to the backseat of his patrol car. She laughed harder. She struggled to regain her composure when the officer backed away from her car with his hand on his holster and mouthed directions over the barking of her dog.

On the road again, she mulled over the officer's words as he handed back her driver's license and registration. A simple remark, but one heavy with implication. "You be careful out there, Mrs. Hudson."

Did he recognize her name? Know who she was?

Who was she anyway?

She'd married at nineteen. Mrs. Hudson, that's who she *was*, but now she wasn't. *Who am I?* She'd turn thirty-four in a blink, high time to figure it out. Find a new path and follow it out of the rut she made of her life.

She knew she was on the right trail when she pulled into a Biscuit City drive-through in Tennessee and was offered mustard with her grits.

Almost home.

55

The sun was a brilliant orb in the hazy blue sky, the air heavy with the humidity of ocean mist. The flat expanse of the beach was sheltered by high dunes, waving flags of hand-planted sea oats in the breeze. One lone beach house stood as a sentinel after hurricane Fran rampaged Topsail Island back in '96. One lone figure stood on the deck looking out at the great expanse of the Atlantic.

The house was old, built around 1953. How it managed to withstand hurricane winds when other, newer structures, were lost without a trace, washed into the unrelenting sea, no one knew or understood. But stand it did. Neighboring homes up and down this stretch of the beach were not only lost to the sea, they were forbidden to rebuild. Only the strongest of ocean front beach houses, ones whose bones withstood the punishment of hurricane Fran, dotted the beachfront. They were few and far between.

In the years following the magnificent power of the storm, homes were remodeled and fortified. Windows and siding were updated, roofs were replaced, and front decking and stairs were rebuilt. Tons of sand, removed from drive-ways and from underneath stilted houses, was bulldozed into a high ridge of dune. It offered added protection from high, storm surge tides, to beach homes sitting a street back from ocean front. Ocean front homes didn't have that added layer of protection; they faced whatever came, head-on.

There were plenty of houses across the street, not ocean front, but due to the hurricane they boasted an unobstructed view of the ocean from their second story decks and high widow walks. While they may not be able to walk down a private set of steps to the sandy shore, they could flip-flop their way across the street to one of the public wooden staircases, steps and planks that rose above the protected banks of sand, to safely cross the rebuilt dunes.

On the outside of the lone beach house, with the lone figure in repose, windows and siding and decking had also been replaced after the storm, but it had weathered into the surroundings. A fresh coat of blue-gray siding stain highlighted the sea-battered exterior. The interior of the stout and sturdy cottage was witness to changing taste in paint color, but the structure itself remained the same.

The main room was one big open space, built ahead of the time designer titled Great Rooms. Hardwood kitchen cupboards lined one wall and were once painted bright yellow, but had faded to a softer butter hue. The bare wood exposed under the handles of drawers and cupboard doors was rubbed naked of color, raw patches of history. A long plank table, flanked with benches for the young and a chair at each end for the old, hosted large groups, but was mainly used to display daily treasures found on the beach.

The floors were wooden, painted with durable high gloss paint. Large rugs, in vivid colors of the outdoor, added cheer. Windows were dressed with wide, white, wooden blinds. Twisted shut only during the heat of the afternoon, the rest of the time they were open, letting in strips of sunlight to waver across the floor.

Furniture that came with the purchase was old and faded, but comfortable, positioned without a decorator's touch. The inspiration behind seating placement was to face the ocean view, in case you were forced indoors by one of North Carolina's angry thunderstorms. They were frequent guests in the heat of the summer, but, even then, you watched from one of the faded chairs, waiting to re-open windows to the ocean breeze, and move life back to the outside deck.

There was a worn sleeper sofa that needed recovering, but was perfect for a nap, with a bright throw tossed over one end, and plump, colorful pillows lining the back. Two painted rocking chairs, one brightly colored upholstered chair and a coffee table made from a tobacco basket, finished the room. Furniture could easily be pushed here and there leaving plenty of floor space for guests rolled into sleeping bags.

The main floor had a short hallway, off which sat two bedrooms, each with a full sized bed, built before bedrooms required over-sized beds to pretend you were sleeping alone. The rooms were freshly painted, airy and light with framed, blown-up prints of sea oats or pampas grass. The headboard, large dresser and simple nightstand in each room were identical and painted white. The bedspreads were crisp white chenille, but the rooms varied with a different colored fleece blankets, folded and spread across the foot of the bed. The shell enriched mirrors above each dresser were each a unique labor of love.

The bathroom was a bunker between the two bedrooms, the old medicine cabinet still on a side wall wearing a fresh coat of paint. A large mirror covered the entire wall above the sink and made the room feel big. An old wooden door had been cut in half from top to bottom and anchored together at an angle, outfitted with triangular shelves. It held rolled, thin, stark white or rich blue towels, with baskets of bathroom toiletries on others. The tub was large and old, surrounded by a brilliant blue curtain, perfect for soaking in, but rarely used. Even showers were taken outside, underneath the stilted beach house in an enclosed shower that was open to the air at the top and bottom.

At the end of the hall was a staircase that led to an upper loft area tucked under the eaves that looked out over the main floor. Once used to house extra guests on cots or in sleeping bags, it had become a bright and airy studio.

Bygie's space.

56

The tumultuous take-down that rocked San Diego became overshadowed when reporters left to cover a juicier, new breaking story. They packed camera gear and loaded their vans, heading to Dallas where a woman claimed to be having an affair with the president. The protesters hitchhiked after the news vans, taking Ruby's name off their signs but leaving the message about Big Man and his power.

At the time, Tom wished he could hitchhike away with them, get lost amongst the unwashed and shout the loudest, but he had too much paperwork to do.

He was applauded for his part in uncovering the corruption, but he refused to be used as a poster boy for truth and justice and requested his name be kept from the press. The city's top brass were relieved and The Pope understood.

Mike immediately flew back to his family; his name was never mentioned. He would have to step forward if the case went to trial, a bridge they would cross when they had to. Word around the department was Ruby was having a hard time adjusting to her new surroundings and was under guarded suicide watch. Tom thought it would be better if they handed her a knotted rope and didn't apologize for feeling that way. You can't fix crazy.

He did reach out to Bygie, once. He called to check on her, but his call was forwarded to a lawyer and he figured the hell with it, he'd stop by. When he took time to drive up the familiar hill, he was stopped at the end of her drive by a shut gate, something he'd never seen her use. He inched forward until the nose of his shitty-van touched the gate, leaving enough space for someone to pass behind. He stepped out, reading the sign posted to the side.

For Sale.

He looked around for a buzzer, not seeing one, he did what the reporters had done before him. He climbed around the gate, up and over boulders, and walked down the drive.

The only sound in the quiet neighborhood was the gentle swoosh of his footsteps. He climbed the front steps, shielding his eyes to look up at the windows of her studio, half expecting to see the silhouette of a waving hand, but it remained empty.

He pushed the doorbell, listening as it echoed inside, feeling the emptiness of the air around him. When no one came to the door on the second ring, he walked to the back of the house on the ruse of inspecting the broken window. The boards were gone, replaced by new glass, and he cupped his hands to peer through.

The room that was nearly empty before, except one side table and a black lacquered box, was completely stark. He sagged against the glass, then fist pumped empty air. He trudged back down the drive with a smile. *Good for her. She's up and moving on.*

He returned to working nights, setting up vice stings and shutting down massage parlors. Without a partner. Weeks and weeks of the same. A never ending loop. He slept fine, but he felt tired.

His eyes popped open one morning, shortly after falling asleep. Dead to the world one minute, eyes wide open the next, he sat up against his headboard. He pulled his laptop from the nightstand and began typing.

***

"I don't know what to say." Pope tossed the piece of paper Tom had handed him. The men sat silent watching as the sheet fluttered across the desk before it tipped off and fell into a trash can. "See? Higher power at work, it'll never happen. It's not meant to be."

"It's happening. I'm going to do it."

"Are you sure this isn't another of your half-baked ideas? The last one didn't turn out so wonderful. How 'bout you move back to homicide instead?"

Tom grinned. "Not gonna happen."

Pope grunted. "Seems like you mean it."

"I do."

"Shit."

"Yes."

"You're not gonna give up a damn thing are you? Just waltz in and drop this on my desk. At least we could discuss it, let me in on our plans. This is pretty big."

"Nope and yep." His smile grew wider.

Pope shook his head, "I gotta hand it to you. This one surprises me." He met Tom's gaze and studied what he saw. "I can see you're serious. It's written on that big goofy face of yours. You mean business." Pope shook his head and used a simple statement to sum up his feelings. "I'm sure gonna miss you."

"Aww, chief, I bet you say that to all the boys."

"Nope." Pope stood and walked around his desk.

Tom came to his feet and they met in an awkward stance, halfway between a hug and a handshake, the history between them calling for one of each.

"Take care of yourself, Hall, and keep in touch, would you?"

Tom answered seriously, "Now that's something I will do."He walked out of the office, his step lighter than it'd been in years.

He'd resigned.

***

On his last day of work, putting his highly specialized detective skills to work, Tom had asked computer whiz, Noah, for a favor. He'd stood over his shoulder, watching as Noah typed and within seconds he had an address is in his hand.

Tom squeezed his shoulder, "Thanks, bud. I appreciate it."

"Heck, you could have done it in seconds yourself, but I don't mind looking brilliant. Hey, good luck, man."

"Thanks again."

He'd been sent off without fanfare. Over twenty years of service and not even an engraved watch to prove his worth. Pats on the back had been sincere, but few and far between. He'd withdrawn from the brotherhood long before resigning, he'd put a barrier between himself and others, a barrier that was easy for him to see in hindsight. Only Becky and Joe were aware of his plans as he put into place motions of moving forward with his life.

And now he was here.

Lost.

Wondering what the hell he was doing as he mopped his forehead. The humidity was unreal and the hot sun baked anything not shaded. Walking into the air conditioned convenience store brought an immediate rash of goose bumps to his bare legs and arms.

He approached a youngish blonde behind the counter. "Hi. I wonder if you could help me? I'm lost."

"Honey, I shore'noughcan. Yur right here at the QuicknGo. Where ya needin'ta be?"

Tom squinted, trying to follow blended words that ran in a southern direction then tipping up at the end like they were headed north.

"I'm looking for North Shore Drive, uhhh, 1427. Something called Hindsight? Does that make any sense?"

She let off a phlegmy laugh. "Makes plenty sense ta me. People 'round here name their houses, yaknowwhatImean? Like, Ships Anchor and it makes ya wonder if their drownin' in debt, or Sandy Dreams like they grew up in a city." Her shoulders shrugged," I don't know where they git 'em but people are plenty creative, yaknowwhatImean?"

He didn't have an inkling of what she meant but nodded agreement. "Do you know where North Shore Drive is? There doesn't seem to be many street signs."

"Ain't that the truth? When they went 'round and named all the little streets that weren't hardly a street atall, I told Jr., that's not gonna help one little bit if they don't go to addin' some signs. Shoot, don't take no rocket man to figur' that one, yaknowwhatImean?" Her head of bouncy curls shook in amazement.

Tom's head was nodding in perfect beat to the sing-song of her speech. "Ahhh, North Shore Drive?"

"Now that's where yur lucky. Yur practically standin'on it, yaknowwhatImean? It's the next road over, right there." She leaned across the counter and pointed across the road towards the beachfront. "Go on back outta the door and drive across. The whole long street that runs by the water is what yur lookin' for. You could walk there if it weren't so hot, yaknowwhatImean? You have a good day now."

With that, he was released back into the wild.

He headed in the direction her arm had indicated, driving down the shoreline, reading the names posted as he passed. Shack Attack, The Chips Ahoy, Dakotah Dream. He focused on newer houses, packed as tight as sardines, on his left. Halting in the middle of the road, he looked back, to his right. He knew it was the place when he saw 'Hindsight' was spelled out in shells.

It stood alone, along the ocean front side of the sandy street.

Backing up, he pulled in behind one of the vehicles tucked up under the house and out of the sun. He sat listening to his car engine ticking in pretense of cooling down, looking at the two vehicles squeezed between pilings that supported the floors above. One was a van, much newer than the one Tom used to drive and the other was the latest model of an economy SUV, not the Miata he halfway expected to see.

What the hell was he doing?

It'd been seven months since Bygie had fled California. Did he not expect her to have moved on with her life? Get a different car for God's sake? Maybe a new husband?

The sweltering heat filling his car forced him to move. He grabbed a laptop from the passenger seat and stepped out, immediately sweating, adding another layer of moistness to his damp clothes. A staircase, leading to an upper deck that disappeared around the side of the cottage, had a shut gate at the bottom.

Should I open it and go up?

Should I get in my car and back away as fast as I can?

He did neither when the tingling sound of voices was carried up and over the dunes by the ocean breeze. He walked past the gate, and clambered up and over the dune, filling his shoes with sand, struggling to remain upright as the sand beneath his feet shifted. Reaching the top, he was momentarily awestruck.

The beach stretched flat and wide, dotted with distant beach umbrellas marking staked out territory for the day. Mounds of shells were being washed by the gentle surf and random, bent bodies, were raking through them, clutching overfilled pails of treasures. He stood in his sand-filled shoes and socks, legs already feeling the burn of the sun, when he noticed a group of people running towards him, frantically waving their arms. *What?*

They shouted through cupped hands. "Get down! Get down!" So he did. He scrambled down the dune side, punching holes through, causing sand slides, barely keeping upright, clutching a stupid laptop to his chest. At the last moment he pinwheeled his arms to keep from falling and the laptop was flung to the sand. He looked at it and looked at the person striding towards him.

Bygie.

In a swimsuit. Chuckling at his careening stumble. "Are you okay?" She bent to pick up the computer, but shot up to face him.

Their first words were disjointed pieces of conversation.

"Oh my god, it's you."

"Yeah. Hi."

"What are you doing here?"

"I, ahhh, bringing you your laptop. You can have it back now."

She looked at it lying in the sand.

Flustered, he asked, "why was everyone yelling at me?"

"You were on the dunes."

"What?"

She switched to the first question. "You brought my laptop?"

"I have another box of stuff in the trunk."

By now, there were children milling around and Moose was sniffing his ankles. He absently patted the dog's head. Tom recognized Jane with a nod.

"You met Jane? This is her husband, Bob. Have you met? No, that's right, you didn't see him when he was in California." Her words were rushed, tripping over themselves to fill the awkwardness, a sense of panic riding up her spine. "These are the kids." She waved her arm, not giving them individual names, like they were all named Kid or they were baby goats. "You're here? Is something wrong?"

This wasn't going like he'd imagined on the long drive. He pictured himself as a calm professional checking on her well-being, not one who pin-wheeled down a dune that he apparently wasn't supposed to be on, and landing at her feet.

He smiled, then surprised himself by giving in to a rusty laugh. "I really am here to return what was taken during the search."

She pushed sunglasses into her salty hair. The air was weighted with unasked questions as she tilted her head and looked at him.

"For real?"

"For real."

Her heart flipped, then flopped, then righted itself in joy.

***

They ate an early dinner of fresh shrimp and homemade coleslaw, insisting Tom stay to eat. Soon after dishes were washed and shrimp shells were wrapped in newspaper to be discarded, Jane and her family were waved off, heading out for the three hour trip home. The children were already falling asleep after the weekend of sun and sand.

Bygie headed around to the front deck and took a seat on one the porch swings. She looked out over the vast ocean and, at last, turned to face Tom sitting in the swing on the other end of the deck. They began talking, hesitant at first, but warming to a comfortable flow. She told him how she had put most of her money into an island clinic and was selling her work on both coasts. He explained his departure from San Diego P.D., and how he was going to visit Mike in South Carolina.

Ruby was mentioned only once, when Bygie stated she'd read Tom's statement and wholeheartedly agreed. You can't fix crazy.

Bygie rose and walked towards Tom. She bent down and kissed his cheek, then turned and went inside, letting the screen door snap shut. Loading a small cooler with ice and beer, grabbing a couple of well worn beach towels, she pushed through the screen door, letting it bang again. The sound of summer.

"Have you ever seen a sunset from the Atlantic side of the world?"

Tom answered from the porch swing, her traitor bilingual dog napping at his feet. "Nope, can't say that I have."

"I haven't either."

"You haven't?"

"That's because it sets in the West."

He looked into laughing eyes.

She swung the cooler. "What say we head down to the beach? I have beer on ice, you can carry the beach chairs."

"I say that sounds like the best invitation I've ever had." He stood up to help, but she backed away, shaking her head.

"No way. First you have to take off those shoes and socks, it's the rule. You can only wear flip-flops with shorts."

He self-consciously obliged.

His feet looked pale and soft. She winced at the pastiness and gave him a broad smile.

"I'll have to teach you about beach life."

Acknowledgments

Dave, Chrissy, Rich, Noah, Ian and Audrey, thank you for being the family I need.

I'm deeply indebted to Tim Hall for law enforcement advice, and to honor him, (I hope) I've named a character similarly. Our lengthy visits about guns and prostitutes at neighborhood cookouts raised some brows. Any mistakes involving crime investigation are mine and mine alone. Tim is a storyteller extraordinaire and should write a novel of his own. Esthi Hall, thank you for never failing to ask when you'd get to read it.

Harriet, I'm honored you took the time to read for me, I'm ready for a walk.

Debby and Bruce, thank you for the early celebration. Let's do it again.

Ron Lee and Kathy Lee, I owe you and will be forever thankful for your generous help.

My readers that went through rough drafts and offered suggestions have been invaluable. They include: my *real* sister Jane, Regina, Carol, Bill and Nancy Service (for two years, Bill never failed to ask how it was going), Linda from La Mesa creative writing, and everyone in my beta-exchange reading group. (Simone, Guy, Reed, Deidre and Sandra.)You each pushed me along the path to publication.

Jim Sprague, are we even? I call a truce.

I would like to thank all of the brave men and women who work in law enforcement. I have the utmost respect for the challenges you face each and every day. I have not walked through your work environment: desks, parking, buildings, etc., everything portrayed is from my imagination.

Jill Shannon is a freelance writer who lives in San Diego and spends time in South Dakota during the warmer months. When she's not at her computer ~~playing solitaire~~ working on her next novel, you'll find her on the Bonneville Salt Flats, or at El Mirage dry lakebed, racing her 1941 Indian.

You can contact the author through Facebook Author pages.

www.ingramcontent.com/pod-product-compliance
Lightning Source LLC
Chambersburg PA
CBHW020336180626
46812CB00001B/229